The River Road

Novels by
FRANCES PARKINSON KEYES

FRANCES PARKINSON KEYES

The River Road

EYRE & SPOTTISWOODE
LONDON

C.23

First published 1946
Reprinted   1950
Reprinted   1955

d9-30-57
HR

This book is printed in Great Britain for
Eyre & Spottiswoode (Publishers) Limited,
15 Bedford Street, London, W.C.2, by
Billing and Sons Ltd., Guildford and London
G9120

Contents

"The description which I have given of a sugar estate, with its vast level fields, like emerald plains, its stately sucrérie, its snow-white Negro village, its elegant château buried in trees, will answer for that of the hundreds which continuously line the two shores of the Mississippi between Baton Rouge and New Orleans. . . . A few yards from the water *runs a beautiful road,* bordered on one side by gardens and houses, and on the other by the River. . . . The whole line of shore, for the one hundred and fifty miles, is a continued unbroken street. . . . This . . . is *the river road,* following in and out every curve of the embanked shore, and level as a racehorse track. Thus, one riding along this road has constantly the green bank, or Levee, on one side, with the mile-wide River flowing majestically by, bearing huge steamers past on its tawny bosom. On the other hand are hedges separating gardens, lawns, cottages, villas, and emerald cane fields, with groups of live oaks, magnolias, lemon, and banana trees interspersed. For miles, all the day long, the traveller can ride through a scene of beauty and ever lively interest."—Taken from "The Sunny South, or The Southerner at Home: Letters embracing five years' experience of a northern governess in the land of sugar and cotton." Edited by Professor G. H. Ingraham, of Mississippi. Published by G. G. Evans, Philadelphia, 1860.

PART I

"Hail the Conquering Hero Comes"

(April, 1919)

I

I

"THERE'S no use going to the window yet, Merry. It's barely five, and you know these things never start on time. I don't believe the parade's left the campus yet."

"I don't suppose it has. But I like standing here where I can see the flags and festoons. Come here and look at them too."

"I've looked at 'em already. Anyhow, our own show windows have got all the other decorations licked to a standstill and we can't see those from here. That backdrop of the battleship with the eagle hovering over her is a knockout."

"Yes, it is. And I like the way the war relics are arranged in front of it between the Victory Loan posters. But the other stores have good displays too, Hazel, and all this bunting floating in the air gives me a big thrill. So do the crowds. I never saw so many people on Third Street. The parade'll be along presently. I don't mind waiting."

"I know you don't. But at that, it doesn't usually get a girl anywhere."

Hazel Wallace spoke in a tone slightly tinged with sarcasm. Everyone in Goldenberg's Store knew that Meredith Randall, Mr. Goldenberg's private secretary, had waited and waited for Gervais d'Alvery to come back from France and marry her. As far as that went, everyone in Baton Rouge knew it, and almost everyone had thought that her waiting would be in vain. But Merry, as they all called her, did not seem to mind. She did not mind having people know that she was waiting, she did not mind having people speak of it, she did not even mind having them feel that her confidence was misplaced. To be sure, she did not air her patience and her trust, she did not bring up Gervais d'Alvery's name of her own accord. But her faith in him was so supreme that her very bearing bespoke it; her love for him had such a shining quality that its glow pervaded her being. Lately, since the grudging but general admission that her confidence had not been misplaced after all, and the further unmistakable evidence that she had reason not

9

only to trust his integrity but to glory in his prowess, this glow had expanded to include everyone around her and actually to transform the drab surroundings of herself and her fellow-workers. Gervais d'Alvery had won promotion for gallant conduct in the face of the enemy; in spite of serious wounds, he had successfully led his men against Hun machine-gun emplacements; after his recovery, the United States Government had conferred the Distinguished Service Cross upon him, and the French Government the Croix de Guerre. His homecoming, late the previous week, had been the occasion of the greatest demonstration that had ever taken place at the Baton Rouge station. Now in the Victory Loan Parade which was about to begin he was the object of excited and concentrated attention. Nearly one hundred officers and men, recently returned from overseas, were to march in the parade. But none of them had made such a record as Gervais d'Alvery; none so dashingly embodied the popular conception of a "hero"; and none, by birth and background, was so logically predestined to become the local idol.

No wonder that Hazel, sauntering over to the dingy window of the crowded cubbyhole where she and Merry did their typing at adjacent clattering machines, said to herself, rather resentfully, that her sarcasm seemed to fall flat. Merry could certainly afford to ignore it. Because everyone had now seen the meeting of her and Gervais at the station. Everyone had known from the avidity with which he seized her in his arms and pressed his face down against hers, and from the lingering reluctance with which he finally released her, with what fervour and intensity he returned her love. Everyone knew that he would rather have gone straight home with her to the jerry-built little bungalow on St. Napoleon Street, where she lived with her shrewish mother, and their eccentric lodger, Miss Mittie Alden, than to have been borne away on the shoulders of cheering men to the music of a big brass band. In fact, a good many people said afterwards that it was a shame the official banquet to which Gervais had so triumphantly been taken had lasted so long, that the Governor and the Mayor and the Secretary of State had all made such long speeches. Because, when these were finally over, it had been too late for Gervais to see Merry again that night. He had been obliged to go straight on to his plantation, Belle Heloise, and the cheering men and the brass band had accompanied him all the way down the River Road. Not that anyone doubted he had managed to get back to see Merry since then. . . .

The door leading from Mr. Goldenberg's private office into the cubbyhole opened quietly and Mr. Goldenberg came out—a thick-set, grey-haired man, immaculate of appearance and formal of manner. He spoke to the girls civilly but conventionally.

"I see you've finished your letters, Miss Meredith. Mrs. Goldenberg and my mother, with two or three of their friends, have come down to my office to watch the parade, and Mrs. Goldenberg has suggested that perhaps you would like to join us. She'd be very glad to have you, if you would. Miss Hazel may come, too, if Mr. Sears can spare her."

Mr. Sears, the merchandise manager, whose office was on the other side of the cubbyhole, was a notorious martinet, and Mr. Goldenberg never interfered with his subordinate's discipline. Hazel had been pouting all the afternoon over the amount of work which he had left her to plough through when he went out. But, after all, he had gone. He was going to march in the parade himself, with other members of the Victory Loan Committee. If he did not find all his letters written when he came back the next morning he could stew and stew, but there would be nothing he could do about it then. Hazel accepted Mr. Goldenberg's invitation with gushing alacrity.

"Oh, Mr. Goldenberg, that's simply sweet of you: I mean it's simply sweet of Mrs. Goldenberg. I'd adore to watch the parade from your office windows. Wouldn't you, Merry?"

"It *is* very kind of Mrs. Goldenberg to ask us. But I think perhaps I ought to wait here for Miss Mittie. I told her this was where she'd find me. She wouldn't know where to look for me, if I left."

"I will keep someone else here in your place, Miss Meredith, to tell your friend that you're in my office. Of course, Mrs. Goldenberg and I will be very pleased to have her join us there, too, when she arrives."

As if the matter were settled, Mr. Goldenberg opened the door of his office again, and the two girls walked in. The cubicles occupied by the minor officials of the store were drab and cluttered, and great naked-looking white water coolers stood in their corners, between the olive-green files. The floors of most of these cubicles were bare, though Mr. Sears had somehow contrived to achieve a shabby, mouse-coloured carpet. The desks were badly battered and perpetually heaped with untidy piles of papers, escaping from beneath glass paperweights, and other miscellaneous packages littered the straight-backed chairs. The walls were undecorated, except for dog-eared sales charts, felt bulletin boards defaced by pricking, and mammoth calendars issued by insurance companies. But Mr. Goldenberg's office was entirely different, and Hazel, who seldom had occasion to enter it, was much impressed. A brightly coloured rug covered the floor, and reproductions of Mr. Maxfield Parish's exotic paintings adorned the walls. There were no files, and instead of the objectionable water cooler, a shining thermos jar, precisely placed with two neat glasses on a matching tray, invited refreshment. The glassed-over desk was orderly and sparsely covered, and the only calendar in the room was a small one, neatly encased in a frame of tooled leather, which matched the frame

containing the photograph of Mrs. Goldenberg in full but re-
strained evening dress which stood on the opposite side of the un-
blemished blotter, near a silver bud vase containing a lonely
crimson rose. Merry was a pretty lucky girl, Hazel thought, to
spend so much of her time in an office like this, working for a
perfect gentleman like Mr. Goldenberg, instead of being cooped
up in a horrid little pen with a sourpuss like Mr. Sears. Just the
same, she did not think Merry had been invited to come to this
office, socially, before. She knew, for a fact, that nothing of the
sort had happened on Armistice Day, because she and Merry had
watched the parade together then. It was that million-volt kiss at
the depot which had got Merry this invitation. Mrs. Goldenberg
knew perfectly well that Captain Gervais d'Alvery of Belle Heloise
would not have kissed Meredith Randall of St. Napoleon Street
like that, for all the world to see, if he had not meant to marry
her; and now that Merry's days as Mr. Goldenberg's secretary
were numbered, and her position as the chatelaine of Belle Heloise
assured, Mrs. Goldenberg felt very differently towards her.

Mrs. Goldenberg came forward to meet the girls and to introduce them to her mother-in-law and her friends. She was a dark,
handsome woman, dressed in dark, handsome clothes, which were
a little heavy-looking for late spring, but nevertheless as elegant
as they were costly. There were advantages in marrying a rich
storekeeper after all, whatever stuck-up girls who would have
nothing to do with anyone "in trade" might say about it. Hazel
was sure Merry would never have diamonds to compare with
Mrs. Goldenberg's, just heirloom jewellery in heavy settings,
cameos and garnets probably, and maybe some seed pearls. Hazel
had noticed the insignificant little ring which Merry had been
wearing the last few days, and though she had it on her right
hand instead of her left, Hazel had no doubt that Gervais had
given it to her. It was just the sort of ring Hazel would have expected of him, made of twisted gold and studded with turquoises,
some of them slightly discoloured. The d'Alverys were not poverty-
stricken, like so many of the old River families who looked down
on the townsfolk and spoke of them sneeringly as "catfish aristoc-
racy," because when the Mississippi receded after it had risen,
quantities of catfish were left on the banks beside Baton Rouge;
but they were not wealthy either.

As far as Hazel knew, Fabian d'Alvery was the only one of
Gervais' kin who was really prosperous, and he had not lived on a
plantation for a long time, but in a cute house on Somerulos Street.
This was right on the edge of "Catfish Town," but no one made
disparaging remarks about Fabian for living there, because he was
a d'Alvery. He was also a lawyer, and furthermore he was making
money fast. Of course he had something queer the matter with
his spine, which had prevented him from going to war, and he had

12

been very bitter about that; but he had kept on getting richer and richer just the same. And he was one of the best speakers in the Parish; he had been in constant demand as a "Four-Minute Man" in every one of the Liberty Loan Drives. He was going to speak that very afternoon, on the corner of Convention and Third Streets, when the parade halted on purpose to admit such addresses. Probably he had done just as much good, raising money by making speeches and giving away a lot himself besides to the Red Cross and other good causes, as Gervais had done getting wounded and killing Huns. Only he did not think so, and Merry did not seem to think so either. That was another reason why Fabian was embittered. Merry respected Fabian and pitied him, but she adored Gervais. And if Merry had only felt just a little differently, or would have pretended that she did, she could have been married at the beginning of the war, when nearly all of the other girls were doing it, and given wonderful parties on Somerulos Street for visiting celebrities, and worn diamonds as big as Mrs. Goldenberg's. . . .

"This is my husband's mother, Miss Randall," Mrs. Goldenberg was saying smoothly, breaking in on Hazel's reverie. "She enjoys a parade beyond anything, so I hope you'll stand right here beside her, and explain everything to her. I'm afraid I don't understand the programme very well. But it begins at the University, doesn't it?"

"Yes, on the campus. The parade must have started already. I think it's headed by the mounted police. If we listen we'll hear the horses coming presently. And the music. There are going to be three bands."

Without self-consciousness or awkwardness, Merry had taken the indicated place beside the elder Mrs. Goldenberg. The old lady looked at her shrewdly, and, at first, rather sharply; but apparently she was pleased with what she saw. Merry's big brown eyes met hers candidly, and there was something so trustful in their gaze that her own glance softened as she continued her scrutiny. She had heard that this girl was a beauty, and she had suffered occasional pangs of maternal uneasiness in thinking of her son's secretary. But now she knew the pangs were needless. There was an almost childlike quality, not only in Merry's guileless gaze, but in the fresh bloom of her skin, and in the dimples which deepened in her cheeks when she smiled. Her hair, which she wore bound with a ribbon and falling in loose waves over her shoulders, enhanced the illusion of extreme youth; it must have been honey-coloured when she was a little girl, for though it was brown now, it was still full of golden glints. But the old lady, who was so carefully appraising all this, likewise saw that beneath its masses of shining hair the girl's head was shapely and erect, and she sensed that beneath the fair flesh the bodily structure was very strong. Here before her was something more than beauty and better than beauty. She could feel Merry's generous vitality flowing out towards her, warming her aged limbs and reanimating her weary spirit, and in like measure she was aware of the girl's integrity and intelligence and steadfastness. She smothered a little sigh, knowing that her son would lose a great deal when he lost the cheer and challenge of such a presence. Then she smiled and gave Merry's hand a little pat, as her daughter-in-law went on with the introductions, belatedly including Hazel in them.

"Mrs. Silver, you've met my husband's invaluable little secretary before, haven't you? Really? Why, I thought—— And this is her friend, Miss—— Oh yes—of course, Miss Wallace: Mrs. Wayland, Miss Randall and Miss Wallace. Mrs. Bourdonnay, Miss Randall and Miss Wallace. It's delightful, isn't it, that we could have some charming young girls added to our little group? I asked Miss d'Alvery and her friend, Miss Hathaway, to join us, because I really think you can get a better view of a parade from this office than from any other point. But it seems they'd already been invited to the Mansion. Governor and Mrs. Pleasant are having a small coffee party. You know Miss Cresside d'Alvery, of course, Miss Randall?"

"No, I haven't met her yet. But I'm hoping to."

Funny that she can talk like that about Gervais' sister, Hazel thought, as if it did not matter at all that Cresside d'Alvery had gone out of her way to avoid meeting Merry. And as for Cresside's bosom friend, Regine Hathaway, she had told all over town that there was nothing in the rumoured engagement, that Gervais had never intended to marry a nobody like Meredith Randall. The scene at the station had put an abrupt stop to her spiteful talk, and Hazel, for one, was glad of it. But still she wasn't easy in her mind about Regine Hathaway; she thought Regine would try to get even with Merry yet. Because, of course, Regine Hathaway had wanted Gervais herself—almost as much as Cresside had wanted Regine's friend, Sylvestre Tremaine, who was up from New Orleans visiting at Hathaway Hall now, and who must have gone with them to the Mansion. Sylvestre Tremaine hadn't been in the war either, though the reason wasn't as obvious as it was in Fabian d'Alvery's case. As far as anyone knew, there wasn't anything the matter with Sylvestre's spine. That is, not really. Though Hazel seemed to remember she had heard someone refer to him as "that spineless slacker."

Hazel's contemptuous reflections were interrupted at this point by the properly heralded arrival of Miss Mittie Alden. No one in Baton Rouge knew much about the Randalls' lodger, beyond the fact that she was an excellent teacher and a strict disciplinarian, and she was generally considered to be as mysterious as she was peculiar. She was a wiry little woman, with unkempt hair and hands, whose clothes were an eyesore, and whose nose always looked as if it were very cold, even in the warmest weather. Among her few friends she had a way of expressing herself that was both quaint and effective, but when she went out among strangers she was silent and constrained, and her cold nose quivered all the time, like a rabbit's. It quivered now, as she made her miserable rounds of the Goldenbergs and their friends, meanwhile casting an accusing eye at Merry, and muttering angrily under her breath, as if to blame the girl for the agonizing experience to which she was being subjected. But Merry, seemingly more and more at ease, blithely ignored this. She made sure that Miss Mittie was placed where there would be the best possible view of the parade, and then herself went on talking to old Mrs. Goldenberg.

"I can hear the music now, can't you? Listen!"

The music was coming nearer and nearer. "We'll be seeing the mounted police any moment. And then the Red Cross nurses, and the canteen workers, and the Boy Scouts——"

"And the Victory Loan Committee," interposed Hazel, speaking up, in spite of herself, for the absent Mr. Sears.

"Yes, the Victory Loan Committee, and hundreds of Standard Oil employees. The Standard Oil has a wonderful band of its own, Mrs. Goldenberg. A man named Sylvester Smith leads it. And there's the fife and drum corps too. Price Mitchell leads that. And the University band——"

"You're not going to forget to mention the Overseas Contingent, are you, Miss Meredith, while you're talking to my mother?"

Mr. Goldenberg still spoke civilly and conventionally in addressing Merry, but somehow it was evident that she had contrived to please him very much. Hazel did not know whether this was because Merry was being so nice to his mother, to whom he was devoted, or whether it was because she was so natural and simple in the presence of his wife and the other important ladies, though a little graver than usual, or whether it was because he too had realized the import as well as the impact of that million-volt kiss at the station. If it were the kiss that had changed his estimate of Merry, however, Hazel felt that the underlying reasons for this were not the same as the underlying reasons for his wife's cordiality. He would not be moved by Merry as the prospective mistress of Belle Heloise; in fact, he would probably go out of his way to indicate that this would make no difference to him, for Mr. Goldenberg was a very proud person in his own right, much prouder than Mrs. Goldenberg, and toadied to no one. But he might well be moved by Merry as a human being devotedly loving and passionately beloved. . . .

When the Overseas Contingent swung into sight, led by Gervais d'Alvery, lean, bronzed, handsome, wearing his captain's uniform and all his medals, Hazel, watching the expression of Mr. Goldenberg's face, knew that in her last surmise she had not guessed wrong.

"If you fellows want to see anything of this parade, you better stop talking politics for a few minutes and come on out. There's the Red Cross unit starting up the street right now and the Overseas Division right behind it."

"I don't give a damn about the Overseas Division. I can't go any-where these days that I don't find the streets blocked by a parade. What I came down here from Caddo to find out, and what I haven't found out yet——"

"I know, Tack, I know. In fact, Jim and I both know why you came down here from Caddo. So does Carruth, for that matter. Just the same, this is only April, and the election doesn't come off till next January. So there's still a little time to spare. We've been talking politics quite a while now to please you. Maybe you'd be willing to humour the rest of us by taking a half-hour off to see the parade. It couldn't do any harm."

Three of the four men who had paused in front of the cash register at "Izzie's" moved unhurriedly towards the sidewalk, and after an instant's hesitation the fourth one, Tack Evans, reluctantly decided to join them. At his invitation the others had been drinking small blacks and eating L.S.U. cream cheese at the counter which ran the length of the tunnel-like room, constituting the politicians' favourite meeting place: "Jim" Bailey, the Secretary of State, who had spoken first; George Favrot, the Congressman from the sixth district, who had retorted to Tack so dryly; and Carruth Jones, the attorney representing East Baton Rouge Parish, whose high-pitched voice seemed to be momentarily silenced. On their way out they had stopped to speak to the beaming, bald-headed proprietor of the little café. Izzie always presided personally at the cash register, in front of a large photograph of himself which was fastened up against a shelf and inscribed across the forehead with the words FAMOUS FOR HIS BRAINS. He was a very short man, so that physically the cash register almost concealed him; the tufts of grey hair encircling his shiny dome and the clean-shaven contour of his rubicund countenance were barely visible above it. But nothing could obscure Izzie's radiant personality or dim the lustre of his fame. Orleanians often said, rather sneeringly, that Izzie's was the only place in Baton Rouge where civilized food could be had, but not one of them denied that you could get it there.

"The Congressman's right, Mr. Evans," he now said encouragingly, noticing that the outsider still hesitated. "You don't want to miss seeing this Overseas Division. It's going to be a great sight. More'n a hundred men in it, all from Baton Rouge. And this young fellow who's leading it, Gervais d'Alvery, he's made a fine

16

record. We're all mighty proud of him in this section. He was in here Saturday, eating some of my specialties, relishing 'em too. Mary's Lamb and Izzie's Yam, that's what I served him. Well, I'm going to have another look at that boy myself. I believe he's going far." While Izzie was still speaking, three or four white-jacketed, white-aproned negro waiters shot past towards the door with unaccustomed alacrity, and Izzie beamed more broadly than ever. "I might just as well," he said. "There won't be any cash coming in to ring up until those boys of mine get back. My customers are out on the sidewalk already. Everybody wants to see Captain d'Alvery at the head of that Division."

He might as well give up the struggle, Tack Evans said to himself, though he stood still for a moment longer, impatiently jiggling the large monogram hanging from his watch chain, and listening unmoved to strains of "Over There." As he had previously remarked, he had not come down from Caddo to see a parade; he had come down because he wanted to know what was brewing in the political pot, who was going to support whom, what the score was on the governorship.

Moving slowly forward, Tack abandoned the monogrammed watch chain, and lighted a cigarette. Jim Bailey was smoking a cigar now, he noticed, Carruth Jones a pipe, and George Favrot was unobtrusively chewing tobacco. Tack pushed his way through the crowd and joined them at the edge of the sidewalk, towering above them all. Bailey was a tall man too, but Evans was long and rangy, more like the traditional Texan than the typical Louisianian. He was proud of his size, as he was of his record, but he knew that neither impressed this triumvirate whose goodwill it was so essential he secure. He was only a hillbilly to them; the others all "belonged."

The Red Cross unit was directly in front of Izzie's now, the first section of it being in the form of a living "Old Glory," woven by nurses. Some were dressed entirely in white, others entirely in red; these two divisions made up the stripes of the flag. The field effect was given by stars in the caps of another division of marchers. The nurses swung rapidly along, their pretty faces alight, their trim persons swaying to the strains of "Keep the Home Fires Burning." The Red Cross unit was followed by a huge white float, with a beautiful girl enthroned at one end. She was dressed in a flowing Grecian robe, and carried an enormous American flag; at her feet, in attitudes of appropriate admiration, were grouped several sailors, soldiers and marines.

The "Miss America" float was the direct precursor of the Overseas Division. Preceded by a band playing "Over There," more than a hundred recently discharged soldiers and sailors were now coming up Third Street. Most of them marched jauntily, responding gaily to the prolonged cheers with which they were greeted; but a few looked straight ahead of them as they marched, their white faces set in grim lines. Several were minus an arm, and several others walked with a limp, struggling and skipping to keep up with the smart pace of their comrades.

What the division as a whole lacked in dash, however, its leaders supplied in abundant measure: Gervais d'Alvery, clad in a full-dress uniform of a Captain of Artillery, was an arresting figure. He was only a little above medium height, and slenderly built; but he carried himself so proudly and erectly that he gave the effect of being a tall and powerful man. He had the high cheek bones, fine features and clear olive complexion characteristic of a Creole aristocrat, and his tan accentuated the fine quality of his skin instead of detracting from it. A small black moustache, closely clipped, shadowed his upper lip, and his rather heavy brows were black too; both added to the striking quality of his handsome face. His magnetism, like his vitality, was inescapable.

III

" 'Oh, it isn't cheerful to see a man, the marvellous work of God,
  Crushed in the mutilation mill, crushed to a smeary clod;
  Oh, it isn't cheerful to hear him moan; but it isn't that I mind,
  It isn't the anguish that goes with him, it's the anguish he leaves
    behind.
  For his going opens a tragic door that gives on a world of pain,
  And the death he dies, those who live and love, will die again
    and again.' "

Fabian d'Alvery raised one arm slowly and shook his hand from left to right as he quoted this verse from a poem by Robert Service. The gesture had seemed both appropriate and effective when he practised it before his bedroom mirror; but somehow, here in the street, it did not go over so well. Besides, he could feel the little wooden stand underneath him tottering as he gesticulated. The stand had been provided to assure him extra height and consequence, raising him above the crowd and setting him apart from it; he needed it, for, unlike his kinsman Gervais d'Alvery, he was unable to cut a fine figure. He had been born with a spinal deformity which not only prevented him from walking in a normal way, but also gave him a hunched appearance when he was standing or sitting. However, at this moment he would willingly have sacrificed the height of the stool if he could have felt the solidity of the sidewalk under his feet. He persevered, fully aware that his position was precarious.

"Today's parade is an appeal to help provide for those who are left behind," he said, trying to speak impressively. His voice was

18

earnest and so was his face. But he did not speak loudly enough, and his grey eyes, which were his finest feature, were wise and honest rather than impelling; aside from them, his thin, refined face was at first glance unremarkable. "Thank God, men are no longer being crushed to smearing clods in mutilation mills," he went on laboriously. "But it is all too true that when they died they opened tragic doors on a world of pain, and that thousands of others, who still survive, are facing destruction and devastation wh'ch is a living death."

Beyond the mob jostling around him and making his position more precarious every minute, Fabian was conscious of the derisive countenance of "College," the Italian who kept the fruit stand on the opposite side of Convention Street. As usual, College was wearing no necktie and his collar was unbuttoned at his throat, which was thrown back a little, adding to the effect of merriment which he gave; his hands were thrust impudently under his exposed suspenders. Everything about his enormous figure, framed with the bunches of bananas hanging in succulent abundance on either side of his wooden shack, bespoke ease, content and amusement. As Fabian unwillingly met his twinkling eyes, his own discomfiture increased apace. But he went doggedly on with what he had to say.

"If we do not rescue these sad survivors from their living death, the heroes who have fallen will have died in vain," he declared. "'They will not sleep though poppies grow in Flanders Fields.' This is a war which has been fought to make the world safe—safe for democracy, as our great President has so often reminded us, and safe in all other ways as well. The dead have done their part. Now we must do ours, in this tumultuous post-war period upon which we are just entering. We must do it in both tangible and intangible ways. We must be as ready to prove our patriotism now as we were in the darkest days of the war."

This time he felt he had really put his idea over and that his words had been respectfully received. He did not glance in the direction of College again, but kept his eyes fixed on the division of the parade which had halted, according to schedule, at Convention and Third. It was a large division, extending far down the street, and consisting of a group of boys and girls in their teens. The group was not in uniform, yet strangely enough there was a certain uniformity in the bearing and expression of these boys and girls, and they gave a greater effect of accustomed unity than many which had passed by. They were not rollicking and roisterous either, like many of the others, but grave and attentive, as if they understood the basic solemnity and importance of the occasion. A great wave of gratitude and recompense welled up in Fabian's heart as he looked at them, and he leaned forward to see the inscription on the banner which their sober young leaders were carrying with so much circumspection. The banner was fluttering in the crisp breeze, and he could not instantly make out the lettering, because it was partially concealed by the shifting folds. Then, with horrible suddenness, it leaped out at him:

STATE SCHOOL FOR THE DEAF AND DUMB

The deaf-mutes! The unfortunate boys and girls, educated at public expense, who could not hear a word that he or anyone else said to them and could not have responded even if they did! Their apparent attention had been a mockery, just as the Italian's grin and shrug had been; their anxious watchfulness for the signal to proceed. Unless their alertness was unremitting, they might miss this, for no sharp command, no blaring bugle, could penetrate the tragic and perpetual silence to which they were doomed. Fabian was still staring at them, with a gaze almost as fixed as theirs, when they caught sight of the awaited signal and began to move, not freely and joyously, but in that monotonous unison which no longer puzzled him. He did not wait to see who would follow after them. He stepped down from his wooden stand, giving it a vicious kick as he escaped from it, and plunged into the crowd. The corroding knowledge that his disappointment was puerile in no way assuaged his overpowering sense of chagrin.

He was still ploughing ahead without any reason or objective, other than avoiding the direction of the fruit stand, when he caught sight of Meredith Randall and Miss Mittie Alden, less than half a block away from him. The girl's arm was linked in that of her queer companion, and she was chattering gaily.

Fabian worked his way sidewise through the crowd towards the kerb-stone. If he could reach it, he could forge forward fast enough to catch up with Merry; and if he could do that, then the day would not be a failure after all. No day could be a failure that was crowned with her presence, no matter what had happened through the burden and heat of it. He called out to her; if he could hear her and Miss Mittie above the noise, surely they ought to be able to hear him.

"Hi, there, Merry! What's your hurry? Wait a sec., can't you?"

He saw her pause and turn her head, trying to locate the source of his call, but unsuccessfully. He had not been able to reach the kerb-stone yet; he was still swallowed up by his turbulent surroundings. But a substantial matron who was in front of him had heard him too. She elbowed out a small circle and turned herself around in it.

"*Why, Fabian!*" she exclaimed delightedly. "I *thought* I recognized your voice! Of course, you have such a *wonderful* voice that I couldn't very well help it! I'm *so* glad to have a chance to speak to you! I want to tell you that your talk was simply *marvellous!*"

"It's terribly kind of you to say so, Mrs. Ingledew. But I know it wasn't really. I know it was an awful flop. I'd rather not talk about it, if you don't mind, especially just now——"

"Why, Fabian, how can you *say* such a thing! It was the most marvellous speech I ever heard in my *life*! Everyone said, when you were in high school, that by and by you would be L.S.U.'s most outstanding orator. When I think of all those debates you were in, about sugar and tariffs and serious subjects like that, and then of your *beautiful* valedictory——"

With desperate determination, Fabian had reached the kerb, in spite of Mrs. Ingledew. Once there, as he had foreseen, he had no trouble in plunging forward. But meanwhile Merry and Miss Mittie must have turned a corner, for they were nowhere to be seen. Fabian sang out again, but the only response to his words came from astonished strangers. Suddenly he felt very tired, and his back hurt him almost unbearably. He could not understand how he had dared to hope, even for a moment, that the day might not be a failure after all. This was not his day. It belonged to his cousin, who could go to war because he did not have a bad spine. Who had been wounded, to be sure, but afterwards decorated for conspicuous gallantry. Who had now come home to be acclaimed as the hero of Louisiana and was the accepted suitor of Meredith Randall. His cousin, Gervais d'Alvery.

IV

"It's good to feel the sun so warm, isn't it, Pascal?"

"Why not? It belongs to be warm in April, don't it, Max? And somehow another it still puts me in mind of Appomattox, even after all this long a time."

"Reckon I might feel the same as you if I'd been there. But I never did get back into the fight, after I was wounded at Donaldsonville. I never even heard what went on at Appomattox till a week after it was all over. Did you, Pres?"

"Yes, I heard. But that's not like I'd been there."

The parade was still coming down Third Street. It would turn presently beside the stereotyped Confederate Monument where these aged veterans were waiting to see it come, and swing up North Boulevard, where it would disband a few blocks beyond the Executive Mansion. But the music from Sylvester Smith's Band and Price Mitchell's Fife and Drum Corps was still distant; the strains of *Buy a Bond, Buy a Bond, Buy a Bond!* were not so loud that the three old friends could not hear each other as they rambled on, talking about old days and comparing these to new ones.

It was the principal pleasure they had left in life. Two of them —Pascal Tremblet and Preston Vicknair—lived in Baton Rouge, Pascal with his married granddaughter, Preston with his bachelor grandson. They were equally in the way and equally aware of it; the wooden bench beside the shell-strewn walk which encircled the monument represented almost their only haven of escape. They came to it every pleasant morning and sat there indefinitely, engaged in endless bickering, contented as long as they could keep it up, saddened when they parted to return to the meals for which they knew they must not be late. Max Stoetzner was more fortunately placed; he had saved a little money when he was younger and more vigorous, and this, with his pension of fifteen dollars a month, enabled him to live peacefully alone, in a small shack ornamented with wooden scrollwork, on the outskirts of Port Allen. When he crossed the River to Baton Rouge, he made a great occasion of it, arraying himself in his faded grey uniform which had been made for him at the time the United Confederate Veterans attended the dedication of the Albert Sidney Johnson Memorial in New Orleans. He took immense pride in the fact that it still fitted him, though this was largely because he could afford no bounty at his bare and lonely table. The uniform set him slightly apart from the others, who always wore the same dingy black suits.

"You know this fellow everyone's making such a fuss about, don't you, Pascal?" Max asked, stroking his goatee softly as he spoke. Since he had the advantage of his uniform, he felt he should accord his friends some advantage also, and he did this by tacitly acknowledging that their acquaintance with local figures and local conditions must necessarily be more thorough than that of a man who lived on the west side of the River, even if this habitation were only four miles away.

"Positively, yes. I know all the d'Alverys, me. They're kin to us in a way. Philogene d'Alvery's sister, Sybelle, married the second cousin of my mother. Philogene was Gervais' father—well, you know about that, at least. But I tell you frankly I don't know Gervais like I know Fabian, or like I knew their grandfather, Lucien Estrade. You take when I was a young boy, nobody called Belle Heloise the d'Alvery Place. It was the Estrade Plantation then. The Estrades been living there, them, ever since 1824."

"They was there a long time, I grant you that," interrupted Pres belligerently, stabbing at the dusty white shells before their bench with his gnarled cane. "But that house wasn't built in no 1824. Nearer 1830, if you ask me, when old man François Estrade, that always lived in New Orleans himself, gave it to his son for a wedding present."

"He gave it to his son for a wedding present, yes, but that was in 1824," Pascal retorted, glowering. "I ain't forgot, even if you have, Pres, how Lafayette got off the boat, him, and visited my kin at Belle Heloise. And that was in January, 1825, when he made his voyage from New Orleans to Baton Rouge. I tell you frankly, I don't like the way you ignore history, my friend."

22

Preston Vicknair muttered something unintelligible, his head bowed over the clasped hands fondling the gnarled cane. Resentfully, he felt himself unequal to the task of challenging history.

"I haven't got used till yet hearing people talk about the d'Alvery Plantation," Pascal continued in triumph; it was not often Pres would admit an error, even tacitly. "Philogene d'Alvery never was more'n a poor relation, taken in out of charity, if he did marry Isabelle Estrade. Sybelle, his sister that I'm kin to, never had so much as a dowry. But I got to admit, me, those d'Alverys always had a way with them, paupers or not paupers. This boy's just running true to form. That's the onliest reason he's gone so far, him."

"He's a mighty handsome young buck. He hasn't just got a way with him. He's got looks too," volunteered Max.

"He must 'a had something else too, if he killed all them Huns. I reckon Pascal won't go so far 's to deny he did kill 'em. Medals like he's got ain't handed out for nothin'," Pres added, recovering his spirits.

"Oh, I grant you, me, he's got medals and all the other trimmin's," Pascal Tremblet retorted, with some bitterness. "People fall mighty hard for heroes nowadays, from the President down. But I can remember when things was different, yes. They never had no parade when Lucien Estrade come home after the war." He did not identify the war. In his mind, and those of his hearers, there was still only one war that really counted, changing the destinies of men and the aspects of civilization. "He was on Beauregard's staff too," Pascal went on, flattered by his friends' attention. "So, like you see, he outranked that grandson of his. But no bands, my friends, not so much as one trumpet. Lucien Estrade never even came into the depot, no. He just picked up a little old brown mule that the damn Yankees must of overlooked, God knows how, and he rode into Baton Rouge like that. Minnie, the mule's name was, and I inform you, there has always been one mule named Minnie at Belle Heloise ever since, out of respect to General Estrade."

"A hell of a mark of respect, should you ask me," jeered Pres, tapping with his cane. Pascal ignored the interruption.

"Minnie carried the General all the way from Natchez down to Woodville and through Bayou Sarah to hit the River Road at Baton Rouge," he continued loftily. "She deserves respect. But they wasn't nobody to meet Lucien Estrade nowhere, and he never expected it, no. Besides, nobody could tell when a man in that war would get home, or how. But the General wasn't studying on parades anyway. All he had on his mind was finding his wife and children and putting Minnie to plough. The poor, poor fellow hadn't got the news till yet how both the little boys were already dead and buried, them. Malarial fever, the summer before. Isabelle was born after he got back."

23

"Seem like a sickly lot, the d'Alverys or the Estrades, whichever way you want to call their name. Isabelle, she lost a couple of children too before Gervais, and another before Cresside came along."

"Well, not to say sickly, no. Overbred, maybe. They've all been marrying their cousins, as far back as I can remember. I tell you frankly, it would do no harm to get some fresh blood into that strain."

"I hear Gervais's got a sweetheart right here in Baton Rouge, and I don't call to mind she's any cousin."

"Nothing of the sort, Pres. You've got everything turned around, same as usual. He is to marry one of the Hathaways, him. Regine, the girl's name is, and handsome? I assure you, my friends —a picture! But I never thought so much of Hathaway Hall, me. Built by Carolinians, if I am not mistaken, or maybe it was just Virginians. I rather see Gervais marry a Louisiana girl. Not so much on account of the d'Alverys. But on account of the plantation. I tell you something, Belle Heloise was a fine place once, and lots of fine people stayed there in the old days, yes. Not just Lafayette either. Henry Clay—Zachary Taylor—Judah P. Benjamin—Jefferson Davis——"

The old voice faltered and trailed wistfully to a pause. The approaching band music swelled and stopped.

"So little was left of the place when Lucien Estrade came home," Pascal continued sadly. "I give you my word of honour, not even gear for Minnie. And I don't know as I would say it ever came back to what it was before the war." Again he did not identify the war. "But it could. The land's rich and there's lots of it." He paused with a chuckle which ended in a sad sigh. "Three thousand arpents altogether and twenty-five just in the 'Small Yard.' That was where they took the passengers from the *Princess* when she busted a boiler in midstream."

"It wasn't the *Princess* busted her boiler in midstream, Pascal. It was the *Mattie Belle.*"

"The *Mattie Belle!*" Pascal exclaimed scornfully. "The *Mattie Belle* never had no explosion, her. It was the *Princess,* I assure you, loaded with sightseers watching the famous race between the *Natchez* and the *Robert E. Lee.* Poor, poor people! There was a tragic end to their merrymaking. But the passengers fished out of the water were each and every one laid down on sheets spread in the Small Yard. I do not recollect, me, how many barrels they broke open to roll those poor scalded people in flour on the sheets. One did not buy a little poke of flour in those days, no. One kept it by the barrel."

"Much good it did to bust up all those flour barrels," Pres said in feeble mockery. "The most of those people died anyway."

"And was that the fault of the Estrades, then?" bristled Pascal.

24

"No, never. In fact, the Estrades gave those that died decent burial right there at Belle Heloise, yes, in the cedar grove alongside the Yankees that died of smallpox, when the Federals used the house as a hospital. They tried to drive the family away, but they didn't succeed—Madame Estrade stood her ground and dared them to put her and her children out. They didn't succeed in shelling the house from the river either—the damned Yankee Commodore who tried to do that was some kind of kin to Lucien, but kinship didn't stop him, darn his rotten hide. Lots of Yankees died on the place though, and their consciences must have hurt them, robbers and usurpers that they were, them. They can't rest too easy in their graves. If I believed in ghosts, me, I could say frankly that many would haunt that place."

"I do not believe in such things either," said Max, looking up at the square crenellated towers of the capitol the Yankees had burned in '62. "But I have many times heard Belle Heloise was haunted."

"Oh, that!" replied Pascal. "That's Angus Holt."

"Never heard of no family by the name of Holt on the River Road," Pres challenged at once. "And I'd have heard of them if they'd amounted to shucks."

"Angus Holt had no family, him," Pascal explained loftily. "He was just a Scotch tramp came up the levee at sunset one night, and asked at Belle Heloise for a drink of water. After he got the water, he asked could he have a hot dinner, and after he got the dinner, he asked for a night's lodging. Imagine it, he never left the place again, no, not until he died. Not even then, at least, for he is buried right there in the garden he tended. What a gardener, my friends! No other could touch him. But he was a man of learning too. He could make anything grow that had a root, him, and he knew the roots of all the languages too. He taught them to Lucien Estrade and Lucien Estrade's children—why, he even taught Lucien how to speak *English*!"

Pascal was warming to his subject. Here was a story that was actually all new to his hearers, which Max could not supplement and which Pres could not dispute.

"Philogene d'Alvery—a wild young buck, that rascal!—used to dress in a sheet, and go prowling around to frighten everybody, pretending he was a ghost of Angus Holt. He was no more than pestering his rich wife's family, I assure you, but his pranks started old women to telling it about that Belle Heloise was haunted. Maybe Angus does really haunt the downstairs room he slept in. The garden room it has been called ever since, because it leads right into the garden he laid out."

"Then he would haunt that too, for certain."

"Maybe." Pascal no longer cared to dispute with Pres. His eyes were fixed on the approaching troops, his foot tapping time to the

25

band music. "I'm not denying, me, Angus Holt might have some kind of a part in the past which goes with an old river house like Belle Heloise," he admitted. "But if he does, he's got a part in the future too—a future that's coming towards us this very minute along with that brass band that's playing 'Over There.'" Softly, in his quavering voice, he began to hum:

> " 'So *prepare, say a prayer,*
> *Send the word, send the word,*
> *We'll be over, we're coming over,*
> *And we won't come back 'til it's*
> *Over, over there.'* "

He could not go on. His voice cracked and broke. He coughed regretfully and rose. "I could have managed all right if it had only been 'Dixie,' " he said in an apologetic way. "I've been waiting for that, but it looks as if I'd have to wait a while longer. And I can still salute. Shall we, my friends? I'm not saying Gervais d'Alvery is any such soldier as Lucien Estrade. But I figure we could owe him that much anyway, for his grandfather's sake."

V

"Well, it certainly was a fine parade. But that seems to be the last of it. Suppose we come into the dining-room and have a little coffee!"

The governor's wife rose, looking at her guests with a comprehensive smile and addressing them as a group. They had been sitting on the lower gallery of the Executive Mansion, a large, rather boxlike white house situated on a street corner at one end of a long lawn. A few japonica bushes bordered the walk between the house and the street, but the bushes were small and the walk was short; the visitors had enjoyed an unobstructed view of the parade as it swung up North Boulevard; they had also enjoyed discussing its principal features with each other.

Some of the guests were so intensively engaged in conversation of this type that they were only vaguely aware of their hostess's suggestion; though they rose, politely, when she did, they made no immediate move to follow her and some of them went on talking among themselves.

"I'm afraid we ought not to linger too long. I'm sure some of you will want to hear Colonel Prescott's stirring address at the conclusion of the parade, and it's going to disband just a few blocks from here."

The governor's wife still spoke smilingly, but there was a little more insistence in her voice this time; she plainly wished to shepherd her guests into the dining-room without further delay. A slim dark girl, exceptionally chic, but piquante rather than pretty, who was perched on a railing at the farther end of the gallery, somewhat apart from most of the other visitors, made a slight grimace as she slid from her seat, and linked her arm in that of another young girl who was standing near her.

"Listen to the old battleaxe, will you, Regine?" she murmured. "Much she cares whether we hear Colonel Prescott's stirring address or not. All she wants is to get us out of the house. Well, I don't think we'll be delayed long in the dining-room—we'll get one small black and one small cookie apiece, if the impending feast is anything like the others I've been to here. I don't think this outfit ever heard of gin, much less champagne. But come on, let's get the orgy over. I want to go down to the river to see those four submarine destroyers that have just come in from the New Orleans Navy yard."

"But what have they come for?"

"To advertise this Loan we're all getting so hot and bothered about. Gervais says they're on the first leg of the run up to Memphis. . . . After I've given them the once over, I'd like to go down to the block dance in front of the Istrouma. Wouldn't you? There may be a little life to that!"

"Hush, Cresside! I do wish you wouldn't talk like that! Someone might overhear and tell. Then you'd never be invited to the Mansion again."

The second girl spoke in a fluttering way which was oddly at variance with her statuesque appearance. Someone had told Regine Hathaway, in her very early youth, that she bore a marked resemblance to the Empress Eugénie; ever since then she had cultivated this resemblance with phenomenal success, considering the handicaps imposed on her by modern fashion. Her hair was always arranged in ringlets, and her carefully planned costumes were always characterized by some touch of elegance suggesting the Third Empire. But evidently it had not occurred to her that her appearance made her manner of speaking seem doubly silly. This had, however, often occurred to Cresside d'Alvery, and though Regine was her best friend, it annoyed her excessively. She made no effort to conceal this annoyance as she answered.

"Now wouldn't I break right down and cry if that happened! You talk as if a coffee party at the Mansion were in the same class as a Carnival ball! Doesn't she, Sylvestre?"

Cresside turned from Regine to a young man, immaculately dressed in the height of fashion, who was standing near them. He had handsome features, a fine figure and a beguiling manner. But it was his colouring which made his appearance especially striking; he had very red cheeks, very blue eyes and very black hair. He smiled engagingly at Cresside, and a look of intimate and ardent understanding flashed swiftly between them. But though he answered lightly and pleasantly, there was a guarded undertone to his voice.

"Oh, I wouldn't go so far as to say that! Besides, there have been some mighty fine parties here in the past, Cresside, and there'll probably be a lot more in the future. It's just as well to keep in with the crowd that's automatically invited to the Mansion in every administration, whether you care for the present one or not. And at the moment we're the guests of the governor's wife. I think we'd be very wise to go on into the dining-room!"

They swung into the end of the line which was now advancing through the wide hallway dividing the double drawing-rooms on one side of it from the governor's study and the dining-room on the other. Their temporary absence had passed unobserved in the midst of the animated chatter which still preoccupied their fellow-guests. But now a few of these detached themselves from their special affinities long enough to speak to Cresside about her brother.

"Honey, I should think you'd be so proud you'd be about to burst! I declare, I get teary myself when I think that one of our own hometown boys got two promotions for gallant conduct in the face of the enemy and medals from two different Governments!"

"Well, I haven't shed any tears over it yet. I still think Gervais a stuffed shirt, just like I always did. I haven't got used to all this hero business yet! . . ."

"You're not looking for Captain d'Alvery to leave here any time soon, are you, Miss Cresside? It would be a great loss to the community if he did. He's got so much to contribute! This State needs men like him. It hasn't got too many."

"I don't know how much he'll contribute, but I reckon he's here to stay. Anyway, I'm afraid so. He's going around Belle Heloise giving Army orders right and left."

Determined to put an end to this sort of thing, Cresside slipped adroitly through the crowd, abandoning Sylvestre and Regine to the gushing enthusiasts, who were uncertain just what to say or do next. They had shared the general impression that there was an "understanding" between Regine Hathaway and Gervais d'Alvery. But now the whole town was buzzing with talk about the way he had greeted another girl at the depot, and here was Regine herself, escorted by that handsome young Tremaine from New Orleans. That is, at one moment he appeared to be her escort; but the next he appeared to be Cresside's. It was all very confusing. Perhaps it would be better to say nothing more, after all. Murmuring something incoherent, the puzzled ladies hurried on to the dining-room, leaving Regine and Sylvestre behind them.

"Let's go into the parlour for a minute," Regine whispered. "No one noticed when Cresside delayed us, so I don't believe anyone would notice if we slipped off now. We haven't had a minute to ourselves all day, Sylvestre."

28

"Are you telling me? I don't know that we can prove much, though, just going in to those great open spaces."

It was true that the double drawing-rooms at the Executive Mansion did not provide a very cosy or secluded spot for an interval of surreptitious love making. The "front parlour" and the "back parlour," furnished identically in tapestried Victorian furniture, led into each other through wide folding doors. The large gilt-framed mirrors, which hung over the twin fireplaces, not only reflected a formidable expanse of room, but everything which took place there. Regine and Sylvestre sat down on one of the stiff sofas ranged between rows of still stiffer chairs, and after glancing carefully about, achieved an uneasy embrace. Then, as no disturbing element appeared to interrupt them, they permitted themselves to unbend a little more. But their period of relaxation was brief. Unanticipated sounds at the front door proclaimed the arrival of a tardy visitor and they had hardly time to get on their feet when Fabian d'Alvery walked unconcernedly into the drawing-room.

"Why, hello, there!" he said. "Is the party over, except for you two? I know it's late. To tell the truth, I forgot until just a few minutes ago that I was supposed to come here after I finished my speech. I was almost home, but I turned around and came back. Evidently it wasn't worth the trouble after all."

"I don't know whether you'll think it worth the trouble or not," Regine said with a giggle. "It hasn't been much of a party. You should have heard Cresside raging on about it. But it isn't over. Everyone else is in the dining-room. We came back here a moment ago to—to look for my handkerchief." Regine giggled again. "It was one of my very best embroidered ones, and I couldn't bear to lose it."

"I see," Fabian remarked rather drily. "Well, now that you've found it, suppose we join the others in the dining-room. You *have* found it, haven't you?"

"Oh yes! Look!"

Regine produced a wisp of muslin and lace from her *petit point* handbag and held it up for Fabian's inspection. He took it from her and regarded it solicitously.

"Yes, that would have been quite a loss," he agreed gravely, handing it back to her. Then, at the sound of light footsteps, he glanced to the rear of the room and saw that Cresside was coming towards them. "Did you lose your handkerchief, too?" he inquired.

"I lose on an average three a day," she said. "I can't find any place to put them in the clothes we wear now. But I don't know what that's got to do with this lousy party—no, don't bother to tell me. How did your speech go off, Fabian?"

"It was a lousy speech—thanks for supplying me with just the right adjective. It sounded all right, when I got it off in the privacy of my own apartment, but of course no one heard it there." He stopped, grinning again. "No one heard it on Third Street, either," he said. "I thought at first I had a very attentive audience. Then I found out that the division I was so eloquently addressing was a group from the State School for the Deaf."

"Oh, Fabian, you didn't!"

For the first time, there was no flippancy in Cresside's voice when she spoke, and none in her pert, provocative little face either. This had softened suddenly, and the expression with which she looked at Fabian was full of sympathy and affection. He regarded her gratefully but whimsically.

"'Pride cometh before a fall and a haughty spirit before destruction,'" he said. "I thought I was quite an orator once, but I know better now. The speech really was lousy, Cresside. I tried talking down to my listeners and that's an insult to any crowd. It's a good thing nobody heard me. It took me a few minutes to realize that too, but eventually came the dawn. I think the whole thing's darn funny, when you get right down to it. And I had another funny experience afterwards."

"I want to hear."

"Well, I saw Merry Randall in the crowd and tried to catch up with her. But who do you think got me into her clutches? That outstanding clubwoman and public-spirited citizen, Mrs. Ivy Mae Ingledew. She stopped me and——"

They strolled back to the dining-room, while Fabian told them about his encounter with Mrs. Ingledew, making a good story out of it. Cresside was laughing unrestrainedly before he finished and presently he laughed too.

"You see, it just wasn't my day," he said. "Not that there's any reason why I should ever have thought it was. Where is the hero of the family, Cresside? I was sure I'd find him here. Hasn't he done his duty to the Great Cause by this time?"

"I reckon so. But he was going straight home to mother after the parade. With a grim purpose, unless I miss my guess. We tried to get him to stay in town for the block dance, but he wouldn't. All the gang is going, and later on we'll probably go somewhere else. You wouldn't come with us, would you, Fabian?"

"Thanks a lot. You know I'm not much of an addition when it comes to dancing."

The merriment had suddenly gone from his manner. He turned away to speak to his hostess, and presently he was swallowed up in a group of other acquaintances. When he looked for Cresside again, she had disappeared; so had Regine and Sylvestre.

II

GERVAIS D'ALVERY was devoutly thankful that no banquet had been planned after the parade, and that he was free to start for home as soon as it was over. Swinging into the River Road, he was acutely conscious, as he always had been when he made the turn, of the immediacy with which the capital merged into the country. The black fields pierced by the tender green of young cane; the flat muddy stretches which later would be rich with rice; the sturdy cattle ranging over the banks of the clover-covered levee; the negro horsemen riding along its ridge; the turbaned women sauntering through the twilight with faggots on their heads; the rickety cabins surrounded by thrifty garden patches; the fluttering fowls and rooting hogs and plodding mules—all these, no less than the sudden coming of quietude, were the unmistakable symbols of the region's abrupt and complete detachment from the city scene. The sky, lightly veiled with small clouds, had the soft colour of pale amethysts. A fluttering breeze scattered the fragrance of the clover. The great river flowed imperturbably on, concealed by the levee, yet omnipresent as any other invisible deity. Gervais could feel its force, its immensity, its continuance. Here, at last, by its shores, was beauty after ugliness, harmony after discord, tranquillity after turmoil, peace after war. . . .

Peace in as far as the countryside could give it, and that was abundantly; still it would not suffice unless the hearthstone which was the core of the countryside was beatified by it too. Instinctively, Gervais glanced away from the levee and saw the immense façade of Hathaway Hall, glistening among the greens and greys of the grove which encircled it. The house was one of the handsomest on either side of the River, both inside and out: the stateliness of its situation, the majesty of its proportions, the delicacy of its carved ornamentation—all this gave it a grandeur which made the simpler attributes of Belle Heloise seem almost humble in comparison. Yet Hathaway Hall, for him, lacked the final quality of charm which would have made it irresistible, either in itself or as a setting for his love. He tried to tell himself that this was because it was not essentially Louisiainan in feeling and expression; its builder had been a Carolinian who had not constructed it on the scale and in the style of either his native or his adopted state, but in a manner which he conceived to be a glorification of both. The result was impressive but it was not enchanting, at least to Gervais, though it was suited to Regine and she to it. This was the sort of house to which she inevitably belonged,

31

quite as much as it was the sort of house which inevitably belonged
to her. Even as a child she had preferred playing alone in its great
galleries to paddling with the others on the sandy shores of the
old barrow pit at the bend of the River near Belle Heloise. Declining the honours of a carnival queen, she had made her début
in the white ballrooms; she would be married in it too, disdaining
the solemnity of the Church; and after her marriage she would
abide at Hathaway Hall and reign there. She would never follow
her husband spontaneously to his home, or merge her life instinctively with his.

Gervais smiled a little wryly and shook his head, thinking of all
this. The rôle of Prince Consort at Hathaway Hall had never
appealed to him; there was not money enough in the world, let
alone on one plantation, to tempt him to repeat his father's mistake. He knew that Philogene d'Alvery had come to Belle Heloise
as the poor relation, the charming wastrel who had not the
stamina or the purpose to strike out for himself; and the kinsfolk
who hastened to give him shelter, also hastened to give him their
daughter, conniving to keep her with them. Gervais knew that this
case was different; but still it was comparable. Strange that his
mother, who must know that he was more her son than Philogene's, had never admitted it, that she had always assumed—or at
all events pretended to assume—that eventually he and Regine
would be married. Very possibly it had been part of her plan that
he *would* leave Belle Heloise, and that it would be Cresside, and
Cresside's future husband, who would stay with her. The wry smile
hardened into a straight line, and he shook his head again, thinking of this. . . .

A small cemetery, dominated by a latticed tower built to house a
tolling bell, lay at the outskirts of Hathaway Hall. Philogene
d'Alvery was buried there, in the same lot with the kinsfolk who
had found him so convenient to kidnap. Even in death he had not
escaped any of the respectable responsible relatives who had remained at Belle Heloise from one generation to another, while
his branch of the family went wandering; and the family tombs
of the Tremaines and Hathaways were divided from those of the
Estrades and the d'Alverys by only the width of a lot, suggesting
another unchangeable and unbreakable tie. Gervais slowed down
his car as he approached the cemetery, and the general appearance
of weediness and neglect which it presented from the road moved
him to get out and walk down the unkempt allée towards his
father's grave, to inspect the condition of this. Horror-stricken, he
recoiled as a snake slithered off and vanished in the tall grass. All
this treacherous grass should be cut early the next morning, he
vowed; and hereafter there should be fresh flowers for the little
Gothic chapel or none at all; savagely he flung out the dark brown
blossoms drooping in front of him and emptied the slimy water in

32

he vase that had held them. The cornice should be repaired too, he inscriptions cleaned and clarified, the iron railing mended and painted. Most of the tombs he had passed had once belonged to families who long ago had left the River Road—the Comerfords, he Simoneaux, the Bovards, the Surcliffes. Some of them had lost heir homes through fire or flood, others through mere neglect, others through poverty or indifference. The Faith Estate, Chelmsford, Cedar Hall—all these places which had once been such proud plantations were only names now; there was no one left on hem to care for either the living or the dead. Only Hackberry Lodge, recently bought by a Bostonian named Charles Boylston, had been redeemed; the general neglect of the cemetery was all too easy to explain. But he would not permit it to continue; henceforth t must take its tone from the families who had possessed the stamina to survive disaster and decay, and stubbornly he had excluded the Hathaways and their kin from this category. It was nothing to him what happened to their simpering statues and heir prickly lambs; but there should be no more snakes slithering through the grass near the place where the Estrades and the d'Alverys were buried.

Still raging with resentment, he walked slowly back towards the road. The light was changing fast; the tottering tiers of brick were already engulfed by the shadows of the cedars which surrounded them, and even the chalk-white tombs looked grey against the grass. But there were still patches of sunshine on his path, and looking down, he saw a four-leaf clover gleaming in the midst of a common cluster. Like most Creoles, he was extremely superstitious, though he himself would have vehemently denied this; and here, at last, was a good omen, after the evil one which had so badly shaken him. He picked the four-leaf clover and folded it carefully away in his wallet; he would have it enclosed in a little gold-rimmed glass locket and give it to Merry. The best luck he had ever had lay in his meeting with her. Now he wanted to share his token of it.

Thanks to his cheering discovery, he left the cemetery happier than he had entered it, after all. And he brightened still further when he heard a joyous shout and saw an old favourite of his, Luigi Tramonte, hastening forward to meet him. Luigi was an Italian peddler, who carried his picayune wares in a deep coarse-woven basket strapped to his shoulders. He had been a familiar figure along the River Road ever since Gervais could remember; his arrival was always hailed with delight in the quarters of all the plantations and he was not infrequently summoned courteously, if condescendingly, into the mansions also. His principal stock-in-trade was a sort of syrup candy, called Johnny Crooks, into which fresh shredded cocoanut had been stirred before it was shaped into balls; but he also dealt in another specialty of the

33

region called "stage planks"—four by eight slabs of hard ginger
bread with thin white icing on one side; also in taffy, liquorice
peanuts, bananas, peppermint stick and other delicacies of lik
nature. All in all, his sweetmeats made so substantial a burden
that his basket was very heavy, and he wore large tufted pads on
his shoulders to prevent the wide leather straps which held this in
place from cutting into his flesh. He was also adept in shifting th
weight of his load, so that this should never rest too long in on
place, and his manner of doing it had developed into a motion
resembling a violent and habitual shrug. He shrugged now, in
series of powerful contortions, before waving his broad-brimmed
hat several times around his dark head and lumbering forward t
meet Gervais.

"'Allo, 'allo, *Capitano*," he shouted delightedly. "Watta goo
luck I have to meeta you this day! I wanta shaka your hand!"

Suiting his actions to his words he hitched over to the car
which Gervais had brought to a standstill, and pumped the youn
officer's arm up and down with unabating vehemence. "We go t
the depot to see you come in," he continued. "Me and my wife
Netta, and my bambino too. I gotta me a beautiful bambino
Capitano, while you were at the war. Fifteen years we been mar
ried, me and Netta, never I getta me a bambino before. But Netta
she pray plenty to Santo Amico, and now I gotta him. We took
him to the depot, so he coulds say, bimeby, when he's bigga man
in war himself maybe, he see *Capitano* d'Alvery coma back from
France. You stay in France alla time, eh, *Capitano*? You no go t
Italy?"

"No, I didn't go to Italy, I'm sorry to say. But I hope I'll ge
there some day yet. All the men who did go there were craz
about it. . . . So you got you a fine bambino while I was away
did you, Luigi? What's his name?"

"His name Riccardo. *Si, si*, one very fine bambino. I holda him
up high at the depot, but you no see him because you're lookin
alla time at one very pretty young lady, eh, *Capitano*?"

Luigi, who was as habitually jolly as he was habitually heavy
laden, laughed heartily, throwing back his head and showing hi
gleaming white teeth. Encumbered though he was with his bi
basket, he managed, amidst his merriment, to poke Gervais jest
ingly in the ribs. But this familiarity, coming from Luigi, someho
lacked the quality which would have made Gervais regard it a
presumptuous, coming from almost anyone else. Gervais laughe
too.

"I'm afraid you're right, Luigi," he said. "I didn't see the fin
bambino this time. I *was* pretty preoccupied. But I hope to see him
some other time, very soon."

"I bringa him to Belle Heloise myself, one day," Luigi sai
proudly. "I gonna teach him my trade. Soon like he can walk, h

gonna go 'long with me on the River Road. Then maybe, bimeby, we make so much money, Riccardo he don' have just a basket with candy in—see? toting it alla day long like his papa. He have nice littla store, sell fancy groceries, all sorts fancy groceries. Well, I gotta go 'long, *Capitano*. I know you wanna get home, and I gotta get to the quarters by Hathaway before gooda sundown. But you leta me give you a package of Johnny Crooks for gooda luck. Next time, when I come to Belle Heloise you buy two Stage Planks to make up, eh, *Capitano*?"

Gervais laughed again, telling Luigi he had just found a four-leaf clover and that he would be glad to add the Johnny Crooks to it; then, with a more serious show of gratitude, he accepted the squashy package which the Italian offered him. Having hitched his heavy basket into position, Luigi stood in the middle of the road waving his hat and cheering as the Captain drove off. Gervais did not have much farther to go now. A stranger, approaching Belle Heloise for the first time, might easily have missed the myrtle-bordered driveway into which Gervais turned. This driveway, leading off the River Road at a sharp angle, was narrow as well as short; and the entrance to it was nearly hidden by clusters of wild palmetto, which likewise almost concealed the squat wooden posts on either side of it; it was as inconspicuous as it was unpretentious, and with the labour shortage which had come during the war, it was also unkempt. The cattle-gap between the posts rattled as Gervais went over it, and he smiled contentedly—the same old rattle, always the first of the familiar home sounds! The next was the cooing of the doves in the twin pigeonniers; these quaint, conical structures, surrounded by overgrown shrubbery, were the singing towers of Belle Heloise. Sometimes, when Gervais was coming in, doves flew across his face in whirring pursuit of each other, or lighted, with a gentle flutter of wings, upon his shoulders. Not when it was as late as this, however; they were now settled in their cotes for the night; only the mild music which they made, drifting drowsily towards him, revealed their continual presence.

A negro boy who had been drowsing by the pump came forward to take the car and put it in the dilapidated shed which served as a garage. This was Amen, the youngest son of Selah the butler, who had always taken the reins from his master when Gervais came back from riding the crops, pridefully leading the palomino back to the stables for special grooming. Now he took charge of the battered automobile with much the same air. Gervais was fond of Amen, and ordinarily he would have stopped to chat with the boy; but for the moment he was bent on seeing his mother with the least possible delay; there had been no chance for a serious talk with her amidst the first hurly-burly of his homecoming, but he was determined that there should be no procrastination in clarifying his position with Merry. So he responded abstractedly to Amen's cheerful greeting, and freed himself impatiently from the two dogs who leaped about him, barking with excitement and delight. This was another of the old familiar sounds, but it failed to evolve such fond memories as the rattle of the cattle-gap and the cooing of the doves. He did not see why they had ever had dogs like these at Belle Heloise in the first place, he told himself irritably, momentarily forgetting his own youthful attachment to Snow, the ageing white collie, and Cornet, the crippled fox terrier; they should have had a *real* dog like Fabian's spaniel Belizaire. He called out after the disappearing negro boy, voicing his irritation after failing to voice any kindliness.

"How many times have I told you to keep the cockleburrs out of Snow's hair? He looks as if he had been rolling in them. Have him combed out by morning, or tell me the reason why. And Cornet's as badly maimed as if he'd been fighting a tiger. You'd better get him to the veterinary before he loses a leg."

Amen stopped the car noisily and stuck his woolly head out of the side. "Yessuh, Mr. Gervais. I didn't disremember what you told me, but I'se done had a fever in my back." The look of beaming expectancy with which he had come forward to meet Gervais had gone, and a hangdog expression of dejection had taken its place. Ordinarily Gervais would have felt compunction for such a change, knowing himself responsible for it. But now he spoke even more sharply the second time.

"Well, then, you'd better go to the doctor yourself when you take Cornet to the veterinary. But get him there. I'm working up a fever too, and it isn't just in one place, either——"

The family cat, a tortoiseshell named Miss Larcella, whose bulging form belied her right to a maidenly title, came padding towards him, purring sonorously and rubbing her sleek sides against his ankles. Again he freed himself, even more irritably than from the dogs, but less easily, for Miss Larcella instantly dug her claws into his skin, clinging to his leg and mewing piteously. Another silly superfluous animal, Gervais thought savagely, restraining with difficulty the impulse to toss the persistent pet out into the shrubbery, as he strode off towards the colonnade forming the gallery that surrounded three sides of the house. It was paved with the same type of mellow brick which made the walls, and his footsteps tapped out a signal of approach on this pavement as he crossed it. But even without the signal Gervais knew that Selah would be watching for him from the doorway. The sight of the old butler's bent figure, standing between the fluted pillars, was another integral part of home-coming. Selah was not the formal butler of tradition, given to platitudes and pomposity; he stumbled a little as he walked, and his clothes were always slightly askew; he gave a general effect of apology and shoddiness. But he belonged.

36

He was as much a part of Belle Heloise as the colonnade, and it never occurred to Gervais that he might not be as permanent.

"Good-evening, Selah. Has Lucie told you how Madame's feeling tonight?"

Contrary to local custom, none of the servants had continued to call his mother Miss Isabelle after her marriage. She had been Madame to them from the time she became Philogene's wife. Gervais had never heard them address her otherwise, and never referred to her himself in any other way.

"Yessuh, Mr. Gervais. She's po'ly, jes lak she alluz is. There ain't no difference. . . . The parade was mighty grand, wasn't it, Mr. Gervais? I reckon there ain't never been anything in Baton Rouge to equal it."

"Well, it seemed to go off all right. . . . Madame is awake, isn't she?"

"Yessuh, she's awake. Lucie don' tole me she waked up extra early this ebenin'. Seems lak she's restless, waitin' for you and Miss Cresside to git home and tell her all about the parade."

"I don't think Miss Cresside will be home until pretty late, Selah. She went to a party at the Mansion this afternoon, with Miss Regine and Mr. Sylvestre, and I have an impression they're going on to another somewhere else after that. Tell Lou Ida not to hold up dinner for her. I'm hungry myself. But I'm going up to see Madame before I eat."

He handed his cap to the old butler, nodded, a trifle less abstractedly than when he had left Amen, and started across the immense hall. It ran the entire length of the house, dividing the library, music-room and the garden room on one side of the parlour, dining-room and service quarters on the other. Though the door at either end of it habitually stood open, the colonnade so shaded it that it was really radiant only during the brief period of sunset; now it was already engulfed in evening shadows. Gervais was used to its dimness, but suddenly this irked him; never had he felt so strongly that the house lacked light and warmth and the simple kindly humanity that was as alien to his sister's flippant coquetry as it was to his mother's arrogant reserve. Light and warmth were what Merry would bring to the house, if he could only get her there without such a struggle that it spoiled the spontaneity of her single-hearted love for him. Those were the qualities that would stamp her as its chatelaine, if he could persuade his mother to step aside for his wife. He had no delusions about the difficulties and delays which confronted him; but because it seemed as if he could not stand the dimness and the cold another moment, he turned sharply, and gave an abrupt order to Selah from the stairway, aware, as he did so, that the fulfilment of his command would alter only the face of the established order, and not its spirit.

"Do turn on the gas, Selah. Tonight and every night. I hate to

37

come home to a dark house. And light some fires. I don't like to freeze to death either, and it's still mighty chilly in the evenings."

"Yessuh, Mr. Gervais. Madame, she's in her room all de time, and Miss Cresside, she's out all de time. It ain't hardly seemed worth while——"

"Well. I'm home again now, and I like a bright house and a warm one. I've had enough gloom and cold in France to last me all the rest of my life. Don't forget. I like a clean one too. And there are cobwebs and dirt-daubers' nests in practically every corner of this place."

"Dey comes right overnight, Mr. Gervais. I cleans 'em out in de ebenin', and dere dey is again, first thing de nex' mornin'."

"Well, clean them out again the next morning too, then."

He went on up the stairs, slightly ashamed of himself for having spoken so sharply to the old servant who was conscientiously trying to save gas and fuel, and who had long lacked anyone to set household standards for him. On the landing he paused briefly, and from force of reviving habit, rather than from any devout impulse, muttered the first few words of an old Latin prayer. There was a niche beside the landing, where an ancient Spanish statue of the Virgin and Child was enshrined. It was a beautiful wooden image exquisitely carved and lavishly gilded, which had originally been brought to Louisiana from Seville, among the belongings of a royal governor. The first mistress of Belle Heloise, who was a descendant of this functionary, had brought it with her when she came to the plantation as a bride, and ever since it had stood in this niche, which had been built on purpose to receive it. Vigil lights were always kept burning in front of it, and on special feast days taller candles were lighted there too, while jewelled crowns and rich robes were placed upon the figures, and flowers on either side of them. The statue was the family's most prized possession, and every succeeding generation was taught to pray before it. Gervais and Cresside had knelt there together countless times, while their mother stood behind them, a detaining hand on the shoulder of each, a meticulous voice prompting their impatient patter. Gervais could not remember that his father had ever stood there too. Philogene d'Alvery had usually been out hunting in the fields or drinking Bourbon in the gallery while his wife guided the children through their reluctant prayers. But Gervais could feel his mother's hand on his shoulder still. He tried to shake it off as he went on up the stairs and knocked at her door. Speaking in French, she told him to come in, and he entered her room.

Like all other rooms at Belle Heloise, this one had high blank walls of white plaster and dark massive furniture. Downstairs, the brocade draperies and Aubusson rugs, the portraits and porcelains, did much to relieve the severity of the walls and the sombre quality of the furniture; but in Madame d'Alvery's room there was no such relief. The curtains at the wide windows and on the mammoth four-poster were made of plain white muslin, and except for a dark braided rug beside the bed, the floor was bare. The mantelshelf was unadorned by vases, and a realistic crucifix, instead of a pleasing portrait, hung over it. Madame d'Alvery herself sat propped up among huge square pillows, the fine linen of her nightgown closing tightly in around her neck and wrists, her hair covered with a fine linen cap. Her long, veined hands lay folded over the smooth sheet in deadly impassivity; they would be folded like that when she lay in her coffin. But her black eyes, which had been the greatest of her many beauties in her youth, glowed from her pale face like dark fire. She waited, silent and motionless, for her son to approach her and address her.

"Hello, *maman*," he said, with forced cheerfulness. "How are you this fine evening? Feeling better?"

"There is no change in my condition, Gervais. I have no hope that there will be. I shall never recover from my crushing loss. But I do not complain. I await in long-suffering a heavenly reunion with your dear father."

She sighed, patiently, and Gervais smothered an ejaculation which was considerably less resigned. He had been puzzled, at the time of his father's death, by his mother's complete prostration; she had never impressed him as a woman whose being was so interlocked with her husband's that the two could not be wrenched apart without disaster to the survivor. In fact, he had always felt that Philogene d'Alvery—improvident, charming, inconsequential —was completely under the dominion of his handsome and imperious wife, and that the only real difference caused by Philogene's elimination from Belle Heloise lay in Isabelle's grievance over having one vassal the less. His bewilderment at his mother's collapse deepened into distrust when the family physician, Dr. Champagne, after a succession of more tactful utterances, abruptly announced one day that he could not deprive those who were really suffering of his services and consume valuable time travelling back and forth over the River Road, merely because it was Madame d'Alvery's whim to lie abed, visited by no one except her doctor and her confessor. If her heart really had been broken—the physician's tone betrayed his scepticism on this point—it would mend again in time, like any other woman's under similar circumstances. As for her body, that was as strong as steel.

At the time this unfeeling pronouncement had been made, Gervais was still willing to give his mother the benefit of the doubt; he at first suggested a consultation of physicians, and upon her indignant refusal to sanction this, asked her to let him seek out someone else who would be willing to take over her case; he was sure that a younger man, less preoccupied and harassed than Dr. Champagne, would be glad to give her all the attention she needed. Madame d'Alvery had proudly replied that she did not propose to have an unskilled youth experiment upon her, furthering his career at her expense; and, in any case, the heartlessness and carelessness of Dr. Champagne had so disillusioned her that she had lost faith in all physicians. From then on, she would bear her afflictions without any attempt to alleviate them. The gravity of these afflictions had long since become a matter of mistrust to her son and of indifference to her daughter; but she herself fostered it with the same relentlessness which marked her every other purpose.

"Your sister did not return with you?" she inquired now, having allowed an effective interval to elapse after the sigh.

"No, I believe she and Regine were going on to some party or other after the parade."

He had been impatient when Selah pleaded with him for an account of the parade, because he was in a hurry to get to his mother and talk to her about Merry. Now, illogically, he wished his mother would ask him some questions. And yet, it was not so illogical, after all, for a man to desire his mother to share his hour of triumph, to reveal pride and pleasure in his achievement. Madame d'Alvery dismissed the parade by asking an irrelevant question.

"Unescorted?"

"Not by a long shot. When you see either of those girls unescorted, you'll see a white blackbird. They had about a dozen boys buzzing around. Besides, of course, Sylvestre in attendance with his usual gallantry."

"I should have said, unescorted by you. I should have thought, Gervais, that you would have wished to remain with your sister— and her friend."

Madame d'Alvery stressed the last three words. The emphasis was unnecessary. Without it, Gervais knew that it was not because Regine was Cresside's friend that his mother wanted him to act as the girls' escort, but because she was predestined as his wife. He decided to plunge into his subject without more delay.

"No, I didn't, especially. As I said, Sylvestre was along. It seems he's visiting at Hathaway Hall again. And if there's one man I can't stomach, it's he. But at least he provides the figure of the protective male that you think is so important. And I was in a hurry to get home. I wanted to talk to you."

"I am very much gratified by your filial devotion. At the same time——"

"I've got something a lot more important on my mind than taking Cresside and Regine to some tame tea. I'm going to get married."

For the first time, the long slim hands which were folded over the white sheet fluttered slightly. Then almost immediately they

40

were still again. But the great eyes burned with increasing intensity in the white face.

"Get married? This is very sudden, my son."

"It isn't at all sudden. It's been going on for years. If I'd had any sense at all, I'd have got married before I went to France. Then I'd have had a wife and child to come home to, like the other men I know. I wouldn't have come back to a great shadowy, empty house that my sister won't stay in and my mother withdraws from. I'd have had someone besides the butler waiting to welcome me. Well, I'm going to have someone from now on!"

Again Madame d'Alvery's hands fluttered momentarily. But she spoke with complete control.

"You are very vehement, Gervais, and very critical. I see no good reason for you to be either. Surely you know that I shall put no impediment in the way of your marriage—if you have made a proper choice. I never would have done so. You could have married two years ago as easily as now. As for the emptiness of the house, I cannot help my infirmities, and it is natural, at Cresside's age, that she should be pleasure-loving."

"Well, suppose we pass over the condition of the house for a moment—especially as I propose to change that. But I don't know whether you will think I have made a proper choice. Not that there's any sound reason why you shouldn't—in fact, you ought to be thankful that a girl of any real calibre will have me. I haven't so much to offer her. . . . I don't need to have you tell me, though, what your idea of a proper choice is. And it isn't the same as mine."

"Then I am very sorry, Gervais. I had hoped you would be guided by my wishes."

"Usually I have been, haven't I?"

"Yes. That is why I am the more amazed—and the more distressed—that you should not be in this all-important instance."

"You chose all my friends while I was growing up. You chose my college and my career. At least you might let me choose my own wife. I *have* chosen her."

"Who is this wife you have chosen, Gervais?"

"Her name's Meredith Randall."

"I do not recall any Randalls among our acquaintances. Has her family ever visited with ours?"

"Not that I know of."

"Then where did you meet her?"

"On the *River Queen.*"

"The *River Queen?*"

"Yes. The dance boat that comes down from St. Louis every winter. You must have heard about it dozens of times."

"If I have, I have forgotten. You met this girl you want to make your wife at a public dance?"

"Good God, don't talk about it in that tone of voice! Everyone in Baton Rouge—at least everyone young—dances aboard the *River Queen* when it's anchored there. There's nothing disgraceful or furtive about it. You make up your own crowd, and it's a good crowd. The same goes for Plaquemine and Donaldsonville that goes for Baton Rouge. Someone in my crowd asked Meredith Randall—I forget now who. As a matter of fact, I think it was Fabian. It doesn't matter anyway. It was the first time she'd ever been aboard the *River Queen*, or to a big dance anywhere—she was just a kid, a sophomore at the Baton Rouge High School. And, gosh, did she eat it all up! Everyone wanted to dance with her, because she was having such a swell time herself that it did something contagious to her dancing. I never saw a girl who had so much vitality!"

He paused, his resentment against his mother momentarily swallowed up in vivid reminiscence. He was remembering the two searchlights stabbing upwards through the river mists, visible for miles away and none the less effective because their manipulation was a clever advertising trick. He was remembering the screaming calliope, drowning out the crackling calls of the tree frogs and the shrill notes of the crickets chirping along the river bank. He was remembering the old-fashioned landing-stage leading from the foot of the levee to the boiler deck, and the ornamental white fretwork banister of the stairway that led to the upper deck where the dance floor was, and where the orchestra began to tune up as soon as the calliope stopped playing. He was remembering the gleaming dance floor itself, not flat, but concave, sloping markedly upward at the bow end. He was remembering the first time he had served notice on the rest of the "bunch" that there wasn't to be any more cutting in when he was dancing with Merry, and the special tune that he and Merry had begun to look upon as their own soon after this —"We'll Go on a Chinese Honeymoon," the name of it was. He was remembering the couples who parked in adjoining chairs on the dark deck outside which was supposedly brightly illumined, but where someone always thoughtfully extinguished most of the overhead incandescents, which were pretty dim at best, by unscrewing them part way in their sockets. He was remembering some of these couples were frequently fused in the single silhouette of a long kiss; and he was remembering, with chagrin mingled with admiration, that when he had tried to draw Merry into such an embrace, she had eluded him, not coyly but almost gravely, and that afterwards she had told him very earnestly how she would have to feel about a man before she would let him kiss her or want to kiss him in return. It was that kiss he had not succeeded in getting which had made him want desperately to hold her in his arms, not as an interlude in an evening's outing, but as a fulfilment and a reward. . . . His mother's measured voice cut coolly across his warm reverie.

"This girl received her education at the Baton Rouge High School?"

"Now that you know what her name is, suppose you refer to her as Meredith. Or Merry—that's what I call her. Yes . . . is there anything wrong with the Baton Rouge High School?"

"I believe not. I believe it does a very worthy work in supplying instruction to a great many young middle-class persons who would otherwise have none."

"I suppose you'd have felt better if I'd have told you Merry went to Convent or Grand Coteau?"

"Much better. It would have assured me that even if she were not a Catholic herself, she had been surrounded by excellent influences. Incidentally, is she a Catholic?"

"No. She isn't."

"There has never been a Protestant at Belle Heloise, Gervais."

"There is going to be one now."

Defiantly, the two pairs of dark eyes met. To his mother's surprise and chagrin, Gervais was able to out-stare her. His gaze was as stubborn as it was piercing. Reluctantly, Madame d'Alvery lowered her white lids, unable to endure the challenge any longer. Aware that he had won the first round, Gervais relaxed.

"I think I'll light the fire. There's no use sitting and shivering, if we're in for a long discussion. What else would you like to have me tell you about Merry?"

Without waiting for an answer, he rose and walked over to the fireplace. The grate was already neatly laid with coal and small kindling, and when he set a match to these, the flame leapt up instantly, alternately illuminating the blank white walls with its radiance and darkening them with its shadow. The eerie quality of the grim crucifix over the marble mantel, and of the still figure on the mahogany bed, was intensified in the weird light.

"And the candles, too, while I'm about it," Gervais went on. "There's no use talking in the dark, either. I told Selah when I came in that I hated a gloomy house. Of course, you'll do as you please about your own room. But I'd appreciate your letting me brighten it up a little when I am in it. Do you mind very much if I smoke?"

Madame d'Alvery made a deprecatory gesture, designed to indicate that in her opinion the suggestion was unworthy of a true Greole gentleman, but that of course he would do as he pleased. She contrived to make this gesture so eloquent that Gervais could almost hear her saying that never, in all the years of their marriage, had her husband smoked in her bedchamber. Gervais reseated himself, crossed his knees, and repeated his question, lighted cigarette in hand.

"What else would you like me to tell you about Merry?"

"I should like to know something about her family and her background, if that is not asking too much."

"Of course it isn't asking too much. She's an only child. At least she is now. She had two brothers, Malcolm and Vail, but they were both killed in the war—one at St. Mihiel and the other at Montfaucon. I reckon they were good fellows, though I don't believe they were quite in Merry's class. Her mother's a widow. She and Merry live in a little house on St. Napoleon Street—you know, the kind that has two front doors, though the façade's so narrow it's taken some planning to get them side by side. The extra door is for the convenience of the lodger."

"The lodger?"

"Yes. Nearly everyone around there has a lodger who occupies the front room. The extra door leads directly into this room, and the lodger goes in and out through it, without disturbing the family. It is a very sensible arrangement."

"And the Randall family takes in lodgers?"

"Not lodgers, just one of them. And you wouldn't call it taking in, exactly. There's no coming and going. Miss Mittie's lived with the Randalls for years—ever since I've known them, and long before that too I reckon. She's quite a character. Came from New England originally. Teaches Latin at the High School. Has an inexhaustible fund of wise sayings and a droll way of getting them off. Dotes on Merry."

Madame d'Alvery actually raised one hand, as a signal to her son that she did not desire to hear anything more about the peculiar Miss Mittie. But she asked another question about the Randalls themselves.

"Since they're obliged to share their home with a lodger, I gather that this family with whom you have become——" She hesitated, quailed for the second time before her son's accusing gazed, and substituted "acquainted" for "entangled," at least aloud. "I gather that this family with whom you have become acquainted is in straitened circumstances."

"I'm afraid they are. I don't know much about the late Mr. Randall. I believe he was some kind of a minor railroad official. Anyway, it's obvious he didn't leave his widow very well provided for. She and Merry live very simply. And Merry's worked ever since she got through High School."

"She *works!*"

"Yes. She's a stenographer at Goldenberg's store. Or, rather, she's risen now to be Mr. Goldenberg's private secretary. I reckon she's made herself pretty nearly invaluable to him. It's going to be an awful shock for the old codger to lose her. I'm sure he figured that if he didn't, at the beginning of the war hysteria, when practically every girl in town was getting married over

44

night, he never would. Well, of course, he should have lost her then. That's when I ought to have married her, as I said before. I don't deserve the luck I've got in having her wait for me."

"And what withheld you then, since you are not withheld now?"

"I'm ashamed to say so, but I suppose it was the same sort of silly inhibition that's cluttering up your mind—the deep-rooted conviction that great River families and mere catfish town nobility shouldn't mix their blood. That I was the last of my line, and that when it came to marriage it behoved me to make a suitable alliance—with Regine Hathaway, or at least some girl like her, exactly as you'd planned. That, of course, I was entitled to a few light love affairs before I settled down, but that when I did——"

"And that was what this was before you went to war? A light love affair with a stenographer?"

"No. This was never a light love affair, *ma mère*. I must ask you to be very sure that you do not make any mistake about that."

Suddenly his voice was steely, as his eyes had been already, and for the first time in his life he was calling her "*ma mère*" instead of *maman*. Madame d'Alvery was horribly aware that this change in address was not accidental, and that its meaning was grave. He went on inexorably.

"There were a few light love affairs in France," he said. "And a few others before I ever knew Merry at all. I'm not at all proud of the fact. It isn't worthy of me or of her. I only mention it in passing to try to show you the difference. . . . I was attracted to Merry the first time I met her, that night on the *River Queen*. I told you, it was her vitality I noticed first. There was something about her enjoyment—the spontaneity and freshness of it—that affected her dancing and made it different from any other girl's. It was so natural and unaffected. Her laugh was that way too, and she laughed a lot. I got so I listened for it, and waited for it. Of course, I liked her looks too. She's very lovely to look at. She has rosy cheeks, with deep dimples in them, and beautiful white teeth and big brown eyes. Her hair's brown too, but there are golden lights in it. She's more than lovely looking. She looks warm-hearted and tender and true, and she is. She's the soul of honour and steadfastness."

Gervais paused, but his mother made no comment. He walked over to the fire and laid more coals on it, and again the flames leapt up, transfiguring the cold walls and the suffering Christ and the bed-bound woman. When he came back, he did not re-seat himself. He stood over his mother and looked down at her.

"I knew all that before I went to France," he said. "The first dance on the *River Queen* was only one incident in our—association. I saw a lot of her after that at dances and elsewhere. And every time I saw her, I liked her better than I had the time before. But, of course, she was just a kid. And she went to the Baton Rouge

45

High School and lived on St. Napoleon Street and there was a lodger in the house. And by and by she graduated at the head of her class and went to work in Goldenberg's store as a stenographer. By that time I wasn't merely attracted to her, I was in love with her. But still I didn't have the guts to ask her to marry me. I was a hide-bound fool. But at least I wasn't enough of a fool to suggest an affair. And at least I had enough sense, before I went away, to ask her if she'd wait for me.

"She said she would, and she kissed me good-bye—it was the first time she ever had kissed me. I realized then how much I meant to her, because—well, because I'd tried to get her to do it before, and she wouldn't. She wrote to me, but we didn't get our mail very regularly, and the letters were sort of shy, especially at first. But from the ones I did get, I knew there must have been others, and gradually they grew less and less reserved. She wasn't afraid, after a while, to tell me just how she felt, and I could see that she felt plenty. But what touched me most of all was her loyalty and her trust. It never occurred to her to look at another man, from the time I asked her to wait for me and she said she would, and it never occurred to her that I wouldn't marry her as soon as I got back. That I wouldn't want to. I do want to. I want to more than I want anything else in the world. If I haven't learned another damned thing in France, I've learned something about values. I'm going to marry her right away, without wasting any more precious time."

Suddenly he smiled, as if the very thought of marrying Meredith Randall made him so happy that he forgot he had set out to be stubborn and stern or that there was any reason why he should be. Then he leaned over and kissed his mother on the forehead.

"You'll enjoy having her in the house," he said. "She'll be pleasant company for you. She'll take the responsibility of the housekeeping off your shoulders. It must have worried you to feel things were being neglected, when you couldn't look after them yourself. She might even help you get well. I thought we'd keep my old room for ours—then you and Cresside could both stay where you are, on this side of the hall, and if Merry and I need to expand later on, we'll have all the space on the other side to do it in. We ought to be able to tuck away any number of grandchildren for you! Is there anything more I can do for you, *maman*, before I do down to dinner?"

III

THE belated dinner which Gervais ate alone in the big square dining-room was very good, and he did full justice to it. A week or so earlier Amen had caught a huge soft-shelled turtle which was crawling unconcernedly along the River Road where this skirted the Small Yard, and Selah had snatched it away from him and saved it for Gervais, whose arrival they knew was impending. Gervais had always been inordinately fond of turtle soup, and Lou Ida had put forth her best efforts in making the one into which the unwary traveller had been transformed. Selah set down the tureen with solemnity, and then removed the cover with a flourish. Gervais sniffed in the steaming fragrance from the succulent dish as he ladled it out into the heated soup plate of gold-banded china which Selah had previously placed on the spotless damask cloth between the neatly laid silverware.

"There's not a soup in France that can touch this, Selah, and they have mighty fine soups there, too," Gervais said enthusiastically. Now that he had spoken his mind and indicated his will to his mother, he was much less tense. Moreover, he was sincerely sorry for his earlier abruptness, and eager to make amends for it by a special show of geniality. He had always talked, incidentally, to Selah when he was eating alone, though he never did so if there were guests or if Cresside were with him, but this time he talked by deliberate intent. "I stayed in one place where we had a different kind twenty-eight nights in succession; but at that, turtle soup wasn't one of the varieties. And there isn't any turtle soup like *this* anywhere in the world except at Belle Heloise. You may tell Lou Ida I said so."

"Yessuh, Mr. Gervais, I suttenly shall. I wish you coulda seen ole Mr. Turtle befo' he went into dat soup, though, Mr. Gervais—crawlin' along down de road lak he never had a care in de world, when Amen cotched him. I disremember I ever seen a turtle big lak he was. He was marked handsome too."

"I'll see plenty of turtles crawling along the River Road from now on. I'm home to stay this time. . . ."

"I'm proud to hear that, Mr. Gervais."

Selah removed the tureen ceremoniously, in the same manner that he had brought it in, and substituted a hot dinner plate for the soup plate which Gervais had now emptied twice. Then he reappeared, bearing an immense ham, its sugar coating spiked with cloves, its pink substance pushed through with herb pockets.

"Lou Ida felt real bad she didn't get to cook your dinner the night you come home, 'cause you wuz to dat banquet. She broilin' a steak for yo' too, Mr. Gervais, but it ain't quite ready. She didn't want it to get to lookin' lak a piece of shoe leather while you wuz enjoyin' your soup, and she thut you mought lak to try dis ham while you wuz waitin'. Our hogs, they'se cured moughty good this year."

"I'm pleased to hear it, but I'm still more interested in our birds. What about those? Any left for next fall's shooting?"

"Yessuh, Mr. Gervais, you gwine to have plenty birds, mebbe more an you know what to do with. Ain't hardly nobody bothered them all de time you'se been gone. Mr. Fabian, he done come out dove-huntin' once or twice, but not bird-huntin'. An' he's a sure enough sorry shot, even on doves."

Having made his disparaging remark, he disappeared quickly in the direction of the kitchen, as if aware that Gervais might resent his reflection on the prowess of any member of his family, and that it might be wisest to retreat. When he returned, he brought with him the steak, now broiled to a turn and imbedded in enormous mushrooms.

"Good Lord, Selah, how do you think I'm ever going to eat that steak when you've filled me full of ham, and on top of that turtle soup, too?"

"Go 'long, Mr. Gervais, you never see de time you couldn't eat steak, 'specially right after Lent, when you done been filled up wid fish for five weeks. This here a mighty fine steak, too. Our beef cattle, they done just as good as our hogs. De grazing's never been better on de levee than this year past. Grass stayed green most all winter, and de clover, it started comin' out in February."

Stifling a mock groan, Gervais helped himself liberally to the steak. Besides the mushrooms, and the mound of flaky rice which automatically accompanied all gravied dishes, there were crimson beets cooked with their own greens, and asparagus heaped on toast in a jade-coloured pile, also a bottle of St. Emilion. As he sipped his sound red wine, Gervais lighted a cigarette and asked Selah for an ashtray. Though the old butler gave it to him without demur, his expression changed, reverting to almost the same look of scorn as when he had spoken of Fabian's marksmanship. He knew that nicotine, like hard liquor, dulled the sense of taste, and he privately considered it an insult to Lou Ida's dinner to do this. But again he changed the plates, this time bringing in an unheated one of fragile porcelain, painted with fruit and flowers; and when Gervais had set aside his finger-bowl, Selah offered him mammoth strawberries from a silver basket ornamented around the side with berry design, and a large silver spoon embellished with a similar design at the end of the handle, with which to scoop them up.

"Good Lord, Selah!" Gervais said again. "The berry-patch must be doing as well as the hogs and the beef cattle. Those strawberries are as big as crab-apples."

"Yessuh, I specks so. Ain't never seen no crab-apples. The milch ows is doin' well too. I done had to bring 'nother of Madame's trawberry spoons to git the cream outin the pitchur with."

Selah spoke gloatingly and truthfully. The cream in the little itcher of garnet-coloured Bohemian glass, ornamented with clear pots surrounded by blue stippling, was so thick that it could not ossibly be poured. Gervais took the second precious old straw-erry spoon and ladled it out, not avidly, as he had ladled out the urtle soup, but with leisurely appreciation and admiration. When he strawberries were almost covered with it, and with the snowy ugar which he sifted slowly over the cream from an antique aster, he looked up at Selah with his charming smile.

"This has been a wonderful dinner, Selah. There's only one rouble with it, and that isn't your fault, or Lou Ida's. I've had to at it alone."

"Yessuh, Mr. Gervais, Ah knows. Mebbe Ah'se got a misconvic-ion, and mebbe I ought not to say it no ways. But Ah believes Madame might pearten up a might, if she jes let herself. And Ah elieves Miss Cresside mought have her a right nice time right ere at Belle Heloise, effen she'd ask nice lady people and nice entlemen people both to come here, 'stead of goin' out other laces with them all de time."

"I believe you're right. I've often thought the same thing my-elf, Selah. But unfortunately neither Madame nor Miss Cresside grees with us. However——"

The charming smile did not wholly fade from Gervais' face. But s he went on, he spoke with increasing gravity, befitting a serious nd highly important subject.

"However, I don't believe I shall have to eat many more meals lone. I'm expecting to be married very soon, Selah. So of course ny wife will be at this table with me, hereafter. I'm sure you'll ake pride in serving her as well as you always have me, and in naking the silver shine as it never did before by the time she gets ere. I'm sure you'll understand now why I want the house to be lean and bright and warm, always. I'm sure you'll be glad to now Belle Heloise is going to have a beautiful young mistress to race it again."

"Ah is, Mr. Gervais, Ah suttenly is. Lordy, if dat ain't de bes' ews Ah'se heard since Ah done foun' out de war ober dere in France done got ended, and you wus comin' home. Is it Miss Regine gwine be your beautiful bride, Mr. Gervais?"

"No, Selah, it isn't Miss Regine. It's a Miss Merry—a Miss Merry Randall."

"Den she libes ober on the west side of de River, don't she, Mr. Gervais? Ah ain't neber heard of any Randall place on our side."

"She doesn't live on a plantation at all, Selah. She lives in Baton Rouge—like Mr. Fabian, you know."

"Yessuh, yessuh. Right in de town? Well, Ah sho'ly wishes yo'

all de happiness in de world, Mr. Gervais, both you and de young
lady dat's gwine to be our new mistress. You don't mind effen A
tells Lou Ida de good news right away, does you, Mr. Gervais?"

Gervais gave his consent gladly, and Selah, having served th
coffee, returned to the kitchen to spread the glad tidings. The tal
clock in the hall struck nine sonorously while Gervais was stil
eating strawberries, and immediately afterwards the ornate gil
timepiece which stood under a *silene* of oval glass on the drawing
room mantel tinkled out a silly tune. When Gervais and Cressid
were little, Philogene had told them that whenever this happened
the heartless girl who leaned provocatively over the dial on th
mantelpiece was mocking the poor old grandfather encased in th
hall, and the children had believed him. Gervais had disliked tha
gilded girl from childhood, and he detested her doubly now tha
she remined him it was too late for him to go back to town an
see Merry again that night.

In spite of his disappointment, however, his deep irritation di
not return. As he went from the dining-room through the parlou
and across the hall on his way to the library, he stopped at th
open door of the house and looked out, drawing in the scented ai
with deep breaths. This should have been his wedding nigh
he thought, and Merry should have been walking with hir
through this magic, scented arch, which might well have serve
as the aisle leading to an altar. His resolution that his marriag
must take place immediately crystallized as he paced slowly bac
and forth, picturing Merry as his bride. Involuntarily, he though
of a story about Isabelle Estrade and Philogene d'Alvery whic
he had inevitably heard over and over again, since it was th
sort of story which no man would choose to hear about his ow
father and mother: after their marriage had been arranged b
Isabelle's parents, it was also arranged that they should not tak
a wedding trip, but spend their honeymoon in the *garçonnièr*
at the rear of the garden where Philogene had made his quarter
during his prolonged visit to his rich relatives. In the dead o
night, however, long after the departure of the last wedding gues
who had made the event so convivial an occasion, Lucien an
Evaline Estrade had been startled by having their daughter burs
into their own stately conjugal chamber, clad only in her long
sleeved, high-necked nightgown, and crying out to them i
hysterical resentment and rage.

"*Je ne peux pas me coucher avec ce cochon là! Il veut m'enleve
la chemise!*"

Somehow they had quieted her, somehow, at that untimel
hour, they had belatedly explained to her the rights and priv
leges of a husband; and before Philogene could start in pursuit o
her, Lucien Estrade had himself led her back to the *garçonnièr*
after Evaline had wrapped a cashmere dressing-gown around he

50

as she murmured a few last words of counsel and consolation in her daughter's ear. As a matter of fact, Philogene had not had the slightest idea of pursuing her. He awaited her return, the circumstances of which he had no difficulty in divining, without undue impatience and with considerable amusement; and, to do him justice, he took no advantage of the shamed and rebellious mood in which his bride was returned to him, either then or later. Philogene, who loved to make a jest of everything, even his own destitution, never derided his wife for the sorry rôle she had played at the moment which should have represented supreme fulfilment to her. Gervais realized this, for he understood his father better than most persons, and loved him better than anyone. But he had always been ashamed of the episode himself. Now he revelled in the realization that his fate would be so different from his father's, that his bride would not only accept his right of dominance and her destiny of surrender without question, but that she would receive him radiantly as well as trustfully, glorifying their union through her ardour even as she quickened it through her acquiesence.

For a long time, as he paced back and forth, in this strange luminescence of the colonnade, he could think only of Merry, and of this rapturous precipitate consummation of his marriage to her. The very conviction that this was at last so close at hand, however, that his long-pent-up passion for her would so soon be assuaged, steadied him instead of increasing his restlessness and impatience; he began to think more quietly about other aspects of their life together. He took immense satisfaction in the knowledge that he would be able to give Merry a home and a tradition so superior to those she had hitherto possessed; he looked forward to seeing her live at leisure in the luxury amidst surroundings distinguished by taste and tradition, in settings of great natural beauty. He visualized her presiding at the head of his table, pouring coffee in his parlour, sauntering through his garden, and—instinctively reverting to his earlier visions—enthroned on his bed. Mentally, he saw her exquisitely arrayed as well as adorably disrobed, adorned with the jewels and laces that had been his grandmother's and his great-grandmother's, tucking the camellias and jasmine in the ribbon which bound the shining masses of her hair and the tulle that veiled the whiteness of her bosom. He saw her too as she would look when she was great with child, bearing herself with such dignity and composure that her condition enhanced her queenliness; and he saw her with the newborn child at her breast, not daunted or prostrated by her travail, but triumphantly nourishing the new life from her own abundant supply of vitality. . . .

Though these visions exhilarated him, however, they did not blind him. He knew that Belle Heloise, beautiful as it was, had escaped only by a hair's breadth the insidious decadence which in the end had destroyed not only countless houses which had been the glory of the River Road, but also hundreds of the men and women who had peopled them. Merry would help him, of course, to avert such a catastrophe here; but if she were to do justice to the part which he yearned to see her play, she must not be handi-capped from the start by problems and burdens which lay essen-tially in a man's province and not his wife's. He must safeguard both the position she would adorn and the home which she would glorify. Still pacing back and forth in the slanting black and white shadows, he seriously considered first the state in which he had found the plantation, and then his general standing in the community. At last, finding that his thoughts were beginning to take him around and around in circles, he went into the library, and, at random, selected one volume after another from the row of old diaries on the top shelf of the breakfront bookcase.

At first he found little to differentiate between the books kept by his grandfather and his great-grandfather. They both attended the races in St. Francisville, they were both sworn in as Police Jurors in Baton Rouge. They both went fishing in the streams and hunt-ing in the swamps and forests, taking bass, deer, ducks and in fact game of every sort. They both kept dogs, which they rubbed with linseed oil, turpentine and sulphur. They both entertained their friends, offering them such modest meals as those comprising "gumbo, boned turkey, young rooster, beef tongue, guava jelly, vegetables, plumb (sic) pudding and syllabub." But gradually Gervais came upon observations in Lucien's diary which had never appeared in François': "War is all the talk"—"Everything at ex-orbitant prices"—"The most dreadful time known to man." Even the vital statistics changed in character: "Many deaths in the Parish. Typhoid fever and pneumonia seem to be the prevalent diseases brought in by the Army."

Gervais shut the volume bearing the telltale date of 1862, put it back in the bookcase, and flung himself into a barrel-back chair. The old entries no longer intrigued him; they revolted him. He did not want to read or hear or think about a war, even a war which was now only a part of history. He felt irritable and restless again as he had earlier in the evening. But he was tired too, and presently he realized that without knowing it, he must have dozed in front of the fire, for he had not heard a car coming in, or a horse's hoofs in the driveway, and the servants had long since gone to bed; yet there were footseps in the gallery now, and the murmur of voices. The footsteps were dilatory, indicating a reluctance to go forward, and the murmur was so low that it suggested secrecy. Every now and then both ceased entirely, and somehow the silence suggested embraces, which seemed to become more and more lingering as they took place closer and closer to the front door. He would have risen and gone to this himself, if he had not felt that any gesture of welcoming a guest might savour of spying on his sister; so he sat still, involuntarily listening, and increasingly uncomfortable as the silences became more and more intensified. He had almost decided that he could not stand them any longer, no matter how maladroit his manner of terminating them might seem, when there was a long drawn out good-night, punctuated by unmistakable kisses. A moment later Cresside tiptoed into the hall alone.

"Don't trip, trying to keep quiet," Gervais called to her. "I can hear you, however cautiously you choose to advance. I can also hear your cavalier cautiously retreating. Why didn't he come in with you? Was he afraid I'd shoot him?"

"You sound mighty silly, Gervais, when you get smart-alecky. It's a little late, isn't it, to go visiting? And how were we to know you were here, anyway?"

"Thanks for the delicate compliment. I reckon that no matter how I get, I don't sound any sillier than you do, when you go creeping along like a cat, or when you stand out on the gallery smacking somebody else's lips along with your own. If you're going to quibble, I'd say it was a little late to be coming in, and I shouldn't think it would take a Sherlock Holmes to guess that if there were a light in the library at this hour, I might be the person who was using it. I don't suppose the servants have taken to literature while I was in France. And as far as I know *maman* hasn't been down the stairs in over two years."

"Oh, for Pete's sake! Haven't you had enough fighting without trying to pick a quarrel with me all the time? You haven't done anything else so far."

Cresside swung herself into a chair sideways and lighted a cigarette, nonchalantly tossing the match, when she had done so, down on the Aubusson carpet. Gervais rose, rather pointedly, and, walking over to the place where the match lay, picked it up, and carried it to the fireplace.

"You've got to be terribly prissy since you went into the Army, do you know it?" Cresside said scornfully.

"No, I don't know that. But I do know that this carpet cost two thousand dollars, and that we couldn't find another like it anywhere, even if we could afford to buy another—which we can't."

"Well, I can remember when you used to throw matches around yourself, like nobody's business, and flick ashes on the carpet too."

Cresside flicked ashes on the carpet now as she spoke, and began to swing her beautiful legs, delicately encased in silk stockings, back and forth over the arm. Her feet, unserviceably but attractively shod in gay high-heeled slippers, were also exquisitely noticeable. Apparently she had gone somewhere and changed her clothes after leaving the Executive Mansion, for she was now wearing a sleeveless beaded evening dress, which came barely to her knees and which clung closely to her flat little figure. Gervais was conscious of a fleeting feeling of amazement that a girl, otherwise provocatively feminine, should have fallen so completely under the influence of the current craze for a "boyish form." But this seemed to him a cause for mild amusement rather than genuine concern; it was her face rather than her figure which really disquieted him. She used more make-up than Regine or any other girl he had seen in Baton Rouge who came into the comfortable category of ladies; but usually she applied it skilfully, if dashingly. Now it gave her a blurred look; the pearly glow of her skin seemed muddied under the rouge, the curving line of her mouth hardened by her lipstick. Her hair, usually so shiny and sleek, was also disordered. She saw him looking at it and tossed back the loose locks.

"All set to play the heavy elder brother, Gervais?"

"No. Just the same I'd be interested in knowing who brought you home."

"Well, just to show you what a sweet little sister I really am I'll tell you. It was Slyvestre."

"Good God, you don't mean to tell me you've really fallen for that muffin hound?"

"I'm sorry you don't appreciate him. In fact, it makes me damn mad. Just as mad as it makes you to have *maman* raise hell about Merry. So you ought to know how I feel."

"I wouldn't compare Merry with Sylvestre, if I were you. And I wouldn't swear quite so much either, if I were a presumably nice girl."

"Well, you're not a presumably nice girl. You're a conquering hero with all the privileges that go with it. Just the same, you might cut out the 'presumably' when you're talking about me. I don't care much for your dirty digs."

"And I don't care much about having you going in for heavy necking with a specimen like Sylvestre. If you think the nature of the tender passages out on the gallery escaped me, you're damn well mistaken."

"No, I don't think so. I think you'd be bound to recognize them. After all, you're in pretty good practice yourself."

Cresside's last remark ended jerkily, not because of any voluntary change in the venomed honey of her tones, but because her brother was shaking her. The impudent swinging of her legs had ceased because he had pulled her abruptly to her feet; neither could she continue her spoken insults with any degree of effectiveness, because she could not get her breath, and she had lost this from amazement as well as fury. Gervais had always been a kind and complaisant brother; even when they were children, he had very seldom teased her, and never before in his life had he touched her roughly. Now, when he stopped shaking her, he continued to grip her shoulders and to force her to look at him.

"See here," he said sternly, "all this nonsense is going to stop.

From now on you're going to behave yourself. Who's supposed to be looking out for you, anyhow?"

"Lucie looks after me. She's my maid as much as she is *maman's*. She's a good one too."

"I'm not talking about a maid, and you know it. Who looks after you in *maman's* place?"

"Mrs. Hathaway. She says it's just as easy for her to look after two girls as one. She's been mighty kind about it. *Maman's* very grateful to her."

"She may have been kind, but I'd say she'd been damn careless, if tonight's a sample of the way she looks after you. I think I'd better have a little talk with her. I'll tell her that when you go out with her daughter, I'd like to have you *stay* with her daughter, and not come streaking in with her house-guest at two in the morning. If I weren't going to get married right away, I'd see if one of our own kinswomen who's got a sharp eye and a strong constitution wouldn't come and make us a prolonged visit. As it is, I don't believe that's necessary. I'll look after you myself until Merry gets here to help me do it. And I'll begin my guardianship with the statement that you can stop this pretty little flirtation of yours before it goes any further."

"It's no more of a flirtation than yours is."

"I'm engaged to Meredith. Are you engaged to Sylvestre?"

"More or less."

"That's not quite definite enough to suit me. Has Sylvestre asked you to marry him?"

"Practically."

"That's not definite enough to suit me either. Unless he's said, in so many words, that he wants you to be his wife, I think it will be very healthy for both of you to stop seeing each other alone."

"Well, he has—in so many words."

"Do you mean what I mean by that, or do you mean rather vague words which you've slanted to suit yourself?"

"I don't see why I should tell you exactly what Sylvestre said to me when he proposed. I bet Merry doesn't go around telling everyone what you said to her when you proposed."

"This isn't a case of telling everyone. It's a case of telling me. You don't have to tell me exactly what he said either. All I want is your word of honour that he has proposed."

"All right. He has proposed."

Cresside's defiant eyes did not drop before her brother's accusing ones, as his mother's had dropped earlier in the evening. She continued to stare at him, boldly, as long as he confronted her. When at last he loosened his hold on her shoulders, she gave a little mocking laugh.

"Now that you've found that out, Paul Pry, suppose you let me go to bed. I could do with a little sleep."

"Yes, you look as if you could. These tense episodes quite often have exhausting after-effects. Well, I won't keep you. But I'll run over to Hathaway Hall tomorrow morning and have a little chat with Sylvestre. As long as he's going to be my brother-in-law, worse luck, we might just as well understand each other at the outset. And one of the things I don't want any *mis*understanding about is a fiancé's prerogatives, as the d'Alverys interpret these."

"Well, of course you're the soul of tact, but I shouldn't think, myself, that a conversation of the sort you have in mind would exactly pave the way for brotherly love. And I don't know just how pleased Mrs. Hathaway would be to have you make a scene in her house. She goes in for dignity with a capital D, and she seems to be feeling a little cool towards you right now. In fact, I shouldn't wonder if she said something to *you* about a proposal, if you gave her the right kind of an opening. I think she rather expected it. Oh, not for herself, of course, but for her dear daughter. You didn't by any chance ever take Regine home on a moonlight night, did you, and loiter for a little while on the way?"

"I've hardly seen Regine since I got home. You know that."

"Yes, but didn't you see her sometimes before you went away? Without the whole family sitting around? Now, now! Don't talk to me about men who raise false hopes in the fluttering breasts of innocent maidens!"

"Don't talk to me like a fool!" Gervais said sharply.

There was no sound reason why Gervais should have been so disquieted. He had never said anything to Regine, in that pre-war period when after all they were both just kids, which she could truthfully have told her mother was "fresh"—that was the way it would have been expressed then. He did not know how the incoming crop of youngsters would define this particular type of conduct, if indeed there was any term of approbrium connected with it; as far as he could see, almost anything went now. If he had ever tried to kiss Regine, either against her will or because she seemed to expect it, the caress had been so casual that he had completely forgotten it. The match-making schemes had been hatched between her mother and his; if Regine had accepted them complacently— and he had an uneasy feeling that she might have—he had never furthered them, at least not consciously. Naturally, he had taken her home from a few parties, since they ran with the same crowd. Probably he had paid her some silly compliments and sent her insignificant little presents from time to time. But none of that amounted to anything. It had nothing to do with his triumphant love for Merry, or with the unfortunate infatuation of Cresside for Sylvestre. There was no reason why he should not go to Hathaway Hall the first thing in the morning and have a plain talk with that skunk. He had half a notion that Cresside had lied to him about the proposal, in spite of the fact that she had sworn, on her word of honour, that she was telling the truth. Well, he would soon find out. . . .

He was unaccountably restless all night, disquieted not only by his own tumultuous thoughts, but by a variety of nocturnal sounds: the cricket-like chirp of toad-frogs, engaged on their amorous occasions in the disused sugar kettle beneath his window; the liquid trill of the mocking-bird which had found daylight all too short for its throat-bursting jubilance; the lonesome wail of a freight engine hauling its mixed string of box and tank cars northward towards Vicksburg; the asthmatic chuff of the *John D. Grace* churning downstream from Baton Rouge to Plaquemine; and sharpening all these, the vicious whine of mosquitoes beyond the screens. Such sounds had once helped lull him to sleep; but for a long time those to which he had listened at night had been different: the chatter of machine-guns at San Mihiel; the roistering at Dufour's *estaminet* in Lille; the rhythmic crash of waters riven by the stem of a transport. The mocking-bird's joyousness seemed ill-timed now, the toad-frog's love-note offensive; they irritated and disturbed him. At last, tired of tossing from one side of the bed to the other, he rose, and going to the plantation desk in the corner of the room, unlocked the drop-leaf front which slanted across the pigeonholes and took out his own diary, which he had left there when he went to France. It fell open at the last entry:

"April 6, 1917. Heavy rainfall. Much needed after long spell dry weather but still too cool for young canes. *Maman* worse, sent for Dr. Champagne, Cresside came home from Convent for Easter Holidays. War declared against Germany. Shall be off tomorrow to enlist."

"There certainly is a deadly monotony about the records the men in this family have kept," he said, half aloud. "Maybe I'd better start in again along different lines." He hesitated, almost tempted to begin the new record then and there. But it seemed an absurd thing to do in the middle of the night, and presently he shoved the old diary back into its pigeonhole, relocked the desk, and got into bed again. But still he could not sleep, and eventually, abandoning the effort, he got up and dressed, long before his usual hour. As he stepped from his room into the upper hallway, Lucie opened the shuttered door opposite his, leading into his mother's bed-chamber. The mulatto maid was wearing her inevitable tignon; she was carrying the customary coffee tray; but there was an unwonted expression of bewilderment on her usually placid face. Gervais noticed it with concern. When Lucie looked like that it was portentous.

"Good-morning, Lucie," he said pleasantly. "How's Madame this morning? I hope I didn't tire her, talking to her so long last evening."

Lucie curtsied. She was very fond of Gervais, and she had enormous respect for him. She had long regarded him as the head of the house, and now that he had come home from the war in heroic guise, his importance in her estimation was still further enhanced.

"No, sir, Mr. Gervais," she said respectfully. 'You didn't tire her out none. I don't know when I seen her so pert like she is this morning. She done tole me she thought she mought try to get out of bed, after while, and lay herself down on de couch in de boudoir instead. She must be feelin' pert if she's aimin' to do that. You knows yourself, Mr. Gervais, that Madame ain't been out of the bed before, not once, since poor Mr. Philogene done died."

IV

THE plantation bell calling the field hands to work was still ringing when Gervais went down the stairs and into the rear of the lower gallery. It was a great bronze bell, suspended from a wooden standard near the corn crib, and its tone, at once impelling and melodious, had increased in richness with age. Like the statue on the stairs, this bell was ancient and honourable and closely associated with the annals of the family. It not only gave the summons to daily toil; it warned of flood and fire, heralded births, pealed for weddings, tolled for the dead. All these functions were habitual on every great sugar estate; the bell was literally the voice of the plantation. But the one at Belle Heloise had served in even more homely and intimate ways: as a child, Lucien Estrade had learned most of his letters from its inscriptions, identifying them, one by one, under the painstaking direction of Angus Holt.

"J stands for justice, laddie. And A for authority, P for patience, another P for peace, another A for amenity, R for rule, T for toil, I for ingenuity, E for energy, N for nobility. Repeat that after me now, and mind you don't forget what I've told you either, you scatterbrain you!"

When he learned his lesson properly, Lucien was permitted to ring the bell for "quitting time," and to this reward he looked forward with eagerness. Then, strangely enough, Philogene d'Alvery had been the one to continue the custom the Scotsman started; he had taught Gervais the alphabet by the bell too, less patiently but more gaily than Angus had taught his pupil, and permitting him to peal it often without rhyme or reason, a practice which threw everyone into confusion. To Gervais, the sound of his father's drollery was for ever intermingled with the peal of the bell.

58

"J pour joie. A pour amour, P pour passion, encore de la passion quand nous trouvons P la deuxième fois, encore de l'amour avec le second A. R pour ravir. T pour tempter, I pour ivresse, E pour xtase—dis donc, Gervais, a tu compris?"

In those days Gervais had always shaken his head, smiling, and Philogene, shaking his head and smiling too, had continued the lesson in a slightly more serious vein. Now, stopping before the bell, which still swayed though it had ceased to sound, Gervais smiled again at the remembrance of those strange lessons, tracing the inscription with his forefinger while he studied it afresh. The bell was ornamented at top and bottom with elaborate scrollwork, and beneath the upper scroll was a plaque, inscribed among further ornamentation with the words:

J'APPARTIEN
A MONSIEUR
FRANÇOIS ESTRADE

It was while pointing to that first word, J'appartien—I belong—that Philogene had told his son J stood for joy and E for ecstasy; but Gervais had known for a long time that there had been little joy and less ecstasy in his father's life, and the mockery in Philogene's voice, which still rang through the peal of the bell, always had a note of bitterness in it. But the bitterness had never silenced his wry jesting for long; after a temporary lapse into gravity, he usually continued his lesson in the same vein that he had begun it, as he went on to the second inscription on the bell, the one which encircled it below the plaque and above the lower scroll:

FONDUE A L'ATELIER DE THIAC-MAIGNAN DURAND
NOUVELLE ORLEANS LE 21 JUIN 1824

Gervais had often wondered about Thiac-Maignan Durand, the man who had cast this bell in his workshop nearly a hundred years before. He had asked Philogene what sort of an artisan Thiac probably was; and Philogene, in his droll way, had said Thiac must have been the sort who put everything hind side foremost, because all the Ns on the inscription were cast backwards, and were weirdly presented as Иs. Ns presented that way, Philogene told Gervais, did not stand for anything, which was the reason he had to skip the last letter in j'appartien, the incomplete word making it all too pointed that he, at any rate, did not belong; whereas, if the Ns had been properly presented, they might have stood for normalcie. It was too bad they didn't, because a little normalcie would not have been amiss at Belle Heloise and would have helped Philogene to belong . . .

Gervais was still staring at the bell and thinking about his father when Lazine Sance, his overseer, came up to speak to him. Sance was a short wiry man, sallow-faced in spite of his outdoor life, with an inverted crescent of a moustache, and thin straggling brown hair. As usual, he was wearing a khaki-coloured shirt, open at the throat, a heavy leather belt, cloth riding breeches, and well-cut though rugged brown boots. The back of his neck was ravined from the sun and his sleeves were rolled up above the elbow. One shirt pocket was bulging with cigars, while from the other protruded an enormous silver watch with a minuscule trace chain attached to this at one end and looped through a buttonhole at the other. His hat, worn at a jaunty angle, was a coarsely plaited affair of palmetto straw, shaped into a somewhat dandified fedora model. He was leading his horse, a small cobby plantation pony, which would never have taken any ribbons on the tanbark, but which carried him interminably along ditch-banks and over head-lands under the broiling Louisiana sun without showing any hint of fatigue, moving in a comfortable little rack equally easy on mount and rider.

"Good-morning, Captain d'Alvery," he said agreeably. The air was crisp, but from force of habit he removed the pseudo-fedora and vigorously wiped first its sweatband and then his own un-beaded brow with his big bandana. "Regular Easter weather, isn't it? I don't recollect a year when the mornings haven't been chilly at Easter, whatever time of year that came. But it'll be plenty warm later in the day. . . . Anything you'd like to tell me before I go out into the fields?"

"Yes. I'd like to tell you that the fence to the mule yard looks in mighty bad condition to me. I'd be willing to bet that the mules and pigs have been breaking out and eating the corn sprouts."

"Well, Captain, you get the barbed-wire and posts and staples I need, and I'll see that the mules and pigs don't get out."

"Very well. I'll take care of that in Baton Rouge today. But your mule shed is in bad shape too. A good many shingles are missing and half the doors from the catchpen are sagging on their hinges."

"Captain, I just haven't been able to get the materials, with the war going on. There are lots of things I'd like to see different myself. For instance, the rats are running wild in the corn cribs, and I need money for traps, and authority to offer bounty to Lou Ida's little boys for every dead one they bring me. Madame wouldn't give me the money or the authority either."

"Well, I'll do it. You can depend on having everything you need from now on. But get that leaking molasses trough fixed right away. All you need for that is a new plug."

While they were talking they had covered the ground between the corn crib close to the bell and the harness-house where the field hands were whistling while preparing the mules to go into the fields. Thirty or more teams were already harnessed for the day's

60

work and the trace-chains were jingling with the singing sound peculiarly their own. By and large the teams presented a fine sight. But Gervais was ready to pick flaws in these also.

"I wouldn't say those mules had been curried any too regularly, and if their manes and tails have been trimmed, I wouldn't know when."

"This time I have to admit I've got no alibi. But it's been too long since there's been anyone around that's shown interest. It'll be different from now on, I promise you, Captain."

"That's the stuff. And maybe in the fall I can take a run up to Missouri and get us some better mules. A lot of these don't even look like cane mules. They're not much bigger than cotton mules."

"The stock has run down some, for a fact, and I don't mind saying it's good hearing to know there'll be a change now that the boss man's come back."

While Gervais and the overseer were talking, the negroes had begun to move out along the headlands with their teams, some of them chanting as they went. One of them, a lanky loose-jointed teen-ager, paused to call out to the near mule of his team in the midst of his carol.

"Get along there, you old Susan you! You'se pure slow this mornin'."

"Susan!" echoed Gervais, turning to Lazine. "Isn't that our head Minnie?"

Lazine chuckled. "Why, Captain, you haven't forgot, have you, that the boys have two names for all these mules? Minnie's that one's stable name all right, but out in the field she goes by Susan. You take that scrubby one she's teamed up with too: her name's Mattie in the mule lot, but as soon as she gets outside the door she's Kate."

"I do remember now," Gervais said, laughing. "But I had forgotten for the moment." Then he added, as an afterthought, "And it wouldn't do not to have a mule named Minnie at Belle Heloise, you know."

The subject of the mules being logically terminated at this point, for the time being at least, Lazine, nodding a friendly farewell, swung one leg over the side of his cobby little pony preparatory to trotting off in the wake of the field hands. Gervais made a detaining gesture.

"Just a minute more, Lazine. I hate to start off by so much variegated fault-finding, but I was a good deal shocked at the state I found the cemetery in yesterday. If you can spare a couple of men, I wish you'd send them down there this morning to cut the grass, and hereafter I'd like it to be kept cut, regularly. A big snake was coiled up on one of the tombs in the Hathaway lot. I shouldn't be surprised if there wasn't a regular nest of them there. Anyway, that long grass is a pretty good place for one. I want it cleaned up."

"Yes, Captain, I see how you feel." For the first time the overseer spoke hesitantly. "I'll get two or three of the boys down there just as soon as I can. But I may as well tell you that I'll have to offer them some kind of inducement or reward. The niggers are scared of that cemetery. It's not just graveyard fright either, like they generally have. There *are* a lot of those snakes, and the niggers are superstitious about them. They say old Miss Regine, that your young lady's named for, used to keep one in her room. The servants kept hearing a queer rustling sound there and it seems that after she died, when they started opening her dresser drawers, there was a snake skin in the place where she kept her paper patterns. The niggers believe that the snake followed her to her grave. . . Well, you could see how it would all work out. Plumb foolishness, of course. But that kind of foolishness is hard to get around."

"I do see that it might present difficulties. But I believe you can get around it. I believe you're good at that sort of thing. And, incidentally, the present Miss Regine isn't my young lady. I've just told my mother, and I'd like to tell you, that I'm engaged to Miss Meredith Randall in town."

"Well, that's fine. The best of luck to you, Captain. And now I'd really better get after those field hands if there's to be any work done today. But you can count on me. I'll see to everything we've talked about."

They had gone forward, spasmodically, as they talked, and now Gervais was almost opposite the sugar house, where he knew his engineer, Etienne Plauché, would be expecting him, for this was the beginning of the repair season and he had not yet been out to inspect the machinery. The sugar house had been built at the same time as the mansion, and though its equipment had been gradually modernized, its appearance, unlike that of any other mill in the vicinity, was essentially unaltered. Its low façade was made of mellow brick, and its simple doorway, flanked on either side by small rectangular windows, was handsomely panelled and surmounted by an ornamental fanlight. At both ends, wide wings of well-weathered wood stretched out beyond the brick, and above it a gabled roof closed down over a spreading triangle of clapboards. The whole effect was quaint, spacious and dignified to a degree more typical of a mansion than of a mill. Even the two square elevations, added to accommodate gigantic new machinery, and rising ungracefully, one over the other, above the gable, did not seriously impair this effect. A line drawing of the sugar mill was stamped on every bag of sugar that went out from Belle Heloise for its owners had always been nearly as proud of the mill itself as they were of its product.

When Gervais opened the door to the mill room, he saw Plauché standing beside the big engine which drove all six rollers and, as he expected, the engineer, a swarthy, thick-set man, whose blue denim jumper was thickly spattered with grease spots, was waiting to speak to him. Unlike Lazine, Plauché himself took the initiative in outlining the need for immediate and urgent improvements.

"Good-morning, Captain. I hoped you wouldn't let another day pass before going over the mill with me. We've got to do considerable repair work here. We had lots of trouble towards the end of the grinding season. Why, this very engine here should have the cylinders bored out. The last mill needs new shells and the front mill should be regrooved. Some of the pumps need new plungers too, and they all need new Garlock packing. Besides, there are new tubes needed for the double effect and——"

"Good Lord, Plauché, stop for breath, can't you? You certainly are unloading a lot of bad news on me all at once!"

"Well, it's better for me to unload it on you than to have you find it out gradually for yourself and think that I've been negligent. I want to get things in shape here so that we can take advantage of the high sugar prices. I look to see sugar hit better than twenty cents within the next year."

"You may be right at that. I know the Belgian sugar mills have all been destroyed, and the ones in France hard hit, because I've seen them. There's bound to be a world shortage. It's a damn shame we didn't go into Germany, and destroy the best factories there the way the Germans destroyed their enemies'. We've been too easy on those Huns from start to finish, and some day we're going to be sorry. They've got every particle of machinery they've ever had, and it's as good as any in the world."

"Is that so? Well, all the more reason for trying to get ahead of them. . . . Now, if you don't mind, Captain, I'd like to walk around and show you just how things are. Let's start in the clarifying department. These heaters are in pretty good shape, but we should have some extra tubes in case they have to be changed during grinding. All the settlin' tanks must be scraped and painted. You know, Captain, the Government is getting mighty particular. Just to show you the way things are, a man from the Department of Agriculture was here the other day, and he said to me, 'You can't use any more paint containing lead in your settlin' tanks.' We can't use red lead, even in making a joint for our pipes, because the Pure Food Department says you can't have lead in anything that's for human consumption."

For the next hour Gervais followed the engineer's lead from one department to another, finding in each its own peculiar evidence of necessity. Finally, realizing the morning would be gone if he did not break away, he interrupted Plauché in a complaint concerning the state of the sugar room, and hastily took his departure, promising to return for a more thorough inspection the next day.

Gervais went back to the house through the sun-dappled walk of the pergola which bounded Angus Holt's garden on the south side. It would do no harm, he thought, to speak to his mother again about Merry before he started for Hathaway Hall. It was still early, by Sylvestre's standards, and Gervais had sense enough to realize that nothing would be gained by bursting in on his future brother-in-law with criticisms of his conduct and imperative demands that this should be rectified, before this wastrel was half awake. Gervais' deep-rooted aversion to Sylvestre and all his ways mounted as he pictured this sluggard lolling among his pillows at a time when any healthy man with an atom of initiative would have been up and doing for hours. Why, in heaven's name, should Cresside, who could have had her pick of the countryside, have made such a sorry selection? And how, again in heaven's name, could she have bestowed her favours so recklessly on the last man who was worthy of either her admiration or her trust?

There was no answer, of course, to either question, and, as far as that went, Gervais was guided by instinct rather than knowledge in gauging the degree of his sister's indiscretion. But he was increasingly convinced that his instincts were not playing him false, and increasingly disturbed by his convictions. He strode through the hall almost unseeingly, and failed to salute the statue as he went up the stairs. The shutter doors of his mother's room stood open, and when he entered it, he saw, as he expected, that the great bed was empty: the white covers were drawn tight across its immense width and its square pillows were smooth. The wide shutters, flanked on either side by gigantic armoires, and dividing Madame d'Alvery's chamber from Cresside's, were tightly closed, and he gathered that his sister was still sleep, or pretending to be. But the smaller door beyond the fireplace, leading into Madame d'Alvery's boudoir, was ajar, and before he could reach it and knock, his mother's voice came to him from beyond it.

"You may enter, Gervais. I was expecting you to come and find out for yourself whether Lucie had told you the truth. Well, you will see that she has."

Madame d'Alvery spoke from a couch covered with dark brocade, on which she lay propped up by brocaded cushions. A purple comfort covered her, and a black satin *peignoir* concealed her linen nightgown. From the black lace cap that covered her hair depended long satin streamers, crossed and fastened under her chin with a diamond and onyx brooch. Her appearance, though still sombre, was infinitely more regal than when she had been engulfed by the whiteness of her big bed, and it was also infinitely more suggestive of action. Her son was quick to feel the pulse of reviving power.

"Yes, I see that she has. Not that I doubted her word. But naturally I was anxious to witness this miracle for myself. You have made a most remarkable recovery, *ma mère*."

64

"I have made a superhuman effort, because circumstances seemed to necessitate it."

"I'm not sure that I understand you."

"On the contrary, I am certain that you do."

Again, as on the previous evening, the two pairs of dark eyes challenged each other. This time it was Madame d'Alvery who triumphed in her gaze.

"I regret that you have obliged me to remind you this is my house. I cannot prevent you from bringing a bride to it. But I can, I hope, preclude its mismanagement by an inexperienced outsider."

"You can prevent me from bringing a bride to this house by ordering me out of it, if you care to do so."

"I resent that retort, my son. It is unbecoming of you to suggest that I would stoop to such a course, merely because the law would permit it."

"It was you who brought up the question of my legal status in this house to begin with. But apparently I care more for the place than you do—it has certainly suffered from lack of supervision during my absence. Moreover, I can assure you Belle Heloise would never be mismanaged by my wife, and I must remind you, in my turn, that, whatever your other rights may be, you are not justified in referring to my fiancée as an outsider."

"I do not feel equal, at this point, to another prolonged argument with you, Gervais."

"I didn't intend to begin one. Just the same, I don't intend to let you speak about Merry like that, either."

"Shall we talk about someone else, perhaps?"

"No. You had better not overtax your strength. I'm just leaving for Hathaway Hall, anyhow. Is there anything I can do for you before I go?"

"Nothing. I hope you will enjoy your visit with the Hathaways. Please give them affectionate greetings from me."

"I'm not going to Hathaway Hall to visit the Hathaways. I'm going there to tell that skunk, Sylvestre Tremaine, exactly what I think of him."

"Isn't that somewhat superfluous as well as distinctly uncivil? You never concealed your dislike for our neighbours' friend, even when you were a child."

"It may be uncivil but I don't think it's superfluous. I think it's important Sylvestre should know what I think of him right now and why. It has nothing to do with the way I felt about him when he and I were both children. But we won't argue about that either."

He left her abruptly, and stopping at Cresside's shuttered door, knocked and called to her. But there was no answer, and after twice repeating his summons he went on downstairs and out of the house. Amen had taken his car from the garage and was waiting patiently beside it, just as he had been accustomed to waiting beside the palomino. He gazed towards Gervais with a grin that was hesitant rather than wholehearted, but Gervais chose to disregard its shrinking quality.

"What are you so cheerful about this morning, Amen?"

"I'se happy about de good news, Mr. Gervais."

"What news?"

"Selah done tole us you'se fixin' to get married, Mr. Gervais."

"Does that make you happy too?"

"Sure it do, Mr. Gervais. We'se all happy when you'se happy, and we grieves when you does."

Amen was telling the truth, and Gervais knew it. It was his own brusqueness that had given the boy that hangdog look the night before and the memory of it that kept his smile so faltering now. Genuinely contrite, Gervais strove to make amends by a special show of geniality.

"You better hurry on and get married yourself. I want to dance at your wedding. Which means you've got to get married out of the book, you rascal, and not just take up."

"Yessuh, Mr. Gervais. That's what I'se fixin' to do, sho' nuff. I don't hold with no taking up myself."

The boy's grin was no longer hesitant; it reached almost from ear to ear. Gervais climbed into his car, smiling too, and started down the driveway, while Amen stood watching him out of sight. It was a glorious morning, bright with sparkling sunshine now, but still crisp enough to be tonic. As Gervais approached the overgrown privet hedge a whir of wings sounded above him, and two cock blue-jays shot zigzagging through the air, one in desperate flight from the other. He looked up to follow the duel with his eyes, fully aware that from the concealing foliage near by a motionless little blue-jay hen was watching it too. Eventually one of the brawlers drove off his adversary, and with a perceptible swagger flew back to the nest which he had just successfully defended or invaded. The brawling was over and tranquillity reigned again in the hedge.

As Gervais walked up the great curving staircase which led, in two graceful branches railed with exquisite ironwork, to the vast galleries of Hathaway Hall, he was struck, as he had been so many times before, by the difference between the atmosphere in this house and his own. Hathaway Hall dominated its surroundings as an entity in itself; Belle Heloise was a part of them—an integral part, without which they could not have survived, any more than the human body could survive unless the heart sent its life blood coursing through all the members; but still only the heart and not the whole. Gervais felt that if the magnificence of Hathaway Hall were diminished or its lustre dimmed, the entire plantation would

66

lose its power and its prestige. But Belle Heloise would somehow triumph over shabbiness and neglect, even over decay. After all, the heart was essentially sound; it would keep on beating till the bitter end. . . .

The gallery which he entered now was empty, but the door leading into the house stood wide open, and Gervais whistled and went in, as he had hundreds of times before. He received a more immediate response than he had anticipated, for, unexpectedly, he found Mrs. Hathaway standing just inside the ballroom at the right of the front door, and she instantly came forward to greet him. It was hard for him to realize that she was only a few years younger than his mother, whom he had long since regarded as an elderly woman. Not a single white hair was visible in Mrs. Hathaway's modish coiffure, not a line in her handsome, expressionless face. Her figure was firm and faultless, and she carried herself erectly and moved briskly; she gave an effect of energy which was somewhat surprising, considering her background and tradition, and this effect detracted from the air of ease and elegance which would have seemed more natural under all the circumstances. She not only looked like a woman with a purpose, but like a woman whose pursuit of her purpose might be relentless. She regarded Gervais politely, but without warmth.

"Why, good-morning, Gervais!" she said in a civil tone. "I didn't hear you coming up the steps. I must have been completely rapt in thought. Come in here and give me your advice. You know that when Regine made her début she and I stood here, just inside this first door. But I have been thinking that if I were planning another important function I should do it differently. I believe I should emphasize the space beyond the archway and the columns. What do you think?"

Gervais regarded the vast vacant space before him unenthusiastically. The white ballroom was appropriately named. The twin mantels, the carved cornice, the high ceiling and the wide walls were all white; so was the graceful arch framed with fluted pillars, to which Mrs. Hathaway had just referred, and which divided the room in two well-proportioned parts. Even the floor had been treated to resemble white tiles, though this effect had actually been achieved by putting paint and lacquer over cypress. The room had never been furnished, and its emptiness added to its immensity. When it was decorated for a function and filled with people it lost its air of emptiness, and in the evening, when the great crystal chandeliers glittered and shone, it acquired a resplendent quality. But in the unrelieved light of morning it looked cold and meaningless. Sumptuously furnished as a drawing-room and constantly chosen as the centre for lavish hospitality, it would have been permeated with genuine splendour; as it was, Gervais felt that its beauty was engulfed in barrenness.

"Perhaps you're right," he said noncommittally. "Of course it would depend on what kind of a function you had in mind."

"Well—a ceremony. And afterwards a reception. I think the participants in the—ceremony—should enter through this door, and file down between the guests into the farther end of the room where the ceremony would take place. Then after this was over they would receive there, and the guests would file down in their turn. I think it would be very effective. Don't you agree with me?"

"Are you by any chance talking about a wedding ceremony, Mrs. Hathaway?"

"You've become very direct since you've been in the Army, haven't you, Gervais? It's a quality I've always greatly admired, and, if you'll forgive me for saying so, it wasn't among your outstanding characteristics when you were younger. Well, since you've put the question to me so bluntly, I'll answer it bluntly too. Yes, I was talking about a wedding ceremony."

"I always had a feeling Regine would want to be married in the white ballroom, but I didn't know she'd begun to make definite plans for it already. Would it be impertinent for me to ask the name of the lucky man?"

"Surely you must have guessed, Gervais!"

"I'm afraid I haven't. You know I've been gone for a long time, and I've been rather preoccupied. I haven't kept abreast of local love affairs as well as I should have. I'd begun to realize that already. I'll have to ask you to enlighten me."

"No one has given you a hint?"

"No, not a hint."

"Why, it's Sylvestre, Gervais!"

Mrs. Hathaway's handsome, unwrinkled face was still expressionless as she turned from her surveyal of the white ballroom to look more closely at her caller, and her tone of voice was still even and polite. But there was now an unaccustomed glitter in her hard eyes.

"They've always been greatly attached to each other, you know that, from the time they were children. But I never gave the matter a second thought, as probably you didn't either. My own suspicions weren't aroused until it dawned on me that they were depending almost wholly on each other for companionship. These last two years they've been almost inseparable."

"I see. When all the other men Regine knew had gone to war, it was natural for her to turn to the one who remained at home."

"Why, Gervais! I hope you're not intimating that Sylvestre wouldn't have been glad to go to war, if he hadn't been prevented by grave physical handicaps, not to mention great financial responsibility! You almost sound as if you were jealous of him."

"No, I'm not jealous of him, and I didn't mean to intimate anything I wouldn't say straight out. Just the same, I did have an idea that he and Regine both had other interests."

"Why, Gervais!" Mrs. Hathaway said again. The exclamation had no vehemence, but by this time her hard eyes were gleaming like agates. "You told me, just a minute ago, that you'd been so preoccupied, during your long absence, that you hadn't had any chance to keep abreast of local love affairs."

"That's perfectly true. But I'll have to admit, after all, that since my return——"

"You've been somewhat preoccupied since your return too, haven't you, Gervais?"

"Yes, somewhat. But that hasn't prevented me from——"

"I'm afraid it has prevented you from being as observant as usual, Gervais," remarked Mrs. Hathaway, who seemed bent on interrupting him. "Otherwise you certainly would have noticed the exceptional degree of congeniality between Regine and Sylvestre. Of course they're both too well-bred to be publicly demonstrative—in fact, I'm sure Sylvestre behaves with complete circumspection towards Regine at all times. He couldn't do otherwise, considering how greatly he respects her. Possibly you've been misled because they didn't seem more romantically inclined. But they are genuinely attached to each other, and very sensibly they have decided——"

"Yes, it does sound sensible, all round, as you outline it," Gervais said, interrupting in his turn. "The Hathaways seem to have lots of sense—I only wish I could say as much for the d'Alverys. Well, congratulations! I must have been blind, as you say, not to notice the drift of things. But I mustn't keep you standing here like this. You'll be all tired out. As a matter of fact, I really came over to see Sylvestre this morning, though, of course, I hoped I'd have a glimpse of you and Regine too. Could you tell me where I could find him? Then I won't detain you any longer."

"I'm not in the least tired," Mrs. Hathaway assured him. "It never tires me to stand. I stand a great deal. And I never lie down. In the daytime, I mean, of course. By the way, how is your dear mother? It's distressing to think of her languishing month after month, with no prospect of improvement."

"Thank you, she's better. She actually got up on her couch this morning for the first time in two years."

"Not really. And Cresside? I hope dear little Cresside didn't get overtired last night. She is so intense about everything she does," Mrs. Hathaway observed, lightly dismissing the subject of Cresside's mother without any apparent surprise at the bedridden woman's apparent improvement.

"She was going strong when I last saw her, which was around three this morning. But I do think that's a trifle late for her to be getting in. I waited up for her and suggested as much to her. I hope you won't mind if I suggest the same thing to you. I under-stand that you've been chaperoning her along with Regine, and it's very kind of you. But I think we'd better have some sort of understanding about the hours she keeps from now on, and also about the matter of escorts. Doubtless you know that Sylvestre brought Cresside home. A very suitable courtesy on the part of her friend's fiancé. But it seems to me it would have been just a shade more suitable if Regine had come along too, and if the whole expedition had taken place a few hours earlier. Of course Cresside must understand exactly how congenial Regine and Sylvestre are at this point——"

"Of course she must," Mrs. Hathaway said, speaking sharply for the first time.

"Yes, there can't be any difference of opinion about that. But she's rather intense, as you said yourself, and the d'Alverys aren't as sensible as the Hathaways, as *I* said *myself*. Suppose we let it go at that. . . . Where did you say you thought I'd find Sylvestre?"

"Why, Gervais, you've been talking so fast about all sorts of irrelevant things that you haven't given me a chance to tell you! Sylvestre left early this morning."

"He *left*! Where did he go?"

"Why, he went back to New Orleans, of course! He was very sorry not to remain for the banquet in honour of the officers on the submarine chasers. He and Regine had counted on going to the canteen ball afterwards, too. But they knew they could count on you and Cresside to take Regine with you, just as Cresside went to the Mansion with Sylvestre and Regine yesterday."

"I'm sorry, but I'm afraid they can't. I've asked Miss Meredith Randall to go to the canteen dance with me. I haven't any idea what arrangements Cresside's made. . . . When is Sylvestre coming back?"

"Really, Gervais, I don't know. After all, he has very extensive business interests. I assume he'll have to give up a good deal of time to them the next few weeks. He's been Mr. Pereira's right-hand man in that huge coffee importing house. And you know when a man's planning to be married——"

Mrs. Hathaway turned her bright gaze from her guest's face and again looked towards the graceful arch and the white pillars at the farther end of the while ballroom. Obviously, she already visualized the brilliant ceremony of which it was soon to be the scene. Gervais himself could see Regine, caparisoned in point lace and diamonds, as the central figure in this scene, with Sylvestre, sleek and safe, on one side of her, and Mrs. Hathaway, satisfied and smug, on the other. He could hear a priest declaring marriage to be a sacrament, and guests murmuring about the wonders of a true-love match. He could even smell the surfeiting sweetness of gardenias and tuberoses, garlanding the room. Momentarily, his bafflement and rage were so submerged in nausea that his head swam. As it cleared, he could hear Mrs. Hathaway still talking brightly.

"Especially when he's planning to wind up all his affairs. He and Regine are going to live at Hathaway Hall. We talked it over, and he agreed with Regine and me that this would be suitable too, so, you see, we'll have a real neighbourhood here presently. Your dear mother, and little Cresside, and that nice girl who lives on St. Napoleon Street—Meredith Randall did you say her name was?—and my daughter and her husband, and you and I. It's nice to think it won't be as lonely on the River Road in the future as it's been in the past, isn't it?"

V

BEFORE doggedly entering Goldenberg's, Gervais had never been in an emporium catering predominantly to feminine cut-price trade. As he walked down the centre aisle towards the elevators, he registered a savage vow that he would never do so again.

His storming of the store was, at best, a last and desperate venture. From Hathaway Hall, he had driven straight to St. Napoleon Street, where he found Mrs. Randall calmly sweeping her small front porch. All the women on that block of St. Napoleon Street were sweeping their small front porches at this hour, unless they had paused from their labours long enough to cross the street or the yard and chat with their neighbours who were similarly engaged; the one exception was an eccentric who year in and year out sat rocking and crocheting, while her porch went unswept. Fortunately for Gervais, Mrs. Randall was, at the moment, undiverted from her sweeping by neighbourhood gossip and Gervais plunged at once into his subject.

"Good-morning, Mrs. Randall. Is Merry home? Could I talk to her for a moment?"

"Good-mornin', Captain d'Alvery. I didn't expect to see you this early. I sure enough didn't. No, Merry isn't home. You know she's at the store daytimes, all but Sunday. She seldom ever gets home until six o'clock."

In his perturbation, Gervais had completely forgotten about the store and its demands upon Merry. For a moment he was nonplussed.

"It was mighty stupid of me to forget about the store, but I did. Well, I wonder if I could talk to you for a few minutes?"

Mrs. Randall looked rather longingly across the street. She had been expecting her friend, Mrs. Resendez, whose husband was part owner of the Fiesole Restaurant, to come over at almost any moment and tell her about a recipe for Ravioli which a cousin who had just come home from Italy had brought to her, and which was said to excel anything of the sort which had ever been eaten in Baton Rouge. She had set her heart on trying out this recipe herself, that very night for supper, and surprising Miss Mittie and Merry with it. However, she knew her duty under the circumstances. If Captain d'Alvery had something serious to say to her, she must listen, for her daughter's sake.

"Why of co'se, Captain d'Alvery, come on into the livin'-room. I'm ashamed to have you see it, the way it looks, but I can't get around to do everything myself, and Miss Mittie and Merry, they both have to start out so early, they can't be any help to me. An' I can't get me any other help, not to save my life. Naturally, I always kept a servant, until the war, but you can't get one now for love nor money. I don't know what we're comin' to, or where all the niggers have gone to. There isn't a woman on this block who's had one workin' for her, as a regular thing, since I can remember. And the wages they ask, at that! Right up to six dollars a week."

Mrs. Randall could not refrain from sighing as she looked across the street, and saw Mrs. Resendez leaning expectantly on her broom. Besides discussing the Ravioli recipe, they were to have discussed the servant shortage, which, like female weaknesses, both physical and moral, and the ruinous cost of living, was a topic of never-flagging mutual interest. She thought that perhaps if Captain d'Alvery noticed her glance, it would suggest the advisability of brevity. But he did not even see it. He followed Mrs. Randall into the disordered living-room, which lay directly beyond the front door, and plunged at once into his subject.

"Mrs. Randall, you know that Merry and I are very fond of each other. In fact, we're engaged. But so far, we hadn't discussed a definite time for the wedding. I want to discuss it with her and with you both. I'd like to get married at once. Well, at least as soon as it could conveniently be arranged."

The final sentence was a concession to the look of sudden dismay, amounting almost to fright, which Gervais had seen on Mrs. Randall's face. As she stared at him dumbly, obviously unable to frame an adequate answer, he went on, trying to speak with less urgency.

"I know a girl needs a little time to get ready. But Merry's so sensible, she won't attach all that much importance to a trousseau, or a big wedding, or anything of the sort. And there's no reason why we should wait. I don't need to tell you I have a beautiful home I can take her to, or that I can support her properly. I hope I don't need to tell you I'll do my level best to make her happy, that I'll try hard to be a good husband. I don't know why I shouldn't succeed. I love her with all my heart and soul. I've loved her for years already. There's nothing on earth I want so much as to have her for my wife."

As he went on, his voice had grown more and more urgent after all, and Mrs. Randall stared at him in greater and greater alarm. But since he could think of nothing more that needed saying, he stopped as abruptly as he had begun, and waited for her to answer him. She opened her mouth, but no sound came out of it. She appeared too paralysed for speech, until the approaching clang of a bell, ringing agreeably but insistently, roused her to relieved utterance.

"That's my vegetable man a-comin'," she said. "And less I rush out the minute he gets opposite this house, he goes right on and won't turn back. He's peculiar that way. If you'll excuse me, Captain d'Alvery, I'll see what he has this mornin'. It'll save me walkin' all the way to market and back to do my grocery shoppin'."

Mrs. Randall hurried from the living-room leaving the front door open behind her. Gervais was certain she had welcomed the diversion, though he was beginning to feel slightly aggrieved and greatly amazed. It had not occurred to him that Merry's mother, as well as his own, might be averse to the marriage, and there was certainly nothing in Mrs. Randall's manner to suggest that she was eager to receive him as a son-in-law. He watched her while she crossed the small porch, flew down the steps and across the sidewalk, and began to bargain with the shabby negro whose unpainted push-cart was piled with wilted vegetables. Life had dealt harshly with Mrs. Randall, and everything about her appearance betrayed this. It was obvious, not only that she did not have much money to spend on her personal appearance, but that she had long since ceased to feel this mattered. Her iron grey hair was gathered up into an untidy knot surrounded by sidecombs, placed more or less at random. Her morning dress, which was hardly more than a wrapper, was also iron grey and hung unevenly over the dingy petticoat which protruded beneath it. Her shapeless shoes were down at the heel. As she argued with the vegetable man, she raised one hand in expostulation, and, even at a distance, Gervais could see how worn and misshapen it was from neglect and toil; her wide, flat wedding-ring, gleaming in the morning sunshine, accentuated its roughness and redness. Gervais thought of his mother's long slim fingers, folded marble-like over her white sheet, and suddenly the contrast between her hands and Mrs. Randall's seemed to symbolize all the differences between Merry's traditions and his own. Never before had he thought of them in that light; never before had they seemed so irreconcilable.

Eventually, Mrs. Randall stopped browbeating the vegetable man, and extracting a small shabby purse from the folds of her grey gingham dress, counted out a few coins, and grudgingly

73

handed them to him one by one. Then she took a bunch of the wilted vegetables from him, and went over to speak to Mrs. Resendez, who was not buying vegetables that morning, and who was still leaning expectantly on her broom. The conversation between the two women went on and on. Gervais began to think that his future mother-in-law had resorted to this expedient in order to terminate the one with him. But at last she turned, with a slowness which contrasted oddly with the speed that had marked her departure, and came back to the living-room and sat down again, placing the wilted vegetables on the table beside her.

"He didn't have anything but carrots and cabbages," she said, referring contemptuously to the disappearing man, whose bell had now become a mere tinkle in the distance. "He seldom ever does. There's another one comes along a little later though, with a horse and wagon. He generally has more of a variety." She gazed longingly out of the door, as if hoping that the second vegetable man might come into view and thus furnish another diversion. Then she sighed again, and forced herself to look at Gervais.

"You've sorta taken me by surprise, Captain d'Alvery, and that's a fact," she said. "Of course I knew you and Merry were keeping company, but I didn't feel so sure it would ever come to anything. I thought if you were really set on marrying her, you'd have done it before you went to France. Merry's never said anything. That isn't her way. But I reckon she was disappointed not to be a war bride, like some of the girls she went with. It's natural for a girl to want to do the same thing other girls are doing." Fleetingly Gervais thought of Cresside, remembering that he tried to excuse her conduct on a similar theory, and the comparison grated. "Why, one girl Merry knew got to go to England to marry her beau," Mrs. Randall went on. "He was a nice fellow too. I think Merry was his first choice. But she did have a crush on you, Captain d'Alvery, from the first time she ever saw you."

"Yes, I had one on her too. But I had an idea it wasn't fair to marry her before I went away."

"Maybe you're right and I wouldn't say you're not sincere. Most generally though, I have noticed that when men talk about it not being fair to marry girls, they're figurin' that's the best kind of excuse they can think up. If they really want to get married, they're not so self-sacrificin' but what they'll do it. They don't stop to think whether it's fair to the girl or not. They're too busy thinkin' of what they'll get out of it themselves, that they can't get any ways else."

Mrs. Randall no longer spoke with shyness and hesitation, but with the increasing confidence inspired by the courage of her convictions. Gervais was annoyed to feel himself flushing.

"I'm sorry I made such a mistake. I realize now that it was a mistake. But I didn't make it because I didn't love her, or because

74

I hadn't always wanted to marry her. And I'm not going to make a mistake like that a second time. I've told you already that I'd like to be married right away. Do you think you could manage a wedding here at the end of this week? Not a large wedding, of course. Just the two families and a few intimate friends."

He spoke in the casual way natural to a man whose household has always adapted itself almost automatically to entertaining. It did not occur to him that for women in Mrs. Randall's category, any kind of a party, but most of all a wedding, represented a complete upheaval in their normal manner of living, even if their hearts were in the project, which obviously hers was not in this case. She had not told him that, except for Merry's disappointment, she would have been glad of his procrastination and that she would have been still more pleased if his intentions had continued to be indefinite. But the growing certainty of this increased his discomfiture.

"I don't see how I could," Mrs. Randall was saying firmly. "I never was one to entertain much, even when I had help. And now without any I wouldn't know how to swing it. Miss Mittie and Merry are both gone all day, like I told you, and they're mighty tired when they get in at night. Besides, maybe you forgot we're in mournin'. I'm not lucky, like your mother, gettin' her son back covered with medals. I lost both of mine."

"I know you did, Mrs. Randall, and of course it's men like your sons who are the real heroes of this war. Malcolm and Vail both were mighty fine fellows, and you've a right to feel proud of them. No one knows that any better than I do or realizes more keenly what a great loss you've had. Of course, I wouldn't expect you to feel like having a large wedding for Merry, so soon after her brothers' death. I'm sure she wouldn't want it herself, and I tried to explain before that I didn't have an elaborate function in mind. But——"

"There isn't space in this house even for a small company," Mrs. Randall said firmly. "It's as much as we can do to find chairs for half a dozen people, when they drop in for Sunday night supper. I don't encourage 'em to do it, but once in a while Merry puts something over on me. We've got quite a lot of kin, and I presume you have too. I don't know how we'd accommodate 'em. . . . Would your mother be able to come? Seems to me I've heard she was puny."

"She's been a bedridden invalid for some years," Gervais said rather coldly. "I'm afraid she couldn't possibly. Aside from her, my sister Cresside's my only close kin. I'd rather like to ask Fabian d'Alvery, but it really isn't necessary—he's only a second cousin. So you see, the family wouldn't take up much room."

"But you'd want to ask your friends, people like the Hathaways, wouldn't you?" persisted Mrs. Randall. "Most everyone in Baton

Rouge thought it was that Hathaway girl you meant to marry. I've heard it said dozens of times. Why, Mrs. Resendez was telling me just now——"

"Like lots of other rumours, that one didn't have a grain of truth in it. As a matter of fact, Regine Hathaway's engaged to someone else."

"I reckon she got engaged to someone else after she found out there wasn't any doubt but what you were engaged to Merry," Mrs. Randall said, again with her deadly air of conviction. "If we were to have a wedding party, I'd ask the Hathaways if I didn't ask another living soul. Well, we could make room for your sister all right, of course. But then she'd naturally want to ask her intended. His name's Sylvestre Tremaine, isn't it?"

The last person whom Gervais wished to discuss with Mrs. Randall was Sylvestre. But he could see all too well that Sylvestre must be invited to the wedding, not on account of Cresside, but on account of Regine. While he was trying to frame an appropriately evasive answer, Mrs. Randall went relentlessly on.

"Maybe you could have the marriage ceremony performed at the parsonage," she said, "and then have a wedding breakfast at Fiesole's Restaurant afterwards. Of course, we'd have to make it small to keep down the cost; but Fiesole's in the habit of catering to wedding parties. There's a private dining-room there, and everything. They even arrange for the decorations, big tissue paper bells and place cards with cupids on them—I'm sure they'd take a special interest in this case, because you see my friend Mrs. Resendez——"

"I hope very much you'll give up the idea of having a wedding breakfast at Fiesole's," Gervais said almost curtly. "It doesn't appeal to me at all. In fact, it ties in with a mental picture of wedding guests tearing through the town in open automobiles, headed by the bride and groom all tooting their horns and singing at the top of their lungs. It may be a good old Italian custom, but it isn't the way the d'Alverys do things. And Merry's going to be a d'Alvery from now on."

"Merry's a Randall through and through," her mother retorted fiercely. "She'll never be anything different. *She's* got backbone." Mrs. Randall had begun to rock, and the sound of the rockers formed a squeaky accompaniment to her strident voice. "I didn't mean to mention it, but since you're so bound and determined that I should go to all the trouble of having a wedding in this house, I may as well tell you that I haven't had a drop of running water since last Saturday. There's something the matter with the pipe between this house and the Serenskys' next door. I reckon it's rotted out. Anyway, I can't get it fixed. It isn't as if we had a public water supply in Baton Rouge, like I hear they do in most places up North, even small places. I can't get the water company to fix it.

76

They claim they're not responsible for the leak, because the pipe's in the driveway and not in the street. I can't get a private plumber either. You ought to know how it is these days—as much as your life is worth to find a mechanic. They're even scarcer than servants. And if you ask me, I think it would be mighty embarrassing if some of the guests should want to use the bathroom and we had to tell 'em to go next door to the Serenskys. I wouldn't think of asking the Serenskys to the wedding ordinarily, but of course I'd have to if my guests used their bathroom, and that's what Miss Mittie and Merry and I been doin' ever since last Saturday. Except that of course at night, we've——"

"I'll speak to the President of the Water Company. I know him quite well," Gervais announced, cutting in again before Mrs. Randall could go into further details concerning makeshift sanitary arrangements. "And I'll find a 'private plumber' too. I guarantee you'll have your pipe fixed before night by someone. I don't know who, but someone. So let's consider that point settled. However, there's another I think we'll have to take up. You spoke, a few moments ago, of having the marriage ceremony performed at the 'parsonage.' I don't know quite what you meant by that, but perhaps I ought to remind you that Merry and I will have to be married by a priest."

"I'll never consent to that, never in this world," Mrs. Randall declared. "You'll be married by our minister, Mr. Hawkins, or you won't be married at all."

"We wouldn't be married at all, according to my faith, if Mr. Hawkins, whoever he is, performed a dozen ceremonies."

"Mr. Hawkins is the pastor of the First Baptist Church. Merry and I have been regular attendants there for years and years. I reckon a girl's got a right to be married by the minister of the church she's always attended if she wants to. What do you mean, you wouldn't be married at all? Of course you'd be married. I'd see to it that you were, all right."

"I'm going to see to it that we are, all right. If you don't think I'm telling you the truth, you might ask your friends, Mrs. Resendez and Mrs. Serensky, what happens sometimes under the sort of arrangement you're suggesting. It's perfectly regular, of course, if the bride and groom are both Protestants. But if the groom's a Catholic, and the bride isn't, he often finds a Protestant ceremony a mighty convenient excuse later on."

"Well, if you're beginning to think up convenient excuses again, Captain d'Alvery—of course, you thought of a considerable number before you went to France—and if you've started all over——"

She rose, bristling with rage. Gervais, no less enraged, also jumped up. But his furious retort was drowned by the clanging of a bell. The second vegetable man, the one who was the proud possessor of a horse and wagon instead of a hand-cart, was now coming down the street. Mrs. Randall rushed out to meet him, in her haste knocking the wilted vegetables she had already purchased from the little table where she had placed them. Gervais stepped on them as he strode after her. If she saw him, as he followed her down the steps, and turned in the direction of North Boulevard, she gave no sign of it. She was already deep in vituperative argument with the second vegetable man.

It was this appalling encounter with his future mother-in-law which had driven Gervais to the doors of Goldenberg's. He was determined to see Merry and to see her at once. He did not care where she was working or for whom; he meant to get her away and take her to some place where he could talk to her, privately, urgently and immediately. He did not see a floorwalker anywhere, and the complete absence of such functionaries served to remind him that floorwalkers were now as scarce as plumbers, and that he had not yet done anything about the Randalls' rusty pipes. Finally he asked the slatternly elevator girl, who sat straddling a stool, staring into space and chewing gum, if she could tell him how he could find Miss Meredith Randall.

"Ah only come yestiddy. I dunno where anything is yet."

"She's Mr. Goldenberg's private secretary. Don't you know where Mr. Goldenberg's office is?"

"No, sah. Ah jus' don' tol' you, Ah only come yestiddy. Ah dunno where anything is."

Her lack of information seemed to be a thing of complete unconcern to her. Her gaze became more and more blank as she continued to chew gum and stare into space, though eventually she condescended to set the elevator in motion. Gervais decided that his only possible course would be to get out on every floor and keep on inquiring with the hope that he might eventually encounter someone who had been in the store longer than a day.

He had reached the sixth floor, and a stage of infuriated desperation, when the unbelievable happened: he saw Merry herself going down the aisle ahead of him. Her back was towards him and she was yards away; but the sheen of her hair, the set of her head and the grace of her carriage were all unmistakable. He did not know another girl who held herself like that or who walked like that, so uprightly yet so harmoniously; no other girl in all the world had so biblical a "crown of glory." He hurried after her and caught up with her, putting a detaining hand on her shoulder.

"Merry!" he said breathlessly. "Merry, I thought I'd never find you!"

"Why, hello, Gervais! What's the matter? Why did you specially want to find me in the middle of the morning?"

She looked at him delightedly, without any effort to conceal her joy in seeing him; but there was gaiety as well as gladness in her brown eyes. Her blithe disregard of the possibility that any serious trouble could have instigated his search was soothing in itself. Nevertheless, he continued to speak excitedly.

"All kinds of things are the trouble. I've got to talk to you about them right away."

"But you can't. I'm in the middle of dictation. I just went out to get the proofs of tomorrow's ads for the *State-Times*. Mr. Goldenberg always o.k.'s them himself the last thing." She glanced down at the sheaf of papers she was carrying, directing Gervais' glance towards them too. "But when I've taken them back to the advertising manager, we've got to go on with the letters."

"You've got to get time off to talk to me."

"I'll talk to you this evening. I thought you were coming to see me this evening, anyway."

"Well, I was. But I decided, last night, that I'd better come to see you before that. And this morning I decided that the earlier I saw you the better."

He spoke not only with increasing urgency, but with increasing harshness. Merry had often heard him speak urgently, but she had never before heard him speak harshly. She continued to look at him lovingly, but a little of the gaiety went out of her look and she regarded him more thoughtfully.

"I'm fairly serious about this, Merry. In fact, I'm in deadly earnest. I want to talk to you right away."

"All right. Let's go to Mr. Goldenberg's office together and tell him so. Perhaps he'll let someone else take the letters. Anyway, we can ask him."

She started down the aisle again, straightening the papers she was carrying as she went. The Department of Draperies and Floor Coverings was in front of the Executive Offices, and several scatter rugs were cluttering up the aisle. Gervais could hardly resist kicking them out of his way, and he was doubly ashamed of this impulse when Merry, who had apparently guessed it, stooped down and put them back in their proper place, folding them neatly. Since there was not a clerk in sight, no one except Gervais appreciated this service.

"We're terribly short-handed," she said, repeating the popular theme song so pleasantly that it sounded inoffensive for once. "But I reckon we won't be much longer. I hear a boy applied for a job this very morning." She smiled, and stretching out her hand caught his in a sudden squeeze. "Don't worry, Gervais," she said softly. "Of course I don't know what the matter seems to be, but I am sure we can straighten it out between us. . . . This is where we turn," she said, nodding towards a huge pulsating red arrow suspended overhead, which pointed towards a corridor running at a right-angle from the Department of Draperies and Floor Coverings. "We have to go through the dingiest part of the store to get to Mr. Goldenberg's office. But I'm used to it so I don't mind it. I hope you won't mind it too much either."

It certainly was dingy, Gervais agreed, and though he did not say so, he found it as depressing as he had found the first floor distasteful. One side of the unpainted wall was lined with a long row of steel lockers; on the other side was a large gaping hole, evidently the opening of the freight elevator—since harsh and creaking sounds seemed to herald the approach of this; beyond was an adjustment bureau, where several portly, vituperative women were arguing with harassed clerks about merchandise they wished to take back. Turning again, Merry led Gervais past the fire escape, and several small glassed-in cubicles labelled in black letters with the names and titles of the functionaries to whom they were allotted. Then, pausing before a sign which read "NO VISITORS ALLOWED," she pressed his hand hard, before releasing hers from his grip with gentleness but determination.

"This is my little cubbyhole, and that's Mr. Goldenberg's office just beyond," she said. "We mustn't go in there holding hands. It wouldn't be the best approach. . . . We'll do it again afterwards, though," she added, with a momentary return of gaiety. Then she opened the door. "Mr. Goldenberg," she said, without any preamble whatever, "this is my fiancé, Captain d'Alvery. I don't think you've met him before. He's sorry to burst in on you like this and I'm sorry to have him. But it's very important for him to have a chance to talk to me for a few minutes. I'd be grateful if he could have it. Perhaps you'd let Hazel take your letters. I don't think she's gone out to lunch yet. I just saw her, when I went down for the ads. And Mr. Sears *has* gone out. Captain d'Alvery and I could step into his office if you don't think he'd mind, and if you wouldn't yourself."

The thick-set, grey-haired man, who had the look of being shaved by an expert barber and manicured by a meticulous operator, turned in his swivel chair and looked appraisingly at his visitor. Gervais noticed that he was dressed with the precision so frequently affected by those who have not had the opportunity of wearing good clothes casually early in life. His high stiff collar had a glazed look. His dark suit was so expertly tailored and so carefully pressed that it gave the effect of being cautiously worn and for the first time.

"I am very glad to have an opportunity of meeting Captain d'Alvery," Mr. Goldenberg said agreeably. "Naturally I went to the station to see his triumphant return. And, as you know, I also watched the parade. But that is not like a personal meeting." His manner was courteous, but somehow he contrived to convey the impression that while he recognized the returning hero in Gervais, he remembered that the d'Alverys and the Goldenbergs had never mingled socially, and that since this was the case, he would not be the first to indicate any desire for a change. He did not rise, himself, and he did not ask his visitor to sit down; his black bloodshot eyes travelled slowly from Gervais to Merry and back again. "Please accept my congratulations, Captain d'Alvery," he went on at last. "I'd heard rumours, but I confess I hadn't listened to them —perhaps because I didn't want to. Miss Meredith's been with me a long time. I don't need to tell you that I consider her services invaluable. Under the circumstances, I suppose I ought to be thankful that you are asking to interrupt them only temporarily. . . . By all means, send Miss Hazel in to me, Miss Meredith."

VI

IN determining to see Merry at once, and to take her to some place where he could talk to her urgently, Gervais had formed no clear mental picture of what this place should be or could be. But certainly he had not visualized a glass-enclosed cubicle beside a public corridor in a department store. There was neither comfort nor privacy in the disorderly little office to which Merry led the way, sitting down in the straight-backed chair which was evidently provided for Mr. Sears' stenographer, and indicating the one by the little old desk for Gervais, after removing a pile of papers from it. Having done this much, she took no further initiative, but sat smiling at him expectantly, waiting for him to speak. His own rebellious impulse to protest against the inadequacy and unsuitability of the setting was curbed only by the certainty that there was no alternative to it, and that he must accept it and make the best of it.

"Merry," he said, and stopped. If they only had been safe from intrusion, if he only could have put his arm around her or even taken her hand, it would not have been so hard, it would not all have seemed so ugly and crude, in spite of the water cooler and the insurance calendars and the misshapen racks standing beside the steel files and hung with limp sample dresses. But he could see two giggling girls pausing to peer into the cubicle as they passed by it, and after they went on their giggles grew louder and were interspersed with whispers. Merry must have heard them too, but they did not seem to upset her as much as they did Gervais.

"Yes, honey?" she said. "What is it, Gervais? How can I help you if you don't tell me what the matter is?"

"I'm trying to tell you. But it's damned hard to do it in a place like this. I get all balled up. I know I'm going to say the wrong thing, because everything else is all wrong."

"I know. You'd like to say it under the colonnade at Belle Heloise in the moonlight. But don't you think we care enough for each other, Gervais, to forget the kind of place we're in, so long as we can be in it together?"

"You make me feel like a fool when you put it like that. Hell, the reason I hate all this so is because of you, and the way I feel about you. If you can't see my point, perhaps I'd better not go on."

"I do see your point. But I can't believe it's the most important one, just now. The most important point was that you wanted to have a chance to talk to me immediately. Well, you've got it. So I think you'd better go on."

"All right. I want you to marry me."

"But I *am* going to marry you. *I* want to marry *you*."

"Enough to marry me right away?"

"Why, I reckon so. What do you mean by 'right away,' honey?"

"I want you to marry me today."

"Why, Gervais?"

She did not shrink away from the bald statement, but her steady eyes grew more searching as she looked at him. He answered with increasing vehemence.

"Because I'm afraid if you don't you won't marry me at all."

"Yes, I will, I promise I will. But I won't marry you today either. If you hadn't completely lost your head you'd know I couldn't do that."

"I haven't lost my head yet. But so many other people seem to be losing theirs that I'm likely to, any minute."

"Is that why you want me to marry you today, Gervais? Because so many people are losing their heads?"

"Yes, partly. Yours is always so clear. You'd help to clarify the others."

"Then what you really mean is that you need me, or think you do? Not that you want me?"

"Good God, Merry, don't talk like that! As if I'd wounded your vanity! I told you I knew I'd do this all wrong. But, hell——"

"You haven't wounded my vanity. You don't really think I'm vain, do you, Gervais? Of course you don't. You know I'm not. But I do want to get this straight. I can't help you if I don't understand. If you want me more today than yesterday, I'd like to know why. And if you don't, if you only need me more than you did yesterday, I'd like to know that too. I'd marry you just as quickly if I thought you needed me more as I would if I thought you wanted me more. But you'd have to tell me the truth about it first."

"All right. The truth is I'm facing a very ugly, complicated situation. If you were my wife, you could help me straighten it out. You'd be in a position to, you'd have a right to. You're not, and you haven't as long as you're only engaged to me."

"Can you tell me what this situation is, Gervais?"

"I can outline it for you. I can't go into details."

"Very well. Outline it for me."

"Primarily it concerns my sister. I'm very much disturbed about her."

For the first time Merry glanced away from Gervais, resting her face on her hand and looking thoughtfully towards the door of the cubicle. The two girls who had passed down the corridor a few minutes earlier were clattering back again now, giggling harder and whispering more brazenly than before. Merry nodded to them, and then spoke to them, briefly but pleasantly. Their bold silly conduct obviously did not upset her, and their untimely appearance did not seem to interrupt her train of thought. When they had gone, their babble dying away in the distance, Merry turned back to Gervais with her steady smile.

"I'm sorry," she said simply. Her tone carried conviction, but no curiosity. Gervais had an idea that this was not only because Merry was incurious by disposition, but also because she was not especially surprised. She probably knew a good deal about Cresside already, and, as far as that went, about Regine too, and he experienced a momentary relief at the thought that he would not have to dwell on Regine's part in the picture, at least not immediately. "I'm very sorry, Gervais," Merry said again. "But I don't know that I could be helpful, just because I'm sorry. I don't think Cresside wants anyone to interfere with her, do you? I don't think she'd let anyone do it."

"No, I don't think she wants anyone to interfere with her. But I do think she may want someone to stand by her. Another woman."

"She has your mother, Gervais."

"My mother's been a recluse ever since my father died. I thought I'd told you that. Anyway, she's been so preoccupied with herself that she's overlooked Cresside's problems. They can't be overlooked much longer. Someone has got to help her solve them."

Again Merry glanced away. This time Gervais went on without waiting for her to make any comments.

"I told my mother, when I went home yesterday, that I was going to marry you. This morning I saw her maid, Lucie, for a moment, and she said *maman* was getting up—for the first time in two years. That seems she intends to resume control of Belle Heloise. Before you can supplant her as its chatelaine."

"She doesn't want me there, Gervais?"

"You've asked for the truth, so I'm going to give it to you. No, she doesn't. She'll make trouble for you, Merry; she'll make trouble for both of us. We can't prevent her making some. But if we get married right away, if you simply step in before she can stop you and begin to take charge before she can get her strength back, we'll avert a good deal. I'll make it as easy for you as I can, and I can make it a good deal easier if we start the struggle right away.

That's the second reason why I'm urging you to marry me at once."

"I see. That is, I think I do."

"Do you really? Gosh, I can't tell you how thankful I am. Merry, you may think I don't realize my own luck, but I do. You're wonderful to take it like this. There isn't a girl in a thousand who could."

"Of course there is. Any girl would, who loved the man she was going to marry as much as I love you. . . . Is there anything else, Gervais?"

"Yes. Yes." His words were coming in a rush now, his need of her piling higher and higher upon his yearning. "A third reason is that your mother's dead set against our marriage too. I can't understand why she could be, but she is. And I don't know how much opposition you can buck without breaking under it, but I should think there might be a limit, if it went on and on. We'd have to put an end to it some time anyhow. It better be right away. It's got to be."

"I beg pardon. Is Mr. Sears out? He told me to let him see this as soon as I could get it ready. He wants to be sure the goods go out this afternoon."

A weedy-looking shipping clerk was standing in the doorway, holding a bill of lading in his hands. Gervais sprang up, swearing under his breath. Merry rose too and walked over to the door.

"I'm sorry, Tim," she said quietly. "Mr. Sears hasn't come back from lunch yet. But if you'll leave that with me I'll see that he gets it as soon as he does come in." She reached out her hand for the bill of lading, and after a moment's hesitation the weedy-looking boy gave it to her, muttering something under his breath as he turned away. Merry laid the bill of lading carefully on the table under a glass paperweight; then she went to the door of the cubicle, closed it, locked it, and came back to Gervais. She did not take his hand again, but she stood so close to him that her nearness was like an embrace.

"I think you're right. I think it has got to be," she said gently. "That is, it's got to be as soon as it can without hurting anyone else more than we have to I'm afraid it's going to hurt your mother so much anyway that it won't matter when we do it. So, as you say, it better be right off, as far as she's concerned. But I've got to think about my own mother. Not about her opposition. I can buck that, whatever you believe, and I will. But about her needs. You see, I support her. I've got obligations and problems too. If I stop earning money, she won't have enough to live on. She hasn't a clear title to our house—it's mortgaged, and Miss Mittie only pays sixteen dollars a month for her room. If there wasn't any other way to manage, would you let me ask my mother to live with us? Of course, I wouldn't do it except as a last resort, because I don't think it would be a good plan. But would you, if I thought I had to?"

"I don't think it would be a good plan either. Not that I'd begrudge her a home, you know that. And there's plenty of room at Belle Heloise. I know it wouldn't work out well, though." With merciless clarity he foresaw the clash of temperaments between Merry's mother and his own. But he gritted his teeth. "I'll let you do anything you want—I mean, anything you think best, if you'll only marry me today," he said desperately.

"Please don't talk as if you were bribing me to marry you, honey," she said. She still spoke gently, but there was a hint of quiet reproof in her tone. "You know I'm not trying to bargain with you. I'm only trying to be fair with everybody. I've got to think of Mr. Goldenberg too. He's always been very kind to me, and very generous. I can't suddenly leave him in the lurch, without anyone to do his work. I'll have to tell him, straight from the shoulder, what you want me to do, and make him understand, without going into detail, that it's important I should. If he says he can spare me, I'll go right to my desk and pick up my things. If he says he can't, I'll have to give him a few days' notice."

"You mean that if Mr. Goldenberg comes across you *will* marry me today?"

"Why, that's what you asked me to do, isn't it? That's what you want, isn't it? We *could* get married today, couldn't we? That is, there isn't any law about waiting after you get a licence, or red tape of any other sort that would prevent it?"

"No," he said hoarsely. "No—that is, I don't think so. Or, if there is, there's probably some way of getting around it, when there's a good reason why anyone should. There's a priest here in town I know very well. Father Navarre, his name is. He's a darn good scout. Comes from the swamp country, but he's been a chaplain in the war, and just now he's in Baton Rouge. I believe he'd understand, if I explained to him. Yes, I'm almost sure he would. Most priests are very understanding, Merry. You'll find that out."

"I'm sure I shall. And you mustn't mind, Gervais, if mother is bitter about your religion. She can't help being. It's just the way she's made. Of course, I'm going to ask her if she won't come with us, to see us married. I think I ought to do that. But if she says no, I'll go with you to see Father Navarre, just the same. We'll do what he tells us to."

Merry glanced towards the closed door and listened intently. There was no one in sight, and there was no sound of footsteps in the corridor either. She came still closer to him.

"I think it would be all right for us to kiss each other now," she said. "And I think it would be nice if we did, too, don't you?"

It was not until hours later, when they were on their way to

Belle Heloise, that Gervais was able to put into words his feeling for what she had done. Merry listened lovingly to what he said as they drove along the River Road in the twilight, with his arm tight around her waist and her head resting quietly on his shoulder. The words sounded very sweet to her, and she was happy to have him speak them; like every other woman, she wanted to hear the man she loved keep on telling her he was certain that no man had ever loved his wife so much before or with so much reason. But she did not require the assurance. No eloquent declaration of passion spoken in the scented moonlight, under the mystic colonnade, could have carried with it the force of the desperate plea which Gervais had made to her in the dingy little cubicle of the merchandising manager. If he had so besought her holding her closely embraced in some bower of beauty, she might have hesitated, fearing that her own stirred senses had confused her to such a degree that she could not see an involved issue clearly, or set on it wisely. But there had been no withstanding a supplication so starkly set apart from romantic appeal. She knew his need of her for what it was, and she could measure it, not by faltering or failure on his part, but by her own need of him.

She moved a little, lifting her head. It had been downcast because at first she had been so overcome by the prodigality of his praise that she could not bring herself to face him. Now she was calmer, and joyously accepting his tribute, she raised adoring eyes to his. Momentarily she had forgotten there was anyone else in the world except her husband and herself. But as she looked up, she became aware of the place they were passing, where a vast house rose like a white palace beyond the green grace of its encircling grove, and of a beautiful girl, who looked like a white-robed queen, standing in the gallery and watching them. Gervais did not see the motionless and mocking figure of Regine. He had bent over to kiss Merry again, and he was still forgetful that there was anyone else in the world. But Merry had already emerged from her fairyland of dreams to confront the menace of reality.

"Come, haste to the wedding, ye friends and ye neighbours!
The lovers their bliss shall no longer delay;
Forget all your sorrow, your care and your labours,
And let ev'ry heart beat with rapture today."

"Ye votaries all
Attend to my call. . . .
And come at our bidding
To this happy wedding!"

This was a favourite selection for festivals along the River Road. Eliza MacHatton-Ripley, who lived at "Arlington," wrote in her book of memoirs: ". . . The 'plantation band' with the inspiring airs of 'Monie Musk' and 'Come, Haste to the Wedding,' put wings to the giddy feet—how the happy moments fled!" It is found in *Songs of England*, edited by J. L. Hatton and Eaton Faning.

PART II

"Come, Haste to the Wedding"

(June 30, 1919)

VII

MEREDITH D'ALVERY stirred sleepily in her big bed and, almost subconsciously, stretched out her arms. It was their emptiness that awakened her. But she was beginning to remember now. . . . Gervais had risen, as usual, when the plantation bell rang. He had done it quietly, trying not to disturb her, and as she half opened her eyes and he had seen her looking at him drowsily but adoringly, he had come to the bedside, telling her to lie down again, like a good girl, and go back to sleep. She had lain down again because he had asked her to; she did everything he requested, not tamely, but exultantly, for nothing made her so happy as to feel she was contributing in any way to his contentment; and she had gone back to sleep again immediately, because nowadays she was unable to set any limits on her hours of slumber. It no longer seemed strange to her to lie in bed, late in the morning, after Gervais was up, as it had in the beginning. If it had not been for that joyous tractability of hers, she would have rebelled when he first told her this was what she was expected to do. But lately it not only seemed natural for her to luxuriate in early morning idleness; it seemed inevitable. She could not rouse herself if she tried. Over and over again she was engulfed by the prolonged, profound slumber of early pregnancy.

She was temporarily emerging from the depths of this gulf now, and in a few minutes she would ring for Creassy, who was Lou Ida's sister and her own maid, assigned to her on the very evening of her arrival at Belle Heloise. The house servants all had their own bells, which hung in a row on the wall of the back gallery, near the kitchen. Each of these bells had a different sound, and the servants could tell by the tone, when they heard one ringing, whether it was for them or not. These little tinkling house bells had not the great importance of the huge bronze bell by the mule shed, which had been cast by Thiac-Maignon Durand in 1824 and was duly inscribed to that effect. But they had their own small and significant place in plantation life just the same.

After Merry rang for her maid, Creassy would bring her coffee and draw her bath and lay out her clothes, and after she had drunk the coffee she would rise and dress in a leisurely way; then she would do a variety of inconsequential, unexacting things until dinner-time. But after dinner she would go to sleep again. She would come back to this beautiful bed, which Creassy would have made up freshly and turned down invitingly; she would stretch out between the linen sheets which were so cool against her skin and drift quietly away into unconsciousness. The room was very restful in the afternoon. There was something about the artificial dimness which Creassy created by excluding the sunlight with shutters which made it seem even more tranquil than it was at night. Its darkness then was different, less uniform, less sheltering and enclosed, more thrilling and provocative. The shutters were swung wide at the open windows then, the moonlight streamed in, the fireflies flitted through the live oaks and camphor trees in the Small Yard, the lights on the riverboats flashed above the levee. Merry could see the fireflies and the boat lights without raising herself from her pillows, and often the moonlight seemed to saturate the very sheets.

These luminous aspects of the night were inescapable. But the afternoon sunshine could not prevail against Creassy's ingenuity. For long hours Merry was oblivious of its quivering intensity. She woke refreshed to face an evening enlivened by the presence of Gervais and an occasional visitor, but otherwise as uneventful as the morning. And then Gervais, who, unlike Merry, had been up early, was ready for bed early too. She was back in the big square shuttered chamber and this time Gervais was with her.

This was one of the reasons, of course, why the darkness of the night was so different from the dusk of the afternoon. She was not alone in the darkness, she was not watching the fireflies and the riverboats by herself, the moonlight did not bathe her in solitary state. And although Gervais' early rising was a convenient parlour pretext for an early bedtime, his pretence of weariness scarcely saw him up the stairs. He was an eager and demanding lover, assured and triumphant from the very first. The unprotesting acceptance of his dominance, which he himself had foreseen, had freed him from all those compunctions which a bride less rapt but more reluctant might have roused, and Merry was unresentfully aware of this. She could have exacted more restraint and gentleness, but in so doing she would have forfeited some of the glory she had gained. Untutored as she was in the ways of love, she knew that this was so; increasingly she rejoiced in the unquenched passion which she now could so ardently return. The darkness of her room at night was the majestic cloak enfolding her with her beloved.

No thought of a child had crossed her mind during the first blissful weeks of her marriage; it had been overflowing with thoughts of Gervais, with love for him, with thanksgiving for the

ulfilment he had brought her. But now that she knew she was
pregnant, she was doubly happy at the realization that she could
ake her place with all the other proud women whose passion had
peen productive and whose children were the visible symbol and
proof of shared rapture and secret communion. More than this:
having been brought, as an outsider, into surroundings where productiveness was the universal rule, she knew she would have remained indefinitely an alien unless she could have met existing
tandards and set now ones. Now she was not only the expectant
mother of an heir to a great heritage, and as such entitled to the
homage which no barren wife could have commanded; she was
conscious of a mystic bond with the joyous fecundity which she
aw on every side.

Even the drowsiness against which she no longer struggled had
been a safeguard and support. Prostrated as she was by it, she could
not supplant her mother-in-law aggressively or offensively. The
course of action on which Gervais, in his anger, had been determined, was perforce delayed, and meanwhile the gradual readjust-
ment of the household was taking place with far less friction than
f he had been able to carry out his original wilful purpose.
Defiantly, he had placed Merry at the head of table when he
prought her home after their precipitate marriage, and she had sat
there, frightened but firm, watching with anxious eyes a ceremonial
which was wholly unfamiliar to her. She knew she must not shame
him before his sister and his servants; and how was he to guess
that never before in her life had she seen a table set with shaded
candles and silver ornaments, that she had never given a signal
for changing plates or displaced a finger-bowl? He had not given
a thought to such matters, because they seemed so natural and
trivial to him, and he would have been astonished and amused to
learn that they could puzzle or agitate his bride. He would have
been equally astonished and amused if he had realized that even
her joy in him had not saved her from chagrin because she had
gone straight to his house wearing the cheap little dress into which
she had hastily changed after leaving the store, a dress in no way
better than the one in which she had worked all day, except that
it was fresh. She had flung two or three similar dresses and some
clean, flimsy underwear into a suitcase that had belonged to her
brother Vail, who had been killed at St. Mihiel, and these had constituted her trousseau. She could not have had much of an outfit
in any case. But with a little time—enough to draw her small
savings from the bank, enough to look around for bargains at
Goldenberg's, enough to do some sewing herself—she could at least
have had something that would have passed for one.

To her surprise, it was Cresside who came to her rescue. Gervais
had not been able to reach his sister before the stark little ceremony which Father Navarre had been prevailed upon to perform:

D

it had been witnessed only by Mrs. Randall, grim and rebellious
by Mr. and Mrs. Goldenberg, who vainly strove to create a les
rigid atmosphere, and by Fabian, who aided and abetted thei
attempts with more success than they achieved themselves. Bu
Cresside happened to be at home when Gervais and Merry arrived
at Belle Heloise, and she shared that first dreadful dinner with
them. After it was over, Gervais went up to his mother's room to
tell her that he was married, and that he would bring his bride to
see her, either that evening or the following morning, whicheve
she preferred; and then Cresside put her arms impulsively around
Merry and kissed her.

"Look here," she said. "I like you. I didn't think I was going to
but I do. I think you've got lots of spunk coming here like this
Not crust—that's what Gervais has bringing you this way. I'd have
told him to go straight to hell, if I'd been you. But I still think
you're swell because you didn't. At that, I know you haven't had
time to take a long breath, much less get clothes together or any
thing. Would you think I was too darn fresh for words if I offered
to step into the breach?"

"I'd think you were very kind. It has all been—well, pretty sud
den. I don't suppose a man realizes. . . . But I'm afraid I don'
understand just what you mean."

"I've got oodles of new clothes," Cresside explained. "A big box
ful came in from New Orleans just yesterday. I don't see why
ever bought so many, but I go haywire like that about once in s
often. Would you let me give you some of them for a wedding
present? Of course I want to give you something, and there's n
use buying you silver, or furniture or anything like that, with al
the junk there is in the house already. Come along into the garden
room. I've got my stuff stacked up in there. And no one will eve
know—*maman* or the servants or that boob Gervais—that th
things didn't belong to you in the first place. We're about the sam
size, though I'm a little more on the skinny side. Just the same,
think you can get into everything I have, the way clothes are cu
nowadays. You've heard that silly riddle, haven't you, about waist
lines? What two French cities they make you think of? No
Toulouse and Toulon! It isn't much of a joke, but it fits . .
Hell, I didn't mean to make a bad pun on top of telling a bad joke
Come on in and change before that dumb brother of mine get
back. He probably won't even see that you've got a different dres
on, but *maman*'ll notice you look exactly right, and she'll be im
pressed. Of course, she won't show that she is or even admit it t
herself. But, believe me, it'll have its effect just the same."

So, thanks to Cresside, Merry had gone into her mother-in-law's
room dressed in a soft and simple white chiffon which had been
fashioned by a master hand; and even Madame d'Alvery's hard

92

eyes, scanning her appraisingly from head to foot, had found nothing to evoke the cold criticism with which she desired to crush the girl. Her son's bride looked like a lady, and what was even more astonishing and disappointing, she acted like one. Her manner was not bold, as Madame d'Alvery uncharitably hoped it would be; but while it was deferential, it was not servile either; this strange little shop girl was respectful to her husband's mother, but not to the degree that would detract from her own self-respect. The first visit was characterized by cool courtesy on both sides, concealing rage on the one and trepidation on the other; and during each succeeding visit which Merry made to her mother-in-law's room, Madame d'Alvery continued to wait watchfully for the errors in conversation or conduct which did not occur. The girl carried herself with dignity, and though to be sure she did not talk much, on the other hand she did not say the wrong thing, and she was the first to lose her sense of constraint. The day came when she took her sewing into Madame d'Alvery's boudoir, and sitting down beside the regal couch, stitched away quietly for an hour or so before gathering up the fine linen on which she had been working and taking her leave with the same apparent ease with which she had come. Gervais was out on the plantation most of the time, Cresside dashing from one festivity to another in town; but Merry, intent on learning the ways of the house, stayed for the most part within its walls. When her drowsiness first came upon her, so that she could no longer spend so much time with her mother-in-law, Madame d'Alvery caught herself, more than once, glancing involuntarily towards the door for the pleasing young figure that failed to appear.

Meanwhile Madame d'Alvery was rapidly regaining her own strength. Vitiated as this was by the years during which she had so stubbornly lain in bed, it was basically indestructible. She began to walk to her couch unsupported, and, before long, to circulate through the second story rooms, making caustic suggestions as to their rearrangement, and to pace slowly back and forth on the upper gallery, issuing an occasional peremptory order to the labourers in the Small Yard. When Gervais was available, she imperiously demanded his support; but after all, Gervais, like Cresside, was seldom in evidence at such times. And Lucie was growing old; her feeble footsteps were oftentimes even more faltering than those of her strong-willed mistress. When Merry offered for the first time to walk with her, Madame d'Alvery did not make her refusal quite as haughty and definite as she intended; and when Merry offered the second time, Madame d'Alvery accepted. So it happened that it was Merry that supported her when at last she went over the stairs, and who urged her to stay down for dinner. Gervais, coming in a little late, found his mother already ensconced at the head of the table again. But his protest was stilled because

Merry reached quickly for his hand and caught it under the long white cloth, pressing it hard.

"You don't know how much I like sitting by you," she said. She did not whisper; she spoke so that not only Gervais but Madame d'Alvery and Cresside and Selah could all hear her too. "It's what I've wanted to do, all the time. Only you never asked me! And I suppose that somebody did have to sit at the other end of this huge table until Madame Mère was well enough to come down again. But I've felt ever so far away from you this time."

It had been her own idea to call her mother-in-law Madame Mère, and the chance choice had been a happy one. She knew only a little schoolgirl French, which she had never put to spoken use; but having hit upon the regal title, she began to try out brief phrases, and to ask her mother-in-law for help in making them more fluent and idiomatic. She was honestly eager to learn, and though now it required real effort to try, she kept on doing so, not as intensively as she had at first, but at least intermittently, during those late morning hours that were filled with such a variety of inconsequential unexacting things. . . .

Her mother-in-law would be waiting for her now, she supposed. It was high time that she had her coffee and rose and dressed. But she put off ringing for Creassy, partly because she was still so sleepy, and partly because there was a good chance that Gervais might come back to their room, and she did not want to risk any distraction from the intimacy they might enjoy. He very often did come back about that time, for he had generally finished riding the crops by then and liked to have his second cup of coffee with her, the first one having been taken alone. It was superb coffee, a blend specially selected and roasted for him by one of his close friends, Billy Pereira, whose father headed the famous coffee-importing firm of Pereira, Ltd., in New Orleans. Merry thought nothing else had ever tasted so good to her. She sat up in bed, beguilingly arrayed in one of the exquisite nightgowns that Cresside had given her, and drank her coffee from a daintily spread tray, while Gervais, still in riding togs, drank his from a small tilt-top table, easily drawn up by the bedside. This was his chosen period for telling her how things were going on the plantation, and for discussing his plans and projects with her. His mother was always with them at dinner and supper now, and, more frequently than in the beginning, Cresside as well; there was no chance for private conversation then, or in the evenings when they all sat in the parlour; and at bedtime Gervais was never in a mood for practical or serious discussion. It was this morning period, which constituted the breathing space between his manifold activities, that seemed ideally suited for such discussions, and that had caused them to become more or less habitual.

94

It was while they were chatting in this way, a month or so earlier, that he had first spoken to her about wanting to entertain at Belle Heloise. Until then, he had been not only satisfied, but eager, to spend every possible moment alone with her. She tried to tell herself she did not mind that this was no longer the case, to make him feel that if the time had come when he craved more conviviality in his home, she would be the first to encourage it. To a greater degree than most brides, under similar circumstances, she had succeeded.

"I've been thinking, Merry, that I'd like to have a few people in for dinner. Not many. Six or so. You won't need to bother about it at all. Lou Ida and Selah will look after everything."

"It wouldn't be a bother. I'd enjoy it." She could say this more sincerely now that candlelight and finger-bowls had ceased to appal her; but still, she had so loved having him to herself! "Do you want to have a party for Regine and Sylvestre? I thought from something your mother said that perhaps you might."

"Hell, no! Why should I want to have a party for them?"

"Well, they're both old friends, aren't they? And Regine's always been a near neighbour besides. And they've both been very nice to us since we were married. It's customary for the friends of engaged couples to give parties for them, isn't it? I mean, when they *stay* engaged long enough to make that possible. Not when they rush off headlong to a priest the way we did!"

She spoke with appealing archness, and usually Gervais would have responded enthusiastically to such an approach. To her surprise, he answered almost abruptly.

"There wasn't anything the matter with the way we got married. Come right down to it, I'm glad we escaped all that special brand of foolishness. And I certainly don't intend to go in for it now, as far as Regine and Sylvestre are concerned. What do you mean, both old friends? I never could endure the sight of that bastard."

"Why do you always call Sylvestre a bastard, Gervais? I thought the Tremaines were very nice people."

"Good Lord, don't take me so literally! I wasn't trying to cast any aspersions on his family. I can call him a skunk, if you like that any better."

"But that isn't complimentary to his family either, is it?"

"I said, don't take me so literally. . . . Incidentally, I'm pretty sure that Sylvestre's sudden decision to became a planter isn't based on a yearning for life on the River Road, or even an abject desire to satisfy Regine's ambition to keep her husband tied to her apron strings. I think he's been fired from Pereira's, the coffee-importing house, where he's been since he faded away from Tulane about halfway through his course. It's a fine old firm, with pretty high standards, and he never did measure up to them. He wouldn't have got into it in the first place if the Tremaines hadn't been very

95

nice people, as you put it. Now all that family influence hasn[
been powerful enough to keep him there. He'd have had to lea[
there with his tail between his legs if the magnificence of Hat[
away Hall hadn't saved his face. Well, I seem to be getting a litt[
mixed in my metaphors, but at least they boil down to the pla[
statement that he's no friend of mine, and that I don't want hi[
at my table, now or ever."

"Do you know I actually guessed that about five minutes ag[
You haven't told me yet who it is you do want, though."

"I thought I'd like to have a stag dinner with poker afterward[
You know I've been in town two or three times to play—not a[
often as if there hadn't been a powerful counter-attraction rig[
here." He set down his coffee cup and leaned over, pulling h[
clustering curls and kissing her upturned face. "But still I've gon[
Now I think it's coming my turn. Besides, I couldn't have a bett[
chance to put over the idea that I'd like to run for the Legislatu[
than after a good dinner at my own house. And, believe me, we[
have a good dinner. I'd send some of the hands up to the barro[
pit for bass, and the river shrimp ought to be at their best pret[
soon. Then we'd have one of the gobblers from the yard and wate[
melon with champagne poured into it before it's chilled. Some[
the 1901 Montrachet with the fish and—well, I'll go the whole ho[
—1892 Ponte Canet with the turkey."

"I never heard of those wines before, but just the same it mak[
me hungry and thirsty to listen to you. However, I'd still like[
know who's going to eat and drink all this."

"Well, Jim Bailey, if I can get him, and George Favrot. I'll fin[
out what night they're free first. Then I thought I'd ask the pres[
dent of the Cotton Factors National Bank, Melvin Bisbee, and th[
Yankee planter, Charles Boylston, who bought the old Surclif[
place, Hackberry Lodge, a piece down the road, while I was ov[
in France. He's a member of the Police Jury now, and I've like[
what I've seen of him. And I suppose I ought to ask Fabian. An[
how, he's better company than you'd guess, when he gets with [
group like that."

"I think Fabian's always good company. I like him."

"Well, he liked you plenty too, if half I've heard happens to [
true. I reckon it would be just as well if I didn't encourage him[
come here too often." Again he paused to pull her curls and to ki[
her. "But this time you won't be much in evidence, you kno[
Just long enough to say hello to all these hairy males before y[
fade gracefully away into the background."

"Won't Cresside say hello to them too? And Madame Mère?"

"Oh, Cresside without a doubt! Cresside wouldn't miss a chan[
to say something, no matter what, to half a dozen men, no matt[
who. I couldn't keep her in her room unless I locked her up ther[
and I don't believe I'll bother to do that. I should think *mam[*

might just as well skip it. No one expects a social resurrection from a woman who's been several years on her deathbed."

"She'll enjoy it, honey, just as much as Cresside will. Not the same way, but just as much."

"Well, I shouldn't have thought so, but I'll take your word for it. You seem to have sized her up better than I ever could and to get along with her better too. And naturally I shan't try to lock her in her room either. But, personally, I'd be just as glad if there was no one besides you with me in the parlour when the guests arrive."

Merry was pleased and proud because he said this and because she knew he meant it. But, personally, she was glad to have Madame d'Alvery on one side of her and Cresside on the other when the Secretary of State and the Congressmen came in together, both easy-mannered and pleasant-spoken, but somehow just a little awe-inspiring just the same. She was grateful to Cresside for giving her another of the pretty dresses from that seemingly inexhaustible supply, a rose-coloured one this time, which Cresside said exactly matched her cheeks. She went into Cresside's room, with Creassy in attendance, to get ready for the party, because Cresside always had some bright ideas about adjusting bows or shifting flowers; and as she looked at her sister-in-law, she thought that Cresside had really been wise not to choose this particular dress for herself, because it certainly would not have matched *her* cheeks. Cresside was very pale, and though she sat longer than usual in front of her vanity, putting on variegated make-up, none of the cosmetics she so skilfully applied wholly concealed her pallor.

"Don't you feel well, Cresside?" Merry finally asked, unable to suppress her concern any longer.

"Of course. What makes you think I don't?"

"You don't look well."

"I haven't got the skin you love to touch, like you have, if that's what you mean. Don't rub it in."

"You know I didn't mean that. You've got lovely skin. I think it's even lovelier when you let it alone. But it's lovely anyway. And that's a mighty pretty spangled dress you're putting on. It's another new one, isn't it?"

"Yep. It's another new one."

"Whatever did you think you could do with so many new dresses, Cresside?"

"Oh, I don't know. I told you I went haywire about clothes every once in so often. When I do, I get dresses by the dozen, just the way some people get eggs. Come on, it's time to go downstairs. All the state officials will be forgathered before we get there if we don't. I think Jim Bailey must have been mighty cute when he was young, don't you?"

Well, cute was not the right word for the Secretary of State, of course, but Merry herself thought that he was still very attractive, and she was sorry she could not have laughed and joked with him and with Gervais' other guests as easily and wittily as Cresside did, or addressed them with her mother-in-law's dignity and composure. She was a little afraid that Gervais would change his mind about wishing she could have received this group alone, because she felt that she made such an inadequate showing, and she thought a good deal about Cresside's sprightliness and about Madame d'Alvery's poise after she had gone upstairs to bed. Madame d'Alvery had gone to bed too, more exhausted by the effort she had made than she would admit, and Cresside had started off "on a hunt of her own," as she had said jokingly when she bade Merry goodnight: Gervais might think he had corralled every man that was really worth having, but she knew better; there were still plenty at large if you knew where to look for them. She did know, and she had a swell date on at the Willows. She would tell Merry all about it in the morning.

Merry knew that Cresside would not tell her all about it in the morning, that she probably would not mention it again of her own accord, and that she would laugh off any specific questions about it. Merry had never been to the Willows herself, but the little she knew about the place did not help to make her happy in realizing that Cresside went there fairly frequently. It was a small café on the short stretch of batture near town, where the willows beyond the levee grew in great luxuriance. A number of small square openings had been cut in these, around one larger clearing where the bar was located. Each of the small clearings was barely large enough to accommodate a little table and some tin chairs, and each was thickly enclosed with abundant growth. Drinks and sandwiches were served in these caches upon request, but when no demand for these was made, the occupants of the little openings were not disturbed. Rightly or wrongly, the café had acquired a bad name. It made Merry miserable to think that Cresside, who was so kind to her, and so gallant and gay, should frequent the Willows. . . .

But she could not go on thinking about Cresside indefinitely. Most of her thoughts centred on Gervais, as they always did, and the sound of his laughter drifting up to her now, together with the aroma of fine cigars and fragments of the talk around the poker table. The early June night was warm, and the shutter doors leading from her chamber into the guest-room behind it and into the upper hall were all open; as to the doors downstairs, those were never closed.

It was Fabian's whimsical voice which she recognized first, as he jested with George Favrot, who had evidently taken in a fat pot "Have you forgotten that we're all constituents of yours, George?" Fabian was saying. "Just for the look of things, you ought to le one of us win a pot now and then, or we'll organize the district against you."

The broad A's of the Bostonian were easily recognizable also: "Somebody better tip off a bank examiner to go over to the Cotton Factors National if Bisbee keeps on losing. It isn't in the realm of reason that any banker could keep on getting rid of his own money without putting up more of a squawk than he's doing. As for myself, I'd like to know if it isn't tough enough on a Yankee to be running for an office that the infidels around here call a police juryship. In all Christian parts of the world it's called a county commissioner's."

There was a pleasant pause, broken first by the tinkle of ice and the hiss of charged water and then by an inquiry, interested rather than anxious, from Boylston: "How are you fixed with prohibition coming along in a few weeks, d'Alvery? Ought we to go easy on this?" Gervais' answer was reassuring: "I haven't even bothered to make a complete check of what I have on hand since I came home. But I don't think we'll ever have to resort to Opelousas corn in this house. My father always kept a fine cellar, whatever else he went without. So I know there's enough to last me and my friends until that crazy law's been repealed. It stands to reason it can't last for ever. . . . Here, let me fill that up!"

"Thanks. And let's talk about something besides politics for a change. The campaign won't start for months."

"As a matter of fact, I'm not so much interested in the gubernatorial race at the moment as I am in my own chances."

Boylston laughed. His laugh, like his voice, was pleasant, but usually it was not characterized by much heartiness; now it had a real ring to it and his amusement sounded through his mock oratory.

"Little as I know about politics in Louisiana, and grateful as I am that your conservation laws include Republicans, and unable as I may be to comprehend how any sugar planter can ever vote anything but a Republican ticket, I can still give you the answer to that one, neighbour. With your war record, all of these little local cliques will be honeying up to you instead of the other way around."

"Hey, there, Boylston, stop poaching on our preserves!"

"Nonsense, Congressman; it's true, isn't it?"

"Of course it's true, but that's no reason for spoiling our little game, which was to keep Gervais on the anxious seat awhile and get a handsome campaign contribution out of him in return for doing something we'd all made up our minds to do long ago. You damn Yankees haven't changed a particle since you stabled your horses in the University buildings."

In the midst of the laughter and badinage which followed this accusation, Merry drifted off to sleep again; after all, she had heard that Gervais' election was practically assured, and this was what most mattered to her. There was no reason why she should stay awake any longer. But the next morning Gervais brought up the subject again himself when he came to have coffee with her, greatly pleased with the results of his stag party.

"I was mighty proud of you, honey," he told her. "You looked just the way I hoped you would, and acted just the way I hoped you would too. I can tell you it made a real impression on all the folks, from Jim Bailey right down the line. And it set me to thinking what an impression you'd make when I took you to the Mansion for parties, and had you beside me on the floor of the House."

"Oh, Gervais, you're not going to do that, are you?"

"You're darn right I am! Why, you must have known we'd be invited to the Mansion! And haven't you heard that every member of the legislature is allowed to have an extra chair set up right beside his?"

"Yes, I reckon I must have. But I never thought I'd be sitting in one of them."

"Well, then, you'd better begin to think of it, because you will be. And you won't be watching parades from the window of a department store, either. You'll be on the Governor's reviewing stand. You're not going to spend the rest of your life snoozing, you know."

"No. Though I suppose——"

"You suppose this isn't the only time you'll ever be in a delicate condition? Well, I hope you're right about that. I hope we'll have a lot of children, Merry, if you're strong enough to stand it, and it looks as if you would be. But far enough apart so that you and I can do things together too. Do you realize the only party you've been to with me this spring was that one given for the officers of the sub-chaser that came up the River? Next year I want to take you to a lot of them, and have a lot of them here too. And I want you to ride around over the plantation with me. My, but we've got a good stand of plant cane this year! I wish you could see it."

"I'll see next year's stand and I'll love doing that. I'd rather learn about our crops than go to the parties, Gervais."

"Well, I want you to care about both. I suppose it's too much to hope that you'll be interested in machinery, but I can tell you, I'm tickled to death with the new tractor we're trying out, and I think the cultivator we're using now is going to be fine. You know I tried to explain about that before. You see, darling, we can't put too much dirt into the cane now, because by and by each stalk will raise its own little family of stalks. 'Suckers,' we call them. Cane's a sociable plant. It likes lots of company. Perhaps that's why sugar planters are a sociable lot too. Living close to the land the way they do, they get habits just like their own suckers."

"I don't think I like to hear you compare yourself to any kind of a sucker, honey, even those that are just little stalks of cane."

"Shucks, I told you before not to be so literal! What I was trying to explain to you is that one stalk comes up first and that presently there are a dozen small shoots around it, making a stool that has to be nourished and fed. That's why we must do so much fertilizing at this time of year. Of course we've got the richest soil in Louisiana right here, because the cream of all that comes from the states draining into the Mississippi Valley has been deposited on the banks of the River. But still we have to use a good deal of nitrogen to hasten growth and phosphate to give early maturity. You know how Lou Ida and Creassy are trying to 'tempt' you right now, because you've got to 'eat for two'? Well, it's just the same with plant life as it is with human beings. Sugar has to be nourished to support its own family. When it is, you wouldn't believe what quick results you get. You can almost see its colour changing from pale jade to emerald green."

"I'd love to see it. It sounds beautiful the way you talk about it. I never thought of cane starting a family, just the way we are, Gervais."

"Well, I want you to, honey. Because that's what it does. And next to our own family, I care more about the cane family than anything else in the world."

She went back to sleep, thinking about the dozen small shoots that came up around the one big stalk and needing to be nourished; and after that she never said no when Lou Ida and Creassy tried to "tempt" her. She remembered, too, that cane was a sociable plant, and she encouraged Gervais to have more company and made the required effort to go out with him the next time he asked her to. But she herself was secretly most content when they were by themselves, and when there were no extraneous diversions to enliven the monotony of the slumberous, prescient days. She still preferred to let time drift past her while she remained sheltered and enclosed by the great shuttered room.

"Well, sleepy-head! If you keep on the way you're doing, presently you won't wake up at all. When I kiss you three times before it takes effect, one of us is certainly slowing up."

So she had not rung for Creassy at all that morning, she had not drunk her coffee, she had gone back to sleep a second time. And here was Gervais bending over her and pretending to shake her, while he looked at her teasingly. She sat up suddenly, rubbing her heavy eyes and shaking her tumbled curls away from her forehead. Then she blinked at him, catching her breath a little, and buried her rosy face against his shoulder.

"You better hide your head in shame!" he said, still teasingly. He had his arm around her now and his fond voice was in itself a caress. "Here it is only a little over two months since I practically had to hold you down to keep you in bed mornings, and now I have to handle you roughly in order to rouse you at ten o'clock. I told Creassy to bring your coffee up with mine. Maybe I ought to tell Billy Pereira to add a little strychnine to the blend for a while in order to stimulate you. . . . Seriously, honey, I didn't mean to startle you so. I didn't suppose you really were all that sound asleep. I'm sorry I made you spring up like that. I don't believe you ought to move around so suddenly now. Hasn't Dr. Champagne told you not to?"

"No. He said I couldn't be getting along better. There's nothing he's forbidden me to do." She raised her face, and shifting her position so that her head was no longer hidden but rested easily on his shoulder, she looked up at him, her loving expression tinged with anxiety. "Do you know, Gervais, I think Cresside really needs a doctor a lot more than I do?" she said. "She doesn't look a bit well to me."

"She might look better if she'd stop running around nights," Gervais said shortly. "She could use a little extra sleep herself. But there's nothing the matter with her, any more than there was ever anything the matter with *maman*. You've got to take care of yourself, though. Because that means taking care of Philogene too."

He had confidently assumed, from the beginning, that the expected child would be a boy, and he had already announced his intention of naming it after his father. He almost never spoke of "the baby," but nearly always of Philogene. It amused and delighted Merry to hear him.

"I'm interested in taking care of Philogene too, Gervais."

"Then don't jump around in bed and don't waste worry on Cresside."

"I hate for you to talk about Cresside the way you do, Gervais. I'm mighty fond of her. She couldn't have been any kinder to me if she'd been my own sister."

"She'd better be kind to you. But that doesn't alter the fact that she lied to me. I don't see how anyone who's the soul of truthfulness, like you are, can stand up for a liar."

"Is it all right for me to ask you what she lied to you about, Gervais?"

"Yes. She lied to me about Sylvestre Tremaine. She told me that he'd asked her to marry him, and all the time he was actually engaged to Regine Hathaway."

"Had you said something critical to Cresside about Sylvestre, Gervais?"

"You're damned right, I had. And I'd told her to stop staying out half the night with him."

"Well, but Cresside may have loved Sylvestre very much, Gervais. And if she did, naturally she'd defend him. If she really had been

102

engaged to him, that would have made it all right for her to stay out late with him. Wouldn't it? She must have told you she was engaged so that you wouldn't think so ill of him."

"Merry, you're crazy, arguing it out that way."

"No, I'm not. I'd have done exactly the same thing myself if anyone had spoken critically to me about you."

"But good God, I *wasn't* engaged to someone else!"

"Cresside couldn't have known that Sylvestre was either. It must have been a terrible shock to her when she found it out. I think she's being very brave about not showing how badly she feels. Of course, I'm sorry she chooses the way she does to cover it up. But I think it's just a phase. I'm sure she won't go on for long running around like she is now with a fast crowd. She really doesn't care about that fast crowd, honey. She *couldn't*. She's not that kind. But she's out to show the world, just now, that it doesn't mean a thing to her that she misunderstood Sylvestre."

"*Misunderstood!*"

"Why, yes! She must have thought he was in love with her, honey. She must have thought he meant to propose pretty soon. She was hoping so hard that he would, she misunderstood, that's all. Plenty of girls make mistakes like that. Because some men say such a lot when they don't mean a thing. Just like some of them mean such a lot, and never seem to be able to open their mouths."

"And you were thinking of just whom when you said that?"

"Well, I was thinking of Sylvestre, for the first kind, naturally. And for Fabian for the other. I sure enough wasn't thinking of you, honey. You say plenty, but you mean plenty too."

Gervais muttered something unintelligible. This was the first time he and Merry had talked so seriously or at any length about Cresside. A dozen times before, when he had been on the point of saying something, an innate aversion to discussing his sister, even with his wife, had withheld him. Now that the secret had been brought into the open, he felt immeasurably relieved. Merry had presented a point of view that was entirely novel to him, and at the same time infinitely reassuring; in explaining Cresside's conduct to him, she had, in a measure, succeeded in excusing it. The day before, he had heard Merry patiently practising her halting French under his mother's direction, and one of the trite proverbs she had been repeating was "*Tout comprendre c'est tout pardonner.*" At the time he had wondered, elatedly, if his mother had perception enough to realize how applicable the old saw was in her own case. Now that she was beginning to understand how wise his choice of a wife had been, she was also beginning to forgive him for having made it, though there were still no prospects that she would admit this. Belatedly he saw that the proverb was applicable in his case and in his sister's also. . . .

"I'm mighty lucky, you know, Gervais, not even to be having

morning sickness," he heard Merry saying. Apparently she had decided, on her own initiative, that for the moment they had discussed Cresside enough, that there was no sense in running the subject into the ground. He followed her lead with the good cheer which sprang from relief.

"I reckon you are at that. And I'm lucky too. I shouldn't think it would add to the general aura of romance surrounding a young couple for the bride to begin the day by up-chucking all over the place."

"Gervais, sometimes I think Cresside's right when she says that Army life didn't improve you. You shouldn't say things like that when you're talking about romance."

"I suppose I shouldn't. But you don't really mind, do you? You ought not to, as a matter of fact. If you don't ever hear me say anything worse than that, you'll be even luckier than you've been in escaping morning sickness."

There was a gentle knock at the shutter door and Creassy entered, watchfully carrying a porcelain coffee service on a silver tray. Without self-consciousness, Gervais released Merry from his embrace, and sat down at the small bedside table, while Creassy arranged Merry's pillows and straightened her covering. Merry looked up at her smilingly.

"Thanks, Creassy. It's a lovely day for Miss Regine's wedding, isn't it?"

"Yes, Miss Merry, it sure is. Such days is well accepted."

"I love to hear you say that, Creassy, the first thing in the morning. It always makes a day begin better for me."

"Ah's proud to hear it, Miss Merry. Could Ah get you somethin' else before Ah goes downstairs?"

"I think we've got everything, but I'll let you know if we haven't." Then, as the maid left the room, beaming, Merry added, handing Gervais his cup, "I hope you're not going to say, like Miss Mittie does, that you wouldn't have minded if it had rained 'cats, dogs and billy goats' on Regine's wedding day, honey. Regine isn't to blame for what happened. We oughtn't to forget that, no matter how sorry we feel for Cresside."

"I'm not so sure. I think Regine *is* partly to blame. I think Sylvestre might have come across if Regine hadn't snatched at him. Not that I wouldn't have hated like hell to have him for a brother-in-law. But just the same——"

Involuntarily, he was reverting to the subject of Cresside after all. This time Merry followed his lead.

"Just the same, you think he ought to have proposed to her. I know. But Cresside wouldn't have been happy, not in the long run, with Sylvestre, honey. She wouldn't be happy with any man who didn't love her as much as she loved him. No girl is. And Sylvestre isn't good enough for Cresside. He isn't much better than the men

104

in this crowd she's running with now. Of course, I wouldn't go so far as you do and call him a—a——"

"A bastard? Or just a skunk?"

"I wouldn't call him any bad names. But I'm glad I don't have to call him kin either. I'm glad it's Regine he's marrying and not Cresside."

"May I come in? Is this billing and cooing I hear mostly verbal? Or is Gervais back in bed, the middle of the morning? I don't want to burst in on anything a nice young girl ought to learn only from the birds and bees. God forbid!"

The shutter door leading into the hall opened slowly again, and this time Cresside came into the room. Gervais, glancing at her covertly to see if there could possibly be any basis for Merry's anxiety, was startled to notice, for the first time, that Cresside's face was not only pale, but haggard, under her make-up, and that there were violet circles around her eyes. As usual, however, she was as smart as paint. Her short linen dress was crisp and spotless, and her scarlet belt and shoes matched her lipstick. She greeted her brother with a nonchalant nod; but she bent over to hug Merry with undisguised affection.

"How are you this morning, precious? Well, I don't need to ask. Dewy with sleep and rosy with kisses! I'd say that marriage and maternity were equally becoming to you. I just dropped in to tell you I'm going over to Hathaway Hall to help with the flowers, and I didn't want you to start dragging the River for me if you found I was missing from the old homestead. Besides, I thought maybe you'd come with me. But I promised I'd be there by ten-thirty, and you won't be as far as the tub by then, from the present look of things."

"Yes, I will. I'd like to come with you, Cresside. I'll hurry. Gervais was just going out again anyway. Weren't you, honey?"

"Well, I wasn't in any particular hurry to get away from you. But now that I see you're eager to get rid of me, so that you can go and gloat over the nearby nuptial garlands, I can take a hint and clear out."

He grinned, kissed her once more and went off, nodding to Cresside with the same nonchalance that had marked her own greeting. But as the morning wore on, he found he could not get her out of his mind. For once the enchanting vision of Merry which was so constantly before him was obscured by the image of his sister's white face, with its scornful scarlet lips and its great violet-ringed eyes. Certainly a healthy young girl should not look as haggard as that, no matter how much running around she was doing. Merry was probably right, as usual. Cresside must be ill, and he would drive into town that afternoon and ask Dr. Champagne to come out and have a look at her. No, curse it, he could not go that afternoon, because he would have to arrive early and stay late at Hathaway Hall. Sylvestre had asked him to be one of the ushers at the wedding, and he had not been able to think up any plausible pretext for declining. Well, anyway, all the Champagnes would be at the wedding and he would manage to draw the doctor aside and get in a word with him edgewise. Then the doctor would come out to Belle Heloise the first thing the next morning and find out what in hell was the matter with Cresside, and give her something that would pep her up. He still could not believe it was anything serious. It was just that she was taking the double-dealing of that bastard too hard. Much too hard. Too damn hard. . . .

He was roused from his reverie by the sound of the plantation bell. There was no logical reason why it should ring at this hour. It was not time for the field hands' dinner. Listening intently, he recognized the special signal which had occasionally been used, before he went to France, to summon him from the fields: three long loud peals, then a pause and two short softer ones. This signal had very seldom been given and he had almost forgotten it. But as he hurried towards the house he remembered that the last time he had heard it had been the morning when his father was suddenly and mortally stricken. And as he came quickly into the Small Yard, Amen ran excitedly out to meet him, with Snow and Cornet barking at his heels.

"Miss Cresside's been bad hurt, Mr. Gervais."

"What do you mean, bad hurt?"

"She was up on a ladder, fixin' flowers in de White Ballroom, and she must of had a swimmin' in de head from bein' up so high, caise she fainted. She done fell down and hurt herself bad."

"Stop saying she's hurt herself bad. Perhaps she's only stunned by the fall," Gervais said sharply. But he quickened his pace, covering the great expanse of the Small Yard in swift strides. Amen, still jabbering excitedly, trotted after him, followed by the dogs.

"No, suh, she ain't stunned no mo'. She done come out of her faint. She don't cry out, but you can tell she's bad hurt."

"Who got her home?"

"Mr. Sylvestre, he brung her home. Looks like he done forgot he was goin' to marry Miss Regine dis very evenin'. He carried Miss Cresside upstairs hisself, and put her on de bed, and stood there lookin' at her for de longes'."

"Is he still there?"

"No, suh, he done gone caise Miss Cresside, she make him. De doctor's dere now. Mr. Fabian come out to see what all he could do to help befo' de wedding, happenin' in jes' when Miss Cresside fell offen de ladder. So he done go for de doctor and brung him back here befo' soon."

The front door opened quietly, and Fabian shuffled down the circular brick stairs and limped towards them. His gait, as usual,

106

was slow and awkward because of his deformity, and he made no evident effort to hurry. He was smiling in his customary wry way.

"Why don't you take those dogs out to the shed, Amen?" he asked pleasantly. "Their barking might disturb Miss Cresside. I'm afraid she's in for a good deal of pain and we've each got to do our part to see that she isn't disturbed." Then, as the negro hastened to follow his suggestion, with the joyous feeling of helpfulness rather than the one of shame which would have been caused by a harsh rebuke, Fabian turned to Gervais. "I'm afraid you've had a nasty jolt, perhaps unnecessarily," he said quietly. "Tante Isabelle insisted on having the bell rung. But I was against it myself. There's nothing you can do for Cresside at the moment. Dr. Champagne isn't even through examining her—she seems to have hurt her back, falling, but he doesn't know yet just how badly. And Merry's with her. Merry was the only person she asked for."

"I don't want Merry upset, just now. You ought to know that."

"I do know that. But Merry isn't upset. She's perfectly calm and collected. And Dr. Champagne himself said he'd like to have her stick around. He wouldn't have done that if he'd thought it would hurt her. Come on into the library, Gervais, and have a drink. I've got one ready for you."

"Damn white of you. But I'd rather get along to my sister."

"Well, of course, if you insist. But she'd rather you didn't. I heard her myself saying, 'You keep Gervais out of here.' It was almost as final as what I heard her saying to Sylvestre."

"And what was that, damn his rotten hide?"

"She said, 'This is your wedding day, Sylvestre. Regine will be waiting for you.' He would've stayed if she'd let him. In fact, he'd have given anything on earth for a chance to stay. You should have seen his face—and hers. He knows at last what a damn fool he's been, just as well as you and I do. Because Cresside's a great girl, and he might have married her instead of that alabaster image hung with diamonds that he's chained too instead. But Cresside's through with Sylvestre, Gervais. She found him out too. She wouldn't marry him if he were the last man on earth. Don't you worry about her, though. She's got the guts to come out all right, by herself."

"Every great war has left in its wake a period of suffering and misery for the vanquished; of extravagance and waste on the part of the victors. The problems to be solved by the world today are complex, and cover nearly every phase of human endeavour. . . .

"As your incoming governor, my earnest appeal to every man and woman in Louisiana is to take a deep interest in public affairs. Remember, it is not only your welfare and happiness, but the future of your children and your children's children which is dependent upon efficient government."—From Inaugural Address of John M. Parker, Governor of Louisiana, delivered May 17, 1920.

PART III

High, Wide and Handsome

(May 8, 1920, to June 20, 1920)

VIII

"I HOPE we won't have to wait much longer for d'Alvery. I'd like to get this thing clinched before that New Orleans crowd gets in on the ten forty-five."

"They ought to be here any minute now, Governor. It was about eight when I got hold of Fabian. He was just finishing his breakfast and he said he'd strike right out for Belle Heloise."

This pronouncement was made, with some pomposity, by Melvin Bisbee, who was extremely flattered at having been asked to help with the conference that was now taking place. He was answered by Hewitt Bouanchaud, the Lieutenant-Governor Elect, a small dark man with jet black hair and a rubicund countenance, so markedly Gallic in appearance that the absence of an accent or colloquialism in his speech came as a surprise.

"Maybe he wasn't as nearly through as he said. If he wasn't, I wouldn't blame him if he took time out to eat before he started. Fabian d'Alvery keeps a good cook. Besides, it may take him longer than we figure to get down to his cousin's. I don't know what shape the River Road's in just now, but it's been pretty near impassable with mud most of the winter, and now it's just the season for seepage. Fabian may have got stuck and had to find a pair of horses to pull him out. What's more, we lost a lot of time because we couldn't get hold of Gervais direct. It's a damn nuisance there's no telephone at Belle Heloise. The place is almost as isolated as if it were in the middle of the Atchafalaya Swamp."

"It's isolated all right, but that's the way for a farmer to live. I won't let them put a telephone on my place at Bayou Sara. I stayed at Belle Heloise several times during the campaign, and I like it there. I like this young fellow who owns it too, and I as good as know he's with us. But I want to be sure how that new representative from somewhere in the seventh district, Gaston Daigle, is going to stand on the speakership vote, and d'Alvery can take care of that better than any man I know."

Having emphasized this point, John Parker, Governor Elect of Louisiana, resumed his study of the legislative list, which he had previously been engaged in checking. He was a well-built man, inordinately proud of the flat stomach which he had succeeded in retaining despite advancing years, doubtless partly because he was so disdainful of Creole cookery, his favourite fare being mustard greens and buttermilk. He had a ruddy face, iron-grey hair and an iron-grey moustache, and in manner and general appearance was curiously like a country merchant wearing "store clothes" with apparent self-consciousness, though he was an outstanding member of the Boston Club in New Orleans, and belonged by both background and breeding in the top social bracket. At the moment he was in his shirt-sleeves, seated on the side of the garish, squeaky brass bed which dominated a musty little room in the Hotel Istrouma at Baton Rouge. The principal conferees were Hewitt Bouanchaud of New Roads and the boss of the third ward in New Orleans, John P. Sullivan, both of whom had settled themselves more or less stably; various others came and went, among them Bisbee and Harry Gamble, who had been Parker's campaign manager.

In spite of the open window, the air was heavy and the room was full of smoke; Sullivan's cigar, one of the sleek Havanas manufactured especially for him, would alone have made this condition almost inevitable. Seated in a mission style rocker of fumed oak, Sullivan puffed away contentedly while Parker studied his check list. The others were all clad in seersucker or white linen, in varying degrees of dishevelment, but Sullivan was magnificently arrayed in superbly tailored Shantung, and wore a Sulka cravat embellished with a diamond and emerald stick-pin which the Elks had given him when he was their Grand Exalted Ruler. He was an enormous man, whose great height was overpowering even when he was seated, and whose vast shoulders seemed to fill the inadequate little room.

"I'm inclined to agree with the Governor on one point. I don't doubt that d'Alvery will vote for our programme straight down the line," he said. If the other conferees had been strangers to him instead of boon companions, they would inevitably have been startled by the rolling basso with which he made his simple announcement, for he had a voice compared to which the percussion of a bass drum sounded like a shrill treble. "I only hope he has as much influence with Daigle as the Governor seems to think. But Daigle was elected on the Stubbs ticket, and while we've got a majority for our man Walker, what we're after is a unanimous vote. And if our side looks strong enough, Hamley won't even go to the post."

"Hold up a second, will you, John? I think someone's at the door now. But I can't half hear when you bear down on that fog horn."

Harry Gamble walked over to the door and flung it open, to disclose Fabian and Gervais standing on the threshold. As always, when the cousins appeared together, Fabian's deformity seemed the more marked. Nevertheless, it was he who entered first, his crooked smile enlivening the sombreness of his expression.

"Sorry we took so long to get here," he said pleasantly. "I've never seen the seepage as bad as it's been this spring. Two or three cars were stuck in that soft spot just below McGregor's store. We had to turn back and go all round Robin Hood's barn to reach town."

"I told the crowd you were probably bogged down," Bisbee responded. "Sorry you were put to so much trouble, but, after all, you River Roaders ought to gang up on the police jury and make them do something about it. . . . Good-morning, Captain. Glad to see you. I don't need to introduce you to the Governor, of course. He's just been telling us how much he's enjoyed being your guest. You know Lieutenant-Governor Bouanchaud too, don't you?"

"Sure. I've known the Captain ever since he was knee-high to a *poule d'eau*," Bouanchaud broke in. "As a matter of fact, his father and I were friends before he was born. How are you these days, Gervais? Still up to mischief? Or had I better ask Fabian to testify on that point?—Though you've probably sobered down now, with all your new responsibilities." He turned to the others in the room. "Possibly the rest of you don't know that Captain d'Alvery's the father of twins."

"Why, you don't say!" The Governor laid down his check list and, rising from the squeaky bed, went over to Gervais and heartily shook his hand. "That's bully. Gives me quite a fellow feeling. My son John has twins too, and, incidentally, I'm a twin myself. Let the grandfather of twins congratulate the father of twins! Both boys, are they?"

"No, a boy and a girl."

"I suppose the boy's a junior? Or did you name him after your father?" Bouanchaud inquired with genuine interest.

"We didn't do either. Both of my wife's brothers were killed in the war, and she wanted to name the boy for them—Malcolm Vail. We call him Vail. The girl's named for my father's sister, Sybelle, and it seemed fair that each side of the family should be represented, when it came to a christening."

"I agree with you. Plenty of time for the second Philogene yet, if you ask me." And as Gervais met his eye, laughing, Bouanchaud also laughed loudly and slapped him on the shoulder. "So it's that way already, is it? How old are the twins?"

"They were born in January."

"And this is only May! Well, you're certainly not losing any time! And how's that pretty sister of yours? I was sorry to hear she'd an accident of some kind."

"Yes, a bad fall. She injured her back pretty seriously. But I'm glad to say she's better now."

"Young fathers are proverbially garrulous, I know," Fabian remarked sardonically. "In fact, they're usually even more tiresome than young mothers. But this is a political meeting, Gervais; it isn't a baby party. I can't believe the Governor interrupted my breakfast and sent me down the River Road to get you, in spite of its horrible condition, merely because you're the father of twins. I think he'd probably like to get along with whatever's on his mind, if you'd give him a chance."

Sullivan, still puffing away placidly at his cigar, shot a surreptitious glance at the speaker. The wry smile, which had made Fabian's face so vivid and winning at first, had completely faded; without this, it was not only sombre but bitter. A queer bird, Sullivan said to himself; something's eating him, not just his deformity at that. But he's nobody's fool; he's a smart man, a damn sight smarter than this showy cousin of his that everyone's making such a fuss about. Finer fibred too. Not just because of the d'Alvery heritage or the Princeton polish either; because of something inside of him that no other man in the room has got. Not even John Parker . . . certainly not John Sullivan. Parker, more bent on action than analysis, broke in on his colleague's contemplation.

"You're right, Fabian. I asked you to bring your cousin here for a very special purpose. Won't you both sit down?"

There was only one vacant chair in the room, which had a straight back and a stamped leather seat, and which stood near the washstand of poisonous pink marble. Gervais promptly seated himself in this. Involuntarily, Fabian met Sullivan's alert eye and a look of swift understanding and instantaneous liking passed between the two men who were so dissimilar. Then the former limped over to a small bent-legged table and leaned against it. Parker also walked over to it and poured himself a drink of ice water from a sweating pitcher standing on a japanned tray.

"I thought perhaps you'd talk to Gaston Daigle," he said, emptying his glass. "We'd like to clinch his vote on the speakership."

"I don't know Daigle too well. And, anyway, I'm not so sure I'd have all that influence with him."

"We thought you might have, both of you being planters and both of you being from sugar parishes," suggested Sullivan pleasantly.

"Well, supposing I had. How do you know I'd influence him the way you want? Seems to me you've taken my vote pretty much for granted."

Gervais' voice had the edginess which characterized it when he felt or fancied anyone had presumed upon his independence. Sullivan, with an amused glint in his eye, glanced first at Bouanchaud and then at Fabian over his cigar. Parker, rising from the squeaky bed, on which he had seated himself a second time, hooked his thumbs in his belt and drew in the flat stomach of which he was so proud.

"Yes, Captain, I think I may tell you I did take it for granted. But not for political reasons," he said, somewhat rhetorically. "Listen, son: you're an L.S.U. man. You know one of the things I've promised to do is build a real university, and by that I mean one that would include a first-class scientific agricultural school. That ought to appeal to you both as a planter and as an L.S.U. alumnus. I'm a practical farmer myself, and you know I want to write a new constitution for this state so that we won't have to use the patchwork of two constitutions we're trying to operate under now."

Still holding his audience with his beady eyes, he bit off a corner from the plug of tobacco which he took from his pocket, and rolled it deliberately around in his mouth before proceeding; he rather liked to parade this habit. "I want to institute a real system of highways for this state too," he continued. "I want to take this state out of the mud. I can't do it unless those legislators who feel the same way I do about it uphold my hands. Unless you give me a Speaker who is my friend and who will appoint my friends to the important committee posts. That's why I venture to take your vote for granted, Captain d'Alvery."

"Well, of course, if you put it that way——" Gervais' voice was no longer arrogant; it was not even reluctant. Without any of the traditional artifices of a spellbinder, without even a struggle, Parker had succeeded in winning his point. "Naturally I don't want to be an administration rubber stamp," Gervais added. "But I see what you mean. You may count on me to help in any way I can."

"Fine! I tell you, us ancestors of twins has got to stick together. There aren't but a few of us."

"No, you're right. There aren't."

Parker rose again and again shook Gervais' hand with great heartiness. "Another thing, we're riding high, wide and handsome right now, with sugar at twenty-six cents. But I don't need to tell you, for all that, that this new mosaic disease which is just beginning to creep in may constitute a terrible problem. We've got to get away from all one-crop systems."

Sullivan's deep laugh suddenly boomed through the room. "That's a great John Parker, isn't he?" the big man chuckled. "He'll be talking about his silos next. But what the hell's mosaic disease, will somebody tell me?"

"It's a disease of the leaf, which is the lung of the plant. When cane's afflicted with it, there's the same terrible results as when a human being is afflicted with tuberculosis, and it leaves other deadly afflictions, just as tuberculosis does—root rot, or red rot, as some call it, for instance. The two almost always go together and root rot is just as disastrous as mosaic disease. I've heard there were

115

some evidences that it was beginning to creep in along your part of the River Road already."

"There are some signs of it at Hathaway Hall right near us, though I'm glad to say we haven't had any of it ourselves."

"Well, you can't put a coffee importer in charge of a sugar plantation and expect too much, especially if he didn't make a go of it in the coffee business. Thanks again for coming, Captain."

The leave-taking was genial, but as Gervais and his cousin went down the dingy hall to the antiquated elevator, Fabian murmured: "The oration of John Parker to the d'Alvery Philistine. That man couldn't talk about the weather without getting a stump to do it."

"I'm no Philistine, whatever you are, and he wasn't up on a stump. This isn't the first time he's talked to me about the future of L.S.U. He told me about his plans for it when he spent the night at Belle Heloise during the campaign. It's about time someone showed a little interest in it too, though I wouldn't expect a Princetonian like you to realize it, or care. The Law School's the only department now that has any standing, and the Pentagon Buildings still look more like the cavalry posts the Yankees used to stable their horses in than a place for students to live and learn."

"My God, are you going to start making speeches too? You'll be kissing babies next, and I don't mean Sybelle and Vail either."

"Oh, shut up! It doesn't matter to a lawyer, I suppose, whether we get an experimental station here or not, but I can tell you it matters a lot to a planter. I'll admit I'm sitting pretty right now, as Parker said, with sugar at twenty-six. But if this darn disease does get in generally, I'm going to be up against it."

"And you really think there are signs of it at Hathaway Hall?"

"There isn't a doubt of it. But again it's like Parker said: why in hell should anyone expect a moron who's made a failure in coffee to be a success in sugar? Especially when he spends the entire winter basking on the Riviera instead of looking after his crops? . . . Well, what do you say we go over to Izzie's and snatch a small black?"

"Very good idea."

They crossed Third Street to Izzie's, where they found the jovial proprietor ensconced, as usual, behind his cash register. He hurried forward to meet them, wreathed in smiles.

"Why, good-morning, Captain! Good-morning, Mr. d'Alvery," he said with great heartiness. "It's a pleasant surprise, seeing you gentlemen so early in the day. I'd like to take this occasion to tell you I voted for you, Captain, and I think I may say I was responsible for several other votes that were cast for you too."

"That's fine, Izzy. I'm very much obliged to you and I'll try to see that you'll never regret it. . . . How about a couple of small blacks?"

"Right away, Captain, right away." Izzie turned to signal one of the white-coated waiters, but that functionary was already drawing coffee from a highly nickelled urn into two tiny white cups. "Sure there isn't anything else you'd like?" Izzie inquired, as the two cousins seated themselves at one of the alabastine-topped tables opposite the counter.

"No, thanks. It isn't long enough since breakfast. . . . All set for the big crowd that'll be battering down your doors when the legislature opens Monday, Izzie?"

"Oh, that!" Izzie made a deprecatory gesture, as if the opening of the legislature were almost too trivial an incident to merit his attention. "Why, that won't be anything—most people from right here in town. The real headache'll begin when folks start coming in from Shreveport, Lake Charles and New Orleans, for the inauguration. But am I fixed for them? . . . Bring me a couple of those new bill-of-fares, the ones that have just been run off on the ditto machine," he called to another waiter. Then he handed one menu to Gervais and the other to Fabian, pointing with bursting pride to a small ornamentally boxed announcement at the top of each:

INAUGURATION SPECIAL
LOIN AND LAMB GET TOGETHER

35c.

"Oh, Izzie! Tampering with Holy Writ!" chuckled Fabian. "And you the son or grandson of a pious rabbi, no doubt!"

"Well, sir," replied the little restaurateur defensively, "Parker has brought all sides together, hasn't he? But you couldn't expect me to serve real lion, so I got the next best thing by just changing two letters. . . . And I expect the Lord'll forgive me, seeing as how it's a good cause."

"Don't let him get your goat, Izzie." Gervais' voice did not indicate the same relish in the situation as his cousin's and he changed the subject, without actual abruptness, but with understandable finality. "By the way, you haven't happened to see anything of Mr. Gaston Daigle around here, have you?"

"No, Captain. I wouldn't, not this early in the morning. But he seldom ever misses an evening, when he's in town. Drop in here again about six o'clock and you'll pretty near be sure to find him."

"I'll do that. And if he gets here before I do, please tell him I'd be much obliged if he'd wait for me, unless he's in a special hurry."

"Certainly, Captain. Another small black? No? Well, don't forget about that new specialty of mine. I want to get your opinion on it." Izzie nodded and meandered back towards his cash register, stopping to speak to patrons at several other tables as he did so. Fabian looked after him with friendly amusement.

"Quite a character."

"Yes—and if there's better coffee than this, I don't know where, except, of course, at Belle Heloise." Gervais put down his drained cup slowly, still savouring its contents. "I'm glad Parker sent you out for me," he said. "Otherwise, Lord knows when I'd have seen you. You're quite a stranger these days."

"Didn't you ever hear the old saying that the law's a jealous mistress?"

"Yes. Personally I never put too much stock in it. But then I'm not an authority on mistresses," Gervais answered, grinning. "If you're all that busy, I suppose it wouldn't do any good to suggest that you might spend the day at Belle Heloise when you take me back," he added as they rose. "I think the road will be patched up well enough to last the day out, and I'd like to have you, if you could. It's a long time since you've been to see us."

"Dying to show off your twins, I suppose?" Fabian inquired, suddenly speaking in the same sardonic tone with which he had broken in at the conference. Then, as if instantly sorry for his satire, he added quickly, "As a matter of fact, I'd like very much to come, and Saturday is always a slack day at the office. The only hitch is I've got guests coming to midday dinner myself."

"Who are they? Couldn't you bring them along too?"

"They'd be tickled to death to be asked, but I don't know how Tante Isabelle would take it. I'm afraid she'd consider them the sort who ought to eat, with gratitude, at the second table."

"Why should she, for God's sake? You're asking them to yours, aren't you?"

"Yes, but I have all sorts at mine. It's one of the many advantages of being an orphan and a bachelor and an eccentric—you can have anyone you like, any time. As a matter of fact, one of these men is a distant kinsman of ours—his second cousin, Cenas Tremblet, married your father's sister, Sybelle. He'd be tickled to death to see the baby that's named after her."

"Funny I never ran across him. But of course *maman's* parents never had much to do with any of us d'Alverys, except the one they captured for their daughter. God, but my father led a miserable life! . . . How did you happen to find Aunt Sybelle's second cousin by marriage?"

"I don't suppose you've ever noticed two old men who spend most of their time sitting on a bench by the Veterans' Monument, quarrelling with each other, have you? This Pascal Tremblet's one of them; the other one's name is Preston Vicknair. . . . They've got a third crony, Max Stoetzner, but he lives over in Port Allen, and only crosses the River on great occasions. Tremblet and Vicknair both live with reluctant relatives, so I've got into the habit of having them to my place once in a while on Saturdays. They know they're really welcome there. We play fantan, and then enjoy putting Belizaire through his tricks. Well, it just seems a generally satisfactory arrangement."

"I'd be glad to have them at Belle Heloise and so would Merry. Cresside won't care one way or the other, but she'll be civil. If *maman* doesn't want to meet them, she can always have dinner in her boudoir. That's what she does when Merry's mother or Miss Mittie comes out—imaginary ill health certainly furnishes a hell of a lot of excuses for anything a woman doesn't want to do! But, as a matter of fact, I shouldn't be surprised if *maman* did come down today. Miss Mittie's all tied up with this suffrage racket she and so many other women have gone crazy over, or you might find her there—Saturday and Sunday are her only free days, of course, on account of her school teaching, and Merry rather makes a point of getting her to Belle Heloise at least twice a month. On the other hand, Charles Boylston is dining with us today, and he's probably *maman's* greatest favourite among my friends, even if he is a Yankee."

"He's a nice fellow. I gathered he was at Belle Heloise a good deal. Is he making any headway?"

"With Cresside? Not a bit. She likes him too, but it doesn't seem to get him anywhere. . . . What do we do, pick up the two old birds at the Monument?"

"Yes, we'll go there first and see how they react to our plan of taking them down to the Plantation. Of course, secretly they'll be delighted, but they may want to put on a show of reluctance for effect. We can't just kidnap them offhand. That wouldn't set just right, even though it's true, as I said, that old Pascal would give his eyeteeth to see little Sybelle! Then, if they agree, I think we'd better stop by at Somerulos Street for a minute too. It's only fair to tell Carmelite I won't be home for dinner with two guests, and incidentally I'd like to get Belizaire. It wouldn't seem just right to deprive Tremblet and Vicknair of the fun they're looking forward to having with him."

"To say nothing of depriving his master of the fun *he's* looking forward to having! You're a fool about that dog, Fabian."

"Well, after all, I haven't got twins, you know."

"If you don't mind, I wish you'd quit talking about the twins in that tone of voice. What's the matter with the twins?"

"Nothing, I suppose, when they're yours. But let's drop the subject, as you suggest."

They rose, simultaneously, and drifted towards the door, their progress halted by the exchange of several hearty greetings and by their stop at the cash register. As they reached the threshold, Fabian hailed another friend, a young man who walked with even more difficulty than he did himself, but was proceeding with apparent buoyancy down Third Street, accompanied by a pretty girl carrying a market basket.

"Hello, Happy!" he called out. "What's your hurry? Can't you stop long enough to say hello to a fellow cripple? Hello, Rett!"

The young couple stopped and laughingly shook hands. Happy's compensation had been late, they said, and they had been living on bread and cheese and kisses for several days; but now the Government cheque had come in, and they were off to buy out Third Street. Their blithe and carefree attitude was infectious; almost everyone who passed by smiled back at them.

"Well, the next time that cheque's late, if you don't come over to Somerulos Street and let Carmelite and me feed you, we'll both consider it a personal insult," Fabian warned them. "So long, and good hunting!" Then, as his friends took their merry departure, he said to Gervais, "Do you mean to say you hadn't met the Seviers before?"

"No, I don't think so. But they're all right. Tell me about them."

"There isn't so much to tell. Happy was in the war, wounded three times. That's why he walked crooked—not because he was born crippled." Fabian paused for a moment, looking after Happy, whose arm was now linked in his young wife's and whose very hobble was jaunty. "You can see he's still pretty badly bunged up," Fabian went on. "But I think he's coming out of it all right. He and Rett were sweethearts from the time they were kids. They were married before he went to France, and she stayed with her folks while he was gone; now they're living in a pocket-size apartment around the corner from me, while he finishes his interrupted law course. They haven't a blessed thing to come and go on, but they're having the time of their lives." Again he paused, trying to follow the Seviers with his eyes. But they had apparently turned in at some shop, for they were no longer to be seen. "Well, shall we go on and pick up our old men?" he asked, changing the subject abruptly.

"Yes, let's do."

The cousins found the two old veterans eagerly watching for Fabian's approach, and, as he had predicted, there was a slight demurrer from them on the subject of going to Belle Heloise. But their objections, though garrulous, were feeble and easily overruled, and Carmelite made none at all. She was a handsome mulatress, possessed of private plans, to which the dinner in any case had been a distinct encumbrance; she was delighted to see it abandoned. The prospect of an outing was also delightful to Belizaire. Having first been informed by Fabian that he could not go with his master, he drooped pathetically. Then, at the reassuring words, "All right, if you really want to, you may come along!" he barked and bounded about with joy, shooting through the front door and catapulting himself into the car. Fabian watched him with an affectionate amusement which he made no effort to conceal, as he hoisted himself awkwardly into the front seat and drew the excited animal down between himself and Gervais, who took the wheel for his cousin, as Fabian always found it difficult to drive. Pascal and Preston, to whom a ride in an automobile was in itself a great event, sat very erect on the back seat, endeavouring to mask, with assumed nonchalance, their pleasure in the expedition, which was actually quite as great as Belizaire's. Until they approached Hathaway Hall they were fairly successful in their endeavour. But at the sight of the vast façade, rising so majestically before them, Preston's enthusiasm got the better of his assumed indifference.

"Say what you will, that's the handsomest place on the River Road," he remarked in an awed voice, gazing at it intently. Pascal dug him indignantly in the ribs.

"You'd better mind your manners, my friend," he muttered in a stage whisper. "Seemingly, you do not recollect, no, that we are on our way to a finer one this minute, one we're invited to, us, which is more than we ever was to that one. I never saw anything so handsome about it anyway, me. Looks more like a picture in a magazine than a real home. The folks that own it don't live in it enough, and that, my friend, is bound to show up, in any house. I hear they were in France most of the winter."

"Are they back now?" inquired Preston, feeling properly rebuked, but still unable to suppress his excited interest in Hathaway Hall.

"Yes, they're back now, but only just, and the rumour is they're going to Hot Springs for most of the summer."

"Miss Regine's been married almost a year, hasn't she? Any prospects in that family?"

"Absolutely not that I have heard of, me. I tell you very frankly, all I did hear was, the crops are not doing so good, no. Mosaic disease."

"Mosaic disease?"

"Yes. You assuredly do not mean to tell me, Pres Vicknair, you have never heard of that?"

Less lyrically but quite as accurately as John Parker had described it to his hearers earlier that morning, Pascal Tremblet embarked upon an exposition for the benefit of his old crony. He was still deep in his subject when he realized that Captain d'Alvery was stopping the car in order to speak to someone on the road. Peering out, Pascal saw that they had overtaken a somewhat grotesque but immensely jolly man, obviously a peddler, who was pushing a cart hung with all sorts of small gaudy wares, in the midst of which was sitting a rather dirty but very beautiful little boy, who had enormous eyes and clustering black curls and who was sucking a long stick of peppermint candy.

"Hello, Luigi," Captain d'Alvery was saying genially. "So you've graduated from a basket to a cart, have you? I suppose that fancy

E

grocery store must be almost around the corner. Just the same, I hope you haven't given up the Johnny Crooks!—And no doubt this is the famous bambino I've heard so much about. I'm glad to see him at last."

"Howdado, *Capitano*! Howdado, Mr. d'Alvery! Howdado, gentlemen!" Luigi responded, saluting the entire group with great heartiness. "Yes, sir, I gotta me a cart now. I have the Johnny Crooks same as alway, taffy and stage planks too. But I no carry justa candy no more. I gotta kitchen ware—fancy dress goods—julery!" In rapid succession he seized various samples of his wares, finally dangling a string of red glass beads before Gervais' eyes. "You taka those for a present to the Missus, please, *Capitano*," he said. "You buya some beads for your sister too, next time I come to the mansion to make up. I gonna go to the quarters today at Belle Heloise, but maybe I don'ta come to the big house, you got so much company already. . . . *Si, si*, this is my Riccardo. Only he's no bambino no more. He's a bigga boy. Ain't you, Riccardo?"

The beautiful child removed the stick of candy from his grimy little mouth, smiled beatifically, and answered his father with the respect that bespoke excellent home discipline.

"Yes, Papa," he said. "I'm bigga boy now. I'm three and a half."

"That'sa right," Luigi said encouragingly. "And when you maka four years, what you gonna do then, Riccardo?"

"I'm not gonna ride in the cart. I'm gonna help push it."

"Good for you, Riccardo. In the meantime, I'm sorry I can't give you and your papa both a lift, especially as the mud's so bad. But my car seems to be pretty full already."

"It is, it is, *Capitano*," agreed Luigi. "And we don't wanna any lift, Riccardo and me. I always walk and pretty soon he's gonna walk too, with me. We donna mind the mud. But sure we sava money for the fancy grocery store all the time, *Capitano*."

"I'm glad to hear it. Mind you don't ever let it run low on sugar. Well, so long, Luigi. So long, Riccardo. Come to the big house soon, even if you don't get there today, won't you?"

An exchange of farewells was characterized by much goodwill on all sides, and then the motor-car started again, leaving the peddler and his child and his cart behind it. The "singing towers" of Belle Heloise were already in sight, and the automobile had turned into the blind driveway before either of the old men were aware of it. Even the rattle of the cattle-gap might have passed unnoticed if Gervais had not turned and spoken to them as the motor clattered over it.

"That rattle gives the signal of my approach, gentlemen. In a second you'll hear our two old dogs, Snow and Cornet, and they'll be jumping all over the car too. But don't let that bother you—they're both perfectly harmless, and after a minute they'll be trying to pick a fight with Belizaire anyway, and forget all about you.

122

My wife generally comes out to meet me, too, so in just about a minute you'll be in the bosom of the family."

The predicted barking began before he had finished speaking, and the next instant the screen of the front door swung open, and a young and very lovely woman appeared between the fluted columns that flanked it, hastened down the brick demilunes and across the gallery. In the comparatively brief period since she had come, so precipitately, to Belle Heloise, Merry had changed, in some respects very markedly. She now wore beautiful and becoming clothes as a matter of course, and her manner, always warm and friendly, had gained immeasurably in poise and graciousness. Her greeting to her husband was unself-conscious, but it was a salutation of welcome rather than an invitation to a prolonged embrace. She freed herself almost immediately to receive her guests with unaffected cordiality.

"Why, Fabian, I can't tell you how glad I am to see you! It seems like months since you've been here. . . . So this is another kinsman, is it? I'm glad to meet you, Cousin Pascal. Fabian's often spoken to me about you. And this is your friend Mr. Vicknair? No, Belizaire, I didn't forget you. I was only speaking to your betters first. Won't you all come out on the rear gallery? That's where we seem to be assembled."

Still chatting pleasantly, she led the way to the front door and through the big hall that bisected the house, with great square rooms opening from it on either side. Essentially the place was unchanged: the same draperies and furniture, the same portraits and ornaments, which had been there for so many years were still disposed as Madame d'Alvery and, before her, a long succession of Estrade ladies had always kept them. But there were more flower-filled vases scattered about, more doors and windows opened to admit air and sunshine. The slight mustiness that had formerly pervaded it was gone and freshness flowed through it; and while it still retained its air of elegance its formality seemed inexplicably tempered. Pascal and Preston, treading cautiously over the soft carpet, cast awed and surreptitious glances into the parlour, the library, the dining-room and the music-room as they passed, hoping against hope that they would have a better look at these glories. Merry, as if reading their thoughts, paused reassuringly.

"We'll come back into the house by and by," she said. "But of course I can't wait to show off my family first. You don't mind, do you?"

Somewhat mendaciously they assured her they did not, and she went on, next swinging open the door to the rear gallery. The old veterans, admitted to Belle Heloise for the first time, had no standards of comparison; but Fabian was quick to notice that here, at least, a tremendous change had taken place. The spacious width, paved with mellow brick, flanked on one side by the house itself and framed, on the other, by the noble columns supporting the upper gallery, had never before been utilized for living quarters. Yet it was ideally suited for this purpose, shielded as it was from the intensity of the sun, but full of the essence of sunlight, and facing the sweep of lawn which merged gradually into the blossoming woods beyond. Now, at last, the delightful possibilities of this gallery, which actually seemed more like a patio, had been recognized and turned to account. Ferns and other plants were scattered about, some hanging, some rising from long boxes, and still others clustering in graceful jars. At one end a refectory table with benches on either side, painted green to match the shutters which enlivened the white walls, suggested that it was frequently used as an alfresco dining-room; while at the other end some spruce rattan furniture, cushioned in bright chintz, indicated its unmistakable habitability as a living-room. Dominating the rest of its equipment was an enormous double cradle in which two bouncing babies were sitting, propped up with pillows, and delightedly, if aimlessly, waving pink and blue rattles. A buxom coloured woman, picturesquely dressed, who rose respectfully at the approach of the visitors, had been sitting watchfully beside this cradle; while bending over it, less quick to look up, was a dark, graceful girl, whose face, even though half hidden, revealed a piquant, almost elfin quality of charm, while her extreme slenderness gave an obtrusive effect of fragility. Fabian went over and put his arm around her shoulder, Belizaire following closely behind him.

"Hello, Cresside!" he said. His flexible voice, which so quickly betrayed the varying moods his sombre face might have masked, took on a new tone when he spoke. It was genial, and at the same time it was curiously gentle. "I brought another worshipper to the shrine. A cousin of Mr. Tremblet's here married our Aunt Sybelle. He wants to see the young lady that's named for her."

"He'll see a mighty fine baby, then. . . . But where have you been all this time, you old wretch?" The latter remark, obviously addressed to Fabian, was made as Cresside straightened up, and when she had done so the excessive thinness of her pretty, pointed little face became more noticeable. Her heavily fringed eyes, large out of all proportion to the rest of her features, still further accentuated this emaciation. But her elfin smile was extremely attractive, and she held out her hand with great cordiality.

"How are you, Mr. Tremblet?" she said. "Take a good look at the Carnival Queen of 1938. . . . And incidentally at her brother. He's nice too," she added, stooping again to divert a rattle which seemed headed straight for the girl twin's eye. "Oh, I'm sorry! I didn't see you had a friend with you. Mr. Vicknair? I used to run around a lot with a boy named Erlo Vicknair. Could it possibly have been a relative of yours? Your *grandson*? *You live with him*? Well, that is a coincidence, isn't it? Give him my best, won't you?

Here, let me get out of the way, so that you can see the twins too."

The two old men bent delightedly over the double cradle. The twins, after staring for a moment doubtfully at the strangers, smiled beguilingly and resumed their gurgling and kicking. Merry had turned back to speak to Gervais, but Cresside and Fabian stood behind the veterans, looking down at the cradle too. The negro nurse, her capable, kindly hands folded quietly over her white apron, continued to watch from a respectful distance.

"I tell you frankly, I never saw a prettier pair of babies, me," Pascal announced at length. "I think you must be a true prophet, Miss Cresside. Most assuredly little Sybelle will be Queen of Carnival when she grows up. And you may say, my friends, it is all imagination, but I think, me, she favours her great aunt, the young lady that married my cousin. But she does not resemble her brother, no. I thought twins always looked alike, but she is fair, yes, and he is dark."

"You don't mean to tell me, Pascal, you ain't never heard that there's identical twins and non-identical twins?" Preston demanded, bridling indignantly. "These here are non-identical twins. That is always the case when one twin is a boy and the other a girl."

"How clever of you, Mr. Vicknair, to know all about that and to notice it right away!" Merry had come up now, her arm linked in Gervais', who was holding her hand. But again she freed herself easily, and picking up little Sybelle, tossed her high in the air, while the baby crowed with glee. "They're identical when it comes to being hungry, though," Merry added. "And it's almost their dinner-time now. I think I'd better take them away before they start howling and spoil the good impression they've made. They can begin to scream right in the middle of a gurgle if they think they're not getting their rights. Especially Vail. Sybelle is quite ladylike even when she cries—if she can keep on that way it'll be a great asset to her later! But Vail bellows. . . . Take him, please, Dinah," she added, turning to the nurse, who immediately gathered the little boy into her comfortable arms. "And excuse us, the rest of you, will you, please, for a little while? We won't be gone long. You'll find out what our guests would like to drink, won't you, Gervais? And I think we'll have dinner out here, unless anyone would rather go into the dining-room!"

"I'd much rather have it here," Fabian said heartily. "This patio is swell, Merry. I hadn't seen it since you fixed it up."

"That's your own fault, isn't it? I've been puttering in it all the spring. I do that instead of sleeping, this time!"

She laughed, and Fabian joined in Gervais' laughing response as Merry left them, quiet, assured, radiant, her baby girl in her arms. The veterans, puzzled but polite, endeavoured to laugh too.

Cresside went over to Dinah, and taking the responsive Vail from her, smoothed down his little dress, which had been hunched up around him when he was lifted from the cradle. Then she handed him back again, and the negro nurse, with a dignity comparable to that of her mistress, followed after Merry, carrying the little boy. Cresside sat down in one of the bright wicker chairs, and, lighting a cigarette, looked fixedly out towards the garden, her black eyes bigger than ever in her white face.

"I suppose it is my fault. I'll try not to let it happen again. 'Time is too slow for those who wait,' you know," Fabian said, answering Merry by speaking to Cresside. "By the way, where's Tante Isabelle?"

"I believe she's having dinner in her boudoir today. The heat, you know."

There was nothing prostrating about the pleasant warmth of May, and again the veterans found it hard to conceal their polite puzzlement. Fabian, however, nodded understandingly.

"And what about Boylston? I thought Gervais said he was coming today too."

"Oh, he's here all right. He arrived before we were through breakfast."

"Cresside, he didn't do anything of the sort. He wasn't here when I went in town with Fabian."

"Well, it seems to me as if he'd been here for ever. I can stand that Boston accent just so long and then it gets me down. Anyway, after listening to an exhilarating conversation for at least two hours, I suggested that he should go and see *maman*. That's where he is now. For all I know he may be reading St. Augustine's Sermons aloud."

"A good Unitarian from Boston? Now, now, Cresside!" rallied Fabian.

"Being an invalid for such a long time didn't cure Cresside of a habit of mockery, Fabian," Gervais said, rather shortly. "I'll let Boylston know we're here, and I'm sure he'll be right down. If this is one of *maman's* bad days, she ought not to tire herself by talking too long, anyway. What will you gentlemen have, a julep or a highball?"

Pascal and Preston eyed each other doubtfully. Cresside answered for them.

"I'm going to make you each one of my special juleps," she said. "You tell me truly afterwards if you don't think it's the best you ever tasted. Then while you're sipping it, why don't we play a game or something? There are five of us—six if the honourable Charles can tear himself away from *maman*. We can play poker. That is, unless there's something you'd rather do."

Again the two old men exchanged glances. Both were still somewhat bound by timidity, but Cresside's breezy friendliness was beginning to take effect, especially on Preston. He was the first to summon courage to speak, unexpectedly finding, once he had begun, that it was easy to go on.

"We wouldn't like to make all that work for you, Miss Cresside, when you've been sick so long," he said apologetically. "Anyone can see you're still puny. We'd enjoy the juleps, of course, but a highball would do just as well, and it wouldn't be half as much trouble. We'd enjoy a game of poker too. We play fantan at Fabian's house; it's been some time though since we've been out in company where there was enough for poker. But maybe you'd like to rest in the bed awhile before dinner, and maybe there's something your brother and Mr. Boylston would rather do too. Me and Pascal, we could walk out and see where those Yanks are buried, them that died of smallpox during the War Between the States. I've always had a hankering to see that graveyard——"

"Then you'd better let Miss Cresside show it to you, and I want to come along and see it too," Fabian broke in. "But not until later in the day, when it gets cooler. Let's have that game of poker now, with the juleps, as she suggests. . . . Didn't I hear something about your fixing up that little old cemetery, Cresside?" he asked, turning to her. "Getting a rustic bridge built over the gully that used to be impassable in wet weather? And then having the stones, that were all broken and battered, straightened and mended? And so on?"

"I don't know what you've heard. I haven't any special affinity for graveyards," Cresside said diffidently. "I only started to do something on the one between here and Hathaway Hall because Gervais wanted it cleaned up and none of the negroes would go near it. As far as that is concerned, Gervais wouldn't either. He's afraid of snakes. I'm not. Then after I cleaned out the nest in the Hathaways' lot, so that ours would be free of them, I started in to see what I could do for the Yanks. I've always felt sort of sorry for them—outliers like that. No relatives ever coming with flowers, or fellow-veterans with bands, or ladies' patriotic societies putting up markers. So I worked down there while Merry was fixing up the patio, and by and by we met in Angus Holt's garden. Maybe that was symbolic or something. I don't know. But I'd be very glad to take Mr. Tremblet and Mr. Vicknair down there later on if they'd really like to go."

"And can't I come along?"

Cresside rose again from her wicker chair, pulling down her belt with the same show of gaiety with which she had adjusted the baby's dress, and once more Fabian was shocked by the revelation of abnormal slenderness. "Oh, you can tag along," she said carelessly. "That is, if you're really intrigued about my handiwork, and not just putting on an act, the way that damned Bostonian is most of the time. Set up a table and get out the cards and chips while I make the juleps, will you, Fabian? Gervais'll have to go upstairs and take another look at the young mother and her offspring before he'll be good for anything else."

IX

THE patio was so peaceful and pleasant that the afternoon was over before anyone could believe that its mellow hours had slipped away. The superlative juleps, presented in great silver goblets and encrusted with frost, had taken a long time to consume; then dinner, served informally but lavishly at the refectory table, had been a leisurely meal, beginning with fish aspic, followed by fried chicken and "fixin's," and ending with peach ice-cream and angel-food cake. There was coffee afterwards, and brandy with the coffee, the coffee-pot and brandy bottle remaining within convenient reach of everyone. Preston and Pascal were both intermittently nodding a little and then rousing themselves in a startled way, when Gervais remarked casually that he always took a snooze after dinner and that perhaps they would like to do the same; if they would, the garden room, where a day bed supplemented the four-poster, was entirely at their disposal. They gratefully accepted his suggestion, and after he had shown them their quarters, by the simple process of opening the door which led directly into these from the patio, he took his leave of the other guests with equal informality, while mounting the adjacent outdoor stairway. Without either apology or explanation, Merry accompanied him; she obviously took it for granted that everyone would expect her to share her husband's siesta. Cresside, left behind with Fabian and Charles Boylston, looked from one to the other with her elfin smile.

"There are three or four more vacant beds in the house," she remarked. "Not to mention any number of stiff sofas. If either or both of you would like to lie down too, it can very easily be managed."

Both men laughingly declined the invitation. Boylston had never succeeded in forming the siesta habit, he said; he did not get up as early as most of his neighbours, but once he *was* up, it was for the day. Fabian had been born with the habit, he drawled; but the war, which had evidently not been carried on with a view of making things easy for civilians, had interfered with it; since he never could brook interference, he had decided to give up the habit. But what about Cresside herself? She looked to him as if she could do with a little sleep.

128

"I can—very little," she retorted. "Don't make such unflattering remarks, Fabian—no girl likes to hear them, even from a mere cousin. . . . It's too bad there wasn't one more person in this gathering, besides us, who could keep awake. If there only had been, we might have had a nice game of bridge."

"What about the Tremaines? Wouldn't they join up? I could run over and find out, if you like. It wouldn't take me ten minutes."

"Thanks, Charles. But you may be sure they're both asleep now too. And, anyway, if they came, we'd have one too many, which is just as bad as having one too few. Why don't you two go ahead and play chess while I do some baby sewing? We're never caught up with that nowadays."

They settled down companionably with ashtrays on either side of Cresside's work basket and a tall pitcher of iced tea within easy reach. Cresside sewed with surprising deftness and daintiness; but the chess game suffered somewhat, because as they played, Boylston watched Cresside and Fabian watched Boylston. He had liked the little he saw of the Bostonian, but he had never before had the occasion or taken the trouble to observe him closely. Now he found it interesting to scrutinize the outsider's appearance and to speculate on his character. Boylston's eyes were grey, very clear and cool, his thin straight hair the somewhat lifeless shade of brown into which a child's pretty flaxen locks so often darken with maturity. He was lean rather than slender, and he carried himself with poise rather than grace. His colour was healthy, though it lacked ruddiness, and his skin indicated almost fastidious cleanliness; his hands were shapely and dexterous. He wore tweeds better than any other planter along the River Road; but he was less distinguished-looking in linens; apparently he had never become wholly reconciled to the Louisiana custom of wearing these from May to October. In conversation he was agreeable, intelligent and cultured; he could hold his own in any group, even if he could not dominate it. He was never profane himself, but profanity did not seem to offend him; he had picked up no colloquialisms during his southern sojourn, and his Boston accent was still wholly unsoftened. Visitors to his house were greatly impressed by the number and quality of his framed diplomas, and his study also contained some very fine family portraits, and a large collection of valuable books; but he himself seldom referred to his education or his background, and then only in the most casual way. No one knew why he had come to Louisiana in the first place, or what had caused him to stay. But he fitted surprisingly well into the local picture; furthermore, he was a man of wealth, an accomplished host and a delightful guest.

Fabian, finishing his appraisal, found it easy to understand that Tante Isabelle would approve and enjoy Charles Boylston above any of Gervais' other friends "even if he was a Yankee." He was the ideal suitor for the daughter of the house, from a conservative and an aristocratic mother's point of view—well-born, well-reared, well-educated, rich, personable and high-principled. If Cresside married a man like this, and continued to live close by, where her position and her prestige would be continually before the eyes of the Capital and the River families, it would more than compensate for Gervais' mésalliance. For Gervais' marriage would always remain a mésalliance in his mother's eyes, despite her reluctant liking for her daughter-in-law and Merry's own phenomenal adaptability and forbearance. Fabian had no delusions on that score; he was not deceived by the surface harmony which reigned at Belle Heloise. Isabelle d'Alvery would never be satisfied until the pomp and circumstance of the Estrades had been restored, and she was counting on Cresside to do this.

Counting vainly, Fabian reflected, shifting his observant glance from Charles to Cresside as he hesitated over a knight's gambit. The Bostonian meant no more to her than he did; he felt sure of that. Cresside, herself so vital, would demand some essential element of vigour which Boylston lacked. That is, if ever again she demanded, or accepted, anything from a man. There were women, Fabian knew, who could not care, as Cresside had once cared for Sylvestre, more than once in a lifetime; and this was all the more likely to be true after a tardy and tragic discovery that the bounty they offered with such prodigality and pride had been taken carelessly or deceitfully. I'm rather sorry for Boylston, he thought, abandoning the gambit, and advancing his queen. But if he weren't such a thoroughgoing polecat I'd be sorrier still for Sylvestre. Not because of what he's done to Cresside, though that's scummy enough, Lord knows. I can't even look at the girl without having something turn over inside me at the sight of her eyes. But because of what he's done to himself. He got a glimmer of it on his wedding day, when he stood looking at her after she was hurt; he'd have given whatever his substitute is for a soul if he could have married her then, instead of Regine. But he didn't really know what frustration can do to a man, through the years, once he's sold his birthright for a mess of red pottage. Some day he'll find out, and then God help him! No, damn him. I hope God doesn't help him, or man either. I hope he gets everything that's coming to him. But I wish Boylston had something coming to him too, something good, because he really is the right kind of people. And I wish Cresside . . .

The door of the garden room opened, and Preston and Pascal came out, looking refreshed and expectant. Cresside laid down the scraps of fine linen and narrow lace which she was whipping together.

"What about some claret lemonade before we start to the cemetery?" she inquired. "I think you'd find it very refreshing. Nonsense, of course it isn't any trouble to make—in fact, I have it half-made already. I'll get Selah to bring it right out. . . . Do you want to see your fellow-Yankees' graves, Charles, or are you going to sit here until the rest of us get back? I think Merry'll be down again any minute now. Gervais generally goes out to see how the hoe gang's coming along as soon as he gets up—Sance is a good overseer, but Gervais doesn't think he keeps the hands' work quite up to the good old Army standards, and we're having a lot of trouble with Johnson grass; so Gervais is out in the field most of the time too. But Merry comes back to the patio to do a little light gardening before supper. Perhaps you'd like to help her."

"I would, sometime. But today I'd like immensely to go with the rest of you to the cemetery, if you don't mind."

"Oh, I don't mind! I suppose it isn't just the thing to say, 'The more the merrier,' when you're going to a graveyard. But please consider that I've expressed the proper equivalent."

The expedition proved a complete success from everyone's point of view. Cresside first led the way through the wicket gate beyond Angus Holt's garden into a narrow allée, bordered on one side by mulberry trees and on the other by elderberries. She stopped for a moment, looking up at the delicate flat clusters of small white flowers which were just beginning to fall.

"We make wine out of those elderberries," she said. "I reckon we'll be making more than ever now. We don't make mulberry wine because there aren't any mulberries. According to Creassy, those are all 'he' mulberry trees. So of course they aren't any more good than other males without normal co-operation."

The corners of Fabian's mouth twitched, and Preston and Pascal both chuckled. Charles Boylston smiled, politely but a trifle forcedly, and Cresside, making a slight *moue* at Fabian, went on towards the cemetery without further frivolous remarks. Beyond the allée the rustic bridge, to which Fabian had referred earlier in the day, spanned a little gully, and on the other side of this the ground widened to form a spacious grove, permeated with the sweet scent of new-mown grass. The greensward was studded with beautiful trees, pecans for the most part, though there were a few cypresses and flowering thorns among them; their trunks were wreathed with vines, their branches draped with moss. Above the dense growth of thickets, the levee was plainly visible. But the River Road itself was concealed by the shrubbery, so that the line of verdure remained everywhere unbroken, and seemed to reach upward towards the sky. The veterans gazed about them in amazement and awe.

"I never saw a more beautiful grove, me," Pascal said. "You wouldn't think there was all this space, either, between the road and the cane fields, would you, now? Is it much farther to the cemetery?"

"But, Mr. Tremblet, this *is* the cemetery! Any number of

131

Yankee dead are buried here—dozens of them died in that small-pox epidemic, and some were killed in battle besides. We don't know whether most of the graves were never marked, or whether the markers disappeared—Creassy says only the officers' graves had tombstones, and that the cypresses were planted to mark the others because it was hard to get marble; but that's just negro hearsay—no one in the family seems to have been interested enough to learn the truth about it. Anyway, there are only four stones here now, and they have no inscriptions on them—they're plain grey marble, very small and simple. But someone must have tried to beautify their surroundings once—there's a big bush of bridal wreath beside one of them, and lemon trees grafted to thorn beside the others. Come, I'll show them to you. They're all on the other side of the grove, not far apart from each other."

Walking silently and slowly, the men followed her. They saw the sheltering trees before they saw the stones, the bridal wreath already past its snowy bloom, the lemon trees already laden with hard green fruit and wreathed with scarlet trumpet vines. While the others stood watching him, Fabian bent over, trying to discover some mark or symbol which would betray the identity of the men whose humble headstones were so pitifully blank. But his search was futile. He straightened up, breaking off a branch of the strange hybrid which had fruit and thorns on the same bough.

"There ought to be a record of these men somewhere," he said. "The War Department must have been functioning when they were here, at least after a fashion, and I shouldn't be at all sur-prised if Madame Lucien Estrade managed to keep some kind of a plantation diary, during her husband's absence in the war. It would have been entirely in character. . . . You've never come across anything of the sort, Cresside?"

"No, never."

"Well, I'm going to see what I can dig up. It might be interest-ing. Meanwhile, let's pretend we know who these men were. . . . Ummmm! Over here would be Colonel McIvor—second genera-tion Scotsman—never let a Sunday newspaper come into the house —if they had Sunday newspapers in those days—always prayed his men into battle, but couldn't pray himself out of the smallpox, poor old devout devil. He'd have hung Jeff Davis to a sour apple tree fast enough, if he'd had his way. And his wife had one black silk dress and no children—a dress that would stand alone. Hail and farewell, Colonel. . . . Next to him would be young Lieutenant Jem—short for Jeremiah—Hawkins, the best dancer in Cincinnati pride of the Burnet House cotillons, if they had cotillons. A gay young rake of a bachelor was Jem, but paying court to the daughter of the bank where he clerked. And he sang tenor around the campfires—just befo-o-o-re the battle, mother. Next to him— well, let's see, that'd be a New Englander, the kind you used to read about selling wooden nutmegs. Had a captaincy in the state militia, and kept a country store in South Scituate, Mass. Wife's name was Hepzibah, of course, and they had nine children, all conceived without taint of sin, regardless of how much sand the old boy used to put into the sugar. Lord, how he hated to give up the store and go off to the wars—with all those government contracts he might have got hold of; but it wouldn't have looked right, giving up his militia commission that way. Wonder if Hepzibah married again. Bet she did. Imagine her introducing his nine stepchildren to the new mister. . . . And finally, over here, is the one real fanatic, a sort of junior John Brown, a black abolitionist who took the sword in one hand and a copy of *Uncle Tom's Cabin* in the other and went out to set the black man free. Calvin Cromwell Stafford was his name—and it's a good thing he didn't survive, for he'd have been the loudest carpetbagger in Dixie if he had, holding down a job of collector of customs at Savannah and burning a candle in front of a picture of Thad Stevens, till he got himself elected to the Senate, where he'd have voted for the impeachment of Andy Johnson. Well—here they are. *De mortuis nil nisi bonum.* They were men of courage and they died far from home. May their rest be ever peaceful. . . ."

None of the others had stirred while Fabian was speaking. Now for a moment no one spoke. Cresside stood looking at him intently, her enormous eyes fixed on his face. her lips quivering slightly. At last Pascal broke the spell which had been wrought partly by the place itself and partly by Fabian's fantasy.

"I could sit here listening to you all night, me. But I think, maybe, if it's convenient for you, Mr. Fabian, we ought to be getting back to town. My granddaughter, she doesn't like to have me late to supper. and——"

"Of course not, Pascal. It's high time I was on my way too. Thanks no end, Cresside, for bringing us here."

They went briefly back to the patio, where they found the twins, refreshed by food and sleep, again happily installed in their cradle, and Merry, as Cresside had predicted, "doing a little light gardening." Charles Boylston decided to stay on and help her with this, but the others made their farewells, leaving good-bye for Gervais, who was still in the field. As they approached Hathaway Hall, Fabian suggested that the two old men might like to drive through the short semicircular allée which separated the house from the road without concealing it, and at their eager assent he turned in among the trees. Instantly he heard someone calling his name, and, looking up, saw Regine, as usual dressed in white, standing in the gallery above them.

"Fabian! Oh, Fabian! Won't you please stop!"

He halted the car and called back to her, mimicking her appeal. "Regine! Why. Regine! I didn't intend to, but of course I will, if you make a point of it. Are you badly in need of help? Is the house on fire or something?"

"Of course I'm not in need of help and of course the house isn't on fire. I want to see you, that's all. Wait, I'm coming down."

Regine came gracefully down the curving steps to meet them, one hand resting lightly on the railing of the balustrade, the other caressing the rose at her breast. She was wise enough to adapt the grotesque fashion of the times to her own type rather than to follow it slavishly, and in spite of her short-skirted, long-waisted dress, she managed to produce a picturesque effect. Her greeting to Fabian was charmingly coy.

"I'm glad I finally succeeded in attracting your attention," she said with a little laugh. "I saw you every time you went by this morning: first alone, evidently on your way to Belle Heloise; then going back to town, with Gervais; finally returning again, with Gervais and these two gentlemen. Mr. Tremblet? Mr. Vicknair? I'm delighted to welcome you both to Hathaway Hall. Won't you all come in where it's cool and let me order you a drink?"

"We've had so many drinks at Belle Heloise that I don't know whether we can hold any more. But we can try," Fabian said agreeably, following her lead up the stairway. "Anyway, we'll be glad to come in. Sorry I didn't see your previous signals—also that I haven't managed to get out here before. I don't seem to have been anywhere lately. Everyone at Belle Heloise has been calling me to task on that score. . . . Well, travel must agree with you, Regine. You look like a million dollars."

"It's probably my new Paris clothes," she said with another little laugh. "But as far as that goes, I don't see how travel could help agreeing with me, when it was made under such ideal conditions! Do you? I want to tell you all about the garden party at Buckingham Palace, and our motor trip through the Dolomites, and our villa at Cannes—oh, everything! But let's get comfy before I begin."

She opened the front door and her visitors followed her into the vast hallway, flanked with Corinthian columns and further embellished with a wide tinted cornice of elaborate plaster work simulating magnolias. As they progressed past the entrance to the White Ballroom, and this was disclosed in all its magnificent emptiness, Preston cast a surreptitious and triumphant glance at Pascal: he had been right after all; there was nothing in the relatively simple style of decoration at Belle Heloise that could be compared to all this grandeur. But once they were seated in the room at the left of the front door he did not feel so certain. Strange that a beautiful young lady, who looked so much like a fashion plate herself, should be satisfied with a parlour of this sort, Pascal reflected; and then decided that, after all, perhaps the young lady was more concerned about being beautiful herself than about making her habitation beautiful. He was sure that Mrs. Gervais d'Alvery felt just the

134

opposite, though she was certainly lovely looking too, much lovelier, when you came right down to it, than this young lady—friendlier, simpler, sweeter somehow. He didn't know just why, but he didn't take to this young lady the way he had to Mrs. Gervais d'Alvery. . . .

"So you've been spending the day at Belle Heloise," Regine went on. She did not say anything more about getting a drink for them, or summon anyone else to do so; instead, she picked up a large fan from the littered centre table and wielded it languidly and grace- fully, her rings and bracelets sparkling with the movement. "I've been rather expecting the d'Alverys to drop in and welcome us back. But we haven't seen any of them yet. How are they?"

"The young couple and their offspring are all flourishing. And Tante Isabelle has certainly staged an astonishing comeback. But Cresside still looks pretty puny, as Mrs. Randall would put it."

"Why, I had no idea she wasn't well! We never corresponded as schoolgirls, so I didn't think it was strange I didn't hear from her while I was abroad. But then, I wasn't paying much attention to letters from anyone, except mamma. And, of course, I wasn't far from her at any time. You know she came to Europe on the *Paris* the week after Sylvestre and I sailed on the *France*, and she stayed at the Berkeley while we were at Claridge's. Then when we went to Cannes, she went to Nice, and so on. She'll be so sorry to have missed you this afternoon—she's gone to play bridge at the Graces'. . . . Why, *cher*, I didn't hear you come in. Fabian's brought some friends to call on us—Mr. Tremblet and Mr. Vicknair."

"How do you do?" inquired Sylvestre impersonally. "Nice of you to drop in." He shook hands, rather limply, with the three callers, and apparently oblivious of the invitation in Regine's upturned face, took some dog-eared magazines off an oak rocker and drew it up beside Fabian. Like Boylston, he was immaculately dressed, though, unlike the Bostonian, he wore his spotless white linens with an accustomed grace. But there was nothing about him to indicate the preoccupied planter. Indeed, his appearance suggested the gentleman of leisure who had been able to devote the entire day to keeping cool, rather than the harassed landowner who had just returned to the house for a hasty shower and a quick change before dinner. Mrs. Hathaway had long entrusted the supervision of the plantation to her manager, Grover Blood, whose personal reputation was unsavoury, but whose professional efficiency had long gone unchallenged, in spite of his predilection for wine, women and song. Mrs. Hathaway did not like changes, and appar- ently Sylvestre had been only too glad to follow the line of least resistance and allow Blood to continue shouldering the responsi- bility and doing the dirty work around the place. "Did I hear you saying something about Cresside as I came in?" he went on, light- ing a cigarette and, as an afterthought, tendering the opened case to his callers. "That she wasn't well?"

"Yes. Possibly you may recall that she had a pretty bad fall the day you were married," Fabian remarked, declining the proffered cigarette, but lighting one of his own.

"Of course we remember! You don't really think we'd be so stupid as to forget that, do you, Fabian?" Regine broke in before Sylvestre could answer. Again she laughed, and this time Pascal realized that one of the reasons he did not like this young lady was because of her laugh. It was tinkling, but it was tiresome. "We didn't know it was serious, though," Regine continued. "That is, we knew she was hurt, but we didn't realize she was injured. Why, all the family came to our wedding, that very same afternoon!"

"Yes, I know," Fabian said dryly. "That is, everyone but me. I figured I'd be the least missed, and apparently I was right—you'd even forgotten I wasn't there, Regine! But I stayed behind with Dr. Champagne. Of course, we knew it would upset your entire programme if one usher dropped out at the last moment, so Gervais decided he ought to come anyway, as long as there wasn't anything he could do for Cresside at that stage—she was under a pretty powerful opiate by then; and you may be sure that whither Gervais goeth, there Merry goeth also, if he wants her to, and he did. Besides, of course, it was a great treat for her to see a beautiful wedding like yours—I'm sure she'll always enjoy going to beautiful weddings. She'll get a vicarious thrill out of them that will partly make up for the one she couldn't get out of her own stark marriage ceremony, worse luck! As to Tante Isabelle, I wouldn't have put it past her to come here that day if there'd been a broken neck instead of a broken back to cope with at Belle Heloise. She'd made up her mind it was to be her first public appearance since her widowhood, and when Tante Isabelle makes up her mind, she doesn't stop for hell or high water."

"What do you mean, a broken back? Cresside didn't *break* her back, did she?"

"She broke a couple of vertebræ. You don't have to break all of them, you know, to suffer the tortures of the damned. She was in a plaster cast for about six weeks, and after that in some kind of a brace. She had to stay in bed for months and months. She's up and around now, but I'm not so sure she ought to be. She doesn't look like herself at all, even yet. She is nothing but skin and bone and eyes."

"Why! Poor, poor Cresside! We had no idea. . . . Of course that explains why the d'Alverys haven't been to see us. We'll go down to Belle Heloise right away."

"It might be a good plan to wait until the road dries out a little. The seepage is pretty bad this year, and there's no point in running the risk of getting stuck in the mud, if you don't have to." Fabian turned from Regine to Sylvestre, changing the subject without preamble. "By the way, how are your crops coming along?

136

There's a rumour going around that you've got mosaic disease here at Hathaway Hall."

"Well, some of the leaves on the new growth do look a little mottled. But I don't believe it's anything to get excited about—anyway, Blood thinks it isn't. . . . Did you say Cresside'd been in bed for a year?"

"No, I didn't say she'd been in bed for a year. I said for months and months, but it must have been darn close to a year, at that. . . . You don't seem to be taking this mosaic disease very seriously, Sylvestre. Have you been getting any of the bulletins the Government's sending out?"

"Yes. I've been getting them. But, to tell you the truth, I've thrown most of them into the wastebasket and turned the rest over to Blood," Sylvestre said impatiently. "The Government's always sending out bulletins about something. It must use up tons and tons of paper that way—not to mention millions and millions of the taxpayers' money."

"Maybe. But it'll also cost the taxpayers of Louisiana millions and millions if this thing spreads."

"Why, Fabian, what makes you bring up such a gloomy subject in the course of a social call? I never knew before that you were this kind of a terrible killjoy! What do you know about sugar anyway? You're not a planter. You're nothing but a lawyer."

"Yes, I know," Fabian said. "I'm nothing but a lawyer, and of course Sylvestre's had all kinds of experience with sugar. Well, we must be getting along. Give my regards to your mother, Regine. Nice to know the family's in residence again. I always hate to see a fine old place empty, and there are so many empty places along the River Road already, worse luck! But I'm glad that one of them, at least, is coming back to its former state. I mean Hackberry Lodge, the old Surcliffe Plantation, that Charles Boylston's bought. You've met him, of course? No? Why, that's too bad. But you're bound to the first day you go to Belle Heloise. He haunts the place, more than any ghost ever did."

"Oh, Fabian, please don't talk about ghosts! I'm simply terrified of them. What do you mean, he haunts the place?"

"Nothing frightening. You don't need to be terrified, Regine." Fabian paused a moment, glancing from Regine to Sylvestre and then at Regine again. "He's taken a terrible tumble for Cresside, that's all. And Gervais and Tante Isabelle have both gone in to bat for him. I only hope Cresside has sense enough herself to know a good fellow when she sees him."

X

"**M**IS-TER SPEAK-ER! Mis-ter Speak-er!"
"The gentleman from Pointe Coupee is recognized."
"I move you, Mister Speaker, that the Committee on Federal Relations be instructed to report forthwith on the resolution ratifying the Federal Suffrage Amendment."

For hours on end—or so it seemed to Gervais d'Alvery—nothing had happened in the somnolent House, now so suddenly electrified. The very atmosphere of the Chamber had been dormant, and the members in that state of torpor for which heavy dinners, warm weather, and complete indifference to legislative routine were about equally responsible. A few insignificant measures were being passed in perfunctory fashion. In each instance, the clerk read the full text of a bill in a rapid monotone; then the Speaker rapped with his gavel, mumbling something unintelligible; finally the clerk called the roll of a hundred and eighteen names and members responded almost mechanically. Gervais, looking lazily about, was convinced that probably no one within earshot of Tallieu's monotone and Walker's occasional mumble cared whether or not Bienville Parish acquired another justice of the peace or whether a certain Julie Becassine were permitted to sue a levee board for the recovery of twenty-eight dollars damages to her property.

An overtone of sibilance was added to the pervading drone by rows of determined ladies, seated on either side of the amphitheatre, who whispered to one another as unremittingly as they fanned themselves. Outstanding on one side were Mrs. Lydia Wyckliffe Holmes, the Misses Badley—Nan and Daisy—and Miss Mittie Alden; they were all looking daggers at the ladies on the other side, whose leaders were Mrs. Ruffin Pleasant, wife of the ex-governor, Miss Jean Gordon of New Orleans, and Mrs. Goldenberg. The animosity of these glances was returned in kind, for "Miss Lyd's" crowd favoured ratification of the Federal Suffrage Amendment, now requiring favourable action from only one more state. Mrs. Pleasant's group, on the other hand, advocated a Suffrage Amendment to the State constitution only. Ostensibly everyone favoured women's suffrage; the method by which it could best be obtained was the only acknowledged issue. But no one was deceived by this pretext. The Anti-Ratificationists were actually Anti-Suffragists as well, and everybody realized that Ferd Claiborne, the member from Pointe Coupee who had so startled the House by his outburst, must have something up his sleeve: what he was saying and what he really wanted were indubitably two entirely different things.

The Ratification Amendment had long since been referred to the Federal Relations Committee, whose chairman, Scott Wilkinson, a young Shreveport attorney, was temporarily away. In his absence, Jules Dreyfous, a short, baldish, scholarly hardware dealer from New Iberia, and an ardent ratificationist, bustled to his feet to take up the Claiborne challenge. Gervais rather admired Dreyfous, who had long made superior wines for his home table, and who continued this practice as placidly as though the National Prohibition Amendment had never been passed; but on the suffrage issue Gervais saw eye to eye with Claiborne. The latter, one of the handsomest men in the legislature, was an attorney, a planter and a professional politician; yet he found time to raise his own strain of fighting cocks, of which he was inordinately proud, and to import from Arabia an occasional blood stallion for his stables. Claiborne's conservative views regarding women's place in politics were wholly in harmony with those of Gervais. According to his tenets—and according to those of practically all South Louisiana sugar planters —a lady had privileges, rather than rights, and the sordid business of voting was not among them, whatever the rest of the country might think. Gervais was more than ready to follow Claiborne's lead.

"We have had this measure before us for five weeks now," the member from Pointe Coupee was continuing vociferously. "Such delay is wholly unreasonable. The House is entitled to dispose of the matter and get it out of the way."

"Mister Speaker, I rise to object. In the absence of the Committee Chairman, no action should be taken."

Dreyfous, still on his feet, spoke insistently, but endeavoured to maintain an attitude of composure and dignity despite the uproar which surrounded him. The clamour for recognition had become general. Everyone was trying to talk at once, everyone was trying to shout everyone else down, no one was listening to what anyone else was saying. The partisan ladies had ceased to whisper to each other and to fan themselves; they had become a part of the general pandemonium. But this subsided as quickly as it had arisen. The Speaker, somehow making himself heard above the hubbub, ruled that the Clerk should inform the Chairman of the Federal Relations Committee on his return that it was the desire of the House to have this resolution reported out at the earliest possible moment. This left matters precisely where they had been before, yet somehow each side indicated by the bearing and demeanour of its members that right had triumphed over the forces of evil and that a notable victory had been won. The two cohorts of fanning ladies on opposite sides of the amphitheatre no longer glared at one another; frankly, openly, each gloated over the defeat of the opposition. The House settled back to its earlier languor.

"The Governor would like to speak to you a moment, Captain

d'Alvery, if it's convenient for you to leave the Chamber just now."

Gervais looked up to see Stanley Ray, Governor Parker's secretary, standing beside his desk. He smiled, suppressing a sigh of relief.

"It's perfectly convenient," he said. "In fact, for the last hour I've been trying to think of a valid excuse to get away. Ferd Claiborne has just stirred up a little excitement, and I'd begun to hope for better things; but it was nothing more than a flash in the pan. Let's go."

He rose and followed Ray up the aisle. The door leading from the Governor's outer office to his private sanctum was open, as always, for it was a point of pride with Parker that this should never be shut, and Gervais entered the inner room without formality.

He found the Governor ensconced at the massive desk which had once allegedly belonged to Maximilian of Mexico. Except for a brief interval at lunch-time, Parker had been there since early morning, for it was another point of pride with him that he never reached the Capitol later than eight o'clock. Now, at five in the afternoon, he was still fresh and alert, and he greeted Gervais with a pleasant briskness.

"Good-evening, Captain. How are things shaping up at Belle Heloise?"

"Almost too well, I suppose. Somehow it doesn't seem right not to be able to complain about the way things are going on a plantation."

Parker chuckled. "Better take advantage of that feeling while you can. You won't have much opportunity to do it. By the way"—he swept a shirt-sleeved arm towards the window in the Norman bay where his desk was placed—"how do you like the way we're cleaning the State House grounds? Regular snake-hole when I took over."

"Looks fine, Governor. You can see the figurehead from the old battleship *Louisiana* now."

"Well—we do what we can. I'm bringing in some goldfish for the fountain down there too. However, I didn't invite you down here to talk to you about landscape gardening. What I wanted to discuss with you very seriously, Captain, if you'll permit me to lay my side of the case before you, is the constitutional convention bill of Representative Chappuis. I am told you have expressed yourself as favouring submission of the new constitution to the voters. Is that correct?"

"Well, yes, I suppose so. I think I might subject myself to a good deal of criticism if I voted that the people had to accept a new constitution whether they liked it or not."

"That's the usual and plausible argument, but it won't hold

water, Captain. No constitution can be written which doesn't offend someone in one or another of its provisions. In order to vote against that one provision, the people must vote against the whole document."

"But that still doesn't answer the argument of those who always talk about the dear people, and what sort of a fix will I be in if I run for re-election and my opponents raise the shout that I'm the one that refused to let them vote on the constitution?"

"The answer to that is simple enough. Let the people elect as delegates to the convention only those whom they can trust to write a constitution which need not be submitted to popular voting when it is finished. There can be no objection to that—no matter what old Gilbert Dupré from St. Landry says to the contrary. He'll be a delegate to the convention himself, you mark my words, even if we pass it without the submission clause."

Gervais nodded thoughtfully. "I guess that might be made a point all right," he agreed. "I'd like to think it over, though, and talk it over too, with Fabian d'Alvery. He's my attorney as well as my cousin and I've got a good deal of confidence in his judgment. I was planning to stop by his house, anyway, before I started home this evening. I want to see if he can't suggest something we planters could do that might induce the Equalization Board to loosen its stranglehold on sugar. I don't for the life of me see why they should be hanging on to it like grim death now that all the other commodities that were controlled during the war have been released."

"Why, that's easy. Because it's the simplest to regulate. The situation would be different if the sugar refineries were scattered from one end of the United States to the other instead of being confined to a few seaports. . . . Well, Fabian might be helpful, though I don't see how anyone here can be; but I'd also be glad to have you talk the other matter over with him. I've a good deal of confidence in his judgment too."

Dismissed as informally as he had been welcomed, Gervais went out of the east door into St. Philip Street, where he came face to face with his mother-in-law. Mrs. Randall had evidently just completed the "grocery shopping" which was one of her principal diversions, for she was carrying, with an air of triumphant weariness, a large string bag full of knobby packages; some dusty greens protruded from one of these, a fowl's yellow feet from another. Her dingy street clothes were vaguely suggestive of the grey wrappers she wore in the house, and her limp hat did not wholly conceal her untidy hair. For the thousandth time, Gervais marvelled that such a drab creature could have borne and reared a radiant being like Merry; the flame which illumined the girl must have been struck from some other spark. Reluctantly, because the antipathy between them was still mutual, he stopped and saluted the drab woman.

"Good afternoon, Mrs. Randall. I'm glad to see that this heat apparently isn't too much for you. Just the same, that bag must be pretty heavy. Better let me get my car and run you home."

"I wouldn't want to take you out of your way, seeing as how I'm still able to walk," Mrs. Randall responded. "Leaving the Capitol early, aren't you, Gervais?"

"I'm on my way to see Fabian about something for the Governor," Gervais answered, chagrined because he felt compelled to acknowledge her implied rebuke by explaining his actions. Then, seizing upon the chance of changing the subject, he added hastily, "By the way, if you have any influence with Miss Mittie Alden, I wish you'd pry her loose from the Suffrage bunch that's rooting for my opponents."

"Miss Mittie's got a mind of her own," declared Mrs. Randall. "She don't need the Governor nor anybody else to tell her what to do. Anyhow, I'm glad to see the old maids sticking up for themselves. Most married women just go around saying amen to their husbands. 'Fraid to do anything else, I suppose."

"If you mean to imply that Merry's afraid of me——" Gervais began.

"No, Merry isn't afraid of you, I'll say that much for her. Just the same, she hasn't got a mind of her own any more. She's wax in your hands," Mrs. Randall retorted, quoting from the latest thriller with which she had beguiled her leisure. "If she hadn't been, she wouldn't have married you as fast as if there'd been reasons why she had to, and she wouldn't be in the family way from one year's end to another. She can't even get out to see her own mother, tied down like she is. She's got a baby in her arms and under her apron both, instead of just one or the other, like the old saying. Well, I must be getting along. Miss Mittie'll be looking for her supper when she gets in from the Capitol, and I have to cook it for her. *She'll* stay to the end of the session all right, and she'll have a right to be hungry."

Having shot this parting bolt, Mrs. Randall walked triumphantly away, one shoulder sagging under the weight of the string bag. Gervais, irritated at his own annoyance, walked on down St. Philip Street and made a series of left turns into Somerulos Street. It was only a short walk, and the sidewalks were abundantly shaded by trees in full foliage. But the day was very warm, and when Gervais reached Fabian's well-ordered little house its quiet and coolness were so amazingly refreshing that he went out of his way to compliment Carmelite on her extraordinary talents for keeping his cousin comfortable. She hoped she knew how to do things right for her white folks, she said, civilly enough; but her tone seemed to imply that her master was more felicitously and intelligently served than his visitor, and she added, without any amiable discursiveness, that he would find Mr. Fabian in the garden with Belizaire. This did not mean that Fabian was reclining in an armchair with a book in his hand and a drink at his elbow, while his dog dozed beside him; it meant that he was down on his knees weeding the walks and flower-beds, while Belizaire spun around snapping at bugs and chasing butterflies. However, Fabian immediately arose, cheerfully dusting off his hands, and saying it was high time he called it a day. Should they stay outdoors or go inside? And what would Gervais like in the way of a drink? Not that it would be as good as he would get at Belle Heloise, since Cresside was not there to mix them. . . .

Inside, Gervais said, because it was so wonderfully cool there; and a gin rickey, if there were any of the real stuff in the house. Fabian assured him that there was, mixed the drinks with adroitness, and listened patiently to everything Gervais had to say about the Governor's theories on the constitutional amendment and the sugar planters' troubles on account of official control. He thought Parker had the situation sized up right, he said; he hoped Gervais would side with him against submitting the constitution to a popular vote. He would like to be helpful, but he did not know, offhand, that he himself could do much about the Equalization Board; he thought the men in Washington—Gay, Rogers and the others—were probably bringing all possible pressure to bear. It was a good thing Louisiana had a sugar planter in the Senate, and, after all, this man had introduced a bill on sugar equalization that was due to come up for approval any day. What, exactly, did Gervais think could be done at this end? Gervais did not seem to know, and Fabian renewed the drinks, waiting patiently for his cousin to bring up some other subject, the first two apparently being exhausted. But for some time Gervais sat rather moodily, speaking fitfully and inconsequentially, and declining to be diverted by Belizaire's persistent antics.

"I seem to sense a slight malaise, as Tante Isabella would delicately define it," Fabian remarked as Gervais finally rose to take his departure, after what seemed to his cousin like somewhat aimless procrastination. "Nothing really wrong, is there?"

"No, of course not. But I just had an encounter with my mother-in-law, and you know how that always affects me. Besides, the Equalization Board does get my goat, and I do get fed up with it all at the Capitol."

"What, so soon?"

"Yes, so soon. This struggle over suffrage is just a wrangle among a lot of termagants. Lord knows how they ever got any he-men into their cat-fight. The worst pain in the neck is that so-and-so Tack Evans, from Caddo. He's hand in glove with the opposition, and he's buzzing around the Capitol most of the time, labouring under the delusion that he's aiding and abetting Mr. and Mrs. Ruffin G.

Pleasant. He'd like to make a hit with them, because he thinks Ruff might get to the U.S. Senate one of these days. But he doesn't really care a damn about suffrage one way or another."

"Well, you should worry about Tack Evans. He isn't a member of the legislature."

"No, but he might as well be, as far as I'm concerned. And there are plenty of members who do get my goat. Take that screwball from along the Texas border, for instance, Brother Ellery Scobell. He started out as a sharecropper, and he's still not so far from where he started. He's laboured to get into the legislature so that he could have the dipping law repealed, and he actually goes around with two ticks in a nickel-gripper purse. He's always coming up with queer laws himself, too, though it's the ticks that he's got his heart really set on. I believe those two devils, Happy Sevier and George Perrualt, egg him on to introducing most of them—the bachelor bill, for instance, and the one subsidizing a lone oarsman to row out to the middle of the Mississippi and pick up drift-wood——"

Gervais was interrupted by a hearty laugh from Fabian. He himself snorted and went on.

"I'm glad you think it's all so amusing. Maybe you wouldn't if you had to sit there and hear it for hours, day after day."

"Listen, Gervais. You'd better develop your powers of endurance, not to mention your sense of humour. There's still a long, long trail a-winding before you reach the Mansion."

"Who said anything about wanting to get to the Mansion?"

"No one. But I rather gathered that was the eventual objective in the back of your mind. Or was it the United States Senate? Or one after the other in swift succession?"

"Some day that vivid imagination of yours is going to get you into trouble, Fabian. I'm not a professional politician, any more than I was a professional soldier. I'm a sugar planter first, last and always. The only reason I wanted to go to the legislature—and you know it—was to see that our agricultural interests got more and better representation than a few sharecroppers like Scobell and you lawyers were giving them."

"All right, all right. Stop weeping about it. You'll be showing your legs to the jury next. This blues-singing of yours is a new line, especially as there can't be much wrong with the plantation either, now that sugar's hit twenty-six."

"No, but there may be, any time, if that god-damned mosaic disease starts to spread. Hathaway Hall is too near Belle Heloise."

"Yes, I've always thought that way about the place myself," Fabian responded. "But, after all, there aren't any signs that the disease is spreading, are there, as yet?"

"No."

"Then what's eating you, for God's sake, besides the astounding

144

discovery that all your fellow-legislators aren't silver-tongued orators and selfless philosophers?"

"Nothing. That is, nothing to speak of. Except that Merry doesn't seem quite like herself."

"There now, we're getting somewhere at last. No wonder you're upset. What seems to be the trouble?"

"She's had to start weaning Sybelle. That was to be expected, under the circumstances. But she's worrying, and when she's upset I am too; it's so unlike her."

"Can't Dinah come to the rescue?"

"Well, that's just the point. Dinah took over Vail almost from the outset. Merry had enough for one, but not enough for two, after the first few weeks. Now she's afraid if Dinah tries to take on two she won't have enough either. Then both babies might suffer for it. Merry can't make up her mind whether to risk it, and to start giving them each one bottle a day, so that the amount could be increased if necessary, or to put Sybelle on cow's milk altogether and let Vail go on with Dinah until the hot weather's over. She's obsessed with the idea that she may not be fair."

"Can't Dr. Champagne make the decision for her and relieve her of the responsibility?"

"Oh, he jokes and says Vail is such a husky specimen that he'd probably get along all right if we started feeding him syrup and rice right now. But then he always adds very pompously that in a case like this a doctor can't lay down the law, that it's a question for the young mother—or the young father—to decide. And Lord knows I'm not an authority on the care and feeding of infants."

Gervais' voice had grown increasingly edgy as he went on. Fabian looked out of the window and drummed on the table with his fingers.

"As a matter of fact, I don't believe the syrup and rice are necessarily a joke," he said at last. "They're pretty well standardized, down on Bayou Lafourche. I wouldn't know, of course, exactly how early in life they make up an accepted diet, but I imagine there must be lots of cases when the kids are pretty small. Families down there usually run about a baker's dozen, and I've often noticed two or three youngsters crawling around the same gallery who seemed to be pretty much of an age. There must be plenty of cases where other young mothers get caught the same way Merry has."

"I don't care for that expression, Fabian. Especially as it's incorrect. Merry wants to have children."

"Sorry. As a matter of fact, I wasn't referring to the same phase of the situation that you were. I meant caught on the horns of a dietary dilemma, not involuntarily prolific. Though at that I should think two pregnancies within a year might try the tranquillity of any woman, even Merry."

"I still don't care much for the way you're talking. These first kids are coming along pretty closely together, but I'm not anticipating the establishment of one of those Bayou Lafourche families you've been talking about. Four or five youngsters would fill up the place very satisfactorily, and I'd like some chance to have Merry to myself. So I think I can assure you the next ones will be farther apart, especially if we get a boy for a Christmas present."

"You're in a hell of a hurry for another son, aren't you? No, don't tell me again that you don't care much for the way I'm talking. At the risk of further rebuke, however, I can't help asking, if you want to have Merry to yourself, why on earth you don't take her off somewhere, before it's too late again? She's never had any kind of a nice trip, as far as I know, not even a wedding trip. And I should think a change of scene might do her no end of good just now—change her train of thought, too, and stop her worrying. It wouldn't have to be a long trip to do the trick—you and she could simply get aboard the *John D. Grace* some Thursday evening after the legislature adjourns for one of its week-ends, and spend the time between sessions in New Orleans. You could blow yourself to a swell suite at the Grunewald and take Merry shopping. I haven't seen her wearing anything yet a modern girl would recognize as real jewellery. I saw Regine the other day and she was simply strung with it. Besides, you know that Billy Pereira would be tickled to death at the chance to show you a tall time."

"If you were married, and had two semi-invalids on your hands, besides twins and a pregnant wife, you might find that little pleasure excursions like the one you're outlining aren't so easy to arrange. In fact, I wish you would get married, if only to try out the practicability of putting all your pleasant little theories into practice, as I said before. . . . Incidentally, Merry'd never consent to taking a trip and leaving the twins."

"To the tender care of Cresside and Dinah? For three days? I dare you to ask her!"

"All right. I will ask her. And I'll drop in tomorrow, just to tell you that you were wrong."

"Don't bother. You all keep badgering me about not coming out to Belle Heloise. I'll be down for the day Sunday, and we can work out the details of your belated wedding journey then."

He arrived to find the place unwontedly silent. The dogs barked briefly when he drove up, but for once they seemed uninterested in picking a quarrel with Belizaire, and wandered aimlessly off again. Amen did not come forward to take the car, and, after parking it himself, Fabian went into the house and drifted through the downstairs rooms without finding anyone. The pleasant patio was empty too, except for Miss Larcella, who was stretched out in a sunny spot, the latest litter of kittens dozing contentedly beside her. But as Fabian started up the outside stairway, leading from the platform by the garden room to the rear of the upper gallery, he met Cresside coming down, her finger on her lips.

"Hello and hush!" she said softly. "Come on back to the patio—unless you'd rather sit among the relics in the drawing-room. But anyway, don't come upstairs. Dinah and I have just succeeded in getting the twins to sleep, after their customary ceremonial visit to *maman*, and I don't want to go through that struggle again. They seem to feel, even if she doesn't, that formal calling went out of vogue with the war, and they resent being thrust into starched dresses, and all the rest of it. Besides, between teething and weaning, they're fussy anyway."

"Where is everyone else?" Fabian inquired, turning to go down the stairs at her side.

"Well, *maman* is in her boudoir, and I believe Lucie is rearranging her hair and washing herself off, where it shows, with Florida water. She takes her daily constitutional in the pergola again now, and, of course, such violent exercise ruffles her locks and brings on profuse perspiration. Dinah is watching over the twins and Lou Ida is getting dinner, rather rebelliously. I don't know whether you'll have anything fit to eat or not. All the other servants, except Lucie and Dinah, have gone to a big baptizing, and Lou Ida wanted to go too. Some of the hands from the quarters are prominently featured in it. In fact, nearly everyone who belongs on the place is down by the riverside breathing the odour of sanctity. I expect some of the most trifling niggers are coming out of the water this minute, shouting, 'I seen de Lord! Glory Hallelujah!'"

"Are Gervais and Merry down on the river bank lending dignity and distinction to this gathering?"

"Oh no. They're attending High Mass at St. Agnes'. You and I are the only apostates of the family, Fabian."

"So Merry goes to St. Agnes' with Gervais now, does she?" Fabian asked, without commenting on Cresside's last statement.

"Sure. That was a foregone conclusion, wasn't it? That she would, I mean. In spite of all her mother's assertions, I think she's already practically forgotten about the Reverend Mr. Hawkins and the Sunday School she attended regularly from childhood. It's only a matter of time before she'll be received into the tender arms of Mother Church. She never even questions anything Gervais wants her to do, apparently. Not that I'm criticizing her wifely docility. Merry's a grand person, and she's got plenty of backbone, too, except where Gervais is concerned. No one realizes that better than I do. . . . What can I get for you? A julep? A Sazerac?"

"Either or both, by and by. I don't know a more beguiling Hebe than you are, Cresside—your ambrosia is one of the chief attractions of Belle Heloise, as far as I'm concerned. But the day's still young. Can't we just sit down and talk for a few minutes, while you drink to me only with your eyes?"

"Yes, of course, if you will pledge with yours." She dropped lightly into one of the chintz-covered chairs, and Fabian, drawing another close to it, lowered himself awkwardly into this. "Perhaps I'd better warn you that I may use my eyes to glare at you, however," Cresside continued. "And that my conversation may take on a pretty acid tone. I understand you're responsible for relegating me to the rôle of the traditional competent old maid aunt."

"Never! What made you think so?"

"Didn't you suggest to that fool brother of mine that Merry might actually like to breathe a little freer air for a change? He hasn't quite said you did, in so many words, but I know he never would have thought of it himself, and he did let out that he'd been seeing you on legal business, the very day he casually brought up the matter."

"So they are going to take a trip?" Fabian inquired, with obvious amusement, but without either denying or accepting Cresside's charge.

"Oh, sure! The *John D. Grace* has orders—and what orders!— to stop here Thursday night; and the royal suite has been reserved at the Grunewald—you know, the one Charlie Chaplin occupied when he was here. And letters dispatched to all our most prominent kith and kin in New Orleans, the ones who have big houses, big cars and big doings."

"I'm very glad to hear it. Merry'll have a lot of fun. Incidentally, so will you, with a free hand during her absence. I haven't done anything to cry *mea culpa* for. I might even suggest it would be a good idea if you took a trip yourself, a little later on. You've stuck pretty closely to Belle Heloise too."

"Well, your first idea wasn't so bad. But don't make a habit of getting these inspirations. You might develop into a sort of Mr. Fixit. I haven't the slightest desire to go away on a trip."

"Well, so long as that's true."

"It is true. Hark, I think someone else is arriving. Probably Charles."

"Is it as easy to guess as all that?"

"Oh yes. He practically lives here. And he has ideas about trips too. Only his are different from yours. He thinks I ought to take them with him."

"Then they're not different from mine. I'd thought of that myself too. He's a good fellow, Cresside."

"Yes, I know. But my ideas *are* different."

"Mind letting me in on them?"

"I think some of your earlier fancies are better than this latest— the one about the competent old maid aunt, for instance."

"Listen, I'm willing to stand back of everything I did say about

148

that trip for Merry. But not back of a single thing I didn't say—or back of anything I didn't think either. And I never in the world thought of you as an old maid aunt, Cresside, in spite of your competence—and you're a darn sight more competent than you like to let on. Because you couldn't be a traditional spinster—no matter how hard you tried."

At the sound of an approaching car, heralded by the barking dogs, Cresside had risen, and before there was time for footsteps to echo through the long hall she had reached the door leading into this from the patio. But Fabian had risen too, almost simultaneously, and now, despite her fleet-footedness, he was almost abreast of her. She swung open the door and slipped through it, half turning to speak to him from the other side.

"Then you have no idea how hard I *can* try, Fabian," she said. There was a slight note of mockery in her voice, but it still sounded carefree, almost gay, as it had ever since his arrival. He had enjoyed every minute he spent with her, for she seemed more like her old self than at any time since her accident. Now, suddenly, there was a change. She did not go forward to meet the expected visitor, but stood so still that she gave an effect of rigidity; her laughing lips stiffened into a hard line, and her big eyes narrowed to half their size. Silhouetted in the doorway, she looked as if she had been transfixed. The sight was the more alarming to Fabian because it was so completely out of character; he had never seen Cresside frightened, and he would have asserted, unequivocally, that there was nothing which she feared. He opened the screen door abruptly, calling her by name and stretching out a reassuring hand. But the seizure was as brief as it was violent; she had almost recovered before he reached her. For an instant she gripped his hand convulsively; then she went quietly through the long hall towards the front entrance, where, instead of Charles Boylston, Regine and Sylvestre were standing.

"Darling!" Regine exclaimed, anticipating any greeting from Cresside. "We just couldn't wait any longer to see you, so we came here, straight from church. How *are* you? Oh, hello, Fabian! Are you spending the day here again?"

"No, I'm not spending the day here again," Fabian answered. "I came out to collect on a bet, and then I just stayed on for a while. But I understand it isn't the best time for visitors—the servants have all gone to a baptizing and the twins are teething. So I'm starting back into town any minute."

"Well, we can't stay but a minute ourselves. We left Regine's mother at Hathaway Hall, and she's expecting us right back. But, as Regine said, we thought——"

Sylvestre's inconsequential remarks trailed away without coming to any definite conclusion. Regine, who had thrown her arms rapturously around Cresside and kissed her excitedly, released her with apparent reluctance, and then, still clasping her hand, but holding her at arm's length, regarded her with playful but close attention.

"Now stand still and let me look at you," she ordered. "A little bird told me you were nothing but skin and bones and eyes, and I want to see for myself. Why, I think you look wonderful! You'll never have to worry about dieting, with a figure like that! And your eyes are gorgeous. I don't wonder you keep the countryside spellbound—oh, I've been hearing about that too! Now let's come and have a nice cosy talk, just you and I—the kind we used to have at slumber parties, don't you remember? Fabian, why don't you take Sylvestre into the library and tell him some more about that queer blight you think's affecting our sugar—the Midas Disease, was that what you called it? Cresside and I want to be by ourselves, because we've got lots more interesting things to discuss than sugar, haven't we, honey? And we don't want any mere men around while we're doing it, do we, darling?"

"I'd be very pleased to take Sylvestre into the library," Fabian said. "At least if that's what Cresside would like me to do. You haven't given her a chance to tell us yet, Regine."

"Why, I know Cresside a lot better than you do, you saucy creature! She always wants to do exactly the same thing I do, when we're together. You don't seem to realize what intimate friends we are, Fabian, or how long we've been parted! We've got to catch up."

"By all means, take Sylvestre into the library, Fabian," Cresside said. Now that she finally had a chance to speak, her voice was as cool as her cousin's, and as collected. "Perhaps you'll get a drink for him—as you said, not very hospitably, the household's slightly upset today; but I know I can depend on you to stay long enough to do the honours." Without having once looked directly at Sylvestre, she turned from Fabian to Regine. "We do have a lot to catch up with," she said. "And, first of all, I'm sure Merry would want me to show you the twins, as she's not here to do it herself. I believe she and Gervais were going to Mrs. Randall's after church —that's why they're not home yet. But, of course, *maman* is, and this is one of her good days. Why don't we go upstairs instead of sitting in the parlour? Then she can see you too, and I'll have Dinah bring the twins into her boudoir."

"I was jes' fixin' to bring 'em down to you, Miss Cresside, while I helps Lou Ida get dinner. They's woke up, and they's fussin some again. Can't nobody quiet 'em like you can."

This unexpected announcement came from the stair landing Dinah, huge, composed, competent, was standing there, a baby cradled on either capable arm, against her ample bosom. She came unhurriedly down the steps, a snowy tignon framing her dusky face, her full skirts brushing against the carpet as she descended

150

Beside her, on the white plaster wall, a long cashmere shawl, centred with scarlet, hung in place of a picture. Behind her, in its niche, stood the ancient Spanish statue, with tall sprays of cape jasmine rising from the silver vases on either side of it, and vigil lights burning before it. For a moment nobody spoke; something about the sight silenced even Regine temporarily. Then Cresside went forward to meet Dinah, and Fabian saw, with an immense wave of relief, that the smile which had left her lips had come back to them. Only it was not mocking any more, or gay either; it was triumphant.

"I'll be glad to take them, Dinah," she said quietly. "You may give them to me here. Then you can go right on out to the kitchen and help Lou Ida. I know she needs you." Cresside slipped a hand under Sybelle's downy head and lifted her gently, while the beautiful blonde baby smiled engagingly. "Hold her for a minute, will you, Fabian?" Cresside asked. "If you're going to be a steady customer of the house, you'd better begin learning how to take care of babies. I think perhaps we might all go out to the patio after all— the day cradle's there." She deposited the girl twin skilfully in Fabian's inexperienced but willing grasp and turned back to Dinah. Vail was already beating the air with chubby fists, and a broad grin of welcome, which disclosed two brand new teeth, illumined his rosy face. He bounded up and down with irrepressible vigour, and as Cresside took him from Dinah he gurgled with glee. She held him high and close to her, his dark hair touching hers, his big blue eyes level with her own.

"What do you think of the d'Alvery son and heir?" she asked. And this time, when she spoke, she did look at Sylvestre.

XI

THE opportune arrival of Gervais and Merry created an almost immediate diversion. Why, she had seen Sylvestre and Regine at St. Agnes', sitting on the Gospel side, in front, Merry exclaimed. If they had only said they were coming to Belle Heloise, she and Gervais would have driven right out themselves, instead of stopping by to see her mother. They could have done that later. Was somebody getting drinks for them? Had they been upstairs to see Madame Mère? Didn't they think the twins were adorable?

Her poise instantly eased the tension which Regine's chatter had only intensified, and carried the visit through to a more harmonious end than the beginning had indicated as possible. But she did not suggest that they should stay to dinner, or urge them to linger when they rose to take their departure after a rather brief call. Gervais went with her to the door when they took their leave, and hardly waited until they were out of sight to give her an exuberant kiss and a hearty hug.

"My, but you handled that beautifully, honey!" he said enthusiastically. "I've been dreading the Tremaines' call ever since they got back, knowing it was on the cards, and wondering how we'd get through with it. But you made it seem smooth as silk. I reckon I'll just have to make good as a politician after all—you'd be wasted as the wife of a mere planter!"

"I'm not wasted as *your* wife, whatever you do, darling. . . . What became of Fabian? He didn't slip off, did he? Of course, I meant to ask him to stay to dinner as soon as Sylvestre and Regine had gone."

"Oh, he's sure to be somewhere around! I think he'd just stay anyhow, whether you asked him or not. He knows perfectly well he's welcome. Don't worry about him—he'll turn up directly. Come on, let's get out of our church clothes and into something cooler."

They started up the stairway, arm in arm. Before they reached the landing where the Spanish statue was enthroned, Merry paused, releasing herself, and called to Cresside: Was she with the twins? Were they all right? Sybelle was in the day cradle on the patio, almost asleep, Cresside called back. She had Vail herself. He was fussing a little again, but he was all right. Both babies were all right. . . .

"I'll bet anything she's walking him up and down in her arms, the way all those new books Dr. Champagne has given us say you mustn't," Gervais muttered, speaking at the same time that he stopped to genuflect, in his customary casual way.

"Yes. I think she probably is. But it doesn't seem to do him any harm and he loves it. You know what Dinah says—'Can't nobody quiet him like Miss Cresside.' Sometimes I think Dinah knows more about babies than the men who wrote those books."

Merry genuflected also, more respectfully and formally than Gervais. He put his arm around her again.

"Maybe you're right. You usually are," he said. "And who's getting to be a darn good little Catholic too, I'd like to know?" he added in a pleased voice. "Didn't I tell you that everything would work out, if you'd just marry me? And it has, hasn't it? That time *I* was right."

"Yes," Merry agreed. "You were. It did work out. Everything's perfect, Gervais—our life at Belle Heloise and now this lovely trip we're going to have together, and next winter the new baby and all——"

They went on to their own room still happily embraced, and oblivious, as they so often were, of everyone in the world but each other. Momentarily they had forgotten about Cresside. But their surmise concerning her had been correct, at least in part. She was walking up and down with Vail in her arms, though she was not doing it, as they had pictured her, in the patio. She had gone into the garden-room, carefully closing the door behind her. It was not until after she had done this that she saw Fabian writing, with his back to her, at the flat-top desk which had come out of the old custom house in New Orleans.

"Why, hello!" he said, turning around, but without rising. "Am I in the way or anything? If I am I'll clear out. It doesn't upset me though, if you just want to change the baby's diapers. I figured I had a little spare time before dinner. And I thought I'd dash off a note to Happy Sevier, while I had the chance. He's gone back to Tallulah, now that vacation's on, and I'm thinking of spending a few days with him on the plantation."

"Good idea. . . . And you're unexpected but you're not *de trop*. And of course it wouldn't upset me to have you here while I changed Vail's diapers. What do you take me for—a pre-war prissy? When it comes to that, I wish you wouldn't talk like one yourself. But, as a matter of fact, Vail's dry, by some miracle. He's wakeful though. His teeth hurt him. I want to get him to sleep, and this is the quietest room in the house."

It's also the most detached room, Fabian said to himself. She was trying to get away and pull herself together, after an upsetting experience, just as I was, though I hope she doesn't realize that. And of course I'd have to stumble into the place she wanted to be. Now I can't very well clear out unless I make it pretty pointed that I know what's the trouble with her. I certainly take the blue for clumsiness. He turned away again, looking out of the window to Angus Holt's pleasant garden, only vaguely conscious, in his distress, of the glossy sago palms and prim brick-bordered flower-beds. But presently he became aware that Cresside had spoken the truth. She really did not mind having him there; in some strange way his presence was soothing to her. She had sought solitude, but what she actually needed was the sense of comfort and support that springs from sympathetic companionship. The realization that he could give this to her was both surprising and rewarding. He sat very still, without trying to talk to her, but watching her with increasing though unobtrusive attention. She was walking slowly up and down, holding the baby closely to her breast and singing to him as she walked. It was years since Fabian had heard the old negro melody:

> "Little David, play on yo' harp, Halleluiah!
> Little David, play on yo' harp, Hallelu.

> "One day, one day I was walkin' 'long,
>   Yes, I heard a reason f'om on high,
>   Say go in peace an' sin no mo',
>   Yo' sins are forgiven an' yo' soul set free.

> "Little David, play on yo' harp, Halleluiah!
>   Little David, play on yo' harp, Hallelu.

> "I pluck yo' feet
>   Out de miry clay
>   An' sot 'em on rock ob eternal age;
>   Where de win' may blow
>   An' de storm may rise
>   But de gates ob hell
>   Shall neber prevail.

> "Little David, play on yo' harp, Halleluiah!
>   Little David, play on yo' harp, Hallelu."

The verses went on and on, punctuated by the refrain, while Fabian listened and watched. Every now and then the baby's eyelids drooped, only to fly wide open again; every now and then he raised his downy head and looked belligerently around him with a sudden yell. He was fighting sleep with the same stubbornness that all the "mule-headed" d'Alverys displayed when they declined to accept a given situation. Cresside continued to walk and to croon, but Fabian could tell both from her step and from her voice that she was getting very tired. He rose from the desk.

"Couldn't I carry him for you a little while?" he asked. "You could go on singing, you know. But you could do it sitting down."

"Yes, I could. All right, take him. Thanks, Fabian."

Fabian could not remember when he had held a baby, except for the instant that he had taken Sybelle at Cresside's bidding, earlier that same day. Momentarily, he felt terribly awkward; but as he walked up and down with the mutinous infant in his arms, the sensation changed. He was gratified to find that Vail did not seem to resent the transfer, but almost immediately cuddled down with a resigned sigh; his eyelids drooped and did not rise again. There was something about the feeling of this warm, relaxed little body, pressed close to his own, that affected Fabian poignantly. So this was what it was like to have a child in your arms, even a child that was not your own! It stirred you to a deeper sense of responsibility and protectiveness than any other human experience—unless it might be the experience of guarding your own child. . . . And that child's mother. Profoundly moved, Fabian looked across at Cresside over the baby's nodding head.

"The inevitable recognition of proper authority, accorded to one male from another," he said, speaking lightly because he did not dare speak otherwise. "This kid shows he can put it over on you, but that he can't on me. I'm a fierce old cousin, not a doting aunt. Just call me in hereafter when you want a slight show of discipline, will you? Meanwhile, now that I've got him to sleep, tell me what to do with him next."

"You could take him out to the patio and put him in the double cradle with Sybelle. That's where he's supposed to sleep, of course. But I'd really rather keep him here—the less he's moved around, the less danger there is that he'll wake up. Suppose you lay him down on the bed. I'll sit here and watch him to make sure he doesn't fall off."

"Right. I'll sit here beside you and watch him too."

Cautiously, having deposited Vail on the four-poster with great care, Fabian pulled up two chairs, placing them side by side near the bed. For a few moments he and Cresside sat quietly looking at the baby without speaking to each other, then Fabian put out his hand and took Cresside's.

"Listen," he said. "Apparently Sylvestre gave you an awful shock by coming here today unexpectedly. Anyway, you acted as if he had."

"I know I did, and I'm sorry. But I got hold of myself right away. I don't think anyone but you noticed that I was shot to pieces."

"I don't think Regine noticed. I'm almost sure Sylvestre did, though. I know this is one of those things that's a lot easier to say than to do. But if I were you I wouldn't ever give him the chance to see you shot like that again."

"I'm not going to. I know I can't keep out of his way. I realize he's a near neighbour now, that the Hathaways are old family friends—oh, all the rest of it! But just the same——"

"Just the same, I hope you'll hang on to yourself the next time."

"I've just told you, I'll try. But why, specifically?"

"Because you've given him a jolt too, and I don't know how he'll react to it—perhaps by trying to 'talk things over,' which I know is the last thing in the world you'd want to do. Up to now I think he was labouring under the comfortable delusion that you and he had just fitted naturally into the post-war scene, and what either of you may have said or done was merely part of the picture. I don't think it ever occurred to him that the very sight of him would hit you like that—as if you'd suddenly seen a spreading adder. Well, I know you're not afraid of snakes, but you get the idea. I mean the way most girls would look if they did."

"I'm not afraid of snakes, but I do loathe liars. And that's what Sylvestre is—a damned dirty liar! He told me he loved me when he didn't. That's the only thing I'm holding against him. But it's plenty. Because I believed him. I wasn't just going in for heavy petting on general principles. I know you think that's part of what you delicately call the post-war scene. That and bathtub gin. But he knew I believed him when he said he loved me."

"I know it too, Cresside. And I never sized you up wrong. But——"

"I told Gervais he wanted to marry me, and I honestly thought he did. It wasn't until afterwards that I found out he'd been engaged to Regine all the time, that I didn't really mean anything to him. But after I'd started lying, I couldn't stop. I had to go on and on. He made a dirty liar out of me too!"

"He lied to you, and you lied about him, because you loved him, but that didn't turn you into a liar, Cresside. I'll grant you Sylvestre is a liar, and lots besides that you haven't called him. But I won't grant that you are. I won't let you call yourself that."

"You won't *let*——"

"No. And I won't let Sylvestre make your life miserable either. But you have to help. You mustn't give him the satisfaction of seeing he can upset you, and you mustn't get him to wondering why he should, so much. If you do, he'll try to find out. You'll have to pretend when you see him it doesn't mean a thing to you, one way or another. And presently it won't. You'll take it in your stride, the same way you've always taken things a lot harder than that."

"You're telling me this just to give me a lift."

"No, I'm not. I'm telling it to you because it's true. You don't think I'd lie to you, do you, Cresside?"

"I know you wouldn't. I know you never lied to anyone about anything that mattered."

"Well, then——"

He smiled at her and pressed her hand. But he did not try to say anything more, and neither did she. They continued to sit side by side in silence watching the sleeping baby, their mutual sense of recaptured tranquillity and new-found companionship merging into deep contentment. They were still sitting there when Dinah quietly entered the room and said that she would watch to see that Vail did not fall while they ate their dinner, which was now ready. There was nothing about her imperturbable and respectful manner to indicate that she had experienced any trouble in finding them or that their joint vigil surprised her. They went out together to join the others, leaving Vail in her safe keeping.

XII

FOR several days after Fabian's warning, Cresside watched guardedly for Sylvestre. But as time went by and she neither saw him nor heard from him, she gradually became less apprehensive. Besides, she was preoccupied in many other ways; she was helping Merry and Gervais with their preparations for departure, and taking over more and more responsibility for the twins. By Thursday evening, when the whistle of the *John D. Grace*, sounding from upstream, heralded its imminent arrival, she joined, with her customary appearance of gaiety, the little procession starting for the steamboat landing.

Considerable bustle attended the d'Alverys' departure: Amen headed the procession, wheeling a barrow piled high with bags, which he intended to place personally in the cabins reserved for his white folks, as he had no confidence in "steamboat niggers." He was followed by Dinah, wearing the costume she reserved for great occasions; but instead of carrying a twin on each arm, as usual, she propelled them in a perambulator veiled with a lace-edged mosquito bar, for at the approach of dusk the mosquitoes began to swarm in a vicious cloud. It was because of these same pests that Merry and Gervais, who came next, carried nothing but mosquito whips of slit palmetto, which they flourished constantly. Following the prospective travellers came Madame d'Alvery in the elaborate wheel chair which she now used when she went about the plantation beyond the pergola. It had a top shaped like a gigantic parasol, and the billowing fringe with which this was edged helped to keep off the insects; so did Lucie, who walked beside Selah as he pushed the chair, and who wielded a large fan, for Madame d'Alvery did not exert herself to the extent of using a mosquito whip. Fabian and Cresside brought up the rear, adequately armed, but somewhat neglectful of their weapons, because they were both trying unsuccessfully to keep Belizaire in line.

The five negro roustabouts who made up the steamboat's deck crew were already standing by the gangplank as the procession went over the crest of the levee, and, entirely uninhibited by the presence of quality, they began to call out eager invitations to Dinah. A trip to New Orleans would not cost her a cent, they assured her; they had space and to spare for the likes of her. The only response which Dinah condescended to make was brief and disdainful: she had a man of her own, not no River trash neither, and she wasn't leaving him right now; when she did travel with her white folks, they'd be paying her passage. While this exchange of compliments was taking place, the captain stepped forward— a burly man badly in need of a shave, who wore a yachting cap on the back of his head, but whose informal attire did not otherwise even suggest a uniform. Tugging at his straggly moustache, he wanted to know whether Captain and Mrs. d'Alvery had dined already. If not, perhaps they'd join the rest of the passengers, who were having steamboat hash in the saloon right now. . . . Oh, very well then! Probably they'd like to see their cabins first thing. Afterwards he'd be very glad to have them go up in the pilot-house, if they'd care to. It was nice and cool there and they'd get a good view of the River. . . . Nonsense, they were not to mention it.

Merry was enchanted with the prospect of going to the pilot-house, and it was the exuberance of her thanks which evoked the captain's disclaimer. He turned away, slightly embarrassed, to give an order to the mate, and Merry, experiencing her first misgivings about leaving the twins, now that the separation was imminent, bent over to kiss them tearfully, while she murmured final admonitions to Cresside and Dinah. When she looked up, she saw that the group at the gangplank had been enlarged; Sylvestre and Regine had joined the others, Sylvestre, looking rather sulky, was carrying a large beribboned basket, and Regine immediately enveloped Merry in one of her comprehensive embraces.

"Darling!" she exclaimed. "We've had such a hectic day we were afraid we couldn't get here, but we were determined to bid you good-bye, and somehow we made it. And look!—I brought you a *bon voyage* basket. Of course, in one way it seems absurd to see your friends off when they're only going as far as New Orleans, but after all, if that's the extent of their travels, why, then you know it seems important to them anyway!"

"Yes. It does seem important to me," Merry answered. "It seems very exciting. The basket's beautiful, Regine! And the captain's so nice! He's asked us to go up to the pilot-house!"

"Oh, that!" Regine said, with a slight shrug of her pretty shoulders. "Why, that's nothing but a little dark room with a bench on one side of it! And you don't see anything when you look out except the River, and the landings at the stupid little places where you stop. Now on an ocean liner, when you go up on the bridge, and see the big harbours as you come into them— Plymouth and Le Havre and, on the way home, New York—why, that really *is* something! Of course, mamma and Sylvestre and I were shown every courtesy on ocean liners. We sat at the captain's table and went to his quarters for cocktails, and naturally we were invited up to the bridge too. It was the most beautiful day, the morning we came into New York, and we saw——"

"How long are you going to be gone?" Sylvestre asked, turning to Gervais and handing him the basket, as Regine went on and on. Though he had not given the effect of interrupting her, since she was talking to Merry, she immediately interrupted herself in order to answer.

"Merry says they're coming back Sunday night on the Gulf Coast Limited," Regine announced. "She says they have drawing-room A. She's actually excited about that, Sylvestre! I've been telling her that you and I never dreamed of travelling without a drawing-room—except of course in Europe, where you have to take *compartements* on the *wagon-lits*. But then we always had two connecting ones, with a lavatory between, so it was even more spacious and convenient than a drawing-room. The European trains are so much better than ours, aren't they?"

"The ones I travelled on weren't," Gervais retorted. "They had accommodations for 40 *hommes*, 8 *chevaux*, and believe me there wasn't anything very spacious or convenient about that arrangement."

"Why, Gervais, you sounded a lot like Fabian the way you said that! I didn't know you ever got so sarcastic! Of course, I wasn't talking about war conditions, I was only trying to describe——"

Her patter was drowned by the whistle blaring the signal for departure; by the twins, whose behaviour so far had been exemplary, but who now howled with fright at this loud and sudden sound; and by Belizaire, who whirled around in circles, barking sympathetically. She clapped her hands over her ears with a playful gesture, backing away from the gangplank; then, after a brief pantomime designed to exact pity for her helplessness in the midst of such pandemonium, she linked one arm affectionately in her husband's, and began waving a lace-edged handkerchief with her free hand. Cresside and Dinah, firmly grasping mosquito whips, were already lifting the twins from the perambulator to soothe them, and calling out reassuringly to Merry, who had turned, halfway to the boiler deck, in a way which seemed to indicate that she could not bear to leave after all; while Gervais, speaking reassuringly also, propelled her on her way.

"They'll be all right in a minute," he said. "I reckon maybe we ought not to have brought them down to the landing. I forgot all about that darn whistle. And it's past their bedtime, anyway. But Cresside'll have them quieted in no time. Come on, honey, we mustn't hold things up any more—there's been a delay as it is, stopping the boat on purpose for us. Gosh, but it's a relief to get away from Regine's everlasting gabble, isn't it? She goes on like a Swiss music box. I'd like to dump this damned basket of hers overboard—we haven't any place to put it or any earthly use for it. Wouldn't you know that Dizzy Dora would come to a grubby little barge with a thing like this? Let's raffle it off at the ship's concert for the sailors' orphans. And now that that's settled . . . Where would you like to go first? To see our quarters, or straight to the pilot-house?"

Merry decided in favour of the former. These were tiny cabins, containing nothing except a single berth and a bowl and pitcher on a small wooden stand, and opening directly on the narrow middle deck, surrounding the dining saloon in a semicircle. A breeze from the River swept through them, cooler than any which reached Belle Heloise from May to November, and infinitely refreshing after the heat of the day; and in themselves they were not un-inviting: the coarse linen sheets on the bunks were very clean, and the well-painted shutters were carefully screened. But Merry's happy face clouded a little when she saw that there was no communicating door between her cabin and Gervais'.

"We're going to be really separated, aren't we, darling? For the first time!"

"Well, it isn't a very serious separation, you know. I can walk out of my door and into yours without much trouble—and I will! But there aren't any double beds on steamboats, worse luck, not even on luxury liners like those Regine keeps bragging about—perhaps that special feature doesn't seem as much of a disadvantage to her as it does to you! So you think you'll really miss me, do you?"

"You know I will. It does seem as if we could have managed somehow, in one cabin."

"Take my word for it, we couldn't! If we could have, do you think I'd have got two? Don't forget, I'm going to miss *you!* . . . Well, now that you've inspected our *suite de luxe,* suppose we go on up to the pilot-house."

Merry was more than willing. But as they stepped out on the narrow deck they found their passage blocked by almost the last person whom they would have expected to find among their fellow-passengers. Luigi Tramonte, wearing "store-bought" clothes and a turquoise stick-pin in his plaid cravat, had just emerged from the cabin beyond Gervais', and hastened towards them, beaming broadly.

"How you do, *Capitano!* How you do, Mis' d'Alvery!" he said heartily. "So you going to the city too? Now, ain'ta that a nice surprise, we meeta like this!"

"Well, it's a surprise to us too, Luigi," Gervais answered. "I generally travel by train, now that the old side-wheelers are gone. But Mrs. d'Alvery thought she'd enjoy the River trip. Do you take the *John D. Grace* often?"

"At first I take him only once a year," Luigi replied. "Now I take him two, three, maybe four time. I no can get alla I need for my trade in Baton Rouge. I gotta go to the city, but it don't costa so much. I gotta relations there, I staya by them. Mike Montagino, he's-a live back of Marrero, him and me is cousins. He gotta nice farm, too. I ride into town every morning on his vegetable truck. One very fine truck, but he can afford it. He's-a make'a plenty money on his farm with four girls and five boys already, and soon his wife have new bambino, make ten to help. He gotta nice house too, plenty room for company."

"That must make things pleasant for you, Luigi," Merry said.

"Ver 'pleasant and ver' cheap too, Mis' d'Alvery," Luigi assured her. "Mike he's a good fellow. I think maybe he make me a fine price on his old truck. He got new one now."

"So you're thinking of getting a truck, are you, Luigi, instead of saving for the fancy grocery store?"

"No, no, *Capitano*. I sava for fancy grocery store alla time. But if I have truck instead of cart, I make'a more money, and then I sava more too, see? Anyhow, I talk to Mike about it. I got plenty time to talk to him and buy what I got to buy. I buy plenty julery wholesale this trip, and Netta, she helpa me pick 'em out." He paused for breath, his jovial face taking on greater animation than ever. "You seen my Riccardo, but you ain't never seen my Netta, no, *Capitano*?" he inquired. "She don't go with me on the cart. She stay home, cook, clean, sew for me and my Riccardo. But always she comes to city with me. She's in-a there with Riccardo right now. I bring her out!"

He turned back to his cabin, and for a few minutes the sound of an unintelligible but heated argument came to the d'Alverys' ears. Apparently Netta was reluctant to present herself to her husband's patrons, and he was insistent that she should. At last he emerged in triumph, with his wife on his arm. Her face was downcast, her manner bashful; she could hardly be persuaded to look up, and, as she understood very little English and spoke less, conversation with her was necessarily limited. But in spite of these disadvantages, there was something very appealing about her. Only her unkempt hands, their roughness and redness accentuated rather than mitigated by her many rings, betrayed the hardness of the work she had always performed; otherwise she gave the impression of a contented and cherished woman, rather than a hard-working one, retaining in maturity, to a surprising degree, the loveliness she must have had as a girl. Besides the rings, she wore an abundance of other jewellery, strings of coral, and cameos in heavy settings which represented considerable value, and great golden hoops hung from her pierced ears. Her beautiful black hair was piled high on her graceful head in a crown of heavy braids, and confined with a tortoise-shell comb. Her dress, subtly suggestive of a peasant costume, set off her trim figure to great advantage, and her skin had the mellowness of a ripe peach. The few words that she was persuaded to utter were spoken in a voice that was sweet as well as shy, and the only time that she raised her head she revealed magnificent eyes and red lips parted in a hesitant smile over fine small teeth. Luigi regarded her with bursting pride throughout the difficult interview, and when she prevailed upon him to permit her return to their cabin he insisted that the d'Alverys should come too and take a look in at the door.

"Looka see, our cabin alla same like yours!" he said proudly. "And looka see Riccardo, whata good boy!"

The good boy was sitting up in the berth, still wide awake, but perfectly placid, and smiled an unembarrassed greeting to the visitors. Obviously he had inherited none of Netta's timidity, and his English was better than Luigi's. His mother helped pick out the jewellery when they went to New Orleans, he told the visitors, with a little prompting from his father; but he helped pick out the toys. He and papa were beginning to carry toys in the cart now, just a few; but when they got their truck, the old one that Cousin Mike was going to let them have now that he had bought a new one, there would be room for lots and lots of toys.

"That's right, Riccardo," Luigi said delightedly. "Next time we come to Belle Heloise, we bringa toys to the twins, don't we? We bringa doll to Sybelle for a present, then maybe the *Capitano* buy a ball for Vail! Now you go to sleep, that's a good boy!"

"*They* seem to be managing all right in one cabin," Merry murmured, after she and Gervais had finally succeeded in taking their leave of the Tramontes without hurting Luigi's pride by doing so too abruptly. "How do you suppose *three* of them can?"

"Oh, I suppose Netta curls up at one end of the bunk and Riccardo at the other! And that Luigi sleeps on the floor. And I don't believe any of them worries too much about washing. Perhaps I ought to say I'd be glad to sleep on the floor for the sake of sharing a room with you. But after all, you and I aren't Italian immigrants, and the sad fact remains that the reason Luigi's doing it is financial, not amorous. He wouldn't think of spending money on two cabins. . . . Obviously he's making money, though," Gervais added thoughtfully. "The next thing you know he'll have a whole fleet of trucks and that fancy grocery store too. Not to mention a house of his own that will knock the daylights out of his cousin's. But that's not our little red wagon! Come on, let's go up to the pilot-house."

It was even cooler in the pilot-house than it had been on the cabin deck, and at first it was very quiet. Evidently none of the other passengers had been invited to sit there, for Merry and Gervais had to themselves the bench Regine so contemptuously described. The pilot, a spare angular man in civilian clothes, nodded to them as they came in, but did not speak; he stood staring out into the deepening dusk, smoking a pipe and spinning his wheel with a nonchalant ease oddly at variance with his general awkwardness. After the boat was well under way, headed downstream towards Plaquemine, a variety of sounds began to drift up from below decks—the clatter of crockery negligently handled as it was washed and put away; the occasional clang of the fire doors leading into the boilers, as these were slammed shut; the rhythmic puff of the blower fan, almost as though the boat were drawing laboured

162

breath; voices of passengers who had finished their steamboat hash and were now seated on the forward deck, talking. But all these sounds seemed to come from a great distance, they were all indistinct and unfamiliar; Gervais and Merry, conscious of an alien atmosphere, spoke to each other in hushed tones, and only occasionally. Once Gervais addressed the pilot.

"Is it all right if I smoke a cigarette?"

"Sure."

Without elaborating on this statement, the pilot relapsed into the silence that had hitherto engulfed him. Eventually it became so oppressive that Merry and Gervais did not speak either. Gervais' cigarette made a tiny point of light in the enveloping darkness, but no other was visible except an occasional beacon until they came within sight of Plaquemine. Then the blaring whistle sounded again and the boat turned, backing water, to make the landing below the locks. A powerfully built, pleasant-faced priest, wearing a travel-stained cassock, disembarked alone, and a rubicund grocery-man standing by a mule-cart was apparently the only white person who had come to meet the boat; but half a dozen negro girls, dressed in flimsy blouses and bright-coloured skirts, were evidently awaiting its arrival with eagerness. Far from maintaining the attitude of contempt with which Dinah had regarded the roustabouts, they immediately opened an exchange of extremely broad jokes with these ribald deckhands, as the men began to carry boxes of groceries down the gangplank, depositing them near the waiting mule-cart.

"Don' yo' want a fella with a strong back fo' liftin' boxes, gal?"

"Huh! Strong back fo' liftin' boxes don' mean nothin'."

"Dat ain't what 'em gals on Rampart Street tells me, and dey done got you skint a mile fo' looks."

"Maybe dey is got me skint fo' looks, but dey don' know real mens like I does. Dem po' N'Yawlins folkses, dey don' never see no real mens like us has got on Bayou Plaquemine."

"Real mens! Some po' ol' cotton chopper, dat's all you's ever got."

This interchange of civilities did not seriously hamper the process of unloading, which was enlivened rather than hampered by it. The mate stood idly by, ostensibly to hurry the process, occasionally giving vent to a phrase or two of listless profanity, and then left the crew to go its own way, while he occupied himself with the placement of some timbers, on which to drive off the two Ford "phaetons" whose disembarkation he proposed to handle personally. The roustabouts, their heads grotesquely draped with gunnysacks which fell shawl-like to their shoulders, kept moving back and forth between the crest of the levee and the boiler deck, with the strange gait which was neither a walk nor a trot nor a shuffle, but which was so peculiarly their own. The boat's electric searchlight playing upon their figures etched these out vividly in the long oval radiance it threw upon the sloping grassy back-drop of the levee, and their shadows, shifting grotesquely about the sward, seemed bent upon a weird dance of their own. The roustabouts did not continuously banter with the bold little hussies who were so ready to jest with them. Some of them chanted, in a singsong as eerie as their gait, and as peculiarly their own.

"We got these twenty boxes to unload."

"Yes, Lord!"

"Twenty boxes offen de steamboat and up on de levee."

"Yes, Lord!"

"Pile gettin' smaller, boys, time to rest is comin' fast."

"Yes, Lord!"

"Only three more boxes left, boys. Oh, possum and cornbread!"

"Yes, Lord!"

"Jes' one mo' time——"

"Yes, Lord!"

The chanting and "coonjining" came to an end only when the unloading was finished. The soap and breakfast food, the salt and canned goods, were all on the crest of the levee then, and the rubicund grocer, having signed the waybills handed him by the mudclerk, was supervising the removal of the commodities he had purchased; the mule-cart began to move slowly down the ramp on the landward side of the levee. The mate, having supervised the adjustment of the timbers to form rails, in a way that was satisfactory to him, was trying to drive the first of the two Ford phaetons up the levee. It did not have power enough of its own to make the grade, and he was obliged to call the roustabouts, who were now resting from their labours, and joking again with the little hussies, to come and push it. The second phaeton behaved better; it bucked triumphantly over the crest and rolled triumphantly down the other side. With the disposal of the phaetons, the stop at Plaquemine came to a logical close. Blaring out one more whistle blast, the boat backed into the stream and floated off into the night; only the beacon lights, upheld by their tripods, pierced the profundity of the darkness.

"Have coffee?"

The taciturn pilot's abrupt question, suddenly shot out of the silence, was startling out of all proportion to its importance. However, both Merry and Gervais managed to answer in the affirmative, and the pilot leaned toward a speaking-tube attached to the wall, and, addressing some unidentified personage below decks, called imperatively for refreshments. An untidy mess boy promptly appeared carrying a tin tray, set with thick white cups, a battered sugar bowl, and a can of condensed milk.

"Take cream?"

Merry and Gervais said that they would; the coffee was very bad and the condensed milk did not improve it, but the travellers swallowed it somehow, feeling it would be ungracious to reject the pilot's expression of hospitality. Fearful lest he might repeat it, however, Merry said that she was beginning to get sleepy, and that she thought it might be a good idea to go to bed. They went carefully down the gangway, finding most of the cabins, including the Tramontes', already in darkness, but seeing the saloon still brightly illuminated. The captain, the mate and the mudclerk, together with three male passengers, were now having a game of penny ante, in which they were agreeably absorbed. None of them even looked up at the d'Alverys' approach; but almost simultaneously a sound of scuffling and sudden oaths, followed by a sharp outcry, came from the forepeak. The mate, swearing himself, vociferously this time, vaulted up and shot out of the door. As he tore past them, Merry shrank back, grasping Gervais' arm.

"What's happened?"

"Some kind of a sudden quarrel among the roustabouts. A knife fight, probably."

"They—they won't get killed, will they?"

"No, of course not. The mate probably has the fighters separated by now. He's used to dealing with that sort of thing—it happens often enough."

"But why should it?"

"It might be over a dice game—but most likely it's about one of those little hellions we saw on the levee. Even white men fight over perfect ladies, sometimes, you know. Come on, honey, let's get to bed. There's nothing to worry about."

She did not feel entirely reassured, but she did not want to seem silly either, so she smothered all further expressions of anxiety and withdrew, reluctantly, to her cabin. In spite of her happiness with her husband, there were still occasional moments when he made her uncomfortably conscious that she lacked experience and sophistication. She knew he did not do this deliberately, but she could never wholly suppress the pangs of regret that she did not, in every way, measure up to his standards; and she stood for a while in the doorway of her cabin, after Gervais had gone unconcernedly into his, wondering, against her will, whether the passage of time would intensify or eliminate the difference between them.

The turmoil on the forepeak had died down quickly, as he had predicted it would, and the interrupted quietude now seemed even more profound than before. The same alien quality in the atmosphere which had hushed her speech in the pilot-house overwhelmed Merry now; so did the unfamiliar attributes of the various landings which, at intervals, continued to interrupt the progress downstream. The blare of the whistle, the backing of water, the "coonjining" of the roustabouts were repeated again and again. At Bayou Goula a woman disembarked who was wearing a widow's veil of rusty crêpe and clutching a large black reticule of well-worn leather; an elderly man, also dressed in mourning, had come to meet her, and an old-fashioned fringed surrey, with an emaciated white-haired negro in the driver's seat, was waiting for her. At Whitecastle the departing passenger was a much-harassed mother, whose three fretful children importuned her incessantly, and whose husband called to her angrily from the shore, for God's sake, would she make those kids shut up. Merry speculated about these other travellers, whom she had never seen before, and would probably never see again; evidently they were all plain people, in even more moderate circumstances than hers had been before she married. All through the night such people would be getting off at landings along the way—Burnside, Donaldsonville, Convent, Vacherie, Lutcher, Edgard. By morning there probably would be no one left on the boat besides Gervais and herself and the Tramontes. Now that the glorious days of steamboating were over, not many through passengers used the River. To most persons these local stops represented convenience as well as economy. Very few went by River for pleasure. But Merry was glad Fabian had suggested the *John D. Grace* and that Gervais had fallen in with the idea, regardless of his scoffing remarks to the effect that stern-wheelers were in the same class as towboats. She was getting a great deal out of the trip; experiences like this would increase her fund of worldly knowledge, and for Gervais' sake she craved this.

At last she closed the door of her cool little cabin, and, climbing into her bunk between the coarse clean sheets, slept peacefully until a "high yellow" girl appeared at her bedside, carrying a red-copper tray set with morning coffee. Then she dressed with the utmost care in her crowded quarters. But she felt vaguely dissatis-fied with the results as she looked in the small blurred mirror hang-ing over the wash-stand. She had never used make-up and it did not occur to her to do so now; but she wished she might look her very best when she met Gervais' New Orleans friends for the first time, and she could not help believing that somehow she might have achieved better results if she had been in a less primitive place. She experimented with her curls, but they fell stubbornly back in their accustomed waves, and she had no better luck with her blouse, which already needed pressing, though it had been spick and span when she left Belle Heloise the evening before. Finally, unable to think of any other preparations or improvements she might make, she went on deck.

She saw no sign of Gervais and Merry decided not to wake him, as it was still very early. Luigi and Riccardo were not in sight either. But Netta was already standing beside the rail, gazing with obvious interest at some cargo ships which had formed part of the World War fleet but were now tied up in a "graveyard." On the other side of the River a four-master, stately even in abandonment, seemed like a great adventuress absorbed in reverie over the magnificent gallantries of the past. Merry had never seen one like it before. She spoke excitedly to Netta, indicating it.

"Look at that sailing vessel, Mrs. Tramonte! She must have been beautiful once, don't you think?"

Netta nodded, smiling assent. She seemed a little less shy than the evening before; her eyes were no longer downcast, and she responded more and more readily to Merry's exclamations of delight as each bend of the river disclosed some new spectacle: the towering grain elevator, with a little freighter flying a Norwegian flag drawn up beside its conveyors; the long low cotton warehouses, drenched in the morning radiance; the spotless liners of the Great White Fleet and the dingy ships from Brazil, respectively discharging bananas and coffee; the Chalmette refinery, looming up in the distance. Finally she spoke, slowly but resolutely, on her own initiative.

"I think Napoli more pretty. But I lika New Orleans best."

"I hope I'll see Naples some day. It must be very beautiful. But I don't believe, myself, that I could enjoy anything more than this. I'm glad you like New Orleans best, Mrs. Tramonte. Is it all right to ask you why?"

"In Napoli very poor. In New Orleans maka much money."

The reply seemed conclusive. Merry, her eyes on the distant silhouette of the sugar refinery, made no immediate attempt to answer it. Netta asked a question herself.

"Your man—he maka money in New Orleans too, no?"

Merry laughed. It was a laugh of contentment and security and pride, and Netta understood it as such.

"I think my husband's going to *spend* it there!" Merry said. "I think we're going to have fun, spending it together!"

XIII

THE *John D. Grace* had almost reached the Bienville Street landing when Gervais joined Merry on deck. He glanced swiftly around the wharf and almost instantly located a swarthy but extremely handsome young man, whose modish attire and slight swagger made him outstanding in the crowd.

"There's Billy Pereira now!" he said. "That lad who looks like a prosperous Spanish *elegant* and damned proud of it!" Then, as Billy Pereira looked up with a dazzling smile, doffing a very fine

167

Panama hat, Gervais called out, "Hello, Don Guillermo! So this is New Orleans!"

"Hello yourself!" Billy called back. "Hello, Mrs. d'Alvery! I'm sure enough grateful to you both for getting me up to see the sunrise. Quite a sight, isn't it? I'd almost forgotten. . . . And speaking of sights, give a look at my new bus, over yonder by the vegetable truck, will you?"

"Not that glassed-in Locomobile showcase!" Gervais followed the exclamation with a whistle. "Man, what bank have you robbed? Or are you just showing off the state of the coffee market?"

"Oh, the boys at the Boston Club paid for that—they thought I had mice in my panelling when I offered to bet on Parker in the election. I hope it didn't teach them a lesson—I'd like a private Pullman of my own—and the city election comes in September. Pretty smooth bus, though, isn't she?"

The Locomobile was certainly very smooth, and the vegetable truck parked beside it—also the latest model of its type—proved to be the one of which Luigi's "relation," Mike Montagino, was the very proud possessor. After the simple process of landing, the d'Alverys and Tramontes exchanged introductions to their respective hosts, who were both slightly staggered by these, then they all parted with mutual expressions of goodwill, and Billy Pereira continued his agreeable small-talk as the Locomobile turned into Canal Street and rolled smoothly along towards the Grunewald.

"I've got you a slick suite. I'm sure you'll like it, for it's really a knockout. We were all tremendously sorry that you wouldn't stay with us, but we understood this was a sort of belated bridal fling. Mother's counting on you for dinner at the house tonight, though, and she's asked a few friends in to meet you. Tomorrow I thought we'd take in the regatta from aboard the *Suzette III* and follow that with the dinner-dance at the Yacht Club—unless there's something else you'd rather do, of course. And father wants you both to come and look over the office—we've just finished remodelling the whole building. Three-thirty's a good time, because everyone knocks off for a cup of coffee then, and you might enjoy having it with the rest. But, of course, you'd be more than welcome whenever you could fit the visit in with your other plans."

They had no other special plans, Gervais said, in a gratified voice, while Merry listened with breathless excitement; they would be more than pleased to fall in with all of these. Of course, he wanted to call on his broker, Mr. Garfield, the first thing, to find out just how much of his sugar was sold and how substantial his credit was. If the news proved as good as he expected, he was going to take Merry to do some very special shopping after lunch, and they would drop in to the office for coffee as soon as they had finished it. Meantime, while he was conferring with Mr. Garfield, he believed Merry intended to look up some clothes. If either Billy's sister, or his mother, would take her to the best places, of course that would be extremely helpful. . . .

The pleasant plans speedily developed into delightful engagements. Billy's sister, Mary Ellen, called for Merry before she had time to unpack, and whisked the visitor away, in her own smart yellow roadster, for an "orgy of squandering," as she herself described it. Breathlessly, almost unbelievingly, Merry bought clothes for the maids, for the twins, for the new baby, for Madame Mère, for Cresside, for herself. Remembering Cresside's generosity, when she had come to Belle Heloise as a dowerless bride, she took a special pleasure in selecting an unusually smart outfit for her sister-in-law. She was going to insist that Cresside should come to New Orleans in the very near future, and have "an orgy of squandering" with Mary Ellen too. It would do her no end of good. Cresside had not "gone haywire over clothes," to borrow her own expression, since her accident, and Merry knew now, for the first time, just what she meant. She had been shut up far, far too long; it was not good for any girl, especially a girl like Cresside, who had so much natural *joie de vivre*. She ought to be getting out among pleasant people, enjoying herself. Merry even began to wonder whether Cresside could not be persuaded to consider Billy Pereira as a suitor, since unfortunately Charles Boylston did not seem to be making much headway. Billy was certainly very engaging, though Merry did not feel sure he was exactly Cresside's type, any more than Charles was. . . .

Gervais was lunching with Mr. Garfield at the Boston Club, so Mary Ellen took Merry to Antoine's, where two other girls, both pretty as pictures and smart as paint, joined them in the Mystery Room. Much of their conversation centred on recipes for home-made gin—"aged in the bathtub, all of five minutes"—and other expedients brought on by prohibition. One of the girls was preoccupied with the romance of Mary Pickford and Douglas Fairbanks, which "thrilled her to pieces." Merry was rather relieved when Gervais, looking very well satisfied with life, came breezing into the Mystery Room while blue flames were leaping upward from the bowl in which *cerise jubilées* were being served and said he was ready to take her away.

"You had a good time, didn't you, honey?" he asked, struck by the fact that she was rather silent, as they turned into Royal Street.

"Ye-es. They were all just as nice as they could be. And so attractive! But Cresside would have fitted in better than I did, Gervais."

"Look here, you haven't let those empty-headed flappers wear you down, have you? If you have, I'm sorry I left you in their sharp-nailed clutches! Which reminds me, I've got something on my own mind I want to talk to you about, when we get back to the hotel. But first we're going to do that very special shopping. Here, this is where we're headed."

"Here" was a fashionable jeweller's, where they were evidently expected, for an unctuous clerk immediately came forward, calling Captain d'Alvery by name, drawing two chairs up to a glittering showcase, and saying that Mr. Straus would be down in just a minute. While they awaited his arrival, Gervais outlined the purpose of their errand, hitherto unexplained.

"Mr. Straus is the head of this firm, honey. I telephoned him from Mr. Garfield's office and said we'd be in. I had very cheering news from my old broker—my credit balance couldn't very well be better. So while we're waiting for Mr. Straus to come I want you to start looking around for an engagement present and a wedding present and the present you had coming to you when the twins were born. Don't ask Mr. Straus how much anything costs. Just tell me what you want."

For a moment she could not answer him. Her eyes brimmed over with tears. which she rarely shed, and her lips, usually so firm, trembled uncontrollably. Gervais would never have believed that jewellery would mean so much to Merry, of all persons. He had not even taken Fabian's hint very seriously at first, and now he hardly knew whether to be pleased or piqued, because the suggestion had proved so felicitous. He did not understand that Merry's emotion was caused less by the prospect of possessing ornaments which almost every man who could afford it gave to his beloved, as a matter of course, than by the long-delayed discovery that he really wanted her to have these tangible proofs of generous devotion.

"Why, Merry, don't look at me like that!" he whispered, amazed in his turn. "If I'd known you were going to take it this way, I'd have warned you beforehand. Come, don't let those people in the store see you cry!" He squeezed her hand, surreptitiously, and leaned over the showcase, putting his head close to hears. "Listen, we'll look at these things together. Of course, the engagement present must be a ring. The only question is what kind."

A diamond solitaire, Merry managed to say, though speaking tremulously; she knew that lots of girls thought these were old-fashioned now, but that was what she had always wanted. . . . Why, they were not in the least outmoded, the unctuous clerk hastened to assure her, and Mr. Straus, appearing himself just then, genially corroborated the statement. A beautiful clear gem in a flat platinum setting—that was what Mrs. d'Alvery had in mind, wasn't it?

With the new solitaire sparkling on her left hand, Merry began to finger the string of pearls now laid out on a black velvet pad for her inspection. It was evident that Gervais felt a pearl necklace was the proper gift for a bride, just as she felt that only a solitaire was

170

exactly right for an engagement present. The chosen string, complete with a diamond clasp, was soon hanging around her neck, and a bar pin having been selected as the third item on the list, she fastened it slantwise to the front of her dress, in the same way she had noticed Mary Ellen wearing one at luncheon. She would feel conspicuous stepping out into the street again, she said, half in jest and half in earnest; she was afraid people would turn around and stare at her, she sparkled so. But she thanked Mr. Straus very graciously for his help and took her departure without too much apparent self-consciousness. Her eyes were brimming and her lips tremulous again as she passed through the door. But she regained her composure without admonition this time, and the call on the senior Pereira passed off with complete smoothness and great satisfaction to all concerned.

The coffee importing house was handsomely located in a beautiful old building ornamented, on the outside, with exquisite grill work which had been carefully preserved, and appointed, on the inside, with furnishings which represented the highest standards of office equipment. Immediately beyond the front door was a large round table with a black marbleized top, to which small swinging basins, uncomfortably suggestive of dental chair attachments, were fastened at regular intervals. At this table a bronzed, crisp-haired man was sitting, dipping, with a long-handled spoon, into some small tumblers which were arranged in front of him, making a strange sniffling sound as he put the spoon in his mouth, and then spitting out the brown liquid to which he had only just helped himself. This man, Gervais explained to Merry in a hasty undertone, was a professional "coffee taster"; the little tumblers contained coffee which he was sampling—"cupping," the process was called. Gervais did not have time to go into further details, for he and Merry were almost immediately swallowed up by the group of clerks eagerly pressing around the urn which dominated a small cupboard directly behind the testing-table. A smiling white-coated negro was deftly dispensing coffee from this urn, and the clerks who crowded around him, after accepting their brimming cups and glasses, began darting in every direction, intent on reaching their favourite spot to sip the fragrant brew. Merry tried to edge in among the other girls, excited at the prospect of sharing this pleasant experience with them; but before she reached the urn, Billy opened the door leading from some secluded sanctum in the rear and hastened towards her and Gervais.

"Hello, there! Father wants you to have coffee with him in his office. Why didn't you bring the missus straight in there, without waiting for me to come out, Gervais?"

"Well, she was getting a great kick out of it right here. So was I, for that matter! I'll say you've done a smooth job of remodelling. I'd hardly know the place, it's so changed since the last time

I saw it. That's a fine fresco, too!" He nodded towards the wall, which was adorned by a highly coloured painting of coffee-gathering peons, but as Billy did not seem disposed to let Merry linger any longer in the crowd, Gervais followed his host from the open offices to one that was completely enclosed, where the elder Pereira —almost as slim and quite as elegant as his son—was awaiting his guests.

"Well, Gervais! Well, young lady! Merry—that's your name, isn't it? I'm not going to stand on ceremony with a pretty girl like you. How do you like our quarters here, Merry?"

"I think they're fascinating. I never dreamed there were places like this in New Orleans—I thought they only existed in Rio de Janeiro, or Bogota, or some other exotic city. It's a sort of story-book place, Mr Pereira—especially this room!"

She looked around her with unconcealed admiration. The modernistic atmosphere of the outer offices had been carefully excluded from this one. It was sheathed in mellow panelling and furnished in richly embossed leather and intricately carved wood. A fine old portrait hung over the marble mantel, and rows of beautiful books, bound in half-calf, filled the shelves of a handsome bureau. The outstanding ornaments of the room, however, were the coffee cups scattered about it, ranging from exquisite gold and silver "miniatures" in glass cases and tiny after-dinner coffee cups, to large costly specimens in Spode, Crown Derby, lustreware and other priceless porcelains. Mr. Pereira, observing the appreciation with which Merry's eyes rested on these treasures of his, addressed her with increasing cordiality.

"I'm delighted that it pleases you so much, my dear young lady, delighted. . . . Yes, we've managed to preserve this room pretty much as it always was—basically, I mean, basically. Of course, we've added the little knick-knacks I saw you looking at ourselves. . . . If you ever run across anything that would fit well into my small collection, don't fail to let me know. Now which are you going to have—iced coffee or hot coffee? Jerry's waiting to take your order."

The smiling negro who had been presiding at the nickel urn was now standing in the doorway, beaming more broadly than ever. Merry said she would take hot coffee, thereby going up a peg further in the old connoisseur's estimation. More or less monopolizing the conversation, and directing it towards her, he went on chatting volubly.

"So you didn't realize how successfully we could compete with Rio de Janeiro or Bogota when it came to an exotic atmosphere? You must persuade your husband to bring you to New Orleans often, my dear Merry, and learn better, you really must. What is there about your part of the State that makes people so loath to leave it? Once they get there, they stay on and on. Now take that

172

handsome young man who had a vague idea he'd like to learn the coffee business—I mean Sylvestre Tremaine. He's the son of two of our oldest friends; in fact, you'll meet his parents at our house to-night. I'd have been glad to push him straight to the top, if he'd only shown the slightest sign of applying himself to the work. But no, his mind was wandering off all the time in the direction of the River Road—well, perhaps I ought to say in the direction of a lovely young lady who lives there. Anyway, he wasn't of any use to me. I finally had to tell him I thought he'd do better in sugar. I hope I wasn't a poor prophet."

Merry looked at Gervais questioningly, uncertain how she ought to reply. He caught the glance and answered for her.

"I'm afraid you were, sir. Sylvestre won't ever make a planter. His place is riddled with mosaic disease right now, and he isn't doing a blessed thing about it."

"Well, well, I'm sorry to hear that. But I suppose one must make allowances for these young husbands. They can't help being pre-occupied. Can they, my dear?"

Merry did not feel equal to discussing this either. She was un-certain whether to say Gervais had never neglected his work for her, or whether to infer that he was so passionately in love with her that their plantation had also suffered from neglect. She was glad when Gervais took up the ball for her a second time, and gladder still when an inconspicuous gesture of his prompted her to give the signal for departure. The chance mention of Sylvestre Tremaine had clouded her enjoyment in the Pereira's unique establishment.

She was also slightly disappointed at finding that the Pereiras did not live in the French Quarter, which she had somehow taken for granted, but in the new "development" at Gentilly, which Gervais explained to her was a corruption of the French Chantilly, adding that a highway leading from there to Versailles, the old De La Ronde plantation on the River, was called the Paris Road. She listened, with polite attention, to these enlightening details as they rolled along in the "glassed-in showcase" which had been sent to take them to the dinner party; but the spacious modern mansion, with a three-car garage and wide-spreading lawns, to which they were driven in such luxury, did not begin to give her the same thrill she would have derived from a house with a quaint old patio, "wing-rooms" and a courtyard kitchen. The assembled company, though unquestionably distinguished, was also slightly overpower-ing; she was self-conscious in the presence of Sylvestre's parents, and her faltering command of French deserted her when the Consul began to talk rapidly to her about the attractions of Paris and the Riviera, which he seemed to take it for granted she had frequently visited. A young man in whom Mary Ellen was obviously very much interested, and a young girl to whom Billy was more complacently attentive than was pleasing to Merry, in the light of her newly hatched plans for Cresside, were the only other persons of their age in the room; the remainder were all important, formidable and middle-aged. Only the realization that the dinner dress which Mary Ellen had helped her to choose that very morning was the prettiest one at the party, and that her new pearls could bear comparison with the string Mrs. Pereira was wearing, helped her to forget that it had been a long day, that she was very tired, and that mentally as well as physically she had digested all she could. She almost went to sleep, on the way back to the Grunewald, with her head on Gervais' shoulder; and she came to herself with a start, when the car stopped, to hear Gervais suggesting that they might go down to the "Cave" and take a few turns before they went to bed.

"The Cave?" she said in bewilderment. "What cave, Gervais?"

"Not the sort that produced the prehistoric gents who clubbed their lady friends into loving them," he said teasingly. "Wake up, honey. It's just one of the features of the Grunewald—a big ballroom a few steps below the lobby level, where the decorations are stalagmites and stalactites, made of papier mâché, *bien entendu*. There's a jazz band and a fine floor show. Come on, let's have a couple of one-steps and see what we can get in a teacup besides tea, if anything. It'll just top off the evening for us."

The anticipation of peace and privacy in their own suite was much more appealing to her, at the moment, than the prospect of the smoke-filled atmosphere of a noisy public room, filled to suffocation with revelling strangers. But she could not selfishly refuse him so small a favour at the end of a day which he had made such a happy one for her. He guided her adroitly through the crowded lobby, nodding casually to several acquaintances as they wove their way along, but not pausing to speak to anyone until they had almost reached the entrance to the Cave. Then, stopping abruptly, he held out his hand to an immense man dressed in superbly tailored Shantung, who almost blocked the doorway.

"Colonel Sullivan!" he exclaimed. "I don't know whether you remember me—Gervais d'Alvery."

"Why, hello, Captain d'Alvery! Of course I remember you. How are you?" Sullivan said cordially, his extraordinary voice booming above the conflicting sounds which made up the tumult in the lobby. "Is your cousin here with you? Oh—Mrs. d'Alvery! Delighted to meet you. Are you staying here at the Grunewald?"

"Yes, for a few days. We were just going down to the Cave. Won't you come with us?"

"Thanks, but my dancing days are over. If you'll come up to the Elks' Roof tomorrow night, though, I'd like to have you as my guests. I've got a pretty good locker there."

"We'd like to very much. We're going to the Yacht Club for the regatta, and taking in the dinner-dance afterwards, but we won't stay late."

"Good. I'll expect you. By the way, I'll be in Baton Rouge again next week. I'm doing what I can to help the Governor on this Constitutional Convention Bill that's coming up. . . . Do you see eye to eye with him on that?"

"I had a talk with him about it a few days ago. He has a way of making me see eye to eye with him."

"That's a great John Parker, isn't he? I think I said that to you before. Well, I mustn't detain you now. But I'll be seeing you to-morrow night and next week too. I was planning to get in touch with your cousin anyway."

"We'd like very much to have you take dinner with us at Belle Heloise, Colonel Sullivan. We'll make it a point to have Fabian there too."

It was rather surprising, Merry thought, as she finally drifted off to sleep after many times "two turns" in the Cave, that Gervais had put it just that way, almost as if he were piqued because Colonel Sullivan had spoken twice about Fabian. After all, Fabian was coming to Belle Heloise with increasing frequency now in any case; the chances were more than even that he would be there whenever Mr. Sullivan came to dinner. And it was not strange that Mr. Sullivan should have taken a liking to Fabian. Everyone liked Fabian. Not that she would have thought he would stand out especially in the same group with Gervais. Probably Gervais wasn't really annoyed. Probably he was only surprised. . . .

It was very late when they waked—so late that, eager as Merry was to crowd everything possible into their brief holiday, she agreed with Gervais that it was not worth while trying to go out that morning. Instead they breakfasted in their bedroom, lingering over their coffee in the pleasant way that had become a habit during the early months of their marriage, when Gervais came in from the fields for his second cup.

"You said, just as we were leaving Antoine's yesterday, that there was something special you wanted to tell me when we got back to the hotel," Merry reminded him, spreading jam over her buttered toast. "Did you forget? Or wasn't there time?"

"No, I didn't forget. There wasn't time. But we'll take time now. . . . I've been thinking for a long while, Merry, that I'd like to do some restoration at Belle Heloise."

"Restoration?"

"Yes. You know those small empty buildings back of the Big House? Of course, they're in a terrible state of dilapidation now, but they're not too far gone to restore, and I'd like to do it. They balance the *pigeonniers* in front—nearly all the old places had some sort of symmetrical design. One of those buildings used to be a storehouse, with a room at one end that my-grandfather and great-grandfather used for an office. My father never cared to spend much time in an office, so he let the whole storehouse fall to pieces. But I'd like to rebuild it—we really need one—and revive the office custom. There really isn't enough space upstairs for me to spread out my private papers—the ones I don't care to keep in the sugar house; there's going to be less and less as our family grows. And, of course, *maman* would shudder at the very thought of having me put the parlour or the library to any useful purpose!"

"I think it would be wonderful for you to have an office of your own, and to use it the way your grandfather and great-grandfather did. . . . What about the other little building?"

"Why, that was the *garçonnière*—all the unmarried sons of the family slept there, in the early days, after they got away from their mothers' apron strings, and all the bachelors who came to the house as guests. My father stayed in it for months and months before he was married, and then he and my mother lived in it until her parents died." Gervais paused for a moment, recalling, with his usual reluctance, the story of Philogene's strange wedding night. He had never told it to Merry, and he did not intend to do so now, but he could not help thinking about it. "Of course, then it ceased to be a *garçonnière*—as a matter of fact, Cresside and I were both born in it. But it never was kept in really good condition after the War Between the States, and when my father and mother didn't need it any more they let it disintegrate, like the office. They thought it represented just one more needless expense."

"But you don't?"

"No. I'd like to rebuild it. I found the old plans, tucked away at the back of the bottom drawer in the plantation desk, not long ago. I didn't say anything to you about them then, because I wasn't too sure how I was coming out for money. But after my talk with Garfield this morning I feel justified in going ahead. Of course, I'd have to modify the interior a little to put in modern plumbing and so on. But the general effect would be the same as it used to be." He paused again, not because of an unpleasant recollection this time, but to give emphasis to his next question. "How'd you like to have a little house of your own, honey? A little house where you and I could be by ourselves? Don't you think that would be fun?"

"Fun! I think it would be heavenly! But are you sure——"

"Yes, I'm sure. I didn't spend the whole morning in Mr. Garfield's office—I talked to an architect for half an hour too. He says he's sure I can find someone in Baton Rouge to do the job, but that if I can't he'll undertake it himself, whenever I say the word. And I'm willing to say it tomorrow morning, if you'll give the plan your blessing."

"Gervais, I don't think I can stand it, if you keep springing surprises on me like this! First all that beautiful jewellery and now a
176

little house of our own! Have you got the plans with you? Can you show them to me?"

"Yes, they're in my suitcase. Wait a sec, I'll set the tray down outside, and we can spread them on this table."

Merry bent entranced over the mottled sheet of paper, brittle with age, which kept curling up at the edges until she weighted down its four corners with toilet articles. The original plan showed three large rooms downstairs, with three dormers above; the rough sketch which the architect had drawn from these indicated that one of the downstairs rooms could be divided to provide for a bathroom, a small dining-room and a kitchen. The other ground-floor rectangles were labelled "living-room" and "master's bedroom," each with a fireplace, those representing the dormers "baby's day nursery," "baby's night nursery," "baby's bath and linen closet." Merry looked up questioningly.

"It's lovely, but it isn't very large," she said. "There wouldn't be room for all of us, would there? We wouldn't take Dinah and the twins with us?"

Gervais picked up the plans, and, re-rolling them neatly, placed them back in the metal tube from which he had taken them. "Well, I don't know," he said slowly. "What do you think? I'm afraid it might be pretty crowded for them and Philogene too, and we'll have him almost as soon as the house is done. We'll have to get a second nurse anyway, and the twins and Dinah are pretty well fixed where they are. Maybe it would be better to leave them in the Big House. But we don't need to decide that right now. Come on, honey, we've got to dress. I'm afraid we've run a little too close to the wind as it is."

The telephone on the little table between their beds rang as he spoke; the doorman was calling to say that Miss Pereira was waiting for them at the Baronne Street entrance. They dressed with frantic haste and dashed downstairs in record time, breathless with apologies. It didn't matter at all, Mary Ellen said, smiling at them from her yellow roadster. They had plenty of time, if they made it snappy; but perhaps they had better shove off now. . . .

They sped out by Canal Street to the cemeteries, whose white tombs rose like tiny marble houses along well-ordered streets; then they turned across the New Basin Canal to the dusty shell road and continued until they passed the huddle of road-houses that fringed a little park along the Lake Pontchartrain wall. Skirting this, they came to the small fenced-in wharf reserved for the use of Yacht Club members, where an imposing bridge-deck cruiser, flashing with paint and brass, was moored alongside.

"Like in the stories about yachting," Merry whispered to Gervais, as a white-jacketed steward showed them aboard through the gap in the yacht's ornate railing and conducted them to the after-deck, where gay wicker furniture was attractively disposed under an ochre-coloured awning. The older Pereira, dressed in white linens, a blue jacket and a yachting cap, rose from one of the orange-painted chairs to greet them.

"Welcome aboard the *Suzette!*" he said heartily. "Make yourselves at home! Gervais, you'd better change that Panama for one of the spare caps downstairs, if you can find your size, or you're more likely than not to lose it at the first good puff of wind. And Merry, I suggest you let Mary Ellen fix you up with a scarf or something, to tie around those pretty curls of yours. . . . Now let me see, do you know everybody here?"

General introductions began and the cap and scarf were both forthcoming before these were finished. Meanwhile the steward approached, and, making a round of the guests, inquired what they would like to drink. Apparently there was a limitless stock somewhere below, for nearly everyone chose something different, yet all were supplied with the greatest liberality. Slowly sipping her Tom Collins, Merry took in the quaint contrasts which the novel scene afforded.

An intermittent procession of schooners, loaded with lumber, shells, turpentine and other produce from the Piney woods section of St. Tammany Parish were moving into the Basin. At one side of its mouth was the spreading yellow-and-white Yacht Club; on the opposite point an octagonal lighthouse; and beside this a couple of shed-like buildings which she learned were rowing clubs. From one of these a quartette of bronzed figures emerged, carrying a long slim shell; and deftly placing this in the water, the oarsmen clove through it towards town at an amazingly swift clip. Another luxury yacht churned past the *Suzette*, bound for the open lake, followed by a dingy lugger which had evidently started life as a sailing vessel. Following the progress of these with a fascinated gaze, Merry suddenly saw something even more extraordinary.

"Look! Do look and tell me what all this is—a parade?"

"Why, those are only the fish boats," Gervais explained, a trifle condescendingly.

"You can't mean that," Merry protested. "I know I'm new to all this, but those lovely little white ships, so clean and all, can't be fish boats! And why are they all in line, tied one behind the other like that?"

Sensing her shy guest's bewilderment, Mary Ellen looked at Gervais reproachfully and hastened to explain. "It's this way," she said. "A while back some of the boys figured that the best way to race was in boats made exactly alike or as nearly as they could be. They thought half the fun was gone when you knew in advance which boat was faster, or when anyone with money enough to get a faster boat could make certain of winning. So they got an architect to design a little sloop, which could be sailed by one man with two others for a crew, and the Club built twelve of them exactly

178

alike. Each was named for a fish, and so they were called fish-class sloops. Now they're called fish-boats for short."

"Thanks," Merry said gratefully. "And where is that grey boat taking them all?"

"That's the Yacht Club Patrol Boat, hauling them out to the lake, so that they won't impede traffic while they're tacking back and forth across this narrow little old Basin, and take forever getting outside. As soon as they're past the breakwater, you'll see them all cast off and put up their sails, each sail with a little red fish on it. And it's a lovely sight! Then the race will be on, and the man who wins will do it because he's sailed his boat best, not because he had the fastest one."

"That's right, Merry," Mr. Pereira said, continuing where his daughter left off. "And you'd be surprised how popular those boats have become. All the Gulf Yacht Clubs have adopted them, and Sir Thomas Lipton was so impressed with them when he visited us a few years ago that he donated a five thousand dollar cup— it's awarded for a year to the club winning the fish-class regatta on Labour Day. We race the little fish-boats every week-end, and the skippers having the highest standing at the end of the season are chosen to represent their club in the Lipton Trophy Race."

"And Billy's right in there near the top," Mary Ellen chimed in. "He's almost a certainty for the Lipton Team this year—he and Billy Porteus and Eddie Keep. We've got some keen skippers. . . . Look, there's our Billy now!"

"Keep your eye on us and give us your moral support!" her brother shouted from the tiller of his little sloop, the eleventh in line when the procession was towed past the *Suzette's* berth. A moment later the smooth string began to break up and bob about in the choppy lake and almost on the instant the line scattered. The cream-coloured sails were hoisted and shaken out, revealing their red insignia, as the vessels heeled to the smart breeze and began to manœuvre. Mr. Pereira called to his skipper.

"Let's go out, Captain!"

Somewhere beneath their feet a starter whirred and motors began to turn. The white-jacketed steward moved nimbly to the foredeck, cast off the bow line, and then hurried aft to cast off the stern line from the bollards along the wharf. Slowly the big yacht took on headway and moved lakeward. At the first chop of the waves Merry glanced doubtfully at Gervais, and he smiled reassuringly.

"That doesn't amount to anything, honey," he told her. "You'll get used to it in no time." But as he spoke a small cannon boomed without warning, and Merry jumped, stifling a small scream.

"The five-minute gun," Mary Ellen said soothingly. "That gives them a chance to jockey for position—knowing that they have five minutes before the race will start. They've all got stop-watches. When I'm in one of the Skipperette races I always think this is the most exciting moment, because usually, at the finish, the boats are too far apart to make it thrilling."

The *Suzette* had been headed for a bobbing metal buoy when the five-minute gun sounded, and by the time the starting gun boomed its message, she had reached a point well along the triangular course. Merry took the second report more calmly than she had the first, but she was confused by the huddle of sails weaving in and out at the starting line.

"They're all going in different directions," she said in a puzzled voice. "Why don't they all go the same way if it's a race?" She turned appealingly to Mary Ellen, who obligingly made a diagram designed to clarify the mysteries of tacking into the wind; but the sketch which her hostess drew so easily seemed very complicated to Merry and after a moment she laid it down.

"It's too much for me," she said apologetically. "But the little ships are beautiful. . . . Where's Billy now?" she added, fearful lest she might have sounded unappreciative.

"He's on the starboard tack," Mary Ellen replied absently, her attention now centred on the approaching flotilla. "Wait till he comes about. You can tell how they stand on the race by the order in which they'll round this buoy. And the same way at the next buoy, and so on. There go the first ones—damn! I think that's Ed Pinac. Billy'll be fourth. Yep—there they go!"

Again the *Suzette* got under way, heading this time for the buoy at the lakeward apex of the triangular course, and, for three laps around the triangle, her passengers watched the progress of the race. Finally the cannon boomed again, for the first yacht had crossed the finish line, with Eddie Keep at the tiller. Merry was on the point of offering condolences, when Mary Ellen clapped her hands delightedly.

"Our Willum's an easy second, children!" she cried. "And that keeps him right up there at the top of the standings. Let's take a little turn around the lake before we go in, Daddy, and give Merry something of a trip. You know how Billy is, he won't want dinner for ages yet. First they'll all go to the bar and sail the race over again. And then somebody'll start a dice game, and finally the showers and all. If we go in now we'd just have to sit around and hear the rocking chair fleet tell about the races they used to sail in the *Calypso* or the *Skimmer*. We can kill a couple of hours better out here."

Mr. Pereira nodded indulgently and gave the necessary orders. Soon they were running eastward past the distant, feathery trees at Citrus and Littlewoods, and sounding the siren imperiously for the drawbridge in the railroad trestle spanning a narrow point in the lake. Then, after a tempting glimpse of Fort McComb in the distance, they turned about. The pastel twilight was deepening over the lake now, and the water was smooth as glass, for the wind had died with the sunset. Beacon lights were beginning to wink along the shore, and from the Yacht Club beamed a strong white shaft of radiance. Merry leaned back in her comfortable chair, contentedly breathing in the soft air, her pleasure no longer marred by perplexity. She was genuinely sorry when they cut past the breakwater to the wharf again, but she was getting tired too, though it was still only the edge of the evening, Mary Ellen told her afterward, as they "freshened up" at the club. The crowd was going to meet for dinner on the broad screened gallery built out over the water, and afterwards there would be dancing inside, with ship lanterns for lights. And Billy would want to show Merry the trophy case with the lovely Lipton Cup that formed the centrepiece, and the photographs of past Lipton teams and famous old yachts. . . .

Somehow Merry braced herself to see it through, and afterwards it all became a glowing memory. But she was almost frantic with fatigue before the dance ended, and when Gervais reminded her that they had promised to meet Mr. Sullivan on the roof of the Elks' Club, she looked at him with entreating eyes and gave a little groan which she made no effort to suppress.

"O.K., if you're sure enough all that tired we'll go back to the Grunewald. But Sullivan's important to me politically, Merry."

"I forgot about that. I reckon I can keep going another hour or so. That would be enough to show we appreciate his invitation, wouldn't it?"

"Plenty. And we can sleep late again tomorrow morning, you know."

It was indeed very late when they woke after their gala evening —so late that the Jesuit Church, where there was a twelve-ten service every day in the year, was the only one where they could still possibly get to Mass. Gervais made this announcement without much enthusiasm, from the bed which was effectually separated from Merry's by a telephone table to which a large metal lamp was immovably affixed. Sitting up herself, so that her view of her husband would not be wholly obstructed, Merry saw that he was still lying on his back, with his arms thrown over his head and his eyes half closed.

"Is it far from here?" she inquired, tossing her curls back from her forehead and reaching for her dressing-gown.

"No. Just across Baronne Street. At that, I don't know we could make it by twelve-ten."

"We can try, can't we?"

"Oh, I suppose so! . . . You're not going to end up more Catholic than the Pope, are you, Merry, after that good Baptist upbringing of yours? Dragging me out to church when I'm still half dead with sleep?"

"I'm not dragging you out. I thought you wanted to go. I thought you told me all Sundays were 'holy days of obligation,' and that unless you were prevented by illness or some other emergency——"

"Oh, hell! I suppose I did tell you that! But I didn't realize you were going to be such an apt pupil. Give me a kiss, anyway, before you force me to get up, without any mercy, after a tall Saturday night."

He smiled at her invitingly, still making no move to rise. Merry slid out of her bed and sat down on the edge of his. He put his arms around her.

"Happy, darling?"

"You know I am."

"Love me a lot?"

"You know that too."

"I need to have you say so, about once in so often, or I'm not easy in my mind."

"I thought things were supposed to be the other way around. I thought it was wives who complained if they weren't reassured on that point often enough, not husbands."

"That's just the popular fallacy. I feel terribly in need of reassurance right now, Merry."

"All right. I love you. I love you more than tongue can tell. But I'd love you a lot more if you'd stop acting like a spoiled child. You don't really need any reassurance; you only want me to keep on flattering you until it's too late to go to church."

"It'll serve you right if the epistle is that one about wives being subject to their husbands. It'll inspire me to demand more docility. I'll get even with you for this yet."

He grumbled, under his breath, until they were actually in their pew, and afterwards in the taxi which they took down to Esplanade, where they dined in state with Madame Omer Estrade, an elderly cousin of Madame d'Alvery, whom she greatly resembled. But considerable merriment was mixed in with his mutterings, and Merry knew that he was not really angry, that he was only teasing her in the way that amused and delighted him. All the other Estrade relatives still living in New Orleans had been bidden to meet them, and again Merry was somewhat overpowered by the importance and dignity of the company in which she was expected to hold her own. The Estrades were all extremely civil to her, but they could hardly be termed cordial; they talked on and on among themselves, while course after course was served, about people and places about which she had never heard, apparently oblivious that they were excluding her from the conversation or indifferent to this fact.

182

"I really believe, Euphrozine, that Lolotte received more presents for her First Holy Communion than any child I ever knew. Not that this surprised me—a little angel, if ever there was one. I could not control my emotion when I saw her going up the aisle of the Cathedral, wearing her white veil, with her hands folded in prayer and her eyes fixed on the altar. I felt as if any moment she might be taken from us and transported to heaven."

"You have reason, Anzolette. My sentiments were the same. But speaking of veils, and of gifts, did you realize that there were more than twenty yards of rose-point lace in Coralie's bridal costume and that she received almost a thousand wedding presents? Those flounces on her skirt, which she inherited from poor, dear Eugénie, were simply priceless, and Vincent de Laune gave her the most magnificent parure of diamonds and rubies I have ever beheld. She did not wear more than half of it at her wedding, for fear of parading too much splendour. But she showed the complete set to me privately, so I know whereof I speak. Nevertheless, had she been my daughter, I should not have approved the match. Of course, the de Launes are very well connected. But they have never been on terms of intimacy with the d'Alverys. And I have heard it said that old Hyacinthe de Laune, Vincent's grandfather——"

"Yes, yes, I know that story too. We can only hope there is not a word of truth in it, for Coralie's sake. It would be terrible if her children . . . And if I'm not mistaken, she is already *enceinte*——"

"She was, but there has been a disappointment. Now she must repose herself indefinitely. First, of course, to recover from this present crisis and secondly to avert similar calamitous episodes. I trust she will be warned by the experience of Justine, who declined to listen to advice from me or anyone else. It is no secret any longer, I suppose, that she has now had a series of mishaps and has had to abandon all hope of a child. I am not surprised that Roland has sought consolation elsewhere."

"Yes, and I hear he has lost heavily at the races besides. Did you not tell me, Dominique, that Roland had not once backed a winning horse this season?"

While this went on Merry sat for the most part in silence, tasting superlative dishes and sipping vintage wines, though Gervais, no longer in a teasing mood, adroitly contrived to bring her into the conversation now and then. The afternoon was already far gone when the Estrades finally filed solemnly from the sombre dining-room to the sumptuous drawing-room, where coffee and liqueurs were served amidst a lavish display of bric-à-brac, marqueterie, gilt-framed mirrors, crystal chandeliers, family portraits and brocaded furniture; and while these refreshments were being passed, fresh cohorts of visitors began to arrive. These, it appeared, were not close relatives like the dinner guests who still lingered on; but they were kin just the same. Merry, whose own family was small and detached, had never before visualized such a circle as this, complete, compact and self-sufficient; she had never before listened to such endless and satisfied discourse on trivialities.

"I cannot understand how Dieudonné ever consented to the sale of Trianon! To be sure, it was in terrible disrepair, and he was so heavily in debt that he could not possibly have repaired it. But I should have let it fall down around my shoulders before I should have sold it to Yankees! Protestants from Chicago!"

"I do not think I even know their names, Simeon."

"North. I have never heard of any Norths in Louisiana. They are doing the place completely over—ten bathrooms, among other superfluous luxuries. Dieudonné is taking Melisande over the Lake. He says he is going to look for a small place at the Pass. I do not see how he could ever have peace there, using the money he got from Trianon to buy a place in Mississippi!"

"Mr. Le Breton offered to send Bertrand on the Grand Tour with his two sons, but René has declined to let him go, very wisely, I think. There is no reason why Bertrand should leave New Orleans. He has never created even the smallest scandal. And with René's practice ready made for him to step into, the way it is——"

This was still going on, with no signs of stopping, when Gervais rose, saying they would not have time to pack, unless they returned to the hotel immediately. Upon hearing this announcement, the relatives apparently ceased to regard him and Merry as outsiders, for they immediately gathered around, making long farewell speeches and sending interminable messages to poor Cousin Isabelle, who was such a patient sufferer, and dear little Cresside, who must be quite a big girl by now, and the sweet, precious twins, who must without fail be brought to New Orleans. As a result of these tardy and prolonged courtesies, the travellers caught their train with only one minute to spare, and Merry stretched out thankfully on the hard little sofa in drawing-room A and slept most of the way to Baton Rouge. When she came briefly to herself from time to time it was to hear Gervais teasing her again.

"I'm sorry that party wasn't more comprehensive. I missed about six families, all told, and they average ten to the family. My great uncle Theodore wasn't there, for instance, and only four of his daughters. He's quite deaf, so that everything you say to him has to be repeated several times. Then there's my second cousin Elaine. She has a slight impediment in her speech, so it's difficult for you to hear *her*."

"Are you trying to tell me what I've been spared, or what I've still got ahead of me?"

"Oh, what you've still got ahead of you! And we didn't even let any of the d'Alvery connection know we were going to be in the city. I'm afraid they'll be very much annoyed when they find out we were there—of course some of the Estrades will tell them. The d'Alverys are much the more numerous of the two families, because there's Fabian's branch and my branch too."

"Oh, Gervais, please stop! I'm too tired to hear about any more relatives, Estrades or d'Alverys either!"

"Glad to be getting back to the peace and quiet of the old plantation after all, are you, honey? Perhaps you'll be satisfied to stay there now, instead of wanting to run all over the countryside."

"Why, I always was satisfied to stay there! Who suggested this trip, I'd like to know?"

"Not me. Fabian. Blame it all on Fabian."

"*Blame* it!"

"Then you did like it, in spite of the relatives?"

"Oh, Gervais, I've adored it all! You know I have! But can't we talk about it tomorrow? I'm so sleepy!"

Amen met them at the station with the olive-green Buick, which had been one of Gervais' recent purchases. The boy seemed glad to see them, but his grin was less expansive than usual, and though he adequately answered the questions which were put to him, he did not volunteer any remarks. "Yes'm, Miss Merry, the little twinses be's doin' fine; seems like dey done got more and more pert every day. Yassuh, Mr. Gervais, Madame and Miss Cresside dey is all right too." After that he did not say much, and, for the most part, the drive along the River Road proceeded in silence. They passed a few parked cars, with engrossed occupants, and Gervais remarked to Merry, the edginess coming into his voice, that this sort of thing seemed to be on the increase all the time—and if the neckers got more numerous, somebody'd better hang red lanterns along the levee, both as a traffic safeguard and a trade mark. Little else had been said when they swung into the driveway, now embowered by crêpe myrtle in full bloom; emerging from this, they caught the first glimpse of the illumined colonnade, framed by moss-draped oaks.

"Do you know what this driveway always makes me think of? The approach to the sleeping beauty's palace!" Merry said, rather hesitantly. Gervais sometimes teased her for her fantasies and she was still a little shy about expressing them. But this time he was attuned to her mood.

"I see what you mean. It does give you the feeling of approaching a place that's enclosed and secret. But there was more of a wood, wasn't there, surrounding the sleeping beauty's retreat? And all sorts of brambles and thickets for Prince Charming to hack his way through, not just privet and myrtle. I don't remember the details. But my father used to read the story to me, in French—*La Belle au Bois Dormant*, the name of it was. That old fairy story book must still be around somewhere. We'll have to dig it up."

"Yes. Besides finding out whether the Belle Heloïse driveway looks like the enchanted wood, we can get ready to read aloud to the twins when they're a little older."

"To the twins and to Philogene too."

He pressed her hand fondly. He was in high good humour, happy to be home again. The trip had been a great success, but no hotel was comparable to Belle Heloise in comfort, no other diversion equal to those it afforded, no other occupations so congenial as those intimately connected with the land. He would have a good sleep in his own big bed, with Merry in his arms, not separated from her by a silly little glass-top table with a telephone on it; and early the next morning he would be out to see Sance and Plauché, before starting for town in time to have a cup of coffee at Izzie's and find out what was going on, so that he would be informed when the legislature met. The Chappuis bill for a Constitutional Convention was to be up for a vote any day now, and old Judge Depré from Opelusas was all set to unlimber his heaviest oratory against its non-submission feature. . . .

Selah was standing at the door, vaguely apologetic and slightly dishevelled, as usual, but more purposeful of expression. He did not help Amen with the bags, but hung about while his son dragged these slowly up the stairs, as if intent on getting something off his mind.

"Good-evening, Selah. Glad to see you. Amen says everything's gone along fine since we've been gone."

"I don' know what he say. I know what I thinks."

"Well, what do you think?"

"Madame, she ain't seemed so well. She been mighty worried and uneasy. Yesterday she never left de bed at all. She be's waitin' up for you, Mr. Gervais. She wants to see you befo' you retires."

"All right. I'll go to see her as soon as I look in on the twins."

"She did say, Mr. Gervais, effin she could speak to you *alone*——"

"*All right.* . . . Good-night, Selah."

"Good-night, Mr. Gervais. Good-night, Miss Merry."

"And now what do you suppose has happened?" Gervais muttered, as he and Merry went up the staircase. "That's a great message to send me by a servant—not that I suppose you care."

"No, of course, I don't care. Why should I? It's natural for a woman to want to talk to her children alone sometimes—I'm sure I shall. And nothing much can be wrong—you worry too much, Gervais. Come, see the cherubs with me and then I'll start undressing while you go in and talk to Madame Mère."

Gervais had declined, from the beginning, to have the twins sleep in his room: it was one thing, he had said, grinning, to share it with a pretty girl like Merry, and quite another to turn it into a family dormitory. So the big bedroom back of his had been made into a nursery; the shutter doors between the two could be opened or closed at will, and Dinah had her own cubbyhole just

186

beyond. Though the twins still used the double cradle in the patio during the daytime, they had now graduated to separate beds upstairs, and slept in beautiful rosewood cribs, representing some of Mallard's finest craftsmanship, with elaborate mosquito bars depending from the testers lined with tufted satin. Merry and Gervais did not raise the mosquito bars, nor light the gas in the room; they tiptoed in very cautiously and peered silently at the sleeping infants. From the first, they could hear the babies' quiet, even breathing, and as their eyes became accustomed to the dim light filtering in from the hall, they could see the two plump, quiescent little forms, stretched out in complete relaxation and repose. The babies did not stir at their visitors' approach, but, quiet as these were, Dinah heard them and appeared at the doorway leading into her own quarters, still fully dressed.

"Dey's done wonderful," she whispered proudly. "Vail, he done cut another tooth, but it come through easy like nothin'. An' Sybelle, she likes her bottle jus' fine. She done stop her fussin' right away after she didn't see you no mo', Miss Merry. I reckon it was a mighty good thing you went to Nyawlins. I'se glad you's all two back, sho' nuff, but I promise you, Miss Cresside and me, we can take care of dem twinses without nobody help us, no time. Yes, *Mam.*"

She was still gloatingly surveying her charges when Merry, completely satisfied as to their welfare, went through the shutter door to her own room and Gervais crossed the hall to his mother's apartment. Selah's statement that Madame d'Alvery was "waiting" up for him had misled him. He had expected to find her in her boudoir, but instead she was propped up against the big square pillows in her great four-poster, the white counterpane drawn up smoothly over her old-fashioned nightgown, as it had been on the night when he had tried to talk to her about Merry. The memory of this interview still rankled, in spite of its apparently felicitous consequences; he did not like to be reminded of it in any way. But he made a genuine effort to speak cheerfully and courteously, as he gave his mother the customary respectful though impersonal kiss.

"Well, *maman*, we've had a fine trip," he said. "I'm sure Merry'll tell you about it in the morning. She can give you details about shopping and parties better than I can. But Selah said you wanted to speak to me about something tonight—alone. What's on your mind?"

"I have reason to be very much disturbed about Cresside, Gervais."

"Why, what's the matter with her?"

"I suppose you would say there is nothing. I feel there is a great deal. And I think we may have to take drastic steps."

"I can't somehow see myself taking 'drastic steps' as far as Cresside's concerned. I never did have much success along those lines, you know. And I certainly can't do anything unless I learn in which direction I'm supposed to move."

"Charles Boylston has come very faithfully to see us in your absence, Gervais. And he has talked to me very earnestly. Of course, he told me long ago that he desired to marry Cresside—in fact, he paid me the compliment of asking my permission to address her." Madame d'Alvery's tone implied that through this act alone Charles Boylston was entitled to a superior place in her esteem, since it set him so far above the rank and file of mannerless modern suitors. "But now he has told me, with great distress, that he is making no headway. Cresside does not even take his proposals seriously. She does not seem to appreciate either his affection, or the very great advantages that the alliance he proposes would bring with it. She declines to listen to him. She even laughs at him."

"I could have told you all of that long ago, and so could Merry. But I still don't see where the drastic steps come in. I like Boylston immensely—under all the circumstances, I don't know anyone I'd rather have for a brother-in-law. But I can't hypnotize Cresside into falling in love with him, or lock her up in her room on bread and water until she consents to marry him whether she loves him or not."

"Then you had better persuade her to go away somewhere. Perhaps a European trip would appeal to her. With the sugar situation what it is, we could afford to give it to her, and no doubt we could find some discreet relative of ours who would accompany her."

"You know as well as I do that I couldn't get Cresside on an ocean liner unless I gave her knockout drops. I know it's the classical custom to send a girl to Europe when you want to break up a love match. But this is the first time I ever heard of doing it to foster one. She certainly won't marry Charles Boylston if you get her halfway around the world from him."

"I am not suggesting that you should send her to Europe to get her away from Charles Boylston. But I am suggesting that unless you can persuade her to accept the protection she would have as his wife, that you do so in order to get her away from Sylvestre Tremaine."

"Sylvestre Tremaine!"

"Yes. Charles Boylston has not been the only visitor since you and Merry went away, Gervais. Fabian has also been here very constantly—so constantly that I almost had the impression he was watching for something to happen. It did happen after he left here Saturday night."

"*What* happened?"

"I am trying to tell you, Gervais. I wish you would not display so much impatience, no matter how you may feel. He and Cresside apparently had a very pleasant evening together. I joined them for dinner, but they started a cribbage game immediately afterwards. Later, I came upstairs, and when Fabian left I heard them laughing and talking on the gallery. I think Cresside went out to his car with him, and watched him drive away. Sylvestre was apparently watching for him to leave too—he must have been somewhere on the place already. Because Fabian had hardly gone when Sylvestre called softly from the garden to Cresside, who was still on the gallery."

"And then you listened?"

"Gervais, I must ask you not to speak to me as if I were an eavesdropper or a spy. The windows were all open. I could not help hearing. Of course, Cresside was taken completely by surprise. Any other girl would have cried out, in alarm. But you know that she is not easily frightened. She spoke to Sylvestre in a controlled way, but very coldly. She told him to leave at once, and never to come back again without his wife. I cannot repeat the exact words she used."

"You don't need to. I have a pretty good idea what they were, anyway. But I don't care much for this vicarious information. I still feel——"

"I do not need to have you instruct me in propriety of conduct, Gervais. I should not have taken advantage of the open windows, nor should I be repeating this to you now if I did not think the occasion demanded it. Sylvestre was not violent in any way. He did not try to touch Cresside—indeed, he promised her, vehemently, that he would not, and I believe he kept his word. But he reiterated that he had to talk to her. He said that he had waited and waited for his chance, and that now Regine had a severe headache, that she had taken a sleeping draught and asked him not to disturb her. So he had seized the opportunity, in spite of the unseemliness of the hour. He implored Cresside to tell him——"

"What did she tell him?"

"Nothing. She spoke to him coldly a second time, and then she walked to the front door, came inside, and locked it. It is the first time, as far as I know, that the front door of Belle Heloise has been locked since the War Between the States."

"That's rather beyond the point. The point is that the time had quite evidently come to lock it. I don't for the life of me see why you're worrying about Cresside and why you think she ought to be sent away if she doesn't get married. It seems to me that she showed a good deal of sense and spirit—more than I'd have given her credit for a few years ago. And, incidentally, I think she can handle this situation better than anyone else can do it for her. I suppose you think I ought to step into the picture now, and go after Sylvestre with a gun, figuratively if not literally. But I can tell you that if I did, I'd only make things a darn sight worse than they are already."

"I am not suggesting that you should go after Sylvestre with a gun, and I admit that Cresside did show sense and spirit. But the after-effects were very serious, and her conduct since then has been extremely strange. I am very sure, Gervais, that she did not sleep at all last night. She was extremely pale this morning, and she has been very silent all day."

"Has Fabian been here again?"

"No. Before he knew when you were leaving, he had invited those two queer old men—the derelict veterans he has so inexplicably befriended—to spend the day with him. He said he did not want to disappoint them. Besides, to do him justice, I must say he undoubtedly felt that there was no special reason why he should return. Cresside was happy and tranquil when he left her last evening. Certainly he could not foresee that Sylvestre would try to reach her late at night, nor had he any reason to suppose that she would be upset today. But she has been, still further."

"For God's sake, how?"

"Regine was here this morning, without Sylvestre. She spoke of last night's headache, and said it was no better when she woke today; so Mrs. Hathaway and Sylvestre went to church without her. But after they had gone she felt so nervous that she did not want to stay in the house alone except for the servants—at least, that was the reason she gave for coming over here. Cresside was obviously disinclined to talk to her, especially by herself; she brought Regine to my boudoir. Regine's manner was very hysterical, Gervais, and her conversation was indelicate. Both were entirely unbecoming a lady."

"Perhaps by now you're not so sorry you didn't get her for a daughter-in-law, after all. I'm only surprised that this is only the first time you've noticed she hasn't any self-control. But what happened, specifically?"

"She said she would not have minded the headache if there had only been a chance that it was one of the first indications of pregnancy; but she knows it was not. She said Sylvestre was very resentful—that is the word she used, resentful—because there were no prospects of a child. While they were abroad, she went on, he was just as thankful as she was that 'they didn't get caught.' I am still quoting, Gervais. But since their return he feels differently, especially since he has seen the twins and learned that Merry is already *enceinte* again. This has apparently given him a feeling of frustration. He reproaches Regine and she retaliates by asking him why he is so sure their childlessness is her fault—that it may very likely be his. I gather that there have been scenes, that these recriminations go on and on. She threw herself about and wept while she described them."

190

"The darn fool! How did you finally get rid of her?"

"Cresside did that. Very adroitly and courteously, I must admit. She succeeded in convincing Regine that it would be much better if she were at home when her mother and her husband returned from church, and also managed to calm her before getting her out of this house. Naturally, I did not hear everything they said after they left my boudoir, but I could hear Cresside's voice, and it was very soothing—almost sweet. I should hardly have recognized it as hers."

"Well, Cresside's voice has changed a good deal this last year—not that it's the only change either. But we still don't seem to be getting to the point of all this."

Madame d'Alvery raised herself slightly on her pillows, and smoothed the already even sheet with her white fingers. Then she looked up at her son with smouldering eyes.

"The point of all this is that after Regine left, Cresside seemed to withdraw further and further into herself, looking paler and paler all the time. Charles came in and stayed for several hours; but Cresside was completely *distraite* all the time he was here; she did not even take the trouble to badger him. And after the twins were in bed she went out. It is the first time she has done so since they were born. She told me she was going, but she did it tersely, with her hand already on the door, and when I called to her she was gone. She has not come back. I have no idea where she went or where she is now."

"A successful sugar planter must possess knowledge or information of many types. He should be an agronomist, a chemist, a mechanical engineer, a surveyor, a veterinary surgeon, a banker (or at least enough of one to know how to get funds for making and saving of a crop!) and finally a lawyer to keep out of the bankruptcy court; but I say above all he should be an optimist and always ready with the encouraging thought of 'l'année prochaine.' He should be one who loves to see the earth turn from the share and the tender shoots of cane mark the long brown rows. He should love to see the fields when they lie like a sea at calm, under the summer sun, and when autumn comes, to see the skilful cutters top and fell the standing cane and cast the purple stalks in even piles ready for the wagons. He should love to hear the sound of rustling leaves and ringing steel above the song of the workers, weird and wild but full of melody. It should fill him with supreme contentment to realize that inside the factory the furnace fires glow and the engines turn endlessly; that the massive rollers crush out the liquid sweets; that the amber juices dance and foam and the machines revolve with lightning speed, until at last emerge the pure and sparkling crystals, finished product of twelve long hard months."—Adapted from a speech made by Hon. Edward J. Gay at Houma, Louisiana, before the American Sugar Cane League, which was taken from the memorial address delivered by Hon. Wilkinson in the House of Representatives, eulogizing Senator Gay's father.

PART IV

The Bastard Grain

(June, 1920, to August, 1921)

XIV

CRESSIDE started down the driveway without any definite plan of action. She did not want to go anywhere or do anything in particular. But she desperately desired to get away from the house, which had seemed, all night and all day, to be closing in on her like a prison. She did not dare stay in the gallery or the garden, for fear that Sylvestre would suddenly appear and accost her again as he had the evening before. The grounds, already shadowed by approaching dusk, seemed to harbour some even more mysterious menace; she had always ranged freely through them, but now she was afraid of something indefinite and none the less threatening because she visualized it vaguely. The idea of escape obsessed her to such a degree that she was unmindful of destination; her mother had not exaggerated in saying she left so swiftly that she could not be stopped.

All the servants except Dinah and Lucie had the evening off, as they usually did on Sunday; therefore Amen was not in watchful attendance as she sped through the colonnade and across the lawn. She backed the first car she saw out of the shed that served as a garage and turned it into the driveway. A cardinal was poised on the nearby ligustrum, and at Cresside's approach he began to dart through the foliage, a scarlet streak weaving in and out of the glossy green. Behind the great oaks, which dominated the west side of the Small Yard, the sky had the rich colour of molten gold, and the Spanish moss, floating from the branches of the trees, looked like grey lace draped against its splendour. Ahead of her the pink plums of the crêpe myrtles made a radiant arch. But she was blind to all this familiar beauty. Despite the roughness of the twisting driveway, she forced the car ahead. Then, having reached the highway, she jammed on the brake, and, for the first time, paused to consider which direction she should take.

Fleetingly, she thought she might go straight to Charles Boylston and tell him she would marry him after all, and the sooner the better. She knew that if she went back to Belle Heloise with the news that she was engaged to him, most of her problems would be solved. But she dismissed the idea almost as quickly as she conceived it. Charles Boylston was not the sort of man to whom a girl, even a girl with whom he professed to be deeply in love, could rush with a declaration like that. He would be startled, even somewhat shocked, if she appeared, unaccompanied, at his bachelor establishment; and his amazement over such a breach of etiquette would temper his pleasure in seeing her. He would receive her courteously, but not ardently, and he would certainly indicate that he assumed only some grave emergency, quite unconnected with her own attitude towards him, could possibly have brought her to his door at such an untimely hour. Moreover, under no circumstances would he wish their marriage to be precipitate or unpretentious. He would want an engagement, first formally announced at some suitable function, and next sufficiently prolonged to admit proper preparation for an elaborate trousseau, an impressive wedding and an extended trip. Cresside felt unequal to facing all the complications which she saw crowding in upon her in connection with Charles Boylston. She did not want to arrange any ceremonies or start any arguments or raise any issues; she only wanted to find understanding and sympathy and refuge, as she had found them that afternoon in the garden room with Fabian. . . .

She turned the car abruptly to the right and swung up the River Road towards the capital, wondering how she could have possibly been so stupid. Of course it was Fabian whom she wanted to see; of course he was the only person in the world who would understand and help. He would be pleased and not shocked to have her come to his house, and even if he were surprised, he would not show it. He might receive her rather gravely, instantly realizing she had sought him out for some special reason, or he might ease the situation by cracking one of his wry jokes; but it would be all right either way. And there would be no ulterior motive in his welcome; he did not want to marry her, he had never thought of her in that way. Fabian had been in love with Merry, but Cresside felt sure that was the only time. She also felt sure that he was not in love with Merry any more, and that this was actually less because, as a man of integrity, he would not have allowed himself to look at his cousin's wife with covetous eyes, than because he had gradually made the discovery that she did not represent his ideal after all. Quoting, as he did so easily and so aptly, he had once said something to Cresside about the type of girl he liked best—

> *"A creature not too great and good*
> *For human nature's daily food——"*

Of course, he did not add that Merry *was* too great and good, and Cresside knew that he admired her sister-in-law immensely and was devotedly attached to her; but the inference was there just the same. Fabian, whose own life was singularly blameless,
196

had infinite tolerance for the weaknesses and misdoings of others, Though naturally there were limits, Cresside said to herself, wincing a little. Well, that was beyond the point. The point was that he would be glad to see her, that he would help her, that he was not in love with her. She knew, now that she realized Fabian was the only person she wanted to see, that she was still as incapable of facing desire as she was of facing ceremony and controversy. Charles Boylston had never told her that he desired her, he had never tried to take her in his arms; but naturally he would, as soon as she consented to marry him. And she did not want to hear his voice shaken with passion, she did not want him to touch her. . . .

She had already passed the cemetery which she had so successfully cleared, and was now approaching Hathaway Hall. As its white immensity, luminous in the twilight, towered before her, she pressed down on the accelerator and sped on. Unbelievable that only a little over a year before, she had been in and out of that house as freely and gaily as she went in and out of her own. Regine had then been her most cherished intimate, and Sylvestre, "the old family friend" of the Hathaway family, her own accepted suitor. Now Regine and Sylvestre were husband and wife, with strife between them already, and she herself was estranged from them both, worse than estranged from Sylvestre. She listened to Regine's chattering and complaining, when she could not escape from it, with contempt untinged by pity; she did not think even Fabian was sorry for this vapid girl who had brought trouble to herself as well as to everyone else, and she marvelled that she could ever have found anyone so silly and selfish good company. She was even slightly ashamed because she had. But she did not dwell on shame, in thinking of Regine, as she did in thinking of Sylvestre. How in the name of heaven could she ever have loved a man like that—shallow, indolent, sensual, insincere? Why had she failed to see him, in that radiant, long-ago Easter moonlight, as she saw him now in the deepening dusk?

She left the River Road and turned into a narrow, uneven side street that crossed the railroad track. Four or five dilapidated negro cabins were scattered along it, their dusty yards and narrow porches overflowing with impoverished but cheerful humanity. Kerosene lamps, shining through the open doorways, revealed further activities inside: groups gathered around rickety tables, drinking and dicing, women in rocking-chairs, holding babies to their bared bosoms, girls wearing bright dresses and held closely embraced. Someone was playing a harmonica, someone else was singing, two or three couples were dancing, and a little boy was plucking white blossoms from a laden bush near a disreputable outhouse. The street, though obviously served by neither electric power nor sewerage, was within the city limits, and the people who dwelt there were subtly different from their country neighbours, who lived such a short distance away; and Cresside had often been told that it was unsafe for a girl to go among them alone, especially at night. But she felt no fear of these negroes. On the contrary, she rather envied them their undemanding lightheartedness, and slowed down to watch them. She thought they all seemed happier than she was, and marvelled at their merriment, seeing their squalor. . . .

She did not have far to go now. Approaching Fabian's pleasant little house from the rear, she passed his garden first, bright with zinnias and gladioli. Then, as she turned the corner, she saw that his car was drawn up before the front door, and that he was on the point of getting into it, accompanied by Tremblet and Vicknair. She called out to him, stopping her car——

"Oh, Fabian! Hello, there! Wait just a minute, will you?"

He looked up, calling cheerfully back to her. The dusk was deepening into dark now, but the light from a street lamp fell on his face, and as she went towards him she could see that he did not look either annoyed or astonished, but quietly pleased. She had kept telling herself that of course he would, but when she saw that he really did, a great wave of relief rushed over her.

"Good-evening, Mr. Tremblet. Good-evening, Mr. Vicknair," she said agreeably. "Was Fabian just getting ready to take you home? Please don't let me keep you, if he was. . . . But you wouldn't mind if I waited till you got back, would you, Fabian? I wanted very much to see you for a few minutes, if I could."

"Of course I wouldn't mind having you wait," Fabian answered. He spoke cordially and simply, as if it were the most natural thing in the world that she should come to see him. "Here, take the key. Carmelite went home a couple of hours ago and Belizaire's in there all alone. He'd be delighted to have your company. But I'm afraid you'll have a rather long wait. You see, I'm taking my guests across the river to Port Allen."

"It's this way, Miss Cresside," Pascal broke in. Now that she looked at the two old men more closely, she saw that their faces were pinched and anxious, and there was a quaver in Pascal's voice that she had not heard there before. "We got a telephone call, us, saying our friend Max Stoetzner was mighty low. He had pneumonia last winter, and he's never got his strength back. Every so often he's had sinking spells, and they've got worse all the time. Now he's bad off."

"We only got the message a few minutes ago." Preston took up the recital which Pascal, apparently, was unable to continue. "Pascal's granddaughter, she telephoned us here—the call came to her house first. So Mr. Fabian said he'd take us to Port Allen. It isn't as if Max was just ailing. It's like Pascal says. He's bad off."

"You wouldn't care to come with us, I suppose, Cresside, instead of waiting here for me?" Fabian asked quietly. The question was entirely unexpected. Cresside looked from her cousin to the two old men in momentary bewilderment.

"Why, yes," she said finally. "Yes, I'd be glad to go. That is, if I wouldn't be in the way. I wouldn't want Mr. Stoetzner to think I was intruding."

"Mr. Stoetzner hasn't any relatives. I'm afraid he's going to be pretty much alone through this bad spell except for these two friends of his. I think they'll agree with me that you wouldn't be in the way and that you might be helpful."

"We'd be proud if you'd come with us, Miss Cresside," Pascal and Preston said, almost in unison.

"All right, then; I will. Would you like me to drive, Fabian?"

"No, thanks; I think maybe you've done enough driving already for a girl who hasn't handled a car in over a year. Come on, let's get going."

He had not answered her curtly, as if she had offended his pride by her reminder that he disliked driving and that it was not easy for him. She knew he appreciated her thoughtfulness, but he was thoughtful too. He could see that driving was far more of a strain for her than it was for him, that while he was awkward and uncomfortable in the driver's seat, he could manage all right and she should not try. Without any protest she got in beside him, folding her hands in her lap and looking straight ahead of her. She could not tell him any of the things she had meant to say, now that the two old men were with them. But that did not seem to matter much. She had been reassured already by his welcome and now she was comforted by his nearness. It was strange that such a crippled body could transmit such a feeling of strength and security. He smiled across at her.

"I take it you told Tante Isabelle you were going out."

"Yes. But I didn't say where. Because at the moment I didn't know myself."

He smiled, a little wryly. "You speak as if it were of no special consequence, just so she has the principal item of information. I'm afraid Aunt Isabelle won't look at it that way. But there's nothing we can do about it at the moment, without a telephone. It's more important for us to be on our way than to relieve her mind."

They were already over the crest of the levee and going down the long ramp towards the ferry landing. The *City of Baton Rouge*, tied to the shore as an "emergency," was nevertheless brilliantly lighted. The *Louisiana*, which was in service, and which was also strung with small sparkling lights, had reached midstream on her eastward passage and was puffing comfortably towards them. Cresside gazed first at one and then the other for a long time, finally turning to Fabian.

"I've always loved a lighted ferry boat. And it's a long time since I've seen one."

He nodded again. "Now that you've made a start, you'll be getting out more. There's no reason why you shouldn't see one as often as you like. We can come down here and look at them together, whether there's any reason for crossing the River or not. I like to see them too, especially when the water's so smooth you get a perfect reflection, and when there's a crescent moon in an amethyst sky, the way there is tonight. Do you wish on crescent moons over your left shoulder, Cresside?"

"I used to."

"Well, here's a good time to begin again."

"I was never one to wish on moons, no," Pascal announced from the back seat. "But I always spit when I see a hearse. There's one right ahead of us now. I kinda wish there hadn't been, seeing that we're going to Port Allen because Max has had this bad spell. Not that there's any connection, of course." He spat, guardedly, out of the rear window. "Some say you ought to spit when you meet a nun too. But I don't hold to that. All the nuns I ever saw were fine women. They didn't bring bad luck to anybody."

"It's just as well to be on the safe side, though," Preston suggested, also spitting guardedly.

The hearse went clattering over the planks and rounded the curve of the open deck. Fabian made a sign to the collector indicating that he did not wish to park directly behind it, and swung his car into the open space at the bow. Most of the other passengers were leaving their automobiles and going off for soft drinks and chocolate bars, but Pascal and Preston huddled together and talked to each other in undertones.

"Wouldn't you like to get out for a minute too?" Fabian asked Cresside. "You can see the moon and the reflections on the water better by the railing than you can from the car."

"Yes. I'd like to very much."

They got out, passing a wide-shouldered negro who sat hunched up in front of him, busily scraping a long horn with a piece of glass. Fabian stopped and hailed him.

"Hello, Willie!" he said cordially. "The way you're working, that horn ought to be super-duper by the time you've finished the job. You must be making it for the head beater himself."

The big negro looked up with a grin. "Why, hello, Mr. Fabian!" he said in a pleased voice. "I ain't seed you in a dog's age. You belongs to come across the ferry about once in so often, whether you's got any call to or not. Us misses you when you doesn't. No, this here blowin' horn ain't for no head beater. But I's gettin' me twenty-five bucks fo' it, and I's bound to give 'em his money's worth. He's that Yankee gemman what's bought de place down near your kinnery on de River Road."

"Well, I'll hope to hear it blowing some day myself then. Mr. Boylston's a friend of mine—he might very well ask me to hunt at his place. And he's a good fellow too, Willie. He just hasn't caught on to our ways yet." Fabian nodded in a friendly manner and went along farther down the bow, with a hand under Cresside's elbow to guide her. "That's quite a character," he explained. "Willie Swan, his name is. Most of the boys around here call him 'Ferryboat Bill'—not to his face though. He's one of the firemen on this ferry. But he'd rather make hunting horns than do anything else. I don't suppose there's anyone around here who can touch him at that sort of work. Did you see those scraps lying on the bench beside him? He collects little pieces like that and fits them together as skilfully as a cabinet maker does fine wood. Then he polishes and carves them and fines them down so that they'll have just the right texture to give a rich tone. When he started out, he'd take any old cow horn he could pick up and tinker with it. Presently he was doing such wonders that he began to get orders from all over the world."

"That's swell, isn't it? I'm glad he's had such good luck."

The rejoinder was adequate enough, as far as the actual words went, but they had been spoken in a voice that was almost expressionless. Fabian saw that this was not the moment for an attempt to rouse Cresside's interest in Ferryboat Bill or in anyone else. He must first give her a chance to tell him what was on her mind. They had reached the railing and were standing side by side, looking out at the sky and the river, and casually, as he had placed his hand under her elbow a few minutes earlier, he now put his arm around her shoulder. This time her response was immediate. Instead of dreading to have him touch her, as she had dreaded the mere thought of having Charles Boylston touch her, she suddenly realized she had been hoping he would. Now that he had done so, his arm felt as if it belonged where he put it and she was not afraid of anything he might say to her either.

"I'm sorry I couldn't get out today," he remarked. "Did you have any other company?"

"Yes. Charles came to dinner and stayed most of the afternoon."

"And no doubt behaved all the time like a *parfait gentil* knight?"

"Oh yes! If you can think of a stuffed shirt in armour. . . . When I decided to go out tonight, I thought first of going to see him."

"Well, I'm rather glad you didn't. Not just because I'm gratified you came to see me instead, though of course I am. But because I'm afraid Boylston may not be at his best if you burst in on him unexpectedly. I have an idea he doesn't care for dropper-inners."

"Yes, that's what I thought too. I bet we're thinking exactly the same things about him."

"I bet we are. He's a good fellow though, Cresside, as I told Ferryboat Bill. Don't make any mistake about that."

"I'm not making any mistake—at least not about that."

"All right, just so you're sure of it. . . . Any other company?"

"Yes. Regine came over this morning, while her mother and Sylvestre were at church. She was trying to get over a bad headache. At least, I don't think she was trying very hard. She cried and carried on. She said Sylvestre was disappointed because he didn't have a child."

"That's a pretty common disappointment, Cresside."

"Yes, I suppose so." She turned away from the River and looked at Fabian; his face was noncommittal as well as grave, and his voice had been unusually expressionless when he spoke. But something sharp, like a knife thrust, went through her when she heard it. So that was one of the reasons Fabian was bitter! Because he hadn't fathered a child, because he thought he never would! He was all over being in love with Merry, but he wasn't all over being a cripple, he wasn't all over . . . And Sylvestre, who was strong and young and handsome, and who could have practically any woman he wanted, was only disappointed because . . .

"I assume you managed to get rid of Regine and her weeping and wailing without too much trouble," Fabian said, still speaking without much expression in his voice.

"Yes. As a matter of fact, it really didn't take very long. I think she wore *maman* down more than she did me."

"And that's church? You haven't any news item beyond the fact that Charles is a shade too conventional and that Regine isn't the least bit pregnant?"

"Yes, I have. Sylvestre came last night, Fabian, after you left."

"I see. . . . Can you tell me about it?"

"There isn't much to tell. Regine had taken a sleeping powder, and he thought . . . He frightened me, Fabian, because he came on me so unexpectedly. But he didn't hurt me. I've got to be fair. He only said he had to talk to me—*had* to."

"And what did you do?"

"I didn't give him a chance. I locked the door in his face."

"I see," Fabian said again. "Well, I don't think he'll come back, Cresside. I don't think you've got a thing to worry about. I'm mighty glad you came in town, though. I was tickled to death to see you myself and I believe you're going to be no end of comfort to these old men. Because I suppose their friend is going to die. You realized that, didn't you?"

"Yes, I realized that as soon as you asked me if I'd come along."

"We don't have much trouble understanding each other, do we? Look, we're almost across. We've got to get back to the car."

He took his arm away from her shoulder and put his hand under her elbow to guide her and steady her. It felt as if it were in exactly the right place there too. And she knew there was nothing more they needed to say to each other.

The little house on the outskirts of Port Allen, at which they finally stopped, was no larger than the negro cabins Cresside had passed on the narrow side street crossing the railroad track. But instead of being characterized by squalor permeated with good cheer, it was characterized by tidiness permeated with tragedy. Everything about it was orderly, from the flowerbeds in the pocket-sized yard and the scalloped edging of the wooden roof over the tiny porch, to the centre table in the front room, which was covered by a yellow plush cloth, and which supported a china vase, a Bible and a photograph album. A corpulent woman, her uncorseted body in a shapeless mass of flesh, but her face gentle and sympathetic, met them at the door.

"I'm Mrs. Hartzberg, a neighbour," she said. "The doctor had to leave on a confinement case, but he said he'd be back as soon as he could. He thought he'd get here in time." She paused to give significance to her last statement. "There's nothing anyone can do, when it comes to that. Poor Mr. Stoetzner's sinking fast. You're the friends he asked for, aren't you?" she added, looking at Pascal and Preston; and, as they nodded, she turned to Fabian inquiringly.

"I'm Fabian d'Alvery and this is my cousin Cresside," he explained. "Mr. Vicknair and Mr. Tremblet were at my home when the bad news was relayed to them, so we took my car and came over. . . . Do you happen to know what brought on Mr. Stoetzner's attack?"

"Well, sir——" she hesitated, looking at Cresside as if uncertain whether she ought to go on. Then, deciding that this was one of those rare young ladies who could face tragedy without hysteria, she continued, "Of course, fifteen dollars a month isn't so much to live on. You don't get so much fuel and food for fifteen dollars a month."

"But Max had his savings, besides his pension!" Pascal broke in. "He could have drawn on those. He always said, him, that he had enough to manage with the two together in any emergency. Didn't he, Pres?"

"I don't know as I ever heard him say he had enough," retorted Pres, unable to agree, even at such a moment as this. "But he did have savings, yes. He could have drawn on them."

"He did have savings," Mrs. Hartzberg repeated. "But he put them all into Liberty Bonds, so there'd be more money to fight the Huns. Because he came from German stock it made him feel that he ought to do more than most in his circumstances. Of course he could have got his money back again, most of it anyhow, but he didn't want to. He was stubborn that way. He wouldn't admit this was any emergency, so he tried to live on his pension. I reckon there was a good many times he just sat around in a cold room without bothering to fix himself anything to eat. He could have come and sat in our kitchen just as well as not, if we'd only known. We always managed to have a good fire, and enough to eat, such as it is. But he was certainly one to keep to himself. He didn't go to church or belong to any organizations, and he didn't have much truck with his neighbours except me and my husband. He never let on he felt puny until he had the second of these spells, and by that time the weather was coming warm and I thought he'd be all right through the summer. But I reckon you don't get over any sickness too easy when you're in your eighties. You keep getting weaker anyway from old age. At least that's what the doctor says. He says it's nobody's fault, and that the old man could have been took with these spells even if he'd had all the money in the world. But I feel real bad. I never realized what it would mean when he couldn't work in his garden and raise vegetables."

"I'm sorry you didn't, Mrs. Hartzberg, for of course we'd all have been glad to help. But I know you've done the best you could. . . . You'd like us to stay here, wouldn't you, until the doctor gets back?"

"If you please, sir. And I'm going home for a while if you can spare me. I haven't got supper for my old man yet and he works on the railroad. I don't want him to leave his shift hungry." She hurried away and Fabian turned to the two old men.

"You'd like to go in and sit with him, wouldn't you?" he asked. "Cresside and I'll stay in here. But please call us if you need us."

Pascal and Preston tiptoed into the bedroom, leaving the door open behind them. Cresside could see a shrunken form on the clean narrow bed, a pointed face with closed eyes and a lifted chin, and hands unlike any others she had ever beheld in both colouring and texture—yellow and wax-like and inanimate. She tried very hard not to shrink from the sight, and not to stare at it either. She watched Pascal and Preston draw two straight-backed chairs up to the bedside, and saw them bending over the dying man, who roused himself briefly, recognizing them and speaking to them; then he drifted away from them again, muttering something wholly unintelligible, and relapsing into silence, broken only by heavy, uneven breathing. Cresside resolutely looked away through a second open door into the kitchen beyond. She could see a small bell-blacked iron stove, with a bright tin tea-kettle placed precisely over one of the lids, and clean red-and-white dish towels hanging from a rack overhead. The place did not look comfortably cluttered, like most small kitchens: no currents of warm air and no appetizing smells issued from it; it looked cool and

204

vacant and disused. Somehow it hurt her to see it, almost as much as it had hurt her to see the emaciated form on the bed, and again she looked away, her eyes travelling this time around the tiny parlour where she and Fabian were sitting on either side of the centre table covered with yellow plush. A cuckoo-clock hung on the wall, and every fifteen minutes a tiny mechanized bird darted out of a little door and screamed; she was so startled the first time this happened that she wondered why the sick man was not roused from his lethargy, but gradually she grew accustomed to the sudden noise of the clock herself. The sounds that drifted in from outdoors, through the window opened to the warm June night, were harder to bear. People were walking up and down the street, gossiping, quarrelling, love-making; they were unmindful, as they passed by this bare little home, of the pitiful old man who lay breathing his life away inside it. Some tipplers, exchanging smutty stories, broke into raucous guffaws; two angry girls, disputing a suitor's favour, began to call each other vile names; a negro, strolling lazily along with his arm around his sweetheart, broke into husky, jubilant song.

> *"Oh, what a night to go co'tin',*
> *Oh, what a night to make love.*
> *Some little white clouds wuz a-floatin'*
> *High up in de blue skies above.*
> *De stars wus a-winkin' an' blinkin'*
> *An' de moon wus a-shinin' so bright,*
> *An' I wus so happy jus' thinkin'*
> *Of my gal on dat wonderful night."*

Cresside tried to close her ears to the melody and the sound of kisses and shrill giggles which followed it, and to focus her distracted mind on the room where she and Fabian were sitting. Besides the cuckoo clock, various other small carved wooden objects were neatly arranged here and there: two miniature bears, a bowl with a fork and spoon lying slantwise across it, a chalet with isinglass windows which she thought was probably a music-box. On either side of the cuckoo clock were photographs of men and women in Bavarian peasant costumes, encased in black oval frames, and on the mantelshelf a picture of Max himself, taken before he was wounded at Donaldsonville. While Cresside was looking at this she heard him speak for the first time, intelligibly though with obvious effort.

"That uniform I had made on purpose for the dedication of the Albert Sidney Johnson Memorial in New Orleans—it's hanging in my closet. It's just as good as it ever was."

Max did not tell his friends how he wanted it used. However, they knew and they reassured him, telling him they would find it, that they would get it that moment and show it to him if he

205

wanted them to. But he had already relapsed into his coma. Cresside looked down at the floor. She was blinded by the tears in her eyes, but she could see that though it was bare, it was scrubbed white. She kept on looking at it until she had regained her self-control, and then she glanced up and saw that Fabian had stretched his arm across the table, that he was reaching for her hand. She put hers out, gripping his hard.

"He—he was in want!" she said in a horror-stricken whisper. "Not somewhere over on the other side of the world—right here in Louisiana, a few miles from the place where we live ourselves, in comfort and luxury."

"Try not to think about it that way, Cresside. He kept what he wanted most—his pride."

I wonder what you want most, Cresside said to herself, momentarily forgetting Max Stoetzner and thinking only of Fabian. Then, remembering what he had said on the ferry about a common disappointment, she believed she knew. Fabian and Sylvestre, otherwise poles apart, were united in one supreme desire. Each wanted a son, a child who would bear his name and appear in his image. Except that of course the child Fabian wanted would not be crippled, but strong and whole as the one in Sylvestre's vision. Surreptitiously she studied Fabian's face, wondering why she had never before realized how vivid and appealing it could be when it lost its look of sombre bitterness. We've all taken Fabian too much for granted, she thought; his deformity, his loneliness, his kindness, everything about him. We've shown him we depend on him, but we haven't shown him we care for him. We haven't done anything to make him forget his deformity or alleviate his loneliness or repay his kindness. But we can begin, if it isn't too late. It is too late though, we can't make up to him now what he's missed. I can't make up to him for anything. There's nothing in the world I can do for Fabian. . . .

"I want you two boys to stop quarrelling." The laboured voice of the dying man suddenly broke the oppressive silence. "I want you to promise. I wouldn't rest easy in my grave if I thought you were all the time bickering there beside the monument, and me not around to stop you."

"Why, we don't quarrel, us. We haven't quarrelled in a long time. Have we, Pres?"

"No, not since I don't know when. Fabian don't hold with no quarrelling neither, and we're at his house a lot now."

Fabian did not hold with quarrelling. He held with pleasant, peaceful things like books and flowers, a bountiful table, a quiet house; and he shared all these with his friends, men who weren't of importance in the state, men who were poor old derelicts like those in the next room. He had no one else with whom to share them; his nearest relatives were distant cousins; his father and mother were long since dead; he had never had any brothers and sisters. He never would have a wife and children. He had his friends and his flowers and his servants and his dogs. That was all. And there was nothing Cresside could do about it. . . .

"There's money put by for funeral expenses. That means the notices too. And I want them to have good wide black borders. It wouldn't hurt any to have them posted up in Addis the same as Port Allen. Maybe Plaquemine and Baton Rouge too."

"We'll get them, Max. We'll have them put on all the telegraph-poles and all the lamp-posts too."

The heavy silence descended again on the pitiful little house. This time it remained unbroken until the arrival of the doctor, a drab elderly man, shabby and stooping. It was plain that he was almost dead on his feet.

"I'm sorry I've been gone so long. It couldn't be helped. A hard birth—high forceps. I was afraid I was going to lose the child, but now I think he and his mother will both pull through. . . . Mr. d'Alvery, isn't it? Reynolds is my name. Good of you to come. But I'm afraid there isn't anything either of us can do here."

The doctor shook hands with Fabian and then with Cresside, saying it was good of her to come too, apparently with no feeling of interest or curiosity about the circumstances of her presence or Fabian's. He went on into the bedroom, closing the door behind him, and asking Pascal and Preston to stand back, with a brusqueness that was a mark of fatigue rather than insensibility. For a few minutes no further sounds reached the little parlour. Then the doctor came back into it again, looking more exhausted than ever.

"Well, he's gone, poor old fellow. His friends are all broken up. I was fond of him and I'll miss him too. But that's a doctor's life—first birth, then death, then birth again. I've got to go to another woman in labour tonight. I'd like to speak to you first though, Mr. d'Alvery, about funeral arrangements and so on—alone if I could. Perhaps the young lady wouldn't mind sitting out in the car for a few minutes."

The wait seemed very long. Cresside sat still, with her hands folded quietly in her lap again, and her head bowed. She was dimly aware of the doctor going out, and a little later of another man going in—a slight mulatto, dressed in black, who moved very quietly. But neither man spoke to her or appeared to notice her. Mrs. Hartzberg returned, walking heavily; apparently she did not see the girl sitting in the car, for she too went by without a word. Cresside felt terribly alone. She tried not to cry, but she could not help it. She wept, thinking about Max Stoetzner, and she wept thinking about Fabian. She did not weep thinking about Sylvestre Tremaine, for the simple reason that she had forgotten all about him. . . .

At last Fabian came out and got into the car again. He did not speak to her either, but his presence gave her the same sense of solace and security that it had before. As he leaned over to turn on the ignition she asked an astonished question.

"Aren't we waiting for Preston and Pascal?"

"No; I'll come back for them in the morning and see if there's anything else I can do at the same time. But I've got to get you home before Tante Isabelle has fits, and of course they'll sit up with their dead friend."

"Of course. It was stupid of me to forget."

She began to think of the night her father had died, when the house had been so suddenly hushed of the gaiety which had been such an integral part of him that it persisted to the very end. She remembered that her mother, clasping a great crucifix, had lain down on her huge white bed, refusing to rise, and that the stricken servants had gone about lighting candles in a dim room and massing flowers beside a still form. Except when he was relieved by Fabian, who was grave and quiet, it was Gervais who had watched ceaselessly by Philogene's side, so shaken with grief that he could not speak; and at intervals Cresside, sobbing too, had sat with her brother, while a solemn priest recited the prayers for the dead, and various black-robed relatives, and innumerable acquaintances whose presence seemed to her intrusive, came and went, holding handkerchiefs and talking in low unnatural tones. Only Fabian, who had come now and then and put his hand on her shoulder, without saying anything, had been of real comfort. But before all this happened there had been an interval when she was sent away, just as she had been tonight. It was not entirely clear to her why, but she remembered that the strange sombre man who had spoken to her then bore a subtle resemblance to the mulatto who had gone through Max Stoetzner's gate. As if he were reading her thoughts, Fabian clarified them.

"The undertaker's there now. I don't know whether you noticed him when he went in—a nice-looking mulatto. It was a surprise to me to learn that there was an undertaker in Port Allen—I thought you and I would have to see about getting one over from Baton Rouge. But the doctor says this man is very highly thought of locally, and that he prepares nearly all white persons for burial here, as well as the dead of his own race. He seems very gentle and soft-spoken. He's lived all his life in a little house right by the cemetery near the ramp, and perhaps that makes him feel at home with dead people. I think he'll make everything as painless as possible for those poor old codgers. But what he has to do is gruesome enough at best. You can't get away from that."

"No, you can't. It's terribly gruesome, Fabian."

"Well, try not to think of it. Think about something else."

"I can't seem to."

208

"Of course you can. Think about the cane coming up all along this road. Think about the fight going on in the Capitol. Think about the twins playing in the patio."

She tried obediently, finding it unbelievably helpful when Fabian suggested she should stand in the bow with him again when they were crossing the ferry. The sickle moon had set, but in the still river the lights from the city beyond were reflected in columns of radiance. They were so beautiful that Cresside was glad the boat pursued a U-shaped course, instead of going straight across, so she could watch them no longer. Fabian put his arm around her again, and kept it there after they got back into the car and until they were within sight of his house. Then he made a commonplace remark.

"If you'll get into your car, Cresside, I'll trail you out to Belle Heloise. I'd ask you to come in and have a drink and a sandwich first, but it's pretty late. I'm afraid Tante Isabelle will be mighty worried about you—Gervais and Merry too, if they're home by now, and I think they must be. You'd better have the drink and the sandwich after you get home."

"All right, I will. Thanks, Fabian, for everything. I'm sorry to put you to so much trouble—all that extra driving."

"Nonsense; it isn't any trouble. And, look here, you must get it out of your head that I mind driving. I don't—not that much."

The stars were very bright and the outline of the road and of the levee was clear; there was nothing menacing or mysterious about the grounds at Belle Heloise when Cresside, closely followed by Fabian, turned into them. The house, coming suddenly into view beyond the avenue of crêpe myrtles, was still brilliantly lighted, the collonade dazzling and luminous in its frame of oaks. As the dogs began their inevitable barking, Cresside thought, resentfully, that Gervais would be out in a minute, that she would have no chance to say anything more to Fabian. To be sure, she had said very little to him anyway, not half what she intended, but she had held the feeling that she could. Now the chance was over. . . .

Fabian got out of his car, slamming the door. He was not even trying to keep quiet. He was telling the household that Cresside was back, and that he had brought her home. But as he helped her out of her car, surprisingly, he put his arm around her again after all.

"You're not sorry I took you, are you?"

"No, I'm glad you did. Not that I was any use."

"You were all kinds of use. Preston and Pascal will never forget that you were willing to go—and that you did. A woman's almost as necessary in a death chamber as at a birthing, even if her purpose there isn't quite as obvious. . . . Look, you're not going to worry any more, are you?"

"No."

"Is that a promise?"

"Yes."

"Cross your heart and hope to die?"

"Yes."

"All right, then—you can go to bed now, like a good girl. . . .
Oh, hello, Gervais! Did you have a good trip this go round? . . .
Why, no, I don't see any reason why you should have worried.
If you think I've brought Cresside back too late, I'll go in and
apologize to Tante Isabelle. But, hell, I took it for granted you'd
know she was all right if she was with me. And you wouldn't have
expected her to be with anyone else, would you?"

XV

ALTHOUGH she herself had succeeded in gaining a stranglehold on her family through pseudo-invalidism, Madame
d'Alvery was inclined to view the bodily infirmities of
others with contempt rather than sympathy. She did not
dislike Fabian, but she had never accorded him a position of importance in the family circle; his deformity, in her opinion, inevitably signified a general lack of stamina, and to her a man
without vigour was also a man without consequence. Cresside's constrained behaviour, precipitate departure and prolonged absence
had seriously shaken her, and gradually her anxiety had turned
into anger. She deeply resented Fabian's casual rejoinder to Gervais' indignant greeting of the truants, which, like everything that
had previously transpired, she heard through the open windows.
In spite of the untimely hour, she sent Lucie downstairs to summon
Fabian to her bedside, and as he did not immediately appear, she
repeated the request, somewhat peremptorily. When he finally
came, looking tired but unconcerned, and carrying a highball in
each hand, she was still further offended.

"Hello, Tante Isabelle," he said, setting the glasses down on her
night-table and pulling up a chair. "We were just pouring out our
drinks when you sent for me, and I hoped you wouldn't mind if
we went on mixing them before I came up. I thought you might
like one too. Gervais said you wouldn't, but I brought it along anyway. The rest of us sure needed them. Apparently Gervais and
Merry have been painting the town red in New Orleans. They're
pretty much all in, especially Merry. And Cresside and I have just
come from a deathbed. It's been a rather devastating experience
for her."

"I have not the least idea to whose deathbed you are referring,

Fabian, or why Cresside should have been present at such a spectacle. I have myself been greatly perturbed by her mysterious absence, and I think you will admit I am entitled to an explanation of it. Since you are apparently responsible, at least in part——"

"Yes, I know. But I thought, under the circumstances, perhaps tomorrow would do just as well." While he was speaking, the tall clock in the hall began to strike in its sonorous way, echoing through the bedchamber, and immediately afterwards the tinkling tune of the parlour timepiece came faintly towards them. "I should have said, later today," Fabian continued. Madame d'Alvery's drink was still untouched, and without urging her a second time to take it, Fabian picked up the second glass and began sipping from it, deliberately. "I still think that would be the best plan—it's pretty late, Tante Isabelle. However . . . you already know that Cresside was upset when she left here and you know why. I do too, because she told me. She felt she had to talk to someone. Almost everybody needs some sort of safety valve, and I'm glad Cresside thought of me in that connection. I'd like to do anything I could to contribute to her peace of mind, especially as I am very fond of her. I couldn't ask her to spend the evening at my house because I was just leaving it myself, in answer to an emergency call. So I asked her to go with me and my old friends, Tremblet and Vickair, to Port Allen. They got word that Max Stoetzner, the third musketeer in that group, was dying. Of course, it never would have occurred to me to take Cresside to Stoetzner's house under ordinary circumstances. Just the same, I don't think the experience will do her any harm, in the long run. On the contrary, I think it may do her some good. It's already taken her mind off some other things that seemed to be worrying her."

He drained his glass and got up, pushing back his chair.

"Not that there's any reason why they should have," he said. "I've tried to tell her that. I don't know whether I've succeeded in convincing her or not, but if I haven't yet, I will, within the next few days. I'll be back for another chat with you too, Tante Isabelle, as soon as I've seen that this poor old codger gets a decent Christian burial, so called, and all that. But if I don't start home now it won't be worth while going to bed at all. That's one advantage you have over the rest of us. You just stay there most of the time, which does away with a lot of bother. You're a mighty shrewd old lady in lots of ways, and believe me I know it. I take off my hat to you."

He smiled, lifting his hand quickly to his forehead and flinging it out, palm raised, in a gesture that was half deferential and half mocking. Then he nodded and left the room without further farewell. Madame d'Alvery blew out the bedside candle, which she still continued to use in preference to gas, and then lay still, slipping her rosary between her white fingers. But the movement was mechanical; there was no urge for prayer in her heart as she did it, only increasing resentment. Gervais and Merry did not come back to say good-night. She heard them go to their room, more silently than usual, closing the door carefully behind them, and she chose to interpret this as another slight instead of giving them credit for trying not to disturb her. She heard Cresside and Fabian moving about downstairs, first in the lower hall and then on the front gallery. They were talking, but in whispers, as if they were guarding against the chance that their words might reach her ears; she strained these futilely, even as she raged against the suspicion of eavesdropping. Finally she heard the girl come back into the house alone, and then the lights went out, one by one, until Cresside's was the only one left.

Through the shutter doors dividing her room and her daughter's, Madame d'Alvery could see the girl's shadow. Cresside undressed wearily, as if the mere effort of stepping from her shoes and letting her slip fall to the floor were too great for her. But she did not blow out her light immediately after getting into her nightgown, as her mother had expected she would. Instead, she stood still for a moment, as if hesitating about something. Then she left her bedside and came slowly across the room, opening the shutter doors.

"Are you asleep, *maman*?" she asked softly from the threshold.

"No, I have not been able to compose myself. How could I?" Madame d'Alvery asked coldly, still fingering her prayer beads.

"Then may I come in?"

"Your request is rather tardy. I should have welcomed you more warmly several hours ago."

"Yes, I know," Cresside answered, unconsciously echoing Fabian. "Just the same, I'd like to tell you I'm sorry I went off at half cock the way I did. That is, I'm sorry as far as you're concerned. It was selfish of me, leaving you to worry about me all evening."

"I am glad you realize that at least."

"Of course I realize it," Cresside said, coming closer to the bed. "I'm darn tired, but that's exactly what I'm trying hard to tell you. I think you've got it coming to you. After all, you've got a right to know what I'm up to when I go out, and you haven't any special reason to suppose that I mightn't be up to mischief. I'm not sorry I went though. If I can do it without going into conversation on a lavish scale, I'd like to make that clear too, before I go to bed. It might be a good thing for both of us if we understood each other a little better. I'm willing to do my share by trying to make you understand me. Then perhaps some time you'll do yours by trying to make me understand you. Not that you ever have yet."

She sat down on the steps beside her mother's bed. In her flimsy nightgown she looked even smaller and frailer than in her trim belted dresses. But she did not look frightened any longer. The expression on her pale face was self-possessed and resolute.

"I don't see why I've been such a fool about Sylvestre Tremaine," she said. "I don't mean a fool to fall for him in the first place. We don't need to go over all that again. I mean by acting like such a sissy since he came back from Europe. I don't wonder you're sore at me. Suppose he does try to talk to me? I don't have to listen if I don't want to. I can keep right on shutting the door in his face, the way I did night before last. Suppose he does try to make passes at me? He can't get very far if I freeze right up, and I do that just at the sight of him. He couldn't touch me with a ten-foot pole. Fabian tried to tell me a while back that I oughtn't to give him the satisfaction of thinking he meant anything to me one way or another. I did try and I hope I put up a fairly good bluff. But it was just a bluff. I dreaded the very sight of him. I don't any more though. He honestly doesn't matter to me, one way or another. He doesn't prove anything at all."

Madame d'Alvery was still silent, but she was no longer withdrawn. Her prayer beads had slipped unnoticed from her fingers. She made a slight gesture, but it was not towards recapturing the rosary; she suddenly felt impelled to stretch out her hands and smooth her daughter's dark hair back from the girl's soft forehead. Her habit of repression was too strong for her, and she did not do it. But Cresside had seen the gesture and sensed its significance. Unexpectedly encouraged, she went on almost boldly, forgetful of her fatigue.

"You know, *maman*, one trouble's been that every time I've seen him this spring, he's given me the feeling that I was stark naked. I don't mean the feeling that I was sitting around somewhere in his presence with nothing on but a nightie, the way I'm sitting beside you now. Or that I was in bed with him, the way Merry is with Gervais this minute—the way that means more than anything else in the world to them both. But as if I were publicly stripped of everything, not just clothes but decency, as if Sylvestre had done the stripping. As if he wanted to keep me exposed. It didn't seem possible to me, when we were with other people, that everyone who saw us together could help knowing what had happened. And when we were alone it didn't seem possible that he wouldn't make it happen again. The Sunday he and Regine came here together, I could almost hear her giggling and whispering, 'Why, Cresside, whatever do you mean, going around bare naked like that?' and when Sylvestre came by himself, night before last, I'd hardly caught sight of him before I felt as if he were fumbling with the fastening on my blouse so that he could get his hands on my breasts."

"Cresside, those are not the thoughts of a modest girl. Or the words," Madame d'Alvery said slowly. But she could not bring herself to speak severely. For out of a distant past, she seemed to hear another young girl, crying out desperately to her parents,

"*Je ne peux pas me coucher avec ce cochon là, il veut m'enlever la chemise.*" That girl's desperation had been silly and groundless, the product of false shame and unenlightened puerility; but the memory of it softened the haughty woman whose daughter had never before come to her in the night with whispered confidences. In Cresside's confession of her sensitivity, her mother recognized a kinship with herself hitherto undivined.

"You're wrong. If I weren't modest, if that's what you call it, I wouldn't care if I was naked," Cresside retorted. "And I do. I care a lot. Isn't that what makes the difference? I mean, between being in love with a real man and being ashamed that you fell for a dirty welsher? If a girl's really in love, I don't believe she's afraid of being stripped. I think she's ready to be revealed."

"Perhaps you are right, Cresside. Yes, I believe that you are," her mother said, speaking still more slowly. She herself had never become ready for revelation; it was in her later relationships that her instinct had failed her, not in her first recoil; and that, she was beginning to realize, was because she had never really cared for anyone as Cresside would still eventually care.

"Anyway, I'm fully clothed at last, mentally," Cresside was saying, speaking more lightly. "You might say that I have on a chemise and a pair of corsets and under-drawers and four petticoats already—in fact, all the things you wore when you were a girl. Now I'm casting around for a set of steel armour—the sort that has spikes on it. And what was that gadget girls wore in the Middle Ages, when their true loves went off to the Crusades and they didn't want any trespassing? The girdle of Venus, it was called, wasn't it? Well, I'm going to have one of those too. When I'm fixed up like that, Sylvestre won't have a prayer of getting at me."

In the dim light which filtered through the door of Cresside's room, Madame d'Alvery could see that Cresside was actually smiling, in her elfin way. She hunched up her knees and clasped her arms around them. "Now that I'm sure I can keep him off, I can stop worrying about other people," she said cheerfully.

"Other people? What other people have you been worrying about, *chère*?" Madame d'Alvery asked, with unwonted gentleness.

"Why, no one special. Almost anyone. I haven't just been thinking about what Sylvestre might do. I've been worrying about what he might say to somebody else. Don't you think Sylvestre belongs to the breed that kisses and tells?"

"Try to put that out of your mind, Cresside."

"Yes, *maman*, but answer me. Don't you?"

Madame d'Alvery hesitated, but she could not escape the girl's earnest eyes.

"Perhaps. Yes, since you ask me, I cannot deny the possibility."

"All right then. That possibility's been an obsession with me.

But I've just realized there's nothing he can tell that wouldn't hurt him more than it would me. If he were given to getting drunk all the time, that would be different—he might very well get chatty in his cups and say plenty that he'd never breathe when he was sober. But Sylvestre doesn't care about liquor, that is, not especially. Looping around isn't his idea of a thrill. It takes something else to give him that."

Cresside spoke with scorn. She looked straight at her mother for a moment, and then she rose from the steps and came closer to the bed, leaning her arms on the counterpane and her head on her arms. At first Madame d'Alvery was afraid that the girl might be crying, but presently she realized that Cresside was only relaxing. She had been very tired, but she had persevered and said everything she had started out to say; now she could rest. This time, almost unconsciously, Madame d'Alvery reached out her hand and began to stroke the girl's dark hair. She did not stop until Cresside looked up again.

"I thought that all through while I was sitting outside Max Stoetzner's house waiting for Fabian to finish talking with the undertaker," she said. "That's why I say I'm not sorry I went off this afternoon. I hope now that I've told you all about it you're not sorry either. I've been so close to the whole darn thing here, I couldn't see any of it straight. Now I think I do, because I got farther away from it and because Fabian got me started on the right track, in another direction. I couldn't have started myself. But I can go on, if he helps me, and he's promised he would. Fabian's wonderful, isn't he, *maman*? I think we ought to be mighty proud that he's our cousin. He's the grandest person I ever knew in my whole life."

XVI

MADAME D'ALVERY lay sleepless and thoughtful for a long time after Cresside finally went back to her own room; but the girl herself immediately fell into a deep and dreamless slumber. The shutter doors were still ajar; through either accident or design, she had failed to shut them, though it had never been her habit to leave them open, or Madame d'Alvery's wish that she should. Nothing about the two bedchambers suggested an intimate or fond association between mother and daughter; they might have been at opposite ends of the house, through the desire of both, as far as any closeness or connection was concerned, except that of architectural design. Now, for the first time, the wakeful woman remained poignantly aware of the sleeping girl's nearness and felt strangely assuaged by it; at the same time, a fierce new desire to protect and support her daughter surged through her proud constricted breast. When Lucie came in with her early morning coffee, she raised a warning hand and spoke in a whisper.

"Put down that tray and close the shutter doors. Miss Cresside got to bed very late and she was very tired. I don't want her disturbed."

"No, ma'am, Mis' d'Alvery, Ah ain't a-gwine disturb her."

Lucie moved soundlessly about the room, her expression as usual impassive and incurious. But still Madame d'Alvery was not satisfied.

"I wasn't referring only to closing the doors and making no noise while you are waiting for me. Don't take her any coffee till she rings for you. And tell Dinah not to count on having help with the twins from Miss Cresside this morning. I suppose Miss Merry will sleep late too. Dinah will have to manage alone or you will have to help her."

"Yes, ma'am, Mis' d'Alvery. Ah done understan' 'bout Mis' Cresside de fust time. You knows Ah be's glad to help wid de twinses too."

Lucie slipped a bed-jacket deftly over Madame d'Alvery's shoulders, arranged her pillows and placed the tray in front of her. Then the maid went into the boudoir and dusted quietly until her mistress had finished her coffee; through the practice of years, she was able to time her return to the minute. Afterwards she waited respectfully for further orders, without making the inquiries or suggestions which would inevitably have come from Creassy.

"I shall remain in the bed until Miss Cresside wakes, Lucie. I believe she intends to go out with Mr. Fabian again—an old friend of his has just died and he may need her help. I shall get up and go to the couch after I know her plans for the day. But I do not want to be in the midst of my toilet when she comes in to tell me what they are."

"Yes, ma'am, Mis' d'Alvery. Ah understands. And don't you worry none 'bout de twinses. Ah's gwine right now to help Dinah with 'em."

Lucie departed, taking the tray with her. Madame d'Alvery picked up her breviary and read the office of the day, conscious from time to time of the normal sounds made by an awakening household without giving them any real attention. Eventually she closed her book and went back to her prayer beads. But her thoughts were still on her child instead of her God, and every now and then her eyes strayed towards the old watch which had be longed to her father and which lay on the night table. It was after ten when she finally heard Cresside stirring, softly and intermittently at first, as if she were still so drowsy that she did not realize the hour, then with a startled swiftness. The girl pattered across the room, knocked lightly on the shutter doors, and then, swinging them open, stood disclosed on the threshold still in her nightgown, her small white feet bare and her dark hair tumbled about her pale face.

"Hell's bells, *maman*, do you know what time it is? Why didn't someone call me? I meant to be across the River by this time! And I've got to see to Vail first."

"Lucie is helping Dinah with the twins. There is nothing for which I require her at this moment. It had occurred to me that you would wish to go out again, and I am glad to dispense with Lucie's services, so that you can. But I thought you needed rest first, Cresside. I gave the orders that you were not to be disturbed."

"Well, I've sure got to get started now, if I'm going to be any use. Look, I don't know what time I'll be back today either. You're not going to worry again, are you?"

"No, *chère*, I am not going to worry again."

Within half an hour Cresside was already tearing down the River Road, and for the next few days she was home so little that Gervais hardly saw her. If he had been less preoccupied himself, with the activities of the hoe gang and the laying by of cane, he would have perhaps attached more significance to her absences and to the subsequent difference in her; but neither made any great impression on him. He learned, without attaching much importance to it, that she had helped Fabian with the arrangements for Max Stoetzner's funeral, after having previously been present at the aged veteran's death and later actively concerned with his surviving friends; and he saw that she was graver and more silent than usual. But he assumed this was only a passing phase, caused by a strange and stark revelation. He did not sense the fact that though she had been sobered by the circumstances of Stoetzner's death, she had been steadied and strengthened by some other experience at the same time.

He did observe that as the summer wore on Fabian was at Belle Heloise more and more, and that he and Cresside were spending a good deal of time in each other's company; but he noticed it without curiosity or interest. The corn was being gathered now, the hay harvested; the remodelling of the *garçonnière* and the storehouse had begun. He had more than a hundred hands at work in the fields, besides the carpenters, masons, plumbers, and electricians in the yard. These men required an enormous amount of direction, and he had little enough spare time on his hands, even for Merry, far less with anyone else; he did not connect the change in Cresside's bearing with Fabian in any way.

For the most part, she still remained on the plantation, giving a good deal of time to the twins, not a little to the supervision of household activities, especially the seasonal one of preserving fruit. This had begun with the ripening of the figs, and soon the laden pear and plum trees would require stripping too. It was hard for Merry to stand over a hot stove now and Cresside did not mind; someone had to supervise Lou Ida, and she was the logical one to do it. But when Fabian came out to Belle Heloise after office hours, she was never too busy to stroll through the garden and grounds with him, and when he suggested they should go as far as the batture and spend the evening there, she consented to this too. There was no reason why Lucie should not continue to help with the twins, Madame d'Alvery said, when Cresside first consulted her; she herself required nothing until bedtime. The girl leaned over to kiss her mother good-bye, and afterwards Madame d'Alvery rose from her couch and went out on the gallery, watching her daughter and her nephew until they disappeared among the crêpe myrtles of the driveway. Later she suggested to Gervais and Merry that it was high time Dinah began training another nurse in her own expert ways, so that the newcomer would not be wholly unfamiliar with them when the expected baby was born. A girl from the quarters, named Lethe, who was the eldest of a large family, and who had shown herself both skilful and tender in the care of her younger brothers and sisters, was brought to the Big House, and the twins took to her kindly from the first. Until the time came when Philogene would need his nurse, there was no reason why Cresside should not come and go more freely.

The walk to the batture was not long or hard. This widened gradually from a strip of hard white sand, which lay beyond the levee directly in front of the house, to a densely wooded triangle about half a mile distant, comprising over three hundred acres. At some points a stretch of sloping ground separated the woods from the sand, and this had long been a favourite daytime picnicking place because it was shaded without being too densely overgrown. Before going to war, Gervais had usually spent a good deal of time on the batture himself, helping Amen with the shrimp boxes and the set lines in the early mornings, picnicking and swimming and dancing in the evenings. But since his return from France, he had hardly been down on the batture at all. It was not important to him, from the viewpoint of productiveness, and Merry's condition, both this summer and the summer before, had automatically precluded her from tramping over rough ground and indeed from practically all forms of amusement which the batture afforded. At first he had been too passionately in love to leave her, and later too preoccupied with plantation problems. Now, when he saw that his sister was beginning to spend considerable time on the batture again, his own dormant interest in it revived.

"You seem to be taking quite a little exercise again these days," he observed, rather tardily, one evening as he met her on the stairs. "Back not hurting you any more?"

"Only off and on. I can take walks all right. And of course I can fish—that doesn't require much strength, mental or physical either, when you do it in a barrow pit. I haven't tried any strenuous swimming yet. Just a little paddling around."

"Good. I'm glad you're having some fun at last. Glad Fabian is too. I'd been trying, for a long time, to get him out here more. But he always put me off. Said he had a jealous mistress."

"You dirty liar? You know damn well Fabian never said anything of the sort!"

"Hold on, spitfire! He did say it. But he was talking about the law. You know he's strong on classical quotations. Well, apparently he's appeased his mistress, and it's a good thing. There's no reason why he should slave himself to death. He's got plenty of money, so he can afford to take it easy. I wish I were in his shoes."

"You'd like to be solitary and deformed and completely disillusioned, I suppose?"

"I said, hold on. Of course, I wouldn't like to be solitary and deformed—the disillusionment's a matter of temperament, not circumstances. But we won't argue over that. I merely meant I envied him his steady income. . . . You know you've given me an idea, going back to the batture. I think I'd like to have a good old-time beer and shrimp party before the legislature closes. I'd ask the whole bunch and the usual hangers-on. None of the new members has ever been down here for one of these shindigs, and not many of the old ones—I don't need to tell you our father never bothered with politicians as such—he only asked the men he really had a liking for. Would you feel like helping me to get up a racket of that kind? Or aren't you equal to it? I don't want you to do it if you aren't, but all my womenfolk seem to be disabled in one way or another."

"I'm not disabled any longer, and of course I'd be glad to help. I think you've got something there—that flea circus down at the Capitol ought to get a great kick out of a Belle Heloise beer and shrimp party. And you better stir your stumps and give as many of that kind as you can while you've still got a free field. By the time you're really a big shot in politics, Sybelle will be down there dancing practically every night with her crowd, and you won't have a look in."

"I'm sure not going to start worrying about what might happen seventeen or eighteen years from now. Whatever made you think of it yourself?"

She made a little *moue* and ran on up the stairs without answering him. She did not tell him, then or ever, that the evening before she and Fabian had been sitting on the sandy strip when the moon rose, and that while they were talking together about dancing, the subject of Sybelle had come up.

"Cresside, wouldn't you enjoy getting out more again?"

"I am getting out more again. We've been fishing twice this week, and we've brought supper with us both times. I could've stayed in the water longer tonight, but those darn shrimps kept nibbling at my legs. That's why I came in. Not because I was tired."

"I didn't mean going fishing and swimming with me. I meant getting out more with other people. Or having them come here. You used to go in a lot for dancing, Cresside. I hope you'll take it up again, as soon as you feel strong enough."

"I shan't, Fabian."

"Why not? You're a beautiful dancer. It would be a shame if you gave it up."

"No, it wouldn't. I have given it up."

"You're very foolish to say a thing like that, at your age and with your natural grace."

"If I don't ever say anything more foolish than that, I'll be doing pretty well. A darn sight better than I usually do."

"Look here, Cresside——"

He stopped. He could not quite bring himself to say, "Cresside, if I could only dance with you myself, I could cure you of this silly notion. But I can't, because I'm a cripple, and so you'll have to cure yourself. You mustn't get too dependent on me, because there are so many limits to the ways I can help you. I wish there weren't, but there are. You must stand on your own two feet unless you let some other man help. But there are dozens who'd be only too glad of the chance, good ones too. Why don't you let them have it?" She knew this was what he was thinking, but she was tongue-tied too. She could not say on her own initiative, "Fabian, I don't need excitement and admiration any more, I don't even want it. I only need and want just what you're giving me now, comfort and strength and companionship. I'd rather go fishing and swimming with you, or just sit on the sand and talk to you, than go dancing with any other man, a man who isn't a cripple, who's strong and whole and handsome. You haven't forgotten, have you, that I did go dancing with another man who was like that and I dreaded the sight of him afterwards, until you made me see that he needn't mean a thing to me any more, one way or another? Well, you don't suppose I want to have anyone else make love to me, do you, after that? You don't suppose I want to go through all that turmoil and anguish again?" Instead she waited a minute, hoping that after all he would go on, and when he did not, she said, "I reckon Sybelle will be the next d'Alvery girl to dance on the batture. She'll look lovely too, if she's as pretty when she grows up as she is now. Can't you just see her on the white sand, with the moonlight shining on her blonde hair?"

"Yes. It'll be a beautiful sight. Some poor boy'll probably go straight off his base over it. But that's still in what's bromidically called the dim distant future. I can see you much clearer and closer. Moonlight looks nice on dark hair, too, you know."

"Well, doesn't it show up enough when I'm sitting still, for the love of Mike?"

"No. It takes motion to really show it off. But I won't pester you about it, if you'd rather I didn't. . . . Apropos of nothing, I've been meaning to tell you that I stopped in at Hathaway Hall a few days ago. I sat through half an hour of Mrs. Hathaway's pronouncements and Regine's giggling chatter and then I went out in the fields and had a little talk with Sylvestre."

"I didn't know he ever went out in the fields. I thought he was one of those lilies who neither toiled nor spun."

"Oh, yes, he goes every now and then. Of course he lets Blood do all the dirty work, and it's plenty dirty, in more ways than one. But Sylvestre has to find some excuse for a means of escape. No man could keep on listening to that giggle indefinitely. He'd go nuts."

"Did you have an interesting conversation with him?"

"Very brief. But very much to the point. I don't think he'll be making you any more unannounced visits after dark when his wife's laid up with a headache. I mention it just in case you're still worrying about that."

"I wasn't. It was swell of you to go there, Fabian. But Sylvestre doesn't prove a thing to me any more, thanks to you. And I might add, thanks to *maman*. There were a few little matters I'd been brooding over and I tried to tell you about them. But, believe it or not, I couldn't—they just weren't the sort of thing any girl says to any man. So I finally broke down and said them all to her, the night after Max died. I went to her room to apologize for rushing off the way I had, because, when I thought it over, I figured she had that coming to her. Then the next thing I knew, I'd started spilling the beans. I don't know who was more surprised, she or I. But it worked. We're getting on like a house afire now, and I've got Sylvestre almost out of my system—not quite, but almost. Near enough so that I'm sure I'm going to."

"Fine. . . . You know, I don't believe Sylvestre and Regine are going to be at Hathaway Hall much anyway, Cresside. They're planning to start for Hot Springs pretty soon. And Regine said they might go back to the Riviera next winter. Once a planter gets the absentee landlord habit, it grows on him."

"And then what happens to the plantation?"

"You ought to know. You've seen enough tumble-down places around here. It doesn't take them long to disintegrate in this climate, once they're deserted."

"Mrs. Hathaway wouldn't let that place disintegrate. She's proud

221

of it, whether Regine and Sylvestre care anything about it or not. And Regine used to have a complex about it too. You know that she insisted on making her début and having her wedding in that great empty white ballrooom. She's always thought it was the zenith of elegance. And she was practically a fixation on the gallery."

"Yes, but that was when she could get away from it whenever she wanted to, in the company of anyone she chose. Especially in Gervais' company. It's been getting less and less of a fixation since she's been tied to a man who doesn't want her and who's bored to death in the country. As for Mrs. Hathaway, she isn't a well woman, Cresside, unless I miss my guess. She's got a mighty queer colour. Of course I didn't mean to intimate, though, that Hathaway Hall was going to disintegrate right away. Blood's a mighty capable manager. But he's also a periodic drinker, and his favourite potion's whisky mixed with chloroform. A combination like that can do plenty to a man's inside, if he sops it up for a week at a time every so often. At that I shouldn't be surprised if Blood came to an untimely end for another reason."

"You mean, one of his numerous lady friends might polish him off some fine night?"

"Yes. . . . There isn't much going on around here you don't know about, is there, Cresside, even if you did spend a year in bed? His little apartment at the rear of the Hathaway boarding house is quite a seraglio. Half the mulatto kids you see stacking cane around that sugar mill are his— there's hardly a trifling negro wench on the place he hasn't had, and there have been two or three pretty ugly rows already—probably you knew that too. Now Blood's started a new system of seduction with a succession of sisters —white girls this time, daughters of those no-count Renos that are squatting on the old Faith estate. He's got rid of Vina, the eldest, already, and passed on to Durice, the second one. But I think he has his eye on the third. Her name's Déette, and she's a handsome little she-devil if there ever was one. Everything's quiet enough on the surface, but I believe the situation's volcanic underneath."

"And you think when the volcano erupts the plantation will go too?"

"I don't say it'll go. But I think it'll cease to produce sugar. And then presently the cane fields will be nothing but rough overgrown pastures, with cattle straying through them. Probably there'll be tenants of a sort in the house for a while, who let chickens and pigs and goats wander in and out through that fine basement— afterwards squatters like the Renos, who'll do worse and come to a bad end themselves. They'll disappear one by one and then the place will be left to the snakes."

"Unless someone else steps into the picture. Someone that cares."

"Yes, of course that might happen. If Gervais had married Regine, the way Mrs. Hathaway and Tante Isabelle planned, instead of marrying Merry to suit himself, of course the two places would eventually have been given Hathaway Hall. But the way things have turned out. . . You can't see Vail eventually living there, can you, Cresside?"

"No. I sure can't," she said shortly. Then, as if to mitigate her abruptness, she added, "But Sybelle might. She might fall in love herself with the boy you thought of who would be watching her dance in the moonlight and he might be the new owner of Hathaway Hall, the one who had rescued it from destruction and decay, besides being a regular fairytale hero. Or don't things like that ever happen except in books?"

"No, I reckon they happen in real life too sometimes—to other people," Fabian said bitterly. Then, as if he too were conscious of ungraciousness, he added, "But maybe Sybelle will meet a real Prince Charming—it's about time some girl had luck along that line in this family. I know it won't hurt your feelings any if I say Gervais doesn't seem to be quite living up to the beau-ideal of a hero, though fortunately Merry isn't on to him yet. And I like your vision of Sybelle dancing in the moonlight. I'm afraid I didn't sound as if I did. But I want you to dance too, Cresside. Do it to please me, if you won't do it to please yourself."

She turned to him quickly. He was not speaking bitterly any longer. Great earnestness had crept into his voice, and, in the moonlight, she could see that his face was very earnest too. She was amazed that it should seem important to him whether she danced or not. But she would have cheerfully walked over red-hot coals if she thought her doing so would mean anything to him. She felt a queer little catch in her throat as she tried to answer lightly so that he would not know how much he had moved her.

"All right. I'll do it to please you. Provided, of course, that you find me exactly the right partner. Come on, it's time we were going in."

Gervais had not the remotest idea that conversations of this type were taking place on the batture. But he was pleased when Cresside mentioned the shrimp and beer party again, at dinner the day after their meeting on the stairs, asking if he had thought of a date for it, and whether he wanted her to help in getting together the provisions. He would see to buying the beer and bread, he told her, outlining his plans to his mother and his wife for the first time. He supposed there were enough pickles in the storeroom; it would not matter if they used up all they had, since a new supply so soon would be made now. He would be grateful if Cresside would oversee the boiling of the shrimps, because he had more confidence in her than in Lou Ida, when it came to a question of

223

seasoning with hot red pepper. He thought perhaps the following
Wednesday would be a good time for the party, but he would let
her know. How much notice did she need?

Oh, not a great deal, she said easily. If he had not looked in the
storehouse yet, to see how many benches they had on hand, she
would be glad to do that first thing. If there were not enough, she
would walk over to the cooperage with Fabian when he came out
that afternoon, to see about having some more made. The tables
would be no problem, since there were always plenty of planks
lying around here and there. . . . A day or two later she asked
him to go down to the batture with her, and showed him the set
up already arranged on the sand—the planks lying across wooden
horses to form long tables, with rough benches on either side of
them, where the guests would eat, and a couple of smaller tables
for the service of whisky, mineral water, coco cola and ginger ale.
Well, she seemed to have thought of everything, Gervais said in a
pleased voice. If the good weather only held, the party was bound
to be a big success. Everyone he'd invited had accepted, and everyone seemed pleased to be asked. The sample of boiled shrimp she
had given him was tops, too. He had been right about her judgment regarding the hot red pepper. He hoped *maman* would not
fuss over the smell of the boiling shrimp. It did have a way of
getting all over the house. But, after all, it did not last long.

There was no question about the success of the party. The guests
who had been invited for eight, began to arrive earlier than that
most of them in cars, but a few in old-fashioned surreys. A runway
of planks had been laid across the ditch and they drove straight
over the levee, parking their automobiles and hitching their horses
on its river side along the batture. Almost without exception, they
were neatly turned out in fresh seersucker and linen suits. But they
readily followed Gervais' suggestion that they should take off their
coats and roll up their sleeves; the discarded vestments were
chucked into the vehicles the guests had just left or draped over
the limbs of trees. Prevailing differences in build and stature were
disclosed in the course of this process. Taken by and large, the
North Louisianians were taller, ruddier and more spare than the
men from the Southern Parishes, many of whom were short and
thick-set, with black hair and olive complexions. Charles Boylston
whose position as a neighbouring planter and a family friend had
indicated his inclusion on the list, but whose acquaintance among
the other guests was limited, stood on the side lines, directing
interested questions at Fabian, who had brought Belizaire with
him and who was waiting until the dog quieted down a little before
attempting to circulate.

"That's John Tanner of Shreveport just going up to Gervais
isn't it? I've met him, but I don't know those two fellows who are
with him."

224

"Why, you must know Tack Evans, Charles. He's around every-where these days."

"That's right, he is. I just didn't connect him with this particular crowd at first. But I remember now, I heard Gervais saying he was going to ask the 'hangers-on' as well as the members of the Legislature, so Evans qualifies all right. What is he stewing about now? The pipe line bill?"

"Yes. Says if somebody doesn't watch them the Baton Rouge cut-throats will get in their dirty work and kill it. Huey Long, the other fellow Tanner's got in tow, says 'improper influences' are being used to defeat Tanner's bill."

"Huey Long? That pudgy-looking geezer with a loose lock hang-ing over his forehead and the diamond tie-pin at his shirt under his bow tie? What does he prove, as Cresside would say?"

"Why, you must know that too. He's one of the Railroad Com-missioners. That doesn't prove much in itself. But Long's smart as a steel trap. He'll go a lot farther before he winds up. Look, Charles, we can't keep on standing over here as if we thought the rest of the crowd had leprosy or something. Belizaire seems to know that he's got to put up with these queer goings on now, and you ought to make it a point to know all these men if you're going to live in Louisiana. Come on and meet Long. I'm inclined to think he's more or less of a scoundrel, but he's a rather intriguing one."

They walked on towards the group standing around Gervais, and Fabian, shaking hands with the various men in turn, embarked on a series of agreeable introductions to which Boylston responded adequately. Everything was now in readiness for the guests; the boiled shrimp, still in the rough, were set out in big bowls that ran at intervals down the length of the makeshift tables. No dressing was served; the high-seasoning of the water in which the shrimp had been boiled took the place of this. Fried chicken, piled in dish-pans, was provided especially for those who might not like sea-food; and between the bowls and pans lay long loaves of bread, opened cartons of crackers, and plates heaped with pickles and mounds of golden butter. The beer bottles were packed in big tubs of cracked ice, and the guests helped themselves to the beer, throw-ing the drained bottles down on the sand; but Amen and Selah were stationed at the two small tables where the hard liquor and soft drinks were being served, opening bottles and mixing highballs. Some of the plantation hands had also been called in from the quarters to make themselves generally useful; they circulated among the guests, passing paper plates and suggesting refills, and when it began to grow dark, they lighted the gasoline torches, shaped like inverted saucepans and equipped with a piece of pipe at the bottom, which had been hooked to the trees beforehand. The legislators ate and drank prodigiously, peeling the shrimp and throwing the shells down on the sand among the empty beer bottles, as they did the chicken bones, in spite of Fabian's muttered warning about keeping these away from dogs. The long loaves of bread, the big mounds of butter, disappeared as if they had been spirited away; in an incredibly short time all that was left on the tables were empty bowls and boxes, a few broken crackers and a few spilled pickles. But the drinks held out. By midnight the guests who had begun by talking about politics and agriculture were telling broad jokes and bursting into carefree song. The pipe line bill and the repeal of the dipping law—another burning issue —were alike forgotten. Men who had been calling each other hard names on the floor of the legislature and secretly manœuvring to outwit each other were carolling with their arms about each other's necks. The party broke up to the strains of "Sweet Adeline" and "Give Me the Moonlight, Give Me the Girl, and Leave the Rest to Me," sung, in some cases, decidedly off key, but in all instances with great heartiness. The old-fashioned surreys and the model T Fords finally went bucking over the levee and down the River Road again, their occupants in a mood so mellow that the echoed evidences of this continued to float back towards the batture. Gervais, delighted at the success of his party, invited Fabian and Boylston to go up to the house with him for a final drink. They left the hands from the quarters to clean up the débris on the beach and put out the torches; but Selah returned to serve the highballs in a silver tray in the drawing-room. Gervais' own room was in darkness, and he felt sure that Merry was already asleep; but seeing that a light was still shining in Cresside's, he called up to her. Wouldn't she come down and join them? They all wanted to thank her for the swell idea she had put into his head. Sure, she called back, she'd be there in a jiffy; she had always thought the best thing about a party was the fun of talking it over afterwards. Her "jiffy" was a little longer than it would have been without Charles, for instead of appearing in a negligee, she got dressed. But for all that she made good time, and she was excellent company when she did arrive. Gervais could not remember when he had seen her in better spirits.

He told Merry so the next morning, adding that he was sorry that she had not been there to give the nightcap its final fillip; and during the next few days he took special pains to tell her the news items which he thought might possibly interest her, partly to guard against giving her the feeling that she had been left out of a pleasant group, in which she logically would have been included, and partly because he was beginning to realize how much of her enjoyment was vicarious in these days. Her condition was already noticeable, and though she appeared to accept her disfigurement philosophically and sensibly, he knew that her natural shyness made her sensitive about it. She stayed close to the plantation, seeing only her family and her most intimate friends, and taking no part whatsoever in the activities connected with the legislative session. But she was pleased because he participated in them, and she loved to listen to his descriptions of the political picture and to his impressions of the main figures in it.

After the close of the legislature, Gervais threw himself, with redoubled energy, into the execution of his plans for improvements on the plantation. A progressive young architect named Arnold Fletcher had recently settled in Baton Rouge, and had done a fine piece of work in restoring and modernizing the beautiful little house near town which belonged to distant kinsfolk of the Hathaways and which had been occupied by Prince Murat during his exile. Gervais had been so much impressed by this achievement that, with the approval of the New Orleans architect he first consulted, he had asked Fletcher to take charge of the restoration programme at Belle Heloise, and Fletcher had accepted the commission with enthusiasm; it was not often that so important a project was entrusted to so young a man. He had thrown himself into the undertaking wholeheartedly and efficiently, and the dilapidated buildings had lent themselves to restoration and adaptation better than Gervais had dared to hope. The interior of the storehouse was now transformed to provide him with two offices, the outer one small and plain, but the other suggestive of a large luxurious library; a shower and a gallery joined these, still leaving some space for storage, and upstairs there were three bedrooms and a bath for male guests. The original *garçonnière* was even more attractive in its new form; it had taken on all the attributes of a charming cottage especially designed for the comfort and convenience of a young couple.

"We'll be all settled in our new home by the time the crops are laid by," Gervais told Merry. "That's when most planters go away on their vacations, because there's a month's leeway before the fall ploughing begins. If it hadn't been for Philogene, we could have gone to Hot Springs ourselves—well, I reckon that wouldn't have been the best choice, with Sylvestre and Regine and Mrs. Hathaway spread all over the place. White Sulphur, maybe, or Asheville. You aren't disappointed, honey, are you, that you're tied down like this?"

"Disappointed! With a new house of our own to move into? We couldn't possibly have as much fun, on any kind of a trip, as we'll have doing that!"

She was entirely sincere in her statement; everything about the transformed *garçonnière* was a source of joy to her: the modern kitchen and bathroom, so much more attractive and convenient than the corresponding portions of the Big House; the large bedroom and the tiny dining-room, which she had equipped charmingly and ingeniously from the stack of discarded furniture rele-

227

gated to the attic; the sunny living-room which she made brighter still with brasses and chintzes and gay prints. She had always scrupulously avoided making or even suggesting changes in her mother-in-law's domain; but this was her own, and her patient transformation of the rear gallery from a catch-all for rubbish to a pleasant and livable patio had given her a good preparation for a more ambitious undertaking. And she did not stop at the *garçon-nière*; she showed the same resourcefulness and put the same care into the appointments of Gervais' offices, rescuing the dilapidated books which she found scattered under the eaves among the broken furniture, and arranging them on wide built-in shelves. Old pictures and old papers came in for the same solicitous treatment; the bare walls were soon adorned with long-forgotten portraits and engravings, and documents which no one else had ever taken the trouble to frame. Even Charles Boylston's impressive study could not compare with Gervais' library in atmosphere and distinction when Merry had finished with it. He was so proud of it that he promptly planned another party to show it off to his friends, and lent a willing ear to Fletcher's suggestion that now the first plans had developed so satisfactorily they should expand their original programme of restoration to include the quarters, the schoolhouse, the overseer's home, and even the old cooperage, blacksmith shop and stables.

"Fletcher says there isn't a place on the River Road, not even Uncle Sam, that could compare with this if it were all put in proper order," he told Merry. "Not many of the plantations had even the quarters made of brick—of course, we had our own kiln here originally; and that mud wall type of construction in Lézine's house is disappearing fast. It would really be a shame not to preserve it. It's beginning to look as if we'd have plenty of use for the old schoolhouse too. If we put it in order now, it'll be ready when the kids are old enough to need it."

He had an equally cogent reason for every proposed item of renovation, and every evening he pored, with increasing enthusiasm, over the blue prints which Fletcher submitted to him in rapid succession. Merry, proud of her own contribution to the improvements, shared his eagerness to go on with them. But with the greater caution of a girl brought up to count the cost of everything she had, she asked one or two anxious questions.

"Won't all this be pretty expensive, honey, if we go into it on such a lavish scale?"

"Yes, but it represents a good investment too. It's poor economy to let a place run down the way this one has. Once it's in really good shape again, it won't begin to cost so much to keep up, in the way of constant patching and tinkering."

"I suppose it won't. But, still, wouldn't it be better to have the work done gradually? I mean, we've done the *garçonnière* and the storehouse this year. Couldn't you do Lézine's house next year and the cooperage and quarters the year after that, and then the schoolhouse last of all?"

"And meanwhile let them get further and further out of repair? No, that's just what I've been talking about. I want to get them all in good order and keep them in good order. I keep telling you, it'll be economy in the end. Besides, I want this restoration work off my mind, so I can concentrate on the crops. As it is, I'm subject to constant interruptions, with all these carpenters and masons running to me every hour or so about this and that. After grinding begins, I'll have to be at the mill all the time; I can't stay at their beck and call. And next year we are going to have a trip instead of a baby, no matter what we do or don't do to be sure we get it."

He grinned at her in his old engaging way. She smiled back at him, her anxiety assuaged by his assurance.

"I'm sure you know best, honey. And of course you know I'd love to see it all done myself. I was only wondering if there was enough money."

"There's enough credit, and that amounts to the same thing."

"Does it really? Hasn't the price of sugar kept on going down since July?"

"Well, yes. But not enough to get nervous over. Listen, Merry, you leave that part to me, and I'll take care of it. You've got enough on your mind as it is."

He picked up the blueprints and put them away, and he did not speak to her again about Fletcher's expanded programme. But the work on it went steadily forward just the same.

XVII

ABSORBED as he was with his project of restoration, Gervais did not permit it to divert either him or his hands from the seasonal occupations of the plantation. The two types of work went forward together. By the time the storehouse and the *garçonnière* had become usable again, repairs on the cooperage, the quarters and the schoolhouse were already under way; after the corn and the hay were harvested, the ditches were cleaned, the wood brought in, and the land prepared for the next year's crop. The seed cane was hauled in mule-carts from the fields where it had been cut to the fields which were ready for planting. Through the earlier part of the summer, all the field work had been done by men; now women and children followed after the mule-carts, straightening the cane which the men had tossed from these, and laying it in six-foot rows the entire length of the field. They squabbled among themselves, and when the cane was not thrown straight, or the division of labour seemed unequal, this wrangling sometimes reached the proportions of a real quarrel. But often the negroes sang too. Gervais, riding over the headland, reined in his horse and listened to the sound of their singing with a feeling of satisfaction comparable to the impulse which produced the song. Dinah's mother, Hester, who had a voice as powerful as her big black body, led the weaker women who followed in her wake and echoed her refrain.

> *"Ah wants to be ready"*—Hester sang—
> *"Ah wants to be ready,*
> *Goin' to Jerusalem,*
> *Jes' lak John."*

And all the others chorused:

> *"Goin' to Jerusalem,*
> *Jes' lak John."*

"I always did like that song," Gervais told Merry when he came in. "I like the sound of it and I like the meaning of it. 'Ah wants to be ready,' too, honey—ready for the grinding season and for everything else that's ahead of us. I'm aiming to be, too—and that's more than can be said of everyone on the River Road," he added, rather self-righteously.

Merry glanced at him with a question in her adoring eyes, and he went on so readily that she guessed he had been hoping she would ask him to explain. "Alphonse Loubat was here yesterday," he said. "You know, the inspector who comes around every year to check the boilers for the insurance company. He thought the safety valves would go through this fall all right, though he was just a shade doubtful about one of them. I told him I wasn't taking any chances. A new safety valve only costs about a hundred dollars, and I'd rather make a clean sweep of them all than to risk having anything go wrong. He said it was certainly a satisfaction to deal with a planter who had such a keen sense of responsibility, and then he added that it was too bad Sylvestre Tremaine didn't have a little more of it. It seems the boilers at Hathaway are in pretty bad shape, but Sylvestre insists he can't afford to do anything about them at present—and look at the money that family throws away, running around from one northern watering-place to another and all over the face of Europe! Between you and me, I believe Sylvestre bribed Loubat to pass the boilers."

"But if Loubat accepted a bribe, wouldn't he be just as guilty as Sylvestre if anything went wrong?"

"Oh, I suppose so! But you'd naturally expect a planter to have higher principles than an inspector. After all, an inspector's only a petty official, with no standing or station to speak of, and a planter's a landed proprietor, personally responsible for the welfare and safety of all his employees. I know of one explosion due to a clogged safety valve which killed half a dozen persons, among them a poor negro who was just patiently sitting on his cane cart, two hundred yards away from the mill, waiting his turn to get up to the carrier. He was hit by a flying tube, and his head was cut right off. . . . There, I ought not to tell you things like that, especially just now. Forget about it, honey. Lightning never hits twice in the same place. There isn't going to be any explosion at Hathaway."

"But was this—did this terrible thing you've just told me happen at Hathaway?"

"No, it happened at Hackberry—years ago, that was; long before Boylston took it over. You may be sure everything's in A 1 condition there now."

"But then, if there *were* an explosion at Hathaway, it wouldn't be a case of lightning striking twice in the same place. It would be the first time."

"Oh, for God's sake, Merry, I've asked you before not to be so literal! I meant the general neighbourhood when I said 'the same place.' I never heard of another explosion anywhere around here. I still don't think there'll be one at Hathaway, in spite of Sylvestre and his criminal carelessness. I was only telling you what Loubat told me."

Merry hesitated before replying. A few minutes earlier she was sure Gervais was waiting for an excuse to talk about Hathaway; now she did not know what he wanted her to do. But besides being horrified, she was reluctantly intrigued. More and more, as it came closer to her time, she was dependent on him for the news of the countryside, and the men and women who figured in it, both righteously and unrighteously. At first she had innocently taken it for granted that this rural region was always tranquil, and that everyone who lived along the River Road was hard-working and high-principled. Gradually she was discovering her mistake, especially in several conspicuous instances. She did not know as much about Grover Blood as Cresside did; nevertheless rumours concerning him were so widespread that some of them had inevitably reached her, and these were lurid enough to rouse her curiosity. She finally ventured to ask another question.

"Hasn't Sylvestre's manager—Grover Blood, that's his name, isn't it?—any more sense of responsibility than Sylvestre? I should think he'd hesitate to take a chance on defective boilers."

"I wouldn't. You could class him in the same general group as the inspector. He isn't a property owner, and he's long passed the point of taking pride in someone else's property. He never did have any lofty ideals or even any especially humane sentiments. Just now he's all worked up over a girl. Of course, you've got to expect that sort of thing, on general principles, among white and coloured both during the slack season that's just coming on. Haven't you noticed Amen mooning around? He's after Creassy, just when you need her most too. And I'm pretty sure that our sugar boiler, Dupuy, is having a little affair with Seraphine, over at the boarding house. But Blood does these things on a different scale. Sance tumbled on a pretty tense scene in the manager's quarters, just the other day."

Again Merry felt that Gervais was waiting to have her inquire what he meant. She asked her next question with less hesitation.

"What sort of a scene?"

"Sance went to see Blood about breeding his mare. He didn't get any answer when he first knocked at the door of Blood's apartment—I don't know whether I've told you, but he's got quite a nice one, as such places go, fixed up on the second floor at the back of the Hathaway boarding-house. Finally Sance tried the door and it wasn't locked, so he walked in. He didn't see anyone at first, but he went along into the next room and there he came full upon Blood in bed with Durice Reno. And this was about three o'clock in the afternoon! . . . Of course, there's nothing wrong about taking a siesta," Gervais added with a grin. "You know I like to do it myself, and to have a certain young lady with me at the time. But mostly men who feel a nap's incomplete without feminine company lock themselves in before they go any further."

"I don't think all that's funny. I think it's revolting, and I don't think you ought to compare——"

"Sorry, honey. I didn't mean to compare, only to explain. But, of course, it would strike you that way. . . . And this was just the beginning of the little episode I started to describe. Do you want me to go on or not?"

"I don't know. Yes, I reckon I do."

"Well, Blood finally roused himself enough to sit up in bed and curse, and just then someone else knocked on the door. Blood couldn't very well get up and go to it, because you see he didn't have much of anything on, and he couldn't nudge Durice and ask her to go, for the same reason. I'll say it must have been damn awkward. Here he was swearing at Sance for stumbling in on him, and he had to choose between having someone else, he didn't know who, do the same thing, or asking Sance to get out, shutting the bedroom door behind him, and stalling off the next visitor for a few minutes."

"And which did he decide to do?"

"He didn't do either, because the next visitor also got impatient and burst in, just the way Sance had. And this next visitor was Déette, the youngest girl in that no-count Reno family. She's just a child, but about as tough as they come—about as handsome, too, in a wild, pagan way. Durice is mighty good-looking herself—all those worthless Renos are. The two sisters must have been quite a sight, together—Durice sitting up in the bed, with a considerable gap between the covers and her hair, and Déette swearing and stamping around in her dirty rags."

He paused, and for the first time since their marriage, Merry felt a swift thrust of misery. During the days when Gervais was in France, she had sometimes suffered such pangs. For all her simplicity, she knew that men, being only human, could not always withstand fleshly temptations, even when they tried, and that they did not always try when such temptations were not only almost inescapable but enticingly presented. Besides, though she had told herself and convinced the world that she trusted him completely, her own hold on the man she adored was then too tenuous to give her a sense of security. But never since he had so urgently entreated her to marry him, and she had consented, had she doubted his wholehearted devotion. She did not really doubt it now. Nevertheless, for a moment she could not help feeling, from something in his voice, that he almost envied his overseer the stolen sight of that beautiful nude girl, and her wild wicked little sister. Reluctantly she realized that even the happiest marriage could not wholly change or subdue every primitive male instinct and craving, and she wished, desperately, that her own body were still beautiful, that maternity had not engulfed her so fast and so completely. Her anxiety and her regret were both ephemeral; the thrust of misery was nothing more than a swift stab, gone almost as quickly as it had come. But afterwards there was a little ache where the sharp pain had been, and every now and then she was conscious of it.

"Déette had been sent to get Durice," she heard Gervais saying now, the tone which had so disquieted her gone from his voice again. He was telling her a story, that was all—a shocking story, but a spirited one, which she had assured him she wanted to hear. "Déette said that Paw had been took bad, that he needed Durice to help nurse him. Vina, she wasn't no use to him, because she was in the bed herself. The quack she went to after Blood got through with her hadn't done such a good job. She was right sick, and if she died, there was going to be hell to pay. Durice had better watch out. If she didn't, she'd be in the same sort of trouble as Vina, and if that happened, there'd be shooting instead of doctoring. She was to come back with Déette straight away, or sick or well, Paw would get up and come after Blood with his gun."

"Do you mean to tell me that this—this girl stood there and said all those things to her own sister with those two men in the room?"

"Sure. And a lot more I haven't told you, too. Finally Blood laughed in an ugly way, and said Durice could go, if she was needed for sickness in the family, but that if she went, Déette had better stay and do for him; he was ready to bet a smart kid like her would be real handy around the house. At that point Sance couldn't stand it any longer. He said he'd never paid Blood any mind before, but he took hold of Déette and shoved her out of the bedroom, calling back to Durice that he would wait for her to dress and take them both to the Faith estate himself. I reckon there were some pretty harsh words exchanged between him and Blood before he left, but he finally got both girls away all right. I don't know how long Durice will stay at home, but I think Blood'll hesitate before he tries to lay his dirty hands on Déette again. For the next year or two, anyway. Sance is good with a gun himself, and Blood knows it. It's time someone stood up to that scoundrel. I'm glad Sance had the guts to do it and I've told him so."

Gervais got up and walked to the window. A hard rain was falling, pouring in sheets from the shrubbery, overflowing the old sugar kettles used as garden ornaments and spattering on the ground. Gervais gazed gloomily out at the downpour, the scene he had just been describing fading from his mind.

"This rain is going to raise hell with the planting," he said. "When you take a hundred people out of the fields, all at once, you get behind with it mighty quick. But Fletcher's getting along fine with the inside of the cooperage. I think I'll swim over there and have a look at the work. Anything I can do for you before I go out, honey?"

"You might see if you can find Creassy for me. She hasn't been here all evening, and she left quite a little pressing undone."

Merry was still eating two meals a day at the Big House, as Madame d'Alvery had expressed a preference for this arrangement, even though Gervais seldom came back from the mill for them. But Creassy continued to bring morning coffee to her mistress, and was theoretically on duty at the *garçonnière* for personal service at all times, except during the night. Until lately she had been faithfulness itself in her attendance, and therefore Merry had been inclined to view her recent derelictions leniently. But Gervais' quick temper was immediately roused by his wife's words.

"Didn't I tell you! She's off somewhere with Amen. I'll find her all right, and bring her back here in short order."

"Don't scold her, Gervais. You know how devoted she's been to me ever since we were married. It's only these last few days that I haven't been able to depend on her."

"Don't *scold* her? I ought to switch her! That's what my grandfather would have done in a case like this. I'm sorry it isn't practical any longer. That's the only thing stopping me."

He turned up his collar, pulled his hat down over his ears and flung himself out of the *garçonnière*, without even stopping for the customary kiss. The house servants, with the exception of Dinah and Lucie, were all quartered in a long plain building that stood at right-angles to the Big House, behind the Satsuma trees. On the ground floor were a laundry, wine cellars and general storerooms; above them, a row of cubicles. Gervais strode off towards this building, his feet sinking into the soggy grass at every step, and then splashing through the puddles which surrounded the quarters. Throwing the door open, he called loudly, first to Creassy and then to Amen. Lethe, who was in the laundry, put down the frilled baby dress she was ironing, and came forward quietly, speaking in her usual gentle way.

"Ain't neither of 'em here, Mr. Gervais. Does you want somethin' Ah could do fo' you?"

"You can go to the *garçonnière* straight off and stay there till I find Creassy. . . . You don't know where she is, I suppose?'

"No, suh. Ah sho' doesn't. Ah ain't seed her since dinner-time."

Gervais did not feel convinced that Lethe was telling the truth, but he knew that there would be no use in arguing the point with her. Besides, the culprits could not be far off. If it had been a pretty day, they would unquestionably have "taken the levee"; in this downpour, however, they would have been drenched to the skin before they could enjoy the delights of privacy. From the quarters Gervais went to the stables; but these were empty too, except for one brood mare who looked at him, above the opening of her box stall, with large reproachful eyes. By this time his rage had mounted to such a pitch that he was ready to ring the plantation bell and institute a general search. Indeed, he actually started towards the mule shed with this drastic action in mind. But as he passed the chicken-house, he caught a glimpse of colour through an opening in this that did not seem to belong there, and almost instantly he connected it with Creassy; a smothered scream confirmed his suspicions. He stepped inside and confronted the dusky lovers.

They had retreated as far as possible into a corner, but they were not wholly hidden, and realizing that they were caught they separated at once and came forward, looking shamefaced, but speaking plausibly and simultaneously.

"Lou Ida, she say she need more aigs for trifle tonight. She done sent me out to de hen-house to gadder dem for her, Mr. Gervais."

"Ah done come out her' to help Amen, Mr. Gervais, caise Lou Ida, she in such a powerful hurry for dem aigs."

"More eggs for trifle! Hasn't she got half a dozen kids she can send after those, any time? You both better think of some better excuse than that for being here. Get out of here quick, you *trifling* wench! If you don't, I'm likely to shake you till your teeth chatter. And I'll do more than that, if you ever leave your mistress again when she needs you."

235

"Yes, suh, Mr. Gervais, Ah's a-gwine fast as Ah can. But Lou Ida, she done send us out to dis here chicken-house and dat's a fact."

Without stopping to pick up a single egg or cast a backward glance at Amen, Creassy whipped out of the chicken-house with unnatural speed, and ran through the rain, her apron over her head. Amen did not attempt to follow her; nevertheless, he began to edge cautiously towards the door. Gervais seized him savagely by the shoulder.

"Didn't I tell you when I first came home from France, you no-count nigger, that I wouldn't have you taking up with anyone on this place?"

"Ah ain't took up with nobody, Mr. Gervais, suh. Me and Creassy, us is fixin' to get married next week, or de week after at de lates'."

"Then how come you didn't mention it to me until I caught you here? Besides, don't you know Miss Merry can't spare Creassy right now?"

"You's allus in such a hurry, Mr. Gervais, suh. Ah doesn't have no chance to talk to you. An' Creassy, she gwine wait on Miss Merry jes lak she allus done. Gettin' married ain't a-gwine make no difference."

"Yes, she was waiting on Miss Merry this evening, wasn't she? And it won't make any difference, I suppose, when she begins to be sick herself?"

"Us ain't a-comin' to de chicken-house no mo', Mr. Gervais, Ah promises you dat. Ah reckon it was jes' de rain made us kinda restless. And Creassy, she didn't know Miss Merry needed her right now. She ain't a-gwine to be sick neither. No, *suh*."

Amen's expression had changed while he was speaking. His face no longer betrayed fear of his master's wrath; it had assumed the look of injured innocence. Gervais, still seething himself, knew that he could talk until doomsday without getting anywhere. Amen's plausibility was impregnable. Nevertheless, Gervais made one last gesture of authority.

"She better not be," he said sternly. "That is, unless you want me to send you both packing. Of course, Mr. Blood might give you a job. But I won't have you around if you don't behave yourselves."

"Us doesn't belong to Hathaway, Mr. Gervais. Us belongs to Belle Heloise."

"Well, then, remember that. . . . If you and Creassy really want to get married, I shan't try to stop you. Very likely Madame d'Alvery will be glad to give Creassy her wedding dress. And I'll speak to Miss Cresside about some kind of a spread for you. But don't you bother Miss Merry about anything right now. And don't you forget again that if you belong to Belle Heloise you've got to act as if you did."

"No, suh, Mr. Gervais, I ain't a-gwine to forgit. Ain't nobody forgits Belle Heloise and Hathaway, dey's different."

The look of injured innocence had faded into one of complete blankness. The negro's voice, respectful throughout the interview, trailed slowly off into silence. He stood still, meeting his master's stern gaze with a vacant stare. But after Gervais had gone out, as Amen stooped to pick up the neglected egg-basket, his thick lips parted in a slow smile and he began to sing to himself:

> "Dere's no hidin' place down dere,
> Dere's no hidin' place down dere.
> Oh, I went to de rock to hide my face,
> De rock cried out, 'No hidin' place,
> Dere's no hidin' place down dere.'
> Oh, de rock cried, 'I'm burnin' too,'
> Oh, de rock cried out, 'I'm burnin' too,
> I want to go to hebben as well as you,
> Dere's no hidin' place down dere.'"

XVIII

WHEN the grinding season opened that year, Merry was already so great with child that she found any exertion an effort. Nevertheless, she went with Gervais to see the blessing of the cane crop.

This ceremony always took place the evening before actual work began in the fields and in the factory. All the hands, clothed in their Sunday best, were lined up in long rows beside the field nearest the sugar-house, with their carts, mules and implements. Minnie and her driver occupied the most prominent place, but all the carts were decorated with stalks of cane in honour of the great occasion. Everything was in readiness when the Bishop, robed in full pontificals and carrying his crozier and a censer, began his walk between the rows, followed by lesser clergy; in their train came the "bossman," the overseer, the chief engineer and various invited guests from town and from neighbouring plantations. As he progressed, the Bishop bestowed his blessing on everyone and everything he passed; he prayed that the workers might be industrious, the mules patient and enduring, the knives sharp, the carts strong, the harvest plentiful. The men stood with bowed heads until he had gone by; they held their hats respectfully in their hands and their dark faces glowed above their clean white clothes. The women, who wore fresh starched dresses, held their children close to them and hushed them if they pointed or asked questions. The negroes at Belle Heloise were nearly all Baptists, but they held the Catholic Bishop in very high esteem; they admired his regalia and his following and firmly believed that his blessing would ensure a good crop.

Merry was also very much impressed with this ceremony, which she watched with her mother-in-law from a parked car, and somewhat overpowered with the responsibility of entertaining the Bishop at dinner afterwards, which the rest of the family took easily, as a matter of course. The grinding season appeared doubly significant to her, when she had seen it ushered in with such solemnity; she understood its importance better than she had before, and her eagerness to learn all she could about sugar-making increased apace. Every day she walked over to the mill to watch the cane arrive, hoping that the more she saw the better she would understand the process which heretofore had baffled and mystified her.

The October days were clear and dry and warm, and beside the shed where the cane was brought in from the fields faster than it could be fed to the carrier, and lay in great piles all around it, dust rose from it as it was dumped on the ground and again when it was lifted up. This dust looked like golden powder, sparkling in the sunshine.

Merry could not understand Gervais' passion for machinery. Only the great black spur wheels, glistening with lubricant, and the strong iron chains turning in endless motion, which she saw when she went inside the mill, were fascinating to her, and this was not on account of their power, but on account of their beauty. She was still confused when Gervais tried to explain their purpose and that of other machinery to her, and he did not encourage her to wander about the mill much these days, in any case. The steps leading from one level to another were very steep and many of them had no handrails; the floors were slippery in spots with oil and water and syrup; much of the machinery was set in deep pits and the borders around these and the mill floor were often obscure. She might easily stumble or fall, and no one had time to stop and look after her. He would prefer to have her keep out.

But he was pleased with the interest which caused her to take her one walk in the direction of the sugar mill, and he hardly ever failed to watch for her, and to come and speak to her for a moment, when she stood looking at the cane while it came in, her head raised, as if she were breathing in the golden dust with delight, and sniffing the fragrance that poured out through the open doors. There was nothing like it in the world, this sour-sweet smell,

238

redolent of the boiling juice and the lime and sulphur which were its clarifying agents. None of the flowers which bloomed so profusely at Belle Heloise—the cape jasmine, the sweet olive, the orange blossoms—gave forth a perfume comparable to it, in his book. When he saw Merry breathing it in with the golden dust, and knew that for her, too, this was becoming the supreme scent of the place, he was immeasurably proud and pleased. It had been the very breath of his nostrils ever since he was born; his love for it was as natural as it was for the land itself. But to Merry, only a year before, it had still been new and strange. Now she loved it too, and this mutual love of theirs was one more mighty bond joining them together. Looking at her uplifted face, radiant with ripening maternity, he thought they had never been closer than they were now, not only because of the burden she bore, but also because the harmony of their bodies was finding constant expression in the harmony of their minds and spirits.

He never stayed with her long on these golden afternoons. Plauché, the chief engineer, and Dupuy, the sugar boiler, did not leave the mill at all during the grinding season; they stayed on duty for indefinite hours and snatched a little sleep as they could in small makeshift rooms, Plauché's on the mill floor and Dupuy's on the pan floor. Gervais was almost equally constant in his supervision; the days when he had come to have mid-morning coffee with Merry at her bedside were now only part of a rapturous past. He slipped from her side before daylight and did not come back to her until the last watch began at midnight, having hastily eaten his dinner and supper at the boarding-house. She waited up for him, keeping the open fire burning brightly in their living-room, and over the hot toddy which she had prepared, they talked together briefly, before he stripped off his clothes and fell into a dead sleep. And this talk was always limited and one-sided. "The Delco got out of order again today. Damn if I don't think the old-fashioned lanterns and flares were better. . . . There's been a choke on the crusher—too much cane fed to the mill," he would say in his edgy voice. "These things ought not to happen." Or, speaking still more irritably, "A chain broke on the cane carrier this afternoon and that meant a thirty-minute delay. Every delay of that sort means a loss of money, and with the price of sugar dropping the way it is, we can't afford to take any kind of a loss." Sugar was now selling at about thirteen cents, half what it had brought when he and Merry took their prodigal trip to New Orleans and began their extravagant programme of restoration and expansion on the plantation. He did not tell her he realized now that he had plunged ahead too rashly, but she knew that the fear of financial embarrassment must be a constantly gnawing worry. He seldom asked her what she had been doing, and sometimes he did not go in to look at the twins for several nights running. Neither did he go anywhere else. Sunday was just like any other day for a planter during the grinding season, he told Merry, though formerly he had been meticulous about taking her to Mass. He played no poker, he asked none of his political cronies to the house, he did not go to Izzie's to seek them out. The mill and the fields constituted his world.

Even when Mr. Harding passed through Baton Rouge on his way to New Orleans, Gervais could hardly be persuaded to join the group invited to meet the special train at Anchorage and accompany the party of the President Elect across the River. Merry, for once overcoming her shyness and self-consciousness, had been eager to accept the invitation to membership on the Ladies' Committee which was to present Mrs. Harding with an elaborate floral offering and spend with her the brief period which her husband would allocate to the local politicians; otherwise Gervais might actually have declined to go. At least, that was what he said at first, insisting that the care of his crops meant much more to him than meeting any Black Republican. Later he seemed to derive considerable satisfaction in helping to plan the arrangements for the visit, and after it had taken place, in talking about the smooth way everything had run.

The glow of his general satisfaction lasted a long time. However, the Harding visit marked the only departure from his rule that nothing should take him off the plantation and that no one should interfere with his work there. The year before it had not been like this. Gervais had made excuses, to himself and to Merry, to come home for his meals, to linger in Merry's company, to discuss their hopes and plans and to tell her—and show her—that he adored her. The crop had not meant so much to him as it did now. This was partly because it had been a better one, perhaps; the stand of cane was not nearly so good this year; the effects of the mosaic disease were showing up all too plainly. But Merry knew that his present preoccupation could not be wholly explained on these grounds or that of financial involvement, and sometimes, as she lay alone in the darkness, she would think longingly of the time when her husband had been so wholly her lover. She reminded herself that her advanced pregnancy had set limits on their intimacy, but this excuse was inadequate too; it was a time for tenderness, now more than ever, even if it were not a time for passion. Honestly, as she was honest in all things, Merry admitted to herself that Gervais would have left her alone, even if there had been no imminent prospect of another child.

There had been no recurrence of the brief pangs which the vision of the Renos had roused; unfearful of the power of any other woman and too generous-hearted for jealousy, Merry had moments of panic because she knew that the land had reclaimed her husband for its own and that perennially it would continue to do so.

In her loneliness she could not always suppress her resentment of this. But the bad moments came only during the long nights, when she was listening and waiting interminably for the whistle blasts to announce the change of watch. They never came when she stood in the dusty sunshine beside the mill, looking at the cane as it came in, and knowing that at any moment Gervais would join her. At these times she was conscious, as he was, of their kinship of interest and purpose, and of the tie which bound them together, strengthened because of this kinship. She knew, indubitably, that they were no longer dependent, as they once had been, and as lesser loves remained, on the satisfaction of the flesh. After the harvest was in and the child was born, the land would give Gervais back to her and she would be ready to receive him. Their reunion would be one of spontaneous gladness. She could afford to wait for it, in rapt anticipation, because the interval which marked their separation was in itself a fulfilment.

Most of the men who came and went while Merry watched the coming of the cane were familiar to her now, and they exchanged brief and friendly greetings with her as they hurried to and from the factory. "Looks like plenty sugar in the cane, Miss Merry," Plauché would say in a satisfied voice. "The boss is bound to give me those new filter presses I want next year." Sometimes it was nice juice pumps he mentioned instead; Plauché was always after more and more replacement, Gervais told her; but he was usually good-natured about doing without when he could not get it. Sance, on the other hand, had a violent temper. Sometimes he came dashing up on horseback to see what had become of his carts, and if these were drawn up in long lines, awaiting their chance to unload, he yelled at Plauché in unbridled rage. "Look here, Chief, what's the big idea playing hell with my work like this?" he bellowed at such times. "The whole damn cane loading crew's had to stop." Then he would pull off his sombrero and add apologetically to Merry, "You must excuse me, Miss Merry; but I've got to have those carts in the fields. If I don't, I might just as well lay off every last one of my niggers."

Merry liked Lézine Sance and he liked her; usually she managed to say something soothing if noncommittal before she turned to greet Seraphine, who was apt to come by at about the same time, carrying a big armful of mish bread. Seraphine was the wife of Tiphane, the night watchman, and she operated the boarding-house. "What are you giving the boys for supper tonight, Seraphine?" Merry would ask her. "Beef stew. But they're getting mighty tired of that. We'll be having cooler weather pretty soon, then I kin give 'em fresh pork. If any of the hogs should get out of the yard, don't you worry none about 'em, Miss Merry. They won't be botherin' you long." Seraphine would have her laugh, in which Merry would join, and then she would lumber on, pausing

241

once to call back over her shoulder, "Want I should send you over some hot cakes when I make 'em tomorrow mornin', Miss Merry? The new people who've just come in, they say they just can't get enough of my hot cakes." "No, thanks, Seraphine," Merry would call back. "I know they're wonderful, but you've got enough to do feeding the big crew you have now without bothering to send goodies to the Big House." There was jealousy between Seraphine and Lou Ida, and Merry knew better, by this time, than to fan it into flame. But with the insatiable hunger of healthy pregnancy she secretly yearned for Seraphine's cakes, which were better than Lou Ida's.

Besides the workmen who came and went, there were frequent visitors from outside. The young people of the locality had a fad for making up "sugar-house parties" and going in groups to the plantations up and down the River Road. Usually they brought baskets with them, eating under the cane shed. Before going to the mill they stopped to snatch stalks of cane from the carrier and lay bets with each other as to who could chew it the fastest. The cane was tender and brittle and juicy; the boys peeled it for the girls, and some of the merry-makers showed surprising skill in making away with large quantities of it in record time. After they tired of this pastime, they went inside, taking tin cups with them from which to drink the sweet juice as it poured from the crusher; without such a drink the visit would have been thought incomplete, and the more daring members of the party also carried hip-pocket flasks and added a jigger or two of whisky to the juice. If the visitors happened to be on good terms with Dupuy, they also brought loaves of mish bread and clusters of oranges, still on the branches of the trees from which they had been plucked, and pocketsful of pecans, trying to time their visit just when a strike was ending. If they were successful in this, and if Dupuy were in a propitious mood, he would put the foodstuffs on his paddle and thrust it into the boiling syrup; coated with this, the bread and oranges became sweetmeats of rare delicacy, to be savoured at leisure, often by couples who retreated to obscure corners and did not join their companions until they were dragged from their hiding-places, to the tune of a good deal of teasing. The group finally departed in high spirits, the sound of their laughter and singing floating back to the mill as the truck in which they were riding went jolting down the sugar-house road.

If there were friends of hers in such groups, as there often were, and if they arrived in the afternoon, Merry went with them into the sugar house. Miss Mittie came often on Saturdays, bringing riotous schoolchildren with her, and Merry tried to keep popcorn on hand for these youngsters; they loved to take it into the mill with them, crunching it as they rushed around, and "popping" the paper bags afterwards. Hazel Wallace, who had worked with Merry in Goldenberg's store, was another familiar visitor. Hazel's fortunes were rising. She was Mr. Goldenberg's private secretary now, and she had a steady suitor, Al Ferrar, who worked in the advertising department. Previously Hazel had never come freely to Belle Heloise; she had always been a little overawed by the Big House and by Madame Mère, and she had not even made any attempt to see the renovated *garçonnière*. But by the stacked cane, with Al at her side, she was at ease and Merry was too. Al gave one arm to Hazel and the other to Merry and they all entered the sugar mill together.

"Gosh, that looks just like a roller coaster, doesn't it?" Al exclaimed, watching the carrier as it sent the stalks endlessly on and on through the giant crushers which shredded the cane more and more finely, while the liquid poured from it in a waterfall to the juice pan below. A powerful negro, wielding a long-handled wooden rake, stood by the juice pan skilfully keeping the flow unclogged, while a jolly-looking little coloured boy reached under the mill with a can on the end of a long pole and collected a cupful of juice. Having done this, he poured the contents of the cup into a numbered tin pail on a shelf nearby and ran off with it toward some unseen destination.

"What are those buckets for?" Hazel asked, diverted from the roller coaster.

"Samples. That was one of our best sample boys. He's taking some juice into the laboratory to be tested. We can go there later on too, if you like."

Merry knew that Gervais would not mind having her walk around with Hazel and Al, because they would watch carefully and see that she did not slip. But Hazel was not interested in the laboratory. She had reluctantly taken a course in chemistry at high school and the very word laboratory still filled her with aversion. Merry made another suggestion.

"Then let's walk back to the furnaces where the bagasse is burned. I think they're a beautiful sight."

"Bagasse?" Al inquired in a puzzled voice. He had only recently come from New Jersey, and all the processes of the sugar mill were mysterious and exciting to him.

"Yes. That's what's left of the cane, you know, when all the juice has been squeezed out. For a long time people used to throw most of it away—they thought it was good for nothing except fertilizer, and Fabian still swears by it for his camellias and gardenias. Then they found out it made wonderful fuel. Come, let me show you. It goes into the furnaces from the top."

They walked on toward the rear of the mill, past the glittering black spur wheels which Merry admired so much and the fast-spinning fly wheels. As they advanced, she indicated a machine shop at their right, saying, with pride, that all the repair work was done on the place at a great saving of time and money. At their left a pile of rubberoid material, from which circles the size of a stove-lid had been cut, cluttered the pavement at one point, and Merry explained that this stuff was sheet packing used in the engines, that some of the cylinders must have just been repacked and that there had not been time to pick up the leavings. They passed a tank, too, filled with frothy liquid, which Merry told them was raw juice. They had all been agreed that the carrier reminded them of a roller coaster, but now they disagreed about the contents of this tank. It looked like the white of an egg, Hazel said, ready to go on a giant floating island; more like whipped cream, Al thought. Merry stood out for ocean foam. They stood discussing it and joking about it for some time, and then Merry reminded the others that they had started out to see the burning bagasse, and they continued their walk towards the rear, where three gigantic brick furnaces stood in a row. Above the iron doors, near the floor level, a round opening showed in each; and through these the leaping flames and the falling bagasse were plainly visible. The bagasse fell fast, in a shower of tiny flakes, gilded by the light from the fire below; the flames became quivering streaks of crimson as they soared. The whole effect was magical but satanic in its splendour.

"Gosh!" Al exclaimed again, in sincere but inarticulate admiration. "Gosh, I never saw anything to equal that, not anywhere."

"There isn't anything to equal that, not anywhere," Merry said proudly. "Anywhere except on sugar plantations, of course. There's a shed in the rear where the surplus bagasse is kept, and you can see it piled up there if you want to. But that's all it is, just a pile. I think perhaps I ought to have let you see the rest of the mill first, before I brought you to the furnaces. I'm afraid you won't find the tanks and the mixers especially thrilling either. Why not come back to the *garçonnière* with me for some coffee and some cherry bounce? You can have a look at the twins too."

Merry kept cherry bounce as well as popcorn constantly on hand these days; freshly dripped coffee and home-made fruit cake were always in readiness too, and usually pralines and new-salted pecans. Her manner of serving refreshments had not the spectacular quality of the notorious Mr. Blood's, but her hospitality was unstinted and spontaneous. It was something of a problem to get the pecans picked, she told Hazel and Al, as they all went towards the house; there were more than three hundred trees on the plantation, and the nuts, falling in the first cool wind, had to be gathered during the grinding season; so none of the hands from the quarters were free for the work. Fortunately the house servants liked to pick; they were allowed to do it on shares, and they were out in the grove every minute they could get. Cresside liked it too; she herself picked and also supervised the negroes, taking the twins to the grove in their big perambulator, and insisting that it was easy to keep them amused there. There was a full crop this fall, much better than last; Gervais had told Merry it was seldom this was especially good two years in succession. The pecans looked beautiful, shining as if they had been coated with wax as they lay on the dark ground. Perhaps the next time Hazel and Al came out they would like to go to the grove themselves. They were welcome to all the nuts they wanted. . . .

Hazel said they would be glad to pick pecans, pleased because Merry seemed to take it for granted they were coming again. But for the moment her attention was fully engaged with the *garçon-nière*. Merry took her two guests through it from top to bottom, pleased beyond measure at their outspoken admiration of her success with interior decorating. Then, settling them before the living-room fire, she served the cherry bounce herself, in small ruby-coloured glasses, and afterwards Creassy came in, bringing the coffee and fruit cake and nuts on a spacious silver tray. Dinah followed with the twins, who had just been brought in from the grove, their cheeks rosy with the crisp air; and Cresside dropped in for a few minutes too, supplementing Merry's spread with a proffer of cigarettes, which Merry had forgotten, as usual, because she did not smoke herself. Hazel had always assumed that Cresside d'Alvery was very high-hat, because when she first came back from the convent she had trained with such a fast crowd, and because since then she had kept so much to herself, until just lately. Not that the poor girl could help that, Hazel admitted tardily, when she had been laid up from such a bad accident; just the same, it was a pleasant surprise to find her as simple and friendly as Merry, who did not put on airs either now that she was Mrs. Gervais d'Alvery instead of Meredith Randall. Cresside had on a pullover sweater and a short woollen skirt, both somewhat the worse for wear, and her hair was all blown around because she had gone out in the grove hatless. Hazel would have felt she must apologize, if visitors had caught her looking like that, and she smoothed down the skirt of her spotless new beige afternoon dress and glanced at her matching pumps and handbag with a feeling of secret satisfaction. But Cresside did not even seem conscious of her old clothes and tousled hair. She sat around and smoked and chatted and drank coffee until she happened to glance at the clock, and said hell's bells, she had no idea it was so late. Fabian would be there any minute to take her to see Annette Kellerman in "What Women Love." He thought she ought to find out. Would the rest excuse her? It had been grand seeing Hazel again and meeting Al.

Merry had enjoyed seeing Hazel and Al too, and when Gervais came in that night she tried to tell him about their visit over the hot toddy. But Gervais had a fresh worry. It was all he could talk about before he went to sleep.

"We had to slow the mill down today because the centrifugals couldn't keep out of the way of the pans."

"Why not, Gervais?"

"We're getting bastard grains in the sugar. There'll be hell to pay if we can't get rid of them."

"I don't think I know what you mean by bastard grains, *cher*. Have you told me about them before?"

"Probably not. We didn't have any trouble to speak of with them last year. In fact, I can't remember that we've ever had much trouble with them at Belle Heloise before."

"But what *are* they?"

He closed his eyes wearily. "They're small-sized grains that appear in the *masse cuite* after the desired amount of granulation has already been secured. If you don't get rid of them they clog the small holes in the centrifugals, and the sugar just won't dry because the molasses can't pass out through those holes."

"But what causes them in the first place?"

"You're asking an awful lot of questions tonight, aren't you, Merry?"

"Only because I'm interested. Only because everything that troubles you or makes you happy is important to me."

"I know. It's extraordinary how quick you've caught on too. I didn't mean to snap you up. Oh, you were asking me . . . Well, the bastard grains might be Dupuy's fault. He may have been careless in graining the pan. Possibly he didn't take in enough grain to start the strike. That's the usual cause of this special kind of trouble. Then, again, it's possible that he and Plauché have been fighting——"

"But why should they?"

"Oh, no special reason that I know of. The sugar boiler and the chief engineer just seem to be natural enemies, and Dupuy's always picking a quarrel about something. Plauché's naturally good-natured, as you know, but once in a while Dupuy gets his goat. If that's what happened lately, Plauché may have slowed down the water pump. That would have caused the pans to heat up and melt away some of the original grains. If the trouble does lie between Plauché and Dupuy and I can't get it patched up, I'll lose a lot more money."

He was not saying a lot of money, he was saying a lot *more*. So he was losing it right along, losing more than he could afford. And sugar had gone down another cent. For a moment Merry sat still, fingering her pearls. Then she folded her hands in her lap, looking down at her beautiful solitaire. She ought to have told Gervais in the first place that she did not want these baubles, she said to herself reproachfully. She ought not to have let him see how much it would mean to her to get away from the Big House and have him to herself in the *garçonnière* either. But it would not do any good to tell him so now. The money advanced on credit was all spent, and they could not get it back. It would sound as if she were reproaching him if she tried to talk about it. Besides, she had begun to think about something else, something which perhaps she might speak of, and find out if her mind had reflected his, as it did so often.

"Strange, isn't it, that this problem should have arisen now, when you've never had it before?"

"Yes, it is." They looked at each other for a moment, both falling silent. Then Gervais got up and put his arm around her. "Don't you get to seeing symbols in everything, like the niggers do," he said. "Come on, honey, I'm dead on my feet. Let's go to bed."

As the season advanced, Gervais was able to take the grinding more easily in his stride, in spite of his varied worries. If the crop was not as good as the year before, at least the weather was better; that more or less evened things up. One warm mellow day succeeded another in leisurely succession. The satsumas hung in golden cosmos and marigolds, flowers of All Saints, bloomed in riotous profusion. The leaves were turning too, and the moss that draped the oaks shone in the sun as it did at no other season; Merry called them "the gold and silver trees." There was no rain and no frost. Labour was plentiful, for many returning soldiers had found no regular jobs awaiting them, and Gervais was able to enlarge his force of factory workers from their ranks. Moreover, women as well as men turned out in prodigious numbers and the fields were full of cutters; their bright garments dotted the landscape, their broad knives sang in the sunshine.

The improvements Gervais had made in the mill were contributing to higher efficiency too. One day the shaft on the Walsh feeder rake, which swept the cane from the cars to the carrier, suddenly snapped, and there was a long delay in consequence; but this was the only major breakdown. Merry sensed the lessened strain in her husband's manner and conversation. He was neither exhausted nor nervous when he came in at midnight, and he stopped speaking solely about mishaps and expenses. Instead he would say contentedly, "The mill ran well today—no stops of any kind," and eventually, with still greater satisfaction, "The sucrose is fine, and we have the cane deliveries in grand shape."

"Couldn't you take things a little easier then?" Merry asked.

"I can't really let up until the whistle blows for the last time. But I thought I might take part of a day off, at least."

"That would be wonderful," Merry began. But he interrupted her.

"Perhaps you'd better let me finish. I didn't mean to spend it at home. I meant to go hunting, if you wouldn't mind too much."

"Why should I mind?" Merry asked. The mental vision of long hours with Gervais had faded as soon as it was formed. But she spoke staunchly. "Were you planning to go 'possum hunting with Cresside?" she asked. During the last few weeks Cresside, who was getting around more and more, had been out several times in mixed groups of six or eight, starting as soon as it was dark and spending most of the night in the woods. The girls as well as the men wore high-laced boots, corduroy breeches and heavy windbreakers on these expeditions and carried flashlights and lanterns. They always took a black boy with them who wore a carbide light fastened to his forehead for the purpose of "shining" the 'possum's eyes and holding the bag into which it was put after it was shaken from the tree. They also took two or three dogs, who first trailed the 'possum and eventually finished him off. Apparently the hunters spent hours at a time sitting around a camp-fire while they waited for the dogs to find the trail, and wiener roasts, hot chocolate, and carefree and casual singing were also features of the night's entertainment. As Cresside described it all afterwards, it sounded very thrilling to Merry, who had never done hunting of any kind. But when she asked her interested question, Gervais answered her contemptuously.

"Lord, no! I outgrew that kind of sport years ago. I was thinking of going on a wildcat hunt. There's a negro named Pinkie Baker that lives over on the other side of town, who's got the best hunting dogs around here, and every now and then he lends them to Parker. The Governor likes cat hunting. He doesn't always follow the run, but he enjoys listening to the dogs after the cat's been jumped. Parker's taking Pinkie's dogs and striking out to Boylston's early Saturday morning—the hunt's going to start from there. The Governor's bringing Fabian along with him, and they'd be glad to stop by for me. Happy Sevier and Ferd Claiborne are going together in another car. And Harvey Lawrason's at Boylston's already. He's driven over from Livingston Parish and brought his own dogs with him, some in the car and some in a trailer—people really go in for hounds where he lives, near Denham Springs. . . That'll make a party of seven or eight all told, and it's a good crowd. I haven't seen Lawrason to amount to anything since I got back from France."

He was making no effort to conceal his normal masculine yearning for congenial male companionship. Merry did not let him down by voicing her equally normal feminine disappointment that he preferred to spend his first time off with these friends instead of with her.

"Parker's been out with Boylston two or three times already," Gervais went on. "It seems that last year when Boylston was hunt

248

ing he had a rather peculiar experience. Cresside said he'd told her about it. I don't know whether he told you too, or whether she did."

"No," Merry answered, leaning over to refill the toddy glasses from a pitcher that stood on a hob by the fire.

"Well, his gyp Diana started a trail, and when he caught up with her, she was standing on her haunches, baying in front of a hollow tree with a big hole in it. Boylston asked her what she was doing, hunting 'possums when she knew he wanted to hunt cats! It's hard to believe, but you talk to these hounds just as if they were humans, and when you start out you tell them what you're after, and they don't trail anything else that day. He'd said 'Scat!' to Diana the first thing after they'd left the house, and it wasn't like her to make a mistake. She answered him by sticking her head into the hole, and when she took it out her face was all scratched up. So Boylston looked in the hole himself, and, sure enough, there was a big cat. He drew back mighty quick, and the cat jumped out and ran like mad, with Diana after her. Boylston says he doesn't know how he happened to look in the hole again, but he did, and there were four kittens! He took up two of them and nicked pieces out of their ears, and then he took up the other two and cut their tails off. Afterwards he called Diana back, so that the cat would have a chance to raise them. All this year he's been hunting the marked cubs. Of course, they're grown cats now. . . . What's the matter? Am I boring you?"

Merry could not bear to see the suffering of any living creature, or even to hear about it. She had flinched when Gervais had mentioned the mutilated kittens, and the happy expression on her face clouded. But she knew there was no use in telling Gervais, or any other born hunter, how she felt. Even Cresside, who was so phenomenally kind to the twins, felt no compunctions about killing doves.

"No, you're not boring me," she said quickly. "I think that's a very interesting story, Gervais. Has Charles caught any of those marked cubs?"

"Yes, he caught one when he was hunting alone, and one the first time Parker went out with Pinkie's dogs. Now he wants to round up the others, and I'd like to be there when it happens."

"Naturally you would. I'm glad Charles has invited you. I'm glad you feel you can go," Merry said, again filling the toddy glasses from the hob.

It was a little earlier than usual when he left her two mornings later, but she was accustomed, by now, to having him slip away in the darkness without a word or a caress. She knew that his silent departure signified neither negligence nor indifference, but a genuine desire not to disturb her; and usually, though she was

249

aware of his leaving, she drifted back to sleep again almost immediately. Now she had been vaguely wakeful and restless for some time already. She snuggled down among the pillows, after the car had rattled over the cattle-gap and the dogs had stopped barking, but she could not seem to get comfortable. For a few minutes she continued to shift her position, with increasing discomfort. Then a sharp dagger-like pain shot without warning through her vitals and trailed away into numbness.

"It can't be that," she said aloud, in bewilderment. "It isn't time yet—not for two weeks at least." But she turned over, and tried to switch on the electricity. Evidently the Delco was out of order again, however, so she lighted her bedside candle and looked at the little clock standing on the night-table beside her. It was exactly four o'clock. She lay down again, without extinguishing the candle, and kept her eyes on the moving hands. At twenty minutes past four the dagger-like pain stabbed her again, harder this time. Instead of leaving her numb, it left her spent. She gave herself a few moments to recover from it; then, putting on felt slippers and a warm woollen robe, she lighted the lamps that were kept in readiness for emergencies, setting one in the window, and, taking a lantern, started for the Big House. It loomed darkly before her, surrounded by eerie black trees, and above them the stars had a far frosty look. It was colder than it had been any night during the fall.

"That's why I'm shivering," she told herself, as she hurried forward. "I'm not frightened, I'm just cold. There's nothing to be frightened about. I'll be all right as soon as I get to Dinah. She said it wouldn't be bad this time."

Merry did not deceive herself. She knew that it would be bad, that it had to be. There was no escape from the dreadful hours which lay ahead of her. But she also knew that she had the strength and courage to meet them undefeated, that no woman's life was full and complete without them, any more than it was full and complete without the hours of rapture which had come before them. Remembering these, she found that she could go on. The third pain, like a vicious auger boring its way through her body, smote her as she reached the gallery. She seized the newel post of the outer stairway, and gripped it hard, smothering a scream. Then, clinging to the railing, she continued to mount the stairs.

XIX

WHEN Governor Parker and the two cousins arrived at Hackberry Lodge, the other men were already gathered around a log fire in Charles Boylston's panelled study, smoking and drinking small blacks. All of them, except Happy Sevier, who had on his old army breeches and puttees, and Boylston, who as usual looked as if his whipcord were the recent creation of a London tailor, were wearing high boots over ordinary well-worn trousers. Harvey Lawrason, the wealthy lumberman from Denham Springs, was outstanding in the group. Though slightly stooped, he was so immensely tall that he still towered over all the others, and his huge bony hands had an unmistakable look of power. He had light sandy hair, and light eyelashes which looked so short that even a casual glance from his pale blue eyes had the effect of a stare. Though he was essentially a man's man, numerous women had figured prominently in his life, and current gossip centred around a pretty widow in Baton Rouge; but hunting was his real passion. Though he had a background of considerable culture, it suited him to talk as if he were utterly unlettered, and he was a teller of tall tales, introducing most of them with the strange expression, "Which-I-God!" and speaking in a high, drawling voice. He was in the midst of a story now.

"Those Walkers of yours look all right to me, Charlie, but I want to see 'em in action. Which-I-God, you can't tell nothing about a dog by looking at him! You take Martin's Choice. There ain't a setter that's worth his salt that don't trace his blood back to him, one way or another, and yet, he was the sorriest-looking bird dog that ever nailed a covey down wind. He had a tail a big rat wouldn't have been ashamed of, and a pinched-in face, but, Lord-in-the mountains! what a nose and bottom! That dog could run his legs off to the elbow and still go after birds. I mind the time Sam Cannell brought him to our little old field trial in Clinton. Well, sirs, I got a thick-headed brother-in-law that thinks he knows all about bird dogs—I ain't apologizing for him; a man ain't responsible for what his sister marries. He used to pay a mint of money for his dogs and brag of what world beaters he had in his kennels. So me and Sam rigged it up how he was going to take Martin's Choice over to my brother-in-law's and offer to sell the dog to him for five dollars. 'Course, everybody knows Martin's Choice was open champion that year, and five thousand dollars couldn't have bought him. Likely his owner would get more than that out of stud fees. Well, sirs, we did it. And my brother-in-law give that sorry-looking pup one disgusted look and says, 'Take that thing off my property. whatever it is. You claim it's a setter all right, but it looks to me like it got a sight of muskrat blood in it. Go on, take it out of here, whatever it is, it might be catching.' Well, it just goes to show there was somebody who thought you could tell all about a dog by looking at him, turning down a chance to buy the national open champion for five dollars."

While Lawrason drawled on, without commanding undivided attention, a drowsy, slatternly coloured girl, who had on a cloth with flapping ends fastened loosely at the back of her head instead of the customary neat tignon, was passing the coffee in a haphazard way. A man's jacket, thrown across her shoulders, partially covered her dingy woollen dress; but she looked cold as well as sullen, and Fabian felt sorry for her. He spoke to her kindly as she stopped to serve him.

"Pretty early to be up on a cold morning, isn't it, Tilda?"

"Sho' is, Mistah Fabian. Don't seem like it's worth while for we'uns to bed ourselves, iffen us has to stir agin so soon."

"We've got to get started early if we're going to hit a trail by daybreak," Boylston said, rather sharply. The remark was addressed to Fabian, but it was obviously aimed at Tilda, who gave her master a resentful glance as she shuffled off with the tray. Boylston paid his servants higher wages than anyone else on the River Road; but he had never learned to make them like him. "I don't want to hurry any of you," he said, speaking this time to the company at large. "But I think if you've finished your coffee, we ought to be on our way."

The guests gathered up their caps and guns and went out into the yard, where the darkies and the dogs were waiting for them. Pinkie Baker's four black-and-tan hounds—Hayes, Crook, Beulah and Fox—had been left in charge of George Dyer, the Governor's chauffeur, when Parker himself went into the house with Fabian and Gervais. The trailer which Lawrason had brought over from Denham Springs, filled with redbones, was parked close beside the Governor's car, enabling Simeon, Lawrason's man, to pass the time of day, more or less obscenely, with George, whose own conversation was less lurid but who was not above listening. Amos Palfry, Boylston's driver, who had brought out his master's pure-bred Walkers, tightly tethered, stood a slight distance away from them. Swung over one shoulder he had Ferry Boat Bill's handsome horn, which was his insignia of leadership and which he wore with great pride; and while he waited for the expedition to get under way, he kept admonishing his dogs. Two younger negroes, Cass and Willie, who also worked for Boylston and usually went hunting with him when he had a sizable group at Hackberry Lodge, were also standing in the yard, discussing the relative merits of the different types of sports common to the countryside.

"Ah sho' wish dis here was a 'coon hunt we was goin' on, 'stead of a cat hunt."

252

"Uh, not me. Ah likes cat huntin' fust rate. Squirrel hunts and 'possum hunts, 'ems for ladyfolks much as menfolks. Don't even no dogs go along, squirrel huntin'. How comes you don't like cat huntin' well as 'possum huntin', Willie?"

"Can't eat no cat, can us? Don't get de hides to sell, neither—bossman keeps 'em for hisself to stuff and den feeds de meat to his dogs. Ain't no better eatin' dan 'possum, nor squirrel neither, and dey keeps de pot full pretty near all through de cold. Ah don't mind havin' ladyfolks on de hunt neither. Leastwise Ah don't mind havin' Miss Cresside. She plumb game on rough goin', and Ah seed her shine four 'possums all in de one night. Now Miss Regine, dat's different. Ah can do without ladyfolks like her jes as well as you can."

"Reckon it's Miss Regine done set me against ladyfolks huntin'. Ain't never forget dat night she come out de woods in dem little high-heeled slippers of hers 'stead of de tall boots Miss Cresside got sense enough to wear. She kept a gettin' stuck in de swamp and a hollerin' after de res', 'Oh, wait a minute! Oh, please come back and get poor little me!'"

Like most negroes, Cass had a considerable gift of mimicry. He mocked Regine's silly way of speaking so effectively that the other darkies all turned around to listen, grinning with appreciation, and some of them snickered under their breath. Willie grabbed his companion's sleeve.

"You hush yo' mouf, nigger, lessen yo' wants to get us into bad trouble. Don't you know Miss Regine done stole Miss Cresside's beau? Ain't none of de d'Alverys forgive her for dat and ain't never goin' to. And dere's Miss Cresside's brudder settin' right inside de house dis minute, lak' as not to come out while you'se talkin'."

The warning had not been given a minute too soon. Just then the door of the house was flung open, and Boylston and his guests came out. Cass and Willie straightened up quickly and came forward respectfully and somewhat shamefacedly. Lawrason, who missed little connected with an outing of this type, glanced at them shrewdly. Then, with his foot on the running-board of his own car, he called out to Dyer.

"Good morning, George! How's Beulah today? Hear she didn't do so well on her last hunt."

"Dat's right, Mr. Lawrason, she sho' was confused. But she don't do dat once in a blue moon. Ain't no better trail dog anywhere, 'ceptin' old Hayes, of course. He's got 'em all beat. But you're goin' to see Beulah doin' fine today, too."

"We won't see any of them 'doin' fine' unless we get started pretty soon," Boylston remarked. It always irked him to have his guests stand around, chatting and joking with the negroes when it was time to be off. "Come on, boys, let's go."

The circle broke up slowly, with some final discussion as to the best division of the guests among the different automobiles. Boylston went with the Governor this time, Gervais with Claiborne and Lawrason, the trailer, packed with barking redbones, in charge of Simeon, attached to their car. Fabian and Happy Sevier followed in one of Boylston's cars, and Amos with Cass and Willie and the Walkers brought up the rear in another. Their route took them over the headland, past the ruins of an old Confederate fort, and the road, cut by the cane carts, was very rough, so that they had to proceed slowly towards the bluffs where they were bound. A little light was beginning to show in the dark sky, paling the stars, but revealing the order and richness of the fields, some already planted with the next season's crop. Parker, peering out over them with his keen, beady eyes, complimented his host on his achievements.

"You've done wonders with this plantation, Boylston. I know the state it was in when you took it over. What yield are you getting to the acre this year?"

"About fifteen tons. Not as much as last year, due to this damn mosaic disease."

"Yes, I'm afraid that's going to play havoc all over the state, and I know it's beginning to show up along the River Road already."

They were leaving the headland, and at a signal from Boylston, George stopped the car. They got out near the edge of a field covered with a brownish plant which was just going to seed. Parker stopped to pull up a handful of it.

"Lespedeza!" he said enthusiastically. "So you've got that too! Nothing like it for cattle and pasture-land, in my book! You can't do better than increase your acreage of this, Boylston."

"I'm planning to, Governor, next year."

Parker selected a stalk of lespedeza from the handful he was still holding and began to chew it reflectively, in much the same way that he chewed tobacco. The two men walked on together towards a pasture overgrown with Cherokee rose, scrub oak and briar thickets, flanked by tall bluffs, where the reddish soil was partially covered with straggly trees. A white frost which gleamed in the pale light coated the bushes and the patches of grass which showed between these; this would disappear with the day, but meantime it gave an effect of eerie loveliness to a scene which in any case would have been peculiarly enticing to the men who had come there.

"Here's the place where Amos saw the cat tracks two days ago," Boylston said. "He'll be along in a minute, but your car makes better time than the rest, Governor." While he was speaking, however, the second car swung into sight, and he added, "Here comes Claiborne and d'Alvery, though. Claiborne's quite a character, isn't he?"

"I'll say he is. And he has some damn original ideas about the duties of a game warden "

254

Parker spoke rather dryly, and as the others got out of the car and came nearer he called out, "Ferd, could you by any chance spare me some of those birds you've got in your cooler?"

"Birds? I don't get you. What birds, John?"

"You get me all right. I'm talking about those my old friend Surget was caught with last week. Somebody took them away from him, but no one's heard what happened to them after that."

"Oh hell, I'm sure they were preserved for a noble purpose. I'm here to defend Ferd on that score," Fabian said pleasantly. The cars had all arrived in the pasture now, and he had come forward in time to change the drift of a dialogue which had begun to take a serious turn. An angry flush was spreading over Claiborne's face, and Parker was no longer speaking jestingly. "Look, we're not any of us here in our professional capacities this morning, are we?" Fabian went on. "We're just so many hunters, and it looks to me as if we're in for some damn good sport."

As he spoke he motioned towards Simeon, who was just getting the redbones out of the trailer, and to Cass, who had already taken the walkers from Boylston's car. All these dogs were still held in leash, but Amos now walked over to the Governor's car, releasing old Hayes and Beulah and turning Crook and Fox over to Willie. With the two trail dogs leaping joyously around him, Amos next began to kick vigorously at the bushes, shouting "Scat!" as he did so. Instantly Hayes and Beulah rushed off into the dark thickets, while the other hounds strained impatiently at their leashes, pulling their drivers around over the rough rime-covered pasture. For a few moments the hunters, now ready and eager for action, remained motionless and alert, listening attentively. Then the sound they had been awaiting came to them through the stillness: old Hayes was giving tongue, his deep voice loud and triumphant.

"Good for him! He's hit the cold trail in record time!" Lawrason exclaimed. "We're off, aren't we?"

The leashed dogs, freed at last, were already tearing after their leaders, their drivers whooping them on. The other men immediately plunged into the brush after them, and for the next thirty minutes pushed forward with perseverance, "cold trailing" the cat which had fed along the way during the night. The ground was very rough, and Fabian and Happy especially found it hard going. But the thrill of pursuit, even more than the cool, crisp air, was a powerful stimulant; they were all tingling with it, and in their excitement they were almost unaware of the impediments to their progress, though they hardly spoke to each other as they first forged forward. But when the dogs, who had been snuffing the scent as they scurried along with their noses close to the ground, raised their heads and began to bay, the hunters turned to each other, proudly identifying their own.

"What's the matter with Mort, Harvey? I haven't heard him sound off yet."

"Listen! There he is now!"

"There goes my little red bitch, Molly, giving tongue too!"

"That's Hayes, Pinkie's prize hound, again! I'd know him anywhere. There's not another dog in the state with that deep bell-like voice."

"Right you are. I'm here to tell you there's no better sport than hunting with him. Just the same, Fox is my favourite."

The light, filtering in through the trees, was brighter now. The men could see, more distinctly, the robin feathers left on the trail, remnants of the cat's final feast before settling down to sleep, and they were pressing ahead with redoubled vigour and enthusiasm. The dogs had begun to circle around a briar patch flanked by a huge fallen log, their voices rising in chorus, and the hunters were all hurrying towards it when Gervais froze in his tracks, shouting a warning to the others.

"Look out! I swear I smell a cottonmouth! Yes, there he is, right alongside that log!"

As he spoke a thick brown and black moccasin, curled up under some fallen leaves, opened its deadly white mouth and then, sluggishly uncoiling itself, slithered away among the bushes. It was gone before most of the hunters were more than half aware of it. But Gervais fell back a little, glancing uneasily at the thickets around him, and several of the dogs, getting the same nauseous scent, recoiled too, as they shrank away, while others snapped at the rustling leaves, breaking the chorusing circle.

"Mr. Gervais, he's done got dem dogs upset," Willie said to Cass in a contemptuous undertone. "He's gwine to have snake jitters all mornin' hisself too. Iffen dis here had been a 'possum hunt now, and Miss Cresside had been along, she'd had old Mr. Cottonmouth kilt before he could 'a' got away. Ah tells you again, Cass, I likes 'possum huntin' de best, and I likes for de ladyfolks to be along, iffen it's de right ladyfolks. I seen just as good spo't an' better 'possum huntin' dan we seen on dis cat hunt yet. Ah don't find no fun just a-ploughin' and a-ploughin' t'rough dese blackberry bushes all day. Iffen we'd been 'possum huntin', we'd a had a couple of 'em treed by now."

"We's a-goin' to have dat ole one-eared cat treed plenty soon now too, big boy. Come on, can't you hear de bossman callin' you?"

The hunters were dividing. From now on the hunt would be even more strenuous than it had been before. The "cold trailing" was over, and the "hot trailing" beginning. The cat, though the hollow log had been located as its bed, had made a swift getaway at the approach of the dogs; but they had lost less than a minute and they were now off in close pursuit, Amos whooping them on more vociferously than ever. Lawrason and Claiborne had followed along after them, without waste of time, and were already crashing through the brush. Boylston and Gervais were still standing near the log, the former because he was too punctilious to leave any of his guests unceremoniously, the latter because he was still shaken by the "snake jitters" of which Willie had shrewdly suspected him. Fabian, grasping the cause of his host's indecision, lowered himself slowly to the log and nodded pleasantly to Boylston.

"This looks like a pretty good stopping-place to me," he remarked. "I'll have the best of my fun sitting down and listening to the dogs, taking it easy while the rest of you wear yourselves out. What about leaving Willie here with me, Charles? You don't really need him, do you, with the other drivers you've got? I wouldn't mind having a good fire to toast myself by. Anyone else staying behind?"

"I am," Happy Sevier answered. "Hard enough to get this far. Pushing a cat's too damn strenuous for me. You've got the right idea, Fabian."

"That's my viewpoint too," Parker said quickly. His decision to remain with the two friends was announced with such promptitude that it seemed to take them out of the cripple class and place them among his preferred companions. As Gervais and Boylston disappeared, he walked in a leisurely way over to the log, took out the plug of tobacco which he always carried in his pocket, and, as usual, bit off a corner of it and rolled it deliberately around in his mouth before he went on with what he had to say.

"I don't know whether you two are especially interested in the Constitutional Convention we're going to have next spring," he remarked at length. "Personally I hope it's going to do great things for this state. You've already heard me speak about my plan for the development of the University, Fabian. The Convention ought to give a good deal of time to a programme for that. And with the River Road the way it is most of the time, I'm sure your cousin would agree that the creation of the State Highway Commission would be a mighty good thing too."

The Governor was off on his pet topic. He continued to talk politics with the two young lawyers beside a cheerful blaze which Willie kept feeding with dry branches, while intermittently muttering to himself that he wished he were 'possum hunting instead of cat hunting. Meanwhile Gervais and Boylston went on, soon catching up with the others. One of the young dogs had already jumped a rabbit, Lawrason told them, and that had caused a delay. Now the cat had evidently got into a thick place, for it was just "babbling around," as Amos described its manœuvres. At all events, the hunt was temporarily more or less at a standstill, and the men, now all drenched with sweat and pretty well winded from their exertions, were not sorry for a short breathing-space, though their enthusiasm was still unabated. Lawrason enlivened their wait with another characteristic story.

"Parker don't never fail to make the gracious gesture, does he? Like he did just now, I mean. No, Which-I-God, I take that back. I heard of one time he wasn't so gracious. Tack Evans was tellin' me about it. Parker's nobody's prissy, but he don't like smut, not even in stories. Well, you all know that. Anyway, the Governor and Tack and a couple of newspapermen were on their way to Alexandria to some damn meetin' or other, and they stopped overnight along the way at one of them little two-storey hotels without any elevator, and the bedrooms, if you could call 'em that, all in a long row on the second floor. The bellhop who was puffing along after 'em with the bags was a funny-lookin' midget, not a boy, you understand, but a queer little ol' dwarf. When he set Parker's bag down, just before he started to unlock the door, this midget tugged at the Governor's coat-tails and says in a hoarse whisper, 'Does you want a lady tonight, sah?' Tack said it was somethin' to see the Governor standing there grim as they make 'em in his pepper-and-salt suit, with an expression on his face that could have froze hell-fire. If some little old dwarf had tried to pander to the Archbishop of Canterbury when he was in full pontificals just ready to go to the Cathedral, it would have been about the same thing."

This time Lawrason's story met with a gratifying response. The hunters were now in the midst of a forest, dense, for the most part, with oak and gum trees and heavy with palmetto and other underbrush; but it was studded here and there by gum ponds and patches of grass where cattle had grazed, and intersected by small creeks. The men finally reached one of these streams, after their first two delays, only to find that the trail had been broken again. The dogs, who were all hot and tired by now, were baying around a tree at the water's edge in a state of disorder and confusion. Amos, quieting them as he glanced around with an experienced eye, pointed to a long limb overhanging the water.

"Look-a-here, Mr. Boylston suh, cat done crossed de creek on dat limb for sure. Dat's how de dogs lose trail. Come on, you no-count hounds, you's gwine swim across dis creek wid old Amos. We's a-gwine find dat one-eared cat yet."

He strode into the water as he spoke, the dogs, eager and excited again, swimming around him, straining up the bank on the far side of the creek, and springing forward once more. Only old Hayes failed to join the rest of the pack. For some moments he remained in the water, lapping it up with calm enjoyment, and splashing around in a leisurely way. The hunters, who were still standing under the long-limbed tree, watched him with varying degrees of anxiety.

"At this rate he'll never pick up the trail again, and there's no telling whether Beulah can get it without him. They're a grand team as trail dogs, and old Hayes is all right alone. But Beulah isn't."

"Don't worry, Charles. Even if Hayes falls down on the job, Mort won't. Nor Molly either."

"Old Hayes ain't a-gwine fall down on no job, Mr. Lawrason. He's full of fat and he gets mighty hot, runnin' lak he's been doin'. Soon as he cools hisself he'll pick up dat trail again right quick. You's a-gwine to see. You'll have your cat most any minute now."

While Amos was still speaking, old Hayes, after pausing to take one last drink, climbed slowly up on the opposite bank and went over to the driver, wagging his tail and lifting his head. Then, as if he were glad to get back on the job again now that he had shown his gratitude in the driver's confidence, he shot off in a different direction from the other dogs. The hunters, fording the creek in their turn, began crashing through the woods once more, to be arrested almost instantly by the renewed sound of his baying, mingled with shouts from Amos.

"Which-I-God he *has* got that stinking cat!" Lawrason exclaimed. "Fast work! He must be somewhere in the clump of oaks."

The hunters tore their way along, closing quickly in around the tree where old Hayes was standing guard, baying with all his might and main at the base of a heavy grapevine which climbed the oak. But the other dogs were nowhere to be seen, and, though it was now broad daylight, the men were not rewarded by the expected sight of a crouching cat, glowering at them from amongst the branches. Boylston spoke to Amos with the sharpness of disappointment.

"Old Hayes must have told us a lie this time. There's no cat in that tree."

"Sho' dey is, Mr. Boylston suh. You don't see it, but it bees dere."

"We'd see it if it were there, all right. That tree's too clean to hide anything."

Claiborne had spoken sharply too. Every bloodthirsty instinct was now fully roused and the seemingly false summons was a sorry slacking of the morning's excitement. Without deigning to answer his master's guest, Amos called old Hayes to him and asked Boylston to step back, while he himslf began to shake the ropelike grapevine. As it vibrated and swung away from the tree, a ball of moss above it suddenly seemed to become animate. Scattering strands of it fell to the ground. The rest, violently rent apart, disclosed an enormous cat which leaped from its hiding-place and hit the ground with almost incredible speed. But Boylston was quick too. Before it could reach cover in the underbrush he raised his rifle and shot. At the same instant old Hayes sprang forward and

259

pounced upon its tumbling form. It gave a vicious snarl and clawed futilely in the air. Then it rolled over and lay still—a huge, wicked, magnificent beast—minus one ear.

For a moment Amos stood still, savouring his moment of triumph; then he turned to Boylston, whose face, stripped of its customary control, was lighted with atavistic satisfaction, and quietly asked whether they were to go on with the hunt. But everyone was agreed that, after the dramatic capture of " one-ear," pursuit of another cat could only end in an anticlimax. The lust to kill was now assuaged; the inevitable let-down had followed. Amos was instructed to call in the other dogs, and, after blowing his horn and allowing them to "wrastle" the cat for a moment, he took it from them to save its hide, and, slinging it over his shoulder, started back towards the pasture with unconcealed satisfaction. Indeed, everyone's return to Hackberry Lodge was marked by high good spirits. Most of the men, delighted by the success of this hunt, were already planning another. Without much difficulty, Lawrason was persuaded that he might as well remain over the week-end, and there was some rather broad joking about his ulterior motives for remaining near Baton Rouge, which he took in good part. . . . The hunt had covered at least fifteen miles, Boylston thought; what did he mean, fifteen? Gervais corrected him; it wasn't really much over five; it just seemed longer; poor Charles, he was just a tenderfoot still when it came to scrambling through briar patches. Maybe Gervais could outwalk Charles, but at least Charles didn't have snake jitters, Fabian remarked in a dry aside. . . .

By the time they had reached the house they were deep in a discussion of the relative merits of different hunting breeds, and this went on while they made their way, without formality, to the dining-room and attacked the hearty breakfast awaiting them. They were all ravenously hungry by this time; the huge platters of pork chops, ham and eggs, and country sausage were soon emptied; the tall piles of hot cakes and hot biscuits, the great mounds of hominy grits melted away. But Tilda, now clad in a formal and immaculate uniform, refilled the coffee-pot again and again, and it continued to circulate as the argument went on and on. It would seem clear enough, from the morning's performance, that Pinkie's black and tans were peerless, Parker contended. Well, he would still stick to his redbones, Lawrason said. Look at the muscle of them and the size! Mort tipped the scales at nearly seventy pounds. And then that rich russet of theirs—where could you match it? It gave colour to any hunting scene. He'd never heard that size and colour were what made a good hunting dog, Boylston remarked. Why, Lawrason himself had rambled on and on about Martin's Choice early that very morning! Now Walkers were smaller than redbones, he was willing to grant that, but they were better shaped and better proportioned and they were a good deal more intelligent. He would never forget a dog he had owned when he was still with the Middlesex Hunt. While he was riding to hounds he had dropped his crop, and, after the kill, Patrick, this dog of his, had gone back over the course by himself and retrieved it. He had come into the house, carrying the crop in his mouth, just as they were all sitting down in their pink coats to the hunt breakfast, and laid it on the rug at his master's feet. Patrick had been the talk of the country for weeks afterwards. . . .

"Well, I reckon that was right smart for a dog, up in Massachusetts," Lawrason drawled. "But I'm here to tell you, we've got hogs over in Livingston Parish smarter than any of your Yankee hounds. Why, I had a hog once that was so smart he'd go to the crib and fetch some corn and put it by a log. Then he'd lie down and wait for the chickens to come along and eat it, and he'd catch them, one by one, and eat them. Naturally this was a razorback hog. These razorbacks never need to exert themselves any. Which-I-God this one's nose was so long he'd be standing on that log where he'd killed the chickens, and dig for roots with his nose in three feet of water."

The laughter which greeted this sally was echoed by the honk of a horn sounding in the driveway. Boylston, already absorbed in the effort to cap Lawrason's tall tale, paid no attention to the sound until Fabian touched him lightly on the arm and motioned towards the window. Boylston looked up in surprise.

"Why, it's Cresside!" he exclaimed, jumping up and hastening through the door. Fabian, stiff from his morning's exertion, rose and followed him, walking even more awkwardly than usual. Boylston's other guests turned in their places to see the girl get out of the car, greet her host and her cousin excitedly, and come swiftly back towards the house with them. She had on a red jacket and skirt, and a small red hat was pulled down over her ears, after the fashion of the moment; but her black hair bushed out irrepressibly underneath it, and her manner was very gay. She stopped on the threshold of the dining-room and waved a buoyant greeting.

"Hello, everybody!" she said. "No, please don't get up. Of course, I'm not here to stay. All you mighty huntsmen will have to excuse me for breaking in on you like this, but I'm out with a search warrant for my brother. . . . Gervais, you've got a son."

"Which-I-God, another?" Lawrason said incredulously, as Gervais, pushing back his chair, rushed over to his sister and began to ply her with imperative questions. Cresside laughed and held up her hands as a signal of her helplessness to cope with his outburst.

"Yes, another!" she said gaily. "That's what I meant, of course. Three children in eleven months is going some, isn't it? Hold on, Gervais, I can't tell you everything at once. Yes, Merry's doing as well as could be expected, and the baby boy weighs nine pounds.

all quite in the best tradition. We've had what you might call a hectic morning, though, I can tell you—no one but you needed to go cat hunting for excitement, Gervais! Merry came in to get Dinah about five, and then Dinah woke me and I woke *maman*—a regular merry-go-round! Hang it, I didn't mean to make a lousy pun like that! We sent Amen into town post-haste for the doctor, but good old Champagne was off on another case, and of course it didn't occur to Amen that he might go and get someone else! He just left a message and came on back to Belle Heloise. Naturally we sent him off again, with ants in his pants, but by that time we knew we'd have to manage as well as we could without him. And were we glad the good old acetylene was still functioning in the Big House and that we weren't dependent on that damn Delco! I sure do hand it to Merry, Gervais. She never once lost her nerve, and if you think most girls wouldn't have, without a doctor or a nurse, or even a husband in the house . . . And she didn't make any mean cracks or do any moaning and groaning because you were off hunting while she was having her baby. . . . I have to hand it to Dinah, too. She's my choice for a midwife, makeshift or not, anywhere, any time. And *maman* stood up to the whole thing like a Trojan, too!"

"I know you'll excuse me if I dash off." Gervais turned to Boylston, his flushed face wreathed in smiles, and wrung his host's outstretched hand, while the others crowded around him, slapping him on the back, and heartily voicing their congratulations. "We weren't expecting this for at least a couple of weeks yet, or of course I wouldn't have been here, and there'd have been a nurse on call in the house. But I can tell you I'm pretty proud of my wife just the same. There's nothing she can't take. Come on, Cresside, you can tell me the rest on the road."

"Have you had anything to eat yet this morning, Cresside?" Fabian inquired.

"Why, no, I reckon I haven't. But that's all right. I hadn't even thought of it."

"Why don't you stop long enough to snatch a cup of coffee, anyway? Gervais can go along in your car and I'll take you home."

"Good idea." Gervais said jovially, answering for his sister. "Look, I must get going. But I hope you all stop on your way back to town, and have a drink with me to make Philogene's hair curl—that's his name, of course. So long."

Gervais flung himself out of the door, followed by the redoubled congratulations of his friends, which were now rising to a chorus of shouts. Cresside sat down in his place and reached for his cup.

"This is all right, isn't it, Charles? That is, I believe it was Fabian who asked me to stay, and after all this is your house. But everyone was making so much noise I couldn't half hear."

"Of course it's all right. I'm very much honoured at having you here. I was trying to tell you so, but in the midst of all this hub-bub . . . Wait, I'll have Tilda bring you some fresh coffee."

He spoke courteously, but with a slight constraint in his voice. Something's wrong, Cresside said to herself, feeling half amused and half angry. Is he annoyed because Fabian came to my rescue, before he thought of it? No, that can't be it. Maybe he's shocked because I stayed. He mightn't recognize Fabian as a chaperon, and he thinks all these other men will be surprised because I'm linger-ing on. When I've been up for hours and taken a long cold ride, without getting anything to eat, not to mention having helped de-liver a baby! If that's the trouble, he's even more of a fool than I've thought he was. And he thinks he's such a man of the world! The rest understand all right. They're my kind of people. Aloud all she said was, "Don't bother, Charles. This is plenty hot. I'll have some more as soon as I get home, anyway."

"But I want you to let me send for some fresh. And I really think you ought to have some toast too. Some toast and some soft-boiled eggs. How long do you like your eggs cooked? About three minutes?"

"No, I don't like them boiled at all. I like them scrambled with hot red peppers and okra. I don't like toast either. I like cakes and cuite. I said don't bother, Charles. I've almost finished already."

She knew that she sounded ungracious and she was annoyed with herself now, rather than with Charles, whose air of formality had changed to one of concern. She realized that she ought to question them about the hunt, to show interest in their outing and enthusiasm at the result. But she could not bring herself to do it. She was too unhappy. She had come in so joyously, openly glad to be the bearer of good tidings, secretly proud of her own share in meeting a hard situation. Now all the radiance was gone from the morning. She took one more long swallow, pushed back her cup and rose, the men rising with her. She looked at them with a com-prehensive smile.

"I'll be seeing you all at Belle Heloise pretty soon, won't I?" she asked, with forced cordiality. "Me, I'd better be running along to get that hair-curling mixture started. Fabian thinks I'm a pretty good barmaid. I hope you'll all agree with him." Then, tardily remembering that Gervais and Fabian had gone to Hackberry Lodge in the Governor's automobile, she turned to Parker in genuine confusion. "I'm terribly sorry, Governor Parker," she said. "I'm afraid I've been assuming too much, and that Fabian has too. I forgot he didn't have his car here, and I'm sure he did, we were both so excited. Will it really be convenient to have me tag along?"

"It'll be more than convenient; it'll be delightful," Parker said instantly. "In fact, your arrival has marked the pleasantest part of the cat hunt for me. I didn't suppose, when I stood listening to the dogs baying, that I'd be hearing something so much more thrill-

ing within a couple of hours. I don't know of any better news than
the assurance that the old River families will be carried on. But it's
high time I was getting back to my office, and I know you're
needed at Belle Heloise. I'm ready to start whenever you are, Miss
Cresside."

"I'd like very much to take Cresside home myself, if you'd let
me, Governor," Boylston began. The constraint was completely
gone from his voice now, and he spoke with unaccustomed eagerness. But the cordial invitation came too late, in the aftermath of
the awkward moment when he himself had been so ill at ease as to
cause Cresside's discomfiture and to make everyone else aware of
the strained atmosphere. The girl shook her head, and linked her
arm in Fabian's.

"You ought to give me a chance to say which I'd rather do," she
answered, speaking gaily again. "And when it comes to a choice
between you and the Governor, you ought to know which it would
be, Charles. My head's completely turned by flattery from such a
high quarter. I'm not planning to even look at any lesser light
than a Congressman from now on."

XX

WHEN Gervais' guests crossed the cattle gap at Belle
Heloise, they found Amen waiting to direct them:
"The Captain says, please, gentlemen, will you all go on
to de *garçonnière*? Dey's keepin' de Big House quiet
as dey kin caise Miss Merry an' de new baby, dey's sleepin' now;
Mis' d'Alvery, she bees restin' too." They nodded, returning
Amen's broad smile, and having circled the satsuma trees, where a
few golden balls still hung, parked their cars near the house servants' quarters and walked through the formal garden. Cresside ran
ahead of the others, snatching off her red cloche and shrugging
out of her jacket as she went; but as she dashed into the living-
room, she saw that Gervais had already succeeded in organizing
his forces without her. The room was decorated with red roses and
Chinese holly, the fire lighted, and steam was rising from the little
brass kettle on the hob beside the hearth; Selah was standing beside
an improvised bar, while Creassy hovered helpfully near him. Hot
toddies and highballs were circulating in no time, and the convivial
atmosphere which had characterized the hunt breakfast became increasingly jocose. But by this time most of the men were disinclined to linger indefinitely over their drinks, they would have to
make it short and snappy now, they told their beaming host.

Governor Parker wanted to get back to the Capitol, Happy Sevier to his wife, Lawrason to the merry widow of the moment and Claiborne to his office, and they confessed this with varying degrees of frankness. Fabian did not indicate or express any special reason for haste, but having gone to the hunt with the Governor, he logically left Belle Heloise with him. Only Boylston continued to stand by one of the built-in bookcases, fingering the mellow volumes with obvious appreciation. The servants removed the glasses, mended the fire and left, and still he did not turn. Finally, Gervais, who was beginning to fidget, asked rather abruptly to be excused.

"You don't mind if I go back to the Big House, do you, Charles? Of course, everything was fine when I last looked in, just before you all came, but I want to have another look——"

"Go right ahead. Merry said something about finding a first edition of *Jorrocks's Jaunts and Jollities* in the attic, and I've been trying to locate it. So far I haven't had any luck. But perhaps Cresside will help me."

Cresside, after exerting herself to be helpful as long as this seemed necessary, had stood for a few minutes with her back to the fire, hitching up her short skirt in the rear, so that the warmth of the flames would toast that portion of her person thus exposed to it. This was a fairly general practice among the girls whom Charles had met locally and it was enjoyed entirely without self-consciousness, but it had never ceased to seem shocking to him. He had avoided looking at Cresside as long as she stood in this position thus engaged. But now she had sunk down on a big sofa by the fire place, and was sitting with one foot tucked under the other knee and her head thrown back against the pillows. Her eyes were half shut and she was smoking a cigarette. She looked comfortable, drowsy and detached, and she answered without stirring.

"Find the darn book yourself. I've had enough activity for one morning. . . . I'll stay here and keep Charles company though, Gervais, if he wants me to, so that his search won't be a lonely one while you're away gazing at your offspring."

Gervais did not give her time to change her mind, which he knew she was quite capable of doing, where Charles was concerned. He hurried from the room, and presently the sound of his impatient footsteps was swallowed up in distance. The servants were still washing dishes in the kitchen, but the living-room was very quiet. Cresside continued to smoke without speaking, and only the flames made a small cheerful murmur. Boylston removed another leather-bound book from a shelf, turned its yellowing pages, and put it back again. He repeated this process until the kitchen clatter subsided and the back door closed behind the departing servants. Then he came over to the sofa.

"I don't care a hang about *Jorrocks's Jaunts and Jollities*, either," he said. "I've got first editions of that and Surtees' other book,

265

Handley Cross, myself. I just wanted to talk to you. I never have a chance."

"You've got a chance now. The book hunt sounded pretty phony to me, right along. I thought you might have something on your mind. I only hope it isn't too far on the serious side. Me, I'm sleepy."

"It's very serious. I hope you'll wake up and listen. And I'd appreciate it if you wouldn't badger me while I'm trying to talk."

Cresside opened her black eyes wide and looked at him with mock gravity. Her expression was quite as trying as a badgering tone.

"Don't, Cresside," he said, almost pleadingly. "I'm in deadly earnest, and I wish you'd try to be, for once. There's nothing funny about what I'm going to say."

"Sorry, Charles. I didn't know you were really so upset. What's the matter?"

"You thought I wasn't glad to see you when you arrived at Hackberry Lodge this morning. I was. I was very glad. But when you came bursting in with your good news, I was so upset for a moment that I couldn't help showing something was the matter. I want to apologize, first of all, for giving you the wrong impression."

"Oh, forget it! I thought you were mildly shocked because I came to your house, and that if you couldn't take it, under the circumstances, you were an awful prissy. But I wasn't offended, or upset, myself."

"I'm very glad. But I want to do more than apologize. I want to explain."

"It isn't all that necessary. Why do you bother?"

"I've just told you, because I want to. I'm jealous of your brother's good fortune, so jealous I can't seem to stand it."

He spoke with gathering intensity. Cresside, who was accustomed to hearing him talk in a calm and measured way, and to whom the change therefore seemed the more ominous than it would have in most men, answered with unusual coolness herself.

"You'll have to, won't you, if there's nothing you can do about it? Lots of other people do, anyway. One of the finest men I ever knew reminded me, not so long back, that childlessness was a pretty common disappointment. And I shouldn't think, in your case, that it had to be a permanent one. You've got almost everything most women would want."

"I don't seem to have enough for the only one I want," he said bitterly. And as she did not answer, he went on, "Besides, it isn't a mere question of childlessness. It's a question of general disappointment and disillusionment."

Cresside still made no reply. It was all too obvious that Charles Boylston was determined to unburden his soul, and though she could not prevent this, she was equally determined not to encourage it.

266

"Probably you wondered how I ever happened to land in Louisiana," he went on vehemently. "I've never discussed the reasons why I left home, because they were too painful. I didn't come here with any set purpose of becoming a planter in the first place. I was just trying to get away from Boston and everything connected with it."

"Well, I can understand that," Cresside murmured.

"Cresside, won't you please stop taking that tone? Of course, I wasn't trying to get away from Boston as a place! I'm very fond of it. I was trying to get away from tragic associations with a girl I had known all my life. Our families had been friendly for generations—they lived in the same block on Beacon Street and had adjoining properties on the North Shore. She went to Miss Winsor's at the same time I went to Noble's, and she came out when I was a junior at Harvard. We always saw a great deal of each other and everyone took it for granted that sometime we would be married. Our engagement was announced the week I graduated, the day before the Beck Hall Spread."

Cresside could not keep the corners of her mouth from twitching. She knew, from Charles Boylston's voice, that what he was saying really had some sad significance for him; nevertheless, the way in which he coupled "tragic associations" with the Beck Hall Spread seemed to her the height of irony. However, she managed to suppress a second flippant remark.

"But no date had been set for the wedding," Boylston continued. "We both took it for granted that we would have a long engagement. I entered law school the next fall and Dorothea went abroad to study at the Sorbonne. Then I decided that I didn't care to go on with my course, and I bought a very nice year round place near Hamilton. I always had plenty of money; one of my grandfathers left me his entire fortune direct. So I wasn't worried about making a living. But Dorothea didn't want to stay in the country all the year round; she didn't care for horses and dogs either. I thought I'd better give her time to get used to my general idea."

"Neither of you thought about trying some kind of a compromise?"

"I didn't, and if she did she never mentioned it. Merry didn't suggest any sort of a compromise to Gervais, did she?"

"No, but he didn't buy a new place out of a clear sky without consulting her; he already had one that he'd inherited, with all its obligations. Besides, he offered Merry a great deal more than she'd ever had before, materially speaking. I think she regarded Belle Heloise as something straight out of a fairy tale—in fact, I'm not sure that she still doesn't. I gather that you and Dorothea had about the same sort of background and about the same amount of opportunity, only different tastes. That might make a lot of difference. You weren't presenting her with a pleasanter kind of life.

You were trying to present her with the kind that seemed to her deadly dull."

"Didn't Merry wait for Gervais all the time he was abroad, even though they weren't formally engaged?" Charles demanded, ignoring Cresside's suggestion. "Wasn't her behaviour exemplary throughout that time?"

"Yes, but I think Patient Griseldas like her are pretty rare, in this day and age. Merry's the exception that proves the rule—to almost everything. Besides, I don't quite follow your line of thought. You started out by telling me that you and Dorothea had both agreed on an indefinite engagement, which doesn't sound to me like such a mighty passion to begin with, if you don't mind my saying so. And now you've apparently switched around to something else. You're not trying to tell me, very delicately, are you, that Dorothea finally got tired of this long engagement, and, being human after all, stooped to folly?"

"That's just what I'm trying to tell you. And I see you intend to treat it as something humorous to the very end."

He turned away from her abruptly and walked towards the door. Genuinely contrite, Cresside sprang up and ran to him, putting her hand on his arm.

"I'm sorry, Charles," she said penitently. "I didn't mean to hurt your feelings, truly I didn't. I know it must have been an awful blow if this girl you'd expected to marry for such a long time went back on you. You're right, Merry wouldn't have done a thing like that. No girl would, who was worth her salt—that is, if she were sure the man really loved her. But don't you think that perhaps, when you didn't urge her, she got the idea you didn't care, and this snake in the grass convinced her that he did, and so——"

"She came to my house and asked me to release her," Charles said hoarsely. "She'd never come there alone before, and I was so glad to see her—I thought she was going to say she was ready to marry me, and everything. And instead of that, she'd come to say she wanted to marry someone else. I didn't realize she'd even seen anyone else—oh, you know what I mean! I thought she was absolutely true to me in every way. I told her that I'd never heard of such nonsense, that I loved her dearly, that of course I wouldn't release her. And then she said that I'd have to—she said she was going to have a child."

Cresside's fingers, which had been lying lightly on his sleeve, closed quickly around his arm.

"I'm terribly sorry, Charles," she said, speaking still more contritely than before. "That must have been a knock-out blow. I don't wonder you feel as if you'd been cheated. I don't wonder you've been embittered. But, after all, Dorothea must have loved this other man very much, or she wouldn't, a girl like that——"

"You're not defending her, are you?"

He swung around and snatched at her hand, suddenly facing her again. Unconsciously Cresside backed away from him a little.

"No, I'm not defending her," she said, in a startled voice. "But I still think she thought you didn't love her any more, and that this other man did. It must have been terrible for her too, having to go to you like that and tell you what she did. . . . Let go my hand, please, Charles, you're hurting me."

"You'll have to forgive me," he said, releasing her instantly. "I wouldn't hurt you for the world, you know that, Cresside. . . . And, of course, you realize I don't love Dorothea any more, as a person. I've never seen her alone since that night, never wanted to. I stayed around until she was married, so that nothing would look queer; in fact, I was one of the ushers at her wedding. Then, after a little, I travelled rather aimlessly, and I was gone so much that eventually I sold my place in Hamilton. Everyone thought I acted very well and that Dorothea treated me very badly, but no one guessed just how badly. . . . Her baby died when it was born, and that gave colour to the report that it was premature. I haven't thought of her for years except as a symbol of everything I've missed. She shattered my life completely—the life I had then. That's why I had to get away from everything that reminded me of it. And one winter when I was in Florida I motored over to Denham Springs for the hunting and met Harvey Lawrason. He told me about Hackberry Lodge, said it could be had for a song, asked me why I didn't buy it, for the fun of the thing. I've never regretted it. I found a new life here, better than the one I left. But still it's terribly incomplete, terribly lonely, bound to be, the way it is. If I only had any assurance that some day it would be different, if I only had any hope——"

"You will have, some time, Charles."

"Is that a promise, Cresside?"

He tried, gently this time, to take her hand again, and again she retreated, speaking in her startled voice.

"No, of course it isn't a promise," she said. "A promise of what? It's just a statement. Nothing is ever hard all the time, for anybody. It can't be, in the nature of things. . . . I'm very much touched, Charles, that you wanted to confide in me. I feel very much honoured. And I'm sorry I was so flip—— I honestly didn't realize at first how deeply you felt. I will, another time. But I'm afraid I've got to ask you to excuse me now. You see, a day like this, there's a lot to be done, and I'm the logical person to do it. Stay here and read for a while if you feel like it, why don't you? I'll look in on you again, by and by. But meantime I've got to run over to the Big House."

She ran so fast and so blindly that she collided with Gervais, who was returning to the *garçonnière* at a more leisurely pace than the one at which he had left it. He took her by the shoulders and regarded her laughingly.

"Hold on, hold on!" he said. "What's your hurry? Come on back to the *garçonnière* and have another drink. Merry and Philogene are both asleep and incidentally so are the twins. 'All is calm, all is bright.' There's not a thing that needs doing at the Big House."

"In that case, I think I'll take a short walk on the levee. I want to get some air."

"Didn't you get enough air, going all the way to Hackberry Lodge and back, for Pete's sake?"

"Well, I got some. But I want some more."

"Look here, you and Charles haven't quarrelled again, have you?"

"No, we haven't quarrelled exactly. But he's trying to propose again, by a new method. He's been telling me all, and I've been a very unwilling listener to the history of his past. He's upset, and he's succeeded in upsetting me too. I want to get away from him for a while, and he hasn't the least idea of going home. I'm sure he thinks that if he keeps hammering away, eventually I'll give in and marry him. But I never shall, never, never, never!"

Her voice broke in something suspiciously like a sob. Gervais regarded her curiously but more sympathetically than usual.

"Look here," he said again. "You're all worn out. You've had a hell of a time yourself this morning. I didn't want to ask you to do anything more, because I know you've done two or three people's work already. But if you really do want to take a walk, would you mind going to the cemetery instead of along the levee? I'd like very much to have some flowers put on our father's tomb today. I suppose you'll think I'm a sentimental fool, but I can't help feeling——"

"I don't at all. I'd like very much to do it. I'll go and pick the flowers straight off. So long, Gervais. And see if you can't get rid of Charles gracefully within the next hour or so, won't you? I can manage to stay away that long, but I don't want to find him here when I get back. You can tell him I've gone to bed, exhausted, without hurting your conscience too much, can't you?"

She stooped to get a flower basket from the tool shed at the rear of the Big House and went on to Angus Holt's garden, her pace now less suggestive of flight, but still rapid. The first white camellias were just coming into bloom; two of the smaller trees were already laden with beautiful blossoms, waxen against the glossy green of the leaves. She gathered a dozen or more, selecting some that were still only half open, bell-shaped buds and others that were already full blown, resembling roses and daffodils in formation, but infinitely more delicate; all were fragile and flawless. Nothing needed to be added to these—they were in themselves a perfect offering. She arranged them carefully in the shallow basket, so that they would not bruise each other, and started down the River Road, her sense of haste and panic already assuaged.

The cemetery never depressed her. Like most Creoles, she felt very near to her dead, and could linger among their tombs with a sense of peace and communion, not only on All Saints' Day but at any time or season. As a child, she had been accustomed to joining the groups making leisurely visits to the family lot, taking her toys and her lunch with her and playing contentedly for hours. Lately she had preferred to go alone; but the feeling of ease and familiarity still lingered. Entering the cemetery now, she went quietly past the chalk-like rectangular blocks nearest the road, the uneven tiers of crumbling red brick and the pretentious mossy monuments, towards the little Gothic chapel which marked the resting-place of the Estrades and the d'Alverys. But, as she approached this, she saw that she was not alone in the cemetery. A man was sitting on the slab adorned with the small recumbent lamb. He was half hidden by the simpering female figure in marble which dominated the Hathaway lot, but Cresside instantly realized who he was. For a moment she stood stock still. Then, bracing herself for the meeting, she went on, calmly confronting Sylvestre Tremaine.

"Why, hello!" she said casually. "What on earth are you doing here?"

He rose from the slab and came up to her. His attitude, when she first caught sight of him, had been one of extreme dejection. Now she saw that his handsome face was stormy and sombre. He neither smiled nor held out his hand.

"Nothing," he said shortly. "But I have to get off somewhere, every once in so often, and this morning a cemetery exactly suited me. . . . Very convenient for a suicide, and I was practically on the verge of that. What are *you* doing here?"

"Just bringing flowers, as you see. To put on my father's tomb. We try to do that fairly regularly, on general principles. But this morning there was a special reason. We've got a new baby at Belle Heloise and his name is Philogene."

"A new baby already!"

"Yes, already. He's a little ahead of time, but he's a fine big boy just the same. Mother and child are not only doing as well as could be expected, but very nicely indeed, thank you."

"Gervais is getting more than his share," Sylvestre said moodily. "Those twins are fine-looking children, especially Vail. I'd give my eye teeth for one such youngster."

"Well, you'll probably have one sooner or later. Most people do. But don't let's talk about it. I've heard a lot on that subject already this morning, and enough is enough."

She nodded, still casually, and moved along towards the chapel

271

again, apparently unconcerned because Sylvestre had moved forward too. He opened the wrought-iron gate of the railing surrounding the Estrade lot, and waited for her to enter. Then he hesitated.

"Could I help you fix the flowers? I'd like to if you'd let me."

"Thanks a lot. But I can do it all right alone."

She unlocked the chapel and went in, closing the door behind her. Sylvestre continued to stand by the gate, swinging it absently back and forth, until it seemed to him Cresside had been gone an abnormally long time. Irrationally worried, he went to the closed door and knocked.

"Cresside, are you all right? What on earth are you doing there all this time?"

"Of course I'm all right. I'm arranging the flowers, that's all. I'll be out in a minute."

Her voice was muffled but composed. After another wait, so long that Sylvestre felt almost irresistibly impelled to tug at the closed door, she came out with the empty basket on her arm, relocked the chapel, and started serenely out of the lot without speaking.

"Cresside," Sylvestre said desperately, "I wish you wouldn't act this way—as if I just weren't here at all."

"Well, you're not, as far as I'm concerned."

"But I am. You can't accuse me of forcing myself on you this time. I hadn't the remotest idea you were coming to the cemetery when I did. Now that we have met though——"

"I'm not accusing you of anything. But there's nothing I want to say to you either. At that, I did say hello."

"There are any number of things I want to say to you. I've wanted to say them a long, long time."

"If you're bound to talk to me, I suppose you will, and I can't very well help hearing you, as long as I'm in this cemetery. After all, you've got just as much right to come here as I have. You came to your family lot and I came to mine. Now that I've been there, I'm going straight home."

"It isn't my family lot. It's the Hathaway family lot. And I wish to heaven every Hathaway was in it!"

He spoke with passionate bitterness. Cresside, making no answer, walked quietly on.

"You wouldn't blame me either, if you knew the life those two women lead me," he said savagely. "It's a hell on earth. And they hate me as much as I hate them. That's my only hope of escape. I think sooner or later Regine will leave me, in a fit of rage. If she does, I may have a chance."

"If you've got to talk, I wish you wouldn't talk about your wife and your mother-in-law, especially like that. And I don't know what you mean by chance."

"I mean a chance to get free, of course. If Regine would only give me the least pretext, I'd get a divorce like a shot."

272

"She won't. You can't get a divorce just because your wife loses her temper, Sylvestre. Especially as you've probably given her all kinds of reasons for doing it."

"I can get a divorce for mental cruelty in some other state, if I can't get one in Louisiana. I will too, if this goes on."

"And where will that get you?"

"Why, I just reminded you. Then I'd be free."

"I still don't get the point."

"Yes, you do. You're only pretending you don't. You know that I'm crazy about you, Cresside, that I always have been. You know I realize what a damn fool I was when I let Regine——"

"I know you're crazy. You can stop right there."

"But Cresside, you did love me, you loved me a lot! You can't have got all over it so soon! I haven't. I want you more than I ever did!"

"Well, that's just your tough luck, then. Because I don't love you any more. I have got all over it. It took me quite a long while, and it wasn't an easy process. I might remind you in passing that you didn't do anything to make it easier. However, we'll let that go."

"But, Cresside——"

They had already passed the pretentious mossy monuments and the crumbling brick tiers and were now approaching the chalk-like rectangular blocks, which were in full sight of the River Road. Involuntarily, Cresside gave a small sigh of relief.

"You'd better go back to your stone slab," she said. "I told you I couldn't stop you from talking to me in the cemetery, but I didn't say anything about letting you walk home with me. If you had that in mind you'd better dismiss it, along with some of these other quaint ideas of yours. Listen hard, Sylvestre, I want you to get all this straight: Regine isn't going to let you go, because she hasn't got anyone else in sight, but even if she did, that wouldn't prove a thing, as far as I'm concerned. I wouldn't believe you if you swore on the Holy Bible that you wanted to marry me. I was a damn fool to believe you once, but at least I'm not such a fool to believe you again. And if I did believe you, and you could marry me, that still wouldn't get you anywhere. Because I don't want to marry you. I wouldn't have you if you were the last man on earth. I hate and despise the very sight of you, and I wish to heaven I never had to see you again, even at a distance. I thought I had all the snakes cleared out of this cemetery. But I see I was mistaken. I see there's one I haven't got rid of yet."

"Nature is fine in love; and where 'tis fine
It sends some precious instance of itself
After the thing it loves."

Shakespeare: *"Hamlet," IV, c.* 1601.

PART V

"Some Precious Instance"

XXI

A S the end of the grinding season approached, the fear that
the drop in the price of sugar might be more than temporary became a sad certainty. In December it was down
to ten point five; in January it hit eight cents even, the
lowest price in five years. At this unpropitious moment, Fletcher,
who had shown great nonchalance on the subject of statements
while the restoration work was still going on, sent in a bill for the
entire amount due him. Gervais had understood that this could be
paid in easy instalments over a long period, but it now appeared
that Fletcher wanted the whole sum at once, and it was a staggering one. When Gervais asked Mr. Garfield, his New Orleans
broker, to advance it against the next year's crop, Mr. Garfield replied, in an unusually brief and formal letter, that this was entirely
out of the question; ten thousand dollars was the largest sum with
which he felt justified in supplying Captain d'Alvery at the
moment and he was really stretching a point to do that. Fletcher's
acceptance of the ten thousand was anything but gracious. He
would be willing to give Captain d'Alvery ninety days in which to
settle, he said, since there had evidently been a misunderstanding
about the instalments; but he had paid for the labour and the
materials himself, while the work was in progress, and that had
been a considerable strain on his own resources. He was sure Captain d'Alvery would understand. . . .

"Unless I have some kind of a windfall pretty soon, I'll have to
get Bisbee to let me have it," Gervais told Merry resentfully, tossing Fletcher's letter over to her as she sat peacefully propped up on
pillows in her bed, nursing Philogene, who was thriving on his
food as the twins had done beforehand.

"Are you expecting any kind of a windfall?"

"Well, no. But that's not saying I might not have one."

"And you're sure Mr. Bisbee will let you have the money?"

"I don't see why not. I went out of my way to be nice to him
when he came to this Parish as a stranger. And there isn't a
bank anywhere around better fixed than the Cotton Factors
National. . . . I don't have to go to Bisbee right off, anyway. I can

K   277 wait a couple of months at least, and see if something doesn't turn up, as I said. But meanwhile there's no getting away from the fact that I'm not much in the mood for reviving an old-fashioned celebration."

The year before, he had been urged by both his overseer and his negro hands to stage the celebration to which he had just referred. He had declined then on the grounds of Merry's imminent confinement, for the grinding season came to an end almost immediately before the birth of the twins. Now that Philogene was already safely in the world, however, and was proving to be such a lusty child, the request had been renewed and he had found no excuse which would prevent him from consenting to the celebration. In his grandfather's time it had been the custom, both at Belle Heloise and at many other plantations, for the "bossman" to give his men a feast the day that grinding was over. The last carts to come in from the field were always gaily decorated with cornstalks and flags, and even the whips and the mules' harnesses were ornamented with a few festive leaves. The negroes were paid in full on this day, and, as many of them had worked overtime, they were "nigger rich," as the saying went. The *vincanne*, made of undistilled rum and fermented cane juice, had been "cooked off" and set aside in great barrels beforehand. Now it was liberally dispensed to the negroes from the corn shed, and added considerably to their high spirits. As the last cane went into the crusher, the men gathered around it, and, with hearty and prolonged cheers, flung their hats into it, too; the battered home-made palmettos, ground up with the stalks, were jokingly said to add something special to the flavour of these. After the final long blast of the whistle, announcing the end of the sugar-making, the negroes produced a chair suitable for such a grand occasion, and looked around for their "bossman," who made a show of hiding. When they found him, they overrode his mock objections, and, installing him in the seat of honour, bore him first around the mill and the quarters and finally around the Big House, at the head of a procession of a hundred or more; and as they marched they sang the songs which they had composed on purpose for the occasion. Finally they deposited him on the front gallery, and clustering around him waited for him to rise and address them. In his speech he always praised them for the hard work which had made the good harvest possible thanked them for their faithfulness, and invited them to go "around to the back" to the "feast" of meat, bread, cheese, cake and red wine that had been prepared for them. Afterwards they returned to the quarters and continued their revelry far into the night, singing, dancing and love-making.

Most of these pleasant customs had continued. The carts were still decorated, the hats still tossed into the crusher, the whistle still blown, the *vincanne* still served, and there was still revelry a the quarters. But the triumphal procession, the flowery address, and the "feast" back of the Big House had long since been abandoned. It was originally Lézine's idea that Gervais could profitably and pleasantly make a special occasion of his homecoming after the war by reviving them, and all the negroes were in hearty accord with this. Because of the inevitable delay in carrying out the plan, Gervais had rather hoped they might forget about it. But their long wait had only served to increase their eagerness. Gervais could not go back on his promise now.

"Cresside's all for the celebration, too," he said, leaning over to insert a finger in the baby's fist, and smiling again as he saw the tiny hand close around it. "She offered to go to the attic and try to find some of grandfather's clothes that I could wear. I believe she's up there now. I wouldn't put it past her to come down with complete outfits for all of us. I'll say this for Cresside, when she really gets her teeth into anything, she doesn't let go until she's done a thorough job. . . . I'd like to know how you feel about it, though—does it strike you as a tremendous bore or an awful effort? If it does, we'll call it all off again. You know I wouldn't be sorry for the excuse."

"Yes, I do know. But wouldn't it be a mistake, Gervais, to disappoint all our people a second time, when they've set their hearts on this? And I think Cresside has the right idea. If we're going in for the celebration at all, I believe we ought to do it up brown. Of course, women enjoy fancy dress more than men do—I know that. But you'd be so wonderful in the rôle of Lucien Estrade, that you ought to be able to stand the strain, for once."

He muttered something unintelligible, but she could tell from his expression that the idea of impersonating his grandfather was beginning to catch his fancy. He picked up the satiated baby, who was already half asleep, and sat down by the bed with his small son in his arms.

"If we go in for costumes and all that," he said, "we'd almost have to make an event of it, for ourselves, I mean, as well as the negroes. And we couldn't ask some of our neighbours without asking all of them. What I'm driving at is, we couldn't invite Charles unless we invited Regine and Sylvestre too. So far we've never been caught quite this way—to give the devil his due, I think Sylvestre started for Hot Springs a week earlier than he intended on purpose to relieve me of embarrassment when I had my beer and shrimp party. But he's home now—they all are. He's made a point of saying he was sticking around until the end of the grinding season, though heaven only knows why—he almost never goes to the mill. I naturally don't care a damn whether his feelings are hurt or not, but I don't want Regine to go around telling everyone Hathaway's been slighted, and starting the whole Parish wondering why."

"I don't think Cresside would mind at all if you invited Sylvestre and Regine, honey," Merry said reassuringly. "I'm almost positive she isn't sensitive about them any more. But why don't you ask her, straight out?"

"Ask her what straight out?" Cresside called from the living-room. "Look here, don't you think it's about time, after all the holy wedlock you've enjoyed, that you two woke up and took notice when someone else comes around? I banged the outside door when I came in on purpose. . . . Never mind, though, for the moment. Just see what I've found!"

She came into the room staggering under an unwieldly armful of old clothes, and, slinging them down on the bed, began to sort them and hold them up for inspection. She had found the suit of elegant grey broadcloth which Lucien Estrade had worn at his wedding, and any number of quaint costumes that had belonged to the various ladies of the family. She herself wanted to wear one of their mother's dresses—a bright plaid taffeta. Of course, that went with a later period, but after all, they weren't trying to be too technical about all this. She was going to take a black brocade that had belonged to Evaline Estrade up to *maman* right now and see whether she wouldn't fall for it. Cresside would come back after a moment to find out if the bridal finery fitted—there was a second day dress, a lovely changeable silk—that would be just the thing for Merry, too. . . .

"By the way, what were you thinking of asking me, when I came in?" she paused to inquire, with her hand on the doorknob again. Merry and Gervais exchanged glances and Merry answered for both of them.

"Gervais wondered how you'd feel about having him invite the Tremaines to the celebration. He thought it would be rather pointed if he didn't."

"Sure it would. Go right ahead. I don't care who's invited. Except that I wish sooner or later we could have one party sans Charles. I'm completely fed up with him. But I know we have to have him this time, worse luck. I only hope he doesn't show up in a uniform of a Yankee officer commanding the First Massachusetts Regiment."

"Cresside's very unjust to Charles," Gervais muttered under his breath as the door closed behind his sister. "I've never known him to say or do a thing that wasn't tactful. Why on earth should she drag in anything as far-fetched as the uniform of a Yankee officer in his connection?"

"I don't know. He just rubs her the wrong way, somehow. But after all, let's be thankful that if she won't fall in love with Charles she isn't in love with Sylvestre any more. That's something."

"Yes, that's something," Gervais agreed. He gave the sleeping baby back to Merry, and, taking off his own coat, picked up the elegant grey broadcloth. "I reckon we can go right ahead and make

280

plans," he said, slipping into it and shaking it down over his shoulders. "I'm beginning to get into the spirit of the thing myself. It isn't as if it were going to cost us much. Of course, if I had that to worry about, it would be different."

He walked over to the cheval glass and surveyed himself with satisfaction; Lucien Estrade's coat fitted as if it had been made for him. But he had to wait a minute before Merry looked up and admired it. She had begun to re-read Mr. Garfield's letter and the tone of it troubled her. It required a real effort for her to dismiss it from her mind.

However, at the time of the celebration she seemed in high spirits. The second-day dress, which Cresside had found for her, was a little too tight; it had been made to fit a slender bride, and Merry was full-breasted, as became a nursing mother; besides, she had put on a little extra weight, which she carried well, after each confinement. But Cresside, who was so handy with a needle, had helped her to let the dress out, and it suited her admirably. Merry looked very lovely as she stood on the front gallery, between her mother-in-law and her sister-in-law, welcoming her guests. The fitful winter weather had moderated, after a hard freeze, and the day was as warm as summer. Tulip-shaped, magenta-coloured buds were tipping some of the bare branches on the Japanese magnolias; here and there scarlet branches of flowering quince blazed among the greenery. Angus Holt's garden had been dotted overnight with purple pansies; the paper-white narcissi, which encircled the oak trees studding the Small Yard, were unfolding in a sudden bloom; and their fresh, provocative perfume scented the balmy air. Regine was exulting in the mildness which had enabled her to wear an elaborate costume which she insisted had once belonged to her idol, Empress Eugénie, and which Sylvestre had bought for her in Paris, paying some fabulous sum for it. Its complete unsuitability for plantation wear, at any period, did not trouble her in the least; she had even gone so far as to insist that Sylvestre should accompany her to the party in the guise of Napoleon III, imperial and all. The fact that his costume could not by any stretch of the imagination be considered authentic, and that his silly little beard seemed perpetually on the point of coming unglued, did not trouble her either. She was still chattering volubly when the sound of shouts and singing announced the approach of the triumphal procession, and when Madame d'Alvery's withering glances failed to silence her, Merry put a gentle hand on her arm.

"Let's all watch and listen," she said. "You know, I never saw or heard anything like this before, Regine. I don't want to miss a single trick."

Regine, who had cornered Charles Boylston, continued to chatter as if she had not heard the request. Sylvestre, touching her arm in his turn, less gently than her hostess, spoke to her with unconcealed annoyance.

"Didn't you hear Merry?" he asked sharply. "Hush up, can't you?"

"Hush up yourself! You know how I hate to be interrupted! Can't you see I'm right in the middle of a story Charles is just dying to hear?"

"I can see you're right in the middle of a story fast enough, but that's chronic. I'm not so sure Charles is dying to hear it."

"Perhaps you'll tell me the end of it later on, Regine," Charles said. "I'd like to hear it very much. But as Merry says, it would be too bad if we missed something because we were absorbed in a story, and all your stories are absorbing. I've never seen a procession like this either, and I've been looking forward to it."

He smiled persuasively as he spoke, and his tact was more effective than either Merry's pleading or Sylvestre's brusqueness. He was looking even handsomer than usual, too, in old-fashioned bottle-green hunting togs, in no way suggestive of a Yankee's uniform. Regine, accepting his courteous attention as a personal tribute, thought Cresside was a fool not to snatch at him, and resolved to tell her so at the earliest opportunity. But there was no immediate prospect of such a chance. The procession was already in sight, winding its way through the grove between the school-house and the Big House. Four huge negroes, all black as the ace of spades, were carrying the massive chair on which Gervais was enthroned. He was in high good humour; his expression was jovial as he waved his grey beaver gracefully above his head while advancing. The bright winter sunshine gave an added sheen to his pearl-coloured clothes, and the contrasting colours and quality of the negroes' jeans accentuated the elegance of their fit and finish. Sance, Plauché and Dupuy walked directly behind him, wreathed in smiles and attired in their Sunday best. Back of them came the plantation "band," made up of instruments owned and played by negroes on the place, and consisting of four harmonicas, three banjos, two guitars and a violin. The musicians, playing entirely by ear, did this remarkably well. After them marched the long double file of field hands in their bright cottons. Some of them carried broad sugar knives in their hands, others long stalks of tasselled cane over their shoulders; all of them were singing—their own song, the one they themselves had composed on purpose for their own supreme festival. They sang it with the zest of natural high spirits; but the *vincanne* in their stomachs and the money in their pockets raised these to a still higher pitch:

> *"Ah is so glad us done got thru at de lastes',*
> *Ol' Satan thought he had me boun' de fastes',*
> *But he miss my soul an' he cotch my sin,*

An' give me a chance for to work an' win,
Now Ah's free from Satan an' Ah's free from sin.
Ah is so glad us done got thru at de lastes'.
Oh, happy day, happy day,
Us done got thru at de lastes'.

"De bossman's glad an' so is us,
Ain't nobody gwine for to fret or fuss,
Caise times is good an' dey won't git wuss—
Sugar makin's done, and us got our pay.
Oh, happy day, happy day,
Us done got thru at de lastes'."

The procession had almost reached the gallery. Merry, at a pre-arranged signal, detached herself from the others and moved forward to meet her husband. As the bearers set down his chair, amidst a chorus of cheers and a round of applause, he stepped towards her and held out his hand. Then they turned and walked together to the demilune of mellow brick which formed the front steps. When they turned again to face their family and friends on the gallery and their people clustering around this, Gervais put one arm around her neat waist and held up the other to command attention.

"I don't want to make a speech," he said. "But on behalf of this lady and myself, I do want to say just a word of welcome to our guests and of appreciation to our workers. I want all our friends who've come out from town and all our neighbours along the River Road to hear me tell our people how grateful I am to them for the faithfulness and industry that made the grinding season which has just ended such a big success. This is a great day at Belle Heloise, and we want everyone to join us in celebrating it."

The applause on the gallery, the cheers from the marchers, broke out again. Everyone was in a mood to enjoy even the most trite remarks, especially when these were spoken with the ease and grace Gervais managed to give them. He smiled engagingly as he went on.

"The crop really is in," he said. "Of course Sance, over there, said it never would be, if the rains kept up. But it is, in spite of Sance, who's a hopeless pessimist."

Everyone looked in the direction of the overseer, cheering and applauding him now; and he grinned sheepishly but delightedly. And Plauché said we wouldn't have sugar worth the name if I didn't get him those fancy new filter presses he's been talking about since God knows when. But we have. We've never made better sugar at Belle Heloise than we have this fall. And Dupuy said the old water pumps wouldn't hold out, and that we might all be blown from here to kingdom come if the new ones I'd ordered didn't get here at the beginning of grinding. Well, those pumps came in just last night—they're down at the depot at Baton Rouge now, so they ought to be ready for us to use next year anyway, unless we have as much trouble getting them set up as we had getting them here by express. But even if we do, I reckon we'll be able to hitch along some way, just as we have this year, in spite of Dupuy!"

Attention shifted from the overseer to the chief engineer and the sugar boiler, and Plauché and Dupuy accepted the "bossman's" ribbing and the hearty tribute of the entire gathering in the same abashed but gratified manner as Sance. Gervais saluted each of them in turn and continued in a slightly more serious vein.

"Most of you know that originally we planned to have this party last year, to celebrate my return from France, and most of you know why we didn't. Well, it's a good thing we put it off, because now we can have a double-barrelled celebration. I feel I have every cause to rejoice because I came out of the hell I'd been through in France, and got back, safe and sound, to the beautiful home I love so much. I'm deeply touched and honoured by your feeling. But I know you'll agree with me that there's an additional cause for rejoicing. Since I came back three children have been born in this house—two boys and a girl. This means that as far as we can look ahead we don't have to fear that some time Belle Heloise will be neglected or fall into alien hands. I want all my people to take a look at their future 'bossman' and his brother and sister today. I hope they'll feel happy, when they do, to think that some day their children will be working for him, just as their grandfathers' children are working for me, helping to carry on the tradition of Belle Heloise. I hope they'll tell me that they are!"

He glanced towards the front door, and, as it swung open, Dinah and the twins came out of it. Vail and Sybelle were now so big that it was almost impossible for her to carry them both at once. But Vail was already beginning to toddle, and, clutching her hand, he managed to make the grade, though his movements were somewhat impeded by the voluminous stiffness of the old-fashioned dress into which he had unwillingly been thrust. Sybelle, similarly attired and enjoying it, crowed and gurgled in Dinah's arms; and close behind them came Lethe, cradling Philogene, slightly resentful at the interruption of his slumbers, and clad in a long lacy christening robe and a tiny close-fitting lace cap. At the sight of the babies the tumult around the gallery increased; the negroes burst into prolonged shouts and loud exclamations of enthusiasm. They could not wave their hats, since these had all been cast into the crusher in accordance with immemorial custom; but they waved their bandanas instead. Gervais took each of the babies in turn and held it up for the guests and the negroes to see. Then he signalled to the nurses to take their charges back into the house, and put his arm around Merry again.

284

"I notice that my family got more applause than my speech," he said, the engaging smile still on his face. "That's fine; that's the way I want it to be. It's a great family and I'm not a great speechmaker. That's one of the reasons I'll never get very far in politics. I'm no orator and no statesman. I'm just a plain planter, just your friend and neighbour, just your 'bossman.'" And as a murmur of dissent began to rise and swell, he held up a hand for silence. "That's all I have to say to you," he said. "But Lou Ida's spent nearly all her time, these last few days, getting ready for this celebration. I think we all better find out what she has for us."

With a few final cheers, the negroes re-formed their processional and started around to the rear of the house. Merry and Gervais, from their station at the front door, motioned to their guests to leave the gallery and come into the dining-room. A large silver bowl, filled with frothing eggnog and surrounded by silver goblets, stood at one end of the long mahogany table; at the other an immense coffee urn rose above a circle of tiny porcelain cups, ornamented with the Estrade crest; the intervening surface, covered with glistening damask, was almost hidden by an endless array of fruit cakes, biscuits, sandwiches, pralines and salted pecans. On the sideboard stood two silver champagne buckets, with fragile and beautiful Venetian glasses between them. Madame d'Alvery seated herself behind the eggnog, inviting Mrs. Hathaway to serve the coffee. Merry, Cresside and Gervais circulated among the guests, supervising Selah, Creassy and Lucie, and accepting congratulations on the great success of the celebration. The babies were briefly brought back and made the rounds of their delighted admirers again. On the surface the atmosphere was carefree, gay and permeated with the spirit of lavish and traditional hospitality. Only here and there a comment was made or a question asked which indicated some underlying disturbance.

"I never drank better champagne," Melvin Bisbee murmured to Charles Boylston in his pinched voice, holding his bubbling glassful of golden liquid up to catch the candlelight. "I'll say this for our host—he knows how to carry on in the grand manner. But lately I've heard rumours that things weren't going so well with him," Bisbee continued, in a lower tone. "I hope that isn't true?"

It was a question rather than a statement, but Boylston did not choose to regard it as such. He regarded the banker with a frosty look in his blue eyes.

"I don't discuss business matters with Gervais," he said, after a marked pause, in a voice as cold as his glance. "I come here because I enjoy the d'Alverys' society. They've always been extremely kind to me. I believe they're rather unusual in that respect, as far as outsiders are concerned. Most Creoles keep a closed corporation."

"Yes, yes, quite so. I am not unmindful of Captain d'Alvery's many courtesies to me. And, of course, I know nothing about sugar. But I understand that this year's crop has been more or less of a failure, in spite of all the satisfaction expressed at today's celebration."

"It isn't quite as good as last year's. That is, mine isn't. As I just said, I don't know so much about Gervais', and he's rather preoccupied at the moment, so I wouldn't think it was the best time to find out. Why don't you ask Tremaine about his?"

Boylston turned away, rather pointedly, and walked over to Fabian, who was sitting alone at the moment, except for Belizaire, upon whose nose he had just placed a sponge drop. Madame d'Alvery had never allowed either Snow or Cornet to come into the house, and she frowned sternly on all visiting animals. But Fabian, nonchalantly observing that was no way to run a plantation anyhow, had serenely continued to bring his dog with him on all occasions, and lately his aunt had refrained from invidious remarks on the subject. Today she had actually stooped and patted Belizaire on the head, and Fabian was now pressing the advantage gained by putting him through a few tricks. Having balanced the sponge drop, he gave the order "Say grace!" and the spaniel immediately put his paws on the chair beside his master and buried his long sensitive nose in them. There he remained motionless until Fabian exclaimed "Amen!" Then he leapt in the air, snapping at the sponge drop with avidity.

"You certainly get away with murder in this house," Boylston remarked, sitting down beside Fabian and handing his empty glass to Selah for a refill. "I wonder what would happen if I appeared here with one of my Walkers. Well, I don't begrudge you your privileges—I'm glad enough to be here under any circumstances. The South certainly survives at Belle Heloise. . . . Incidentally, Gervais tells me that the next party is to be a christening. I'm glad to hear it. I remember feeling disappointed last year that there was no celebration when the twins were baptized, because this house is such an ideal setting for a ceremony of that sort. Of course, Cresside was still incapacitated then, though."

"Yes—but hasn't she staged a grand comeback?"

Fabian glanced across the room, and Boylston followed his gaze. Cresside was standing by the fireplace, engaged in lively conversation with Harvey Lawrason, who was visiting at Hackberry Lodge again, and who was obviously enjoying himself immensely. The quaint plaid dress, with its full skirt and tight bodice, was extremely becoming to her, both in colour and in style, and unlike the changeable silk which Merry was wearing, it had required no alterations, for Cresside was still slim as a reed. But her look of gauntness and emaciation was gone and her sparkling eyes were no longer black-ringed in a haggard face. Framed by the orna-
286

mented marble mantel, with the glowing firelight for a background, she made a picture that was not only vivid but enchanting. Instinctively Boylston rose and took a step in the direction of the hearth.

"I want to show you another trick of Belizaire's," Fabian suggested. "I think it's about his best. Wait here just a sec, will you, Charles?" He rose too, but instead of going towards the fireplace, limped out into the hall, his dog at his heels. Presently he returned, and, reseating himself, addressed Belizaire as quietly as he might have spoken to a child. "I left my cigarettes out there," he said. "Go get them for me, will you?" And when the dog bounded off, to return with the package in his mouth, Fabian added, "Oh, but I forgot the matches too. . . ."

"Very diverting," Boylston said a little dryly, as Belizaire returned triumphantly a second time. "But, after all, there's no reason why I should concede that Harvey's also a privileged character, even if you're willing to." He nodded and sauntered on towards the fireplace, and Fabian, after looking at him quizzically for a moment, returned to the dining-room. Madame d'Alvery and Mrs. Hathaway were still sitting at their posts, though the demands for refills were now few and far between, and the guests had scattered informally through the parlour, library and music-room. Fabian drew up a chair and sat down by Mrs. Hathaway, who forestalled any remark he might make by a rather captious one of her own.

"Fabian, tell me whether you do not agree with me. I have just been saying to your Aunt Isabelle that while this celebration has been delightful, on the whole, I feel that part of Gervais' speech might well have been omitted. Of course, I have in mind his reference to the security of this plantation."

"'As far as we can look ahead, we don't have to fear that Belle Heloise will be neglected or fall into alien hands.' Is that what you mean, Mrs. Hathaway? Why, I thought that was one of his best lines! I wrote it for him myself."

"There was nothing the matter with the line, as you call it, in itself. But it was based on the fact that three children have been born here within the last year. In view of the fact that Regine and Sylvestre are childless, and that we are all so deeply disappointed because of this, I think Gervais would have been more tactful if he had made no such reference to it in our presence."

"Well, I don't know. My view was that he was talking primarily to his people, rather than to his guests. After all, this was the negroes' celebration. The rest of us were only onlookers. Don't you agree with me, Tante Isabelle?"

"Completely, Fabian. You analysed the situation exactly as I did —in fact, I said the same thing to Mrs. Hathaway before you came in. Naturally, all of us here would be extremely sorry if there were

287

never an heir to Hathaway. But that cannot prevent us from re-joicing that we have been so greatly blessed at Belle Heloise."

She rose, and Fabian immediately went over to her and offered her his arm. She smiled at him with unaccustomed graciousness as she took it.

"I think we may safely join the group in the music-room now," she said. "Unless, of course, dear Mrs. Hathaway, you would prefer the group in the parlour or the one in the library. But I believe we are to have some spirituals before the party breaks up, and the music-room always seems the most appropriate place for those. Besides, Dinah has taken the twins there, at Sylvestre's suggestion —he said he wanted to get better acquainted with them. But we must not leave him indefinitely to their mercies—at this time of day, when they begin to get tired, they are sometimes riotous also, especially Vail. . . . If anyone desires more coffee or eggnog, Selah may take it around as he is still taking champagne. I believe my son is planning to make quite an occasion of the christening. Of course, we shall count on your presence for that too, *chère*."

XXII

PHILOGENE'S christening was indeed a great event, but it marked the last of the entertainments reviving the tradi-tional hospitality at Belle Heloise.

A few days after it took place, Gervais received a letter from Arnold Fletcher, saying that he would greatly appreciate another payment of ten thousand dollars on account. He had not forgotten that he had agreed to a ninety-day delay for full pay-ment; but it did so happen that he was unusually pressed himself, and he was sure Captain d'Alvery would be glad to accommodate him with this small sum. A year earlier, Gervais would readily have agreed that ten thousand dollars was a small sum; but it did not look that way to him now, and he was sure, from Garfield's latest communication, that it was futile to look for further advances from that quarter. Ruefully, he went to Bisbee and asked him for the money, and without apparent hesitation Bisbee let him have it on an open note. The transaction was so much easier than Gervais had expected, despite the confident way which he had spoken about it to Merry, that he tried to tell himself there was no reason why he should worry any more: if Bisbee would let him have that much without formality, he would let him have a larger amount with satisfactory collateral. He allowed Fletcher's ninety-day limit to pass without mentioning it and without undue concern; and he felt safer still when the deadline went by and the architect did not immediately send him a reminder that it had. Then he was suddenly and rudely shaken from his sense of security.

One pleasant Sunday in April, Melvin Bisbee came out to Belle Heloise. He had been meaning to pay a party call ever since the christening, he said—in fact, he had two or three party calls on his conscience! He certainly always had been entertained like royalty on the River Road! He went first to the Big House, where Madame d'Alvery received him graciously, saying she was sorry Cresside was out, but that Merry and Gervais were fortunately both at home; she would send Selah to the *garçonnière* immediately to let them know they had a visitor. Meantime, she and Mr. Bisbee would have a glass of port together while they awaited the arrival of coffee and the other members of the family.

The call passed off agreeably, but tepidly. Gervais and Bisbee discussed the recent decision, made by two members of the Railroad Commission in the absence of the third, granting an increase in rates to the Cumberland Telephone Company.

Madame d'Alvery and Merry took very little part in this conversation, but as neither objected to the rôle of listener, there was no awkwardness because of this. They continued to sip small blacks and to eat little frosted cakes with composure while Gervais and Melvin Bisbee discussed Huey Long. It was not until he rose to leave, and inquired rather tardily for the children, that Merry got in a word edgewise.

"Wouldn't you like to see them? We'll have them brought in if you would."

He was either oblivious of the eagerness in her voice or indifferent to it. He had never been especially interested in children or intimately associated with them, and the two recent celebrations at Belle Heloise, with which the three youngest d'Alverys had been so closely connected, had already taxed his powers of expressive admiration. He shook his head with attempted archness, his pinched voice cracking a little as he answered.

"Suppose I postpone that pleasure until my next visit? It's such a pretty day, as you say around here, I've been hoping that Captain d'Alvery would ask me to take a turn in the fields with him before I went back to town. And unfortunately I haven't time for both today."

The last thing that Gervais desired was to take Bisbee "for a turn." The fields were grassy because of excessive rains, and the cane had come in to a very poor stand. The young growth which should have been so fresh and green was already streaked with yellow. Bisbee, who was originally a Hoosier, might not grasp the exact significance of all these telltale signs, but, after all, now that he had reached the standing of a prominent banker in a sugar parish, he must have learned what most of them meant. Gervais explained that the ground was very wet and that he was afraid his visitor might find the going rather rough. But it appeared Bisbee had come prepared for this; his rubbers were in the car. He said good-bye to Madame d'Alvery and Merry and went out to get them. . . .

A week later Bisbee wrote to Gervais and asked for collateral on the open note. Of course, he explained, this was only a formality. But since the loan had been made, the board of directors had met and decided that they must observe such formalities more rigidly than in the past, owing to the general financial situation. . . .

Merry had seen Gervais lose his temper many times by now. But she had never seen him as angry as he was on receipt of this letter. He strode up and down their pleasant little living-room, shouting and swearing.

"He came out here on purpose to spy, the dirty sneak! He pretended he was making a social call, and all the time he was just snooping around to see what the prospects were for a good crop!"

"They're pretty bad, aren't they, Gervais?"

"You're damn right, they're bad! But that doesn't excuse Bisbee. I ought never to have let the bastard inside this house! I ought to have seen his stripe from the beginning."

Merry listened, silent and miserable, as Gervais ranted on and on. Her own career in the business world had been brief and limited; but her good sense told her that however reprehensible Bisbee's conduct might have been as a friend, as a banker he was only acting with proper prudence. However, she was wise enough not to voice this opinion. She waited until the worst of Gervais' anger had spent itself, and then she asked one or two cautious and hesitant questions.

"You can let him have the collateral, can't you, honey?"

"Yes, of course I can. . . . Some kind of collateral. I don't at the moment know just what."

"Is there some other bank you could go to that wouldn't ask for it?"

"Of course, there must be—but I wouldn't know which, offhand. I've done all my business with the Cotton Factors National for years. If they treat me like this, then——"

"What about Fabian? Would you mind asking him to help you?"

"I'd mind like hell. He's kept telling me, ever since I got back from France, that I ought to try a different kind of seed cane—as if there *were* any different kind I could try! The land's worked out, that's what's the matter."

"Wouldn't it help if you raised two or three kinds of crop, instead of one?"

"Oh, it's supposed to! You must have been listening to Fabian yourself, Merry. You don't know anything about land. Of course, it's possible to raise cotton and rice. I don't need to tell you that—

290

you've seen them both growing here and there along the River Road. But if I tried to do that, I'd raise the cost of my overhead without any assurance that those crops would do better than the sugar, and it's hard enough to keep one complicated set of machinery paid for and in order without trying to tackle two or three. If you're a millionaire, like Boylston, it doesn't matter about the cost of your overhead, and when one crop fails you can take it in your stride and wait for another. That's why he can afford to dabble around in every sort there is."

She was afraid he was going to say, "If Cresside would only marry Boylston, everything would be all right. She could ask him for the money I need, and he'd give it to her. After all, she has an interest in Belle Heloise and he'd want to protect his wife's property." As a matter of fact, the words were already on the tip of Gervais' tongue; something in Merry's expression stopped him from saying them.

"We've had a series of unbelievably bad breaks in the weather, too," he said. "First days and days of rain, then a long stretch of drought; first a heat wave, and then one freeze after another. Not just one season either—year after year. There's nothing any human being can do about that. It's an act of God—or the devil."

"But Fabian *could* help you, couldn't he?" persisted Merry, not to be diverted.

"Oh, he could, all right. Fabian's very well off and he doesn't spend anything except on those damn camellias of his. He hasn't got anything to spend it for—it isn't as if he had three or four hundred thousand dollars' worth of machinery to keep up and more than a hundred hands to pay and a big family to provide for. One dog doesn't cost much, and Belizaire's his only interest, except his garden and that little insignificant house."

"I shouldn't be surprised if he gave away a lot of money to people who need it, in a quiet way, and he's always seemed very interested in his family, and very kind to me."

"Now get this straight, Merry. I'm not asking Fabian for money. We're not quite in the class of deserving paupers even yet. And I won't have him coming here all the time, knowing I'm in debt to him, and feeling uncomfortable every time I look him in the face."

Again she had the wisdom to be silent, instead of asking what he did intend to do, if he could not go to his broker or to another bank and would not go to Fabian. But she lay awake most of the night worrying; the next morning Philogene was fretful, because she did not have enough milk for him. Then the following day still another letter came in from Arnold Fletcher, and this one tersely called attention to an account past due and abruptly demanded the balance owed for the work of restoration.

It was so long since Merry had been to town, or even spoken of going, that Cresside was taken completely by surprise when her sister-in-law, who had never learned to drive a car, asked her for a ride. However, she managed to answer in her usual casual and cordial way: sure, she said, she had thought of going in herself, anyhow; it would be fun to have Merry along. About what time? Right after Philogene's three o'clock feeding, Merry answered. She did not add that Gervais would be out in the fields then, but something about the flushed, almost frightened look on her face suggested to Cresside that he had not been told of the plan, and that there was some special reason why Merry did not want him to know about it. Cresside asked no further questions, but she regarded Merry covertly during the course of the ride, and what she saw moved her to sympathy. Merry's expression was still as sweet as ever, her features as faultless; but some sort of a blight had fallen on the bloom which had been her greatest beauty. The slight excess weight, the slight weariness of carriage, the slight look of dowdiness caused by ill-fitting and outmoded street clothes—none of these could quite account for this faded look. That fool brother of mine has done this to her, Cresside said to herself savagely; I don't know how or what, but somehow and something. I'd like to wring his damn neck. That's all any man's neck is worth, wringing; almost any man's neck, she added to herself, with one swift and tender mental reservation; and she wanted desperately to say aloud, *"I'm sorry, Merry. Is there anything I can do to help?"* Instead, as they neared town and she slowed down the car, she merely waited for Merry to tell her where to go.

"Oh, I forgot!" Merry said in confusion. "Would it be convenient for you to take me to the store? If it isn't, just drop me at the first corner."

"It's perfectly convenient for me to take you anywhere you want to go. But you'll have to tell me which store."

"Oh! I forgot!" Merry said again. "I meant Goldenberg's. We never called it anything but 'the store' when I was working there. Of course, it was silly of me not to think——"

"It wasn't silly. It was perfectly natural. I'm the dumb one, not to understand right away what you meant. About how long do you want to be there?"

"I shouldn't think more than half an hour. But I want to go over to my mother's for a minute afterwards, and I'd like to walk. Why don't you meet me there, any time you like, just so I get back before six?"

"Right. Let's say five-fifteen, so that we won't run too close to the wind."

"But what are you going to do in the meantime? Won't it be awfully dull for you, waiting around?"

"Oh, I can always count on a date at the Confederate Monument, you know! Or I can go to Fabian's house and play with Belizaire.

I might even drift into Fabian's office and read law. You know, there's no telling to what lengths the modern girl will go."

She was off with her usual gay salute, and Merry went through the revolving doors and entered Goldenberg's store. She had hardly set foot in it since her marriage, and she had not once returned to Mr. Goldenberg's office after resigning as his secretary. She had no sense of ease and familiarity as she took the elevators to the sixth floor, and her feeling of strangeness tightened the lump which already constricted her throat, and made the hollow at the pit of her stomach seem deeper. The slatternly but cheerful coloured girl, who had formerly run the elevator, and who had never failed to greet her with a grin, had been replaced; the new operator was a young man who wore his smart uniform as if he had grown accustomed to similar clothes in the Army, and he held himself with military precision and aloofness. But as Merry went through the Department of Rugs and Draperies, and saw the scatter rugs cluttering the aisle as they always had, she stooped down and put them in their proper places, folding them neatly. This trivial service, performed almost instinctively, made her feel more at home again. However, when a lounging clerk, after regarding her with a disapproving air, came haughtily forward and asked if he could show her something, she flushed and answered with acute embarrassment.

"No, thank you. I used to work here, and I straightened the scatter rugs whenever I went down this aisle. It seemed natural to do it again, that's all. . . . I'm on my way to Mr. Goldenberg's office."

"Have you an appointment?"

"No, but I'm sure he'll see me, if he's there."

"He may be in conference. Of course, you can ask his secretary."

"I'm going to. She's an old friend of mine."

She turned under the pulsating red arrow, and went past the steel lockers, the freight elevator, the adjustment bureau and the fire-escape to the cubby-hole at the end of the glassed-in cubicles. Hazel was typing busily, but Merry saw a small diamond twinkling on her left hand, and guessed that Mr. Goldenberg might soon be looking for a secretary again. Hazel jumped up in a startled way when Merry spoke to her.

"Why, Meredith Randall! What on earth are you doing here? Why didn't you let me know you were coming, instead of just walking in on me like that?"

"I didn't have any way of letting you know. I decided to come very suddenly, and you know we haven't a telephone. . . . Is Mr. Goldenberg in, Hazel?"

She ought to have asked after Al before saying anything else, she realized after she had spoken. But her nervousness had added to her sense of urgency. Now that she had made up her mind what she was going to do, she did not want to postpone the evil moment; she wanted to have it behind her. Hazel, though a little disappointed by Merry's directness, was unresentful; she had not forgotten how cordial Merry had been to her and Al when they went to the sugar house. She rose immediately.

"Yes, he's in. I'll tell him you're here. I know he'll be glad to see you."

She went into the private office, leaving the door open behind her. Merry could hear her speaking to Mr. Goldenberg and his cordial and instantaneous rejoinder. He came to the threshold himself with an outstretched hand.

"Why, Miss Merry, this is a great pleasure. How are you? I haven't seen you in a long time!"

Again the lump in Merry's throat tightened. Gervais had never invited the Goldenbergs to Belle Heloise himself, and when she had first suggested doing so, he had answered vaguely that it wasn't just the best time; later, when she pressed the matter, he had said rather shortly that he did not think his mother would particularly care to have the Goldenbergs at Belle Heloise, and, as it happened, he shared her viewpoint for once. The fact that Mr. Goldenberg must be aware of this viewpoint made her mission all the harder now. Merry's hands had grown terribly cold, and her voice shook a little as she answered.

"Yes, I know. I don't get in town very often. But I came today on purpose to see you."

"I'm very much honoured. Won't you sit down and tell me what I can do for you?"

She was thankful for the seat, but she was not sure things were any easier because he realized this was not a social call, that she would not have come if she had not wanted to ask a favour. The situation, stripped of all pretence, became horribly bald. She took a moment to gather her forces, fixing her eyes on the glassed-over desk, which she saw was still adorned with the bud vase, the picture of Mrs. Goldenberg, and the small neat calendar in a frame of tooled leather. Then she looked up and faced Mr. Goldenberg.

"My husband's in trouble," she said. "Bad trouble. He doesn't know which way to turn. I've been trying and trying to think of some way I can help him. Finally I thought of coming to you and telling you all about it. Gervais doesn't know I've come. I'm afraid he may be very angry when he finds out. It's the first time I've ever kept anything from him, and of course I'm worried about that too. Just the same, I thought it was better not to let him know until afterwards."

"I'm very glad you thought of coming to me. I'm very much honoured," Mr. Goldenberg said again. "Is this trouble of your husband's financial?"

"Yes. He spent too much money last year. He made a great

many improvements on the place because he thought that would be a good investment in the long run. And, anyway, sugar was so high that he had every reason to feel he could afford what he was doing. Then the price of sugar fell—of course, you know that. And now the new crop is a failure—the cane is riddled with mosaic disease. His factor won't advance him anything and the bank he's always gone to won't lend him anything."

"I'm very sorry to hear that he's had such difficulties and that they've made you so unhappy. Was there any special way you thought I could help?"

"Yes. I remembered that you were a director in another bank. I used to transcribe letters about loans for you sometimes, you know. I'm sure you have a great deal of influence with the other directors. I thought perhaps you might be willing to bring up the question of a loan to Gervais at the next board meeting."

"Yes, I would be willing." At the unhesitating reply a great wave of relief engulfed Merry, leaving her assuaged but limp; the dreadful tautness, the dreadful sensations of cold and choking were gone; but now she wondered how she could summon the strength to say anything more. "Of course, I can't tell you how the other directors would feel about the matter," Mr. Goldenberg went on. "And even if they were willing to make a loan, I don't know whether your husband would be satisfied with the terms of it. They might seem pretty harsh to him. Money's very tight these days, I'm sorry to say."

"I realize all that. I know we have to go ahead just a step at a time. But if you proposed a loan, we'd have taken the first step anyway."

"Very well, Miss Merry. I'll propose the loan at the next meeting of the directors. It's on Monday."

He drew a small pad of scratch paper towards him and picked up a pencil.

"I'll have to ask you a few questions," he said. "Not that your answers will affect my promise—it's merely that I need more information than I have. How many acres are there on your plantation?"

"Gervais always speaks about arpents. I think there are around three thousand. An arpent is a little smaller than an acre, isn't it?"

"Yes. . . . And how many tons of cane, approximately, did the plantation produce last year, Miss Merry? Do you know?"

"Nearly forty thousand. Of course, the year before was much better."

"I'm taking it for granted that since you're suggesting this loan you would be willing to sign a paper waiving your homestead rights? Is that correct?"

"I am not just sure what you mean, Mr. Goldenberg. But, of

course, I'm willing to sign anything to get Gervais the money he needs."

Her voice did not tremble any longer, though she felt so tired. It was firm and eager. Mr. Goldenberg raised his searching, bloodshot eyes and looked at her with admiration.

"I'm afraid your husband is going to need a very large sum, in order to clear up the indebtedness for the improvements he has already made and to meet the running expenses of getting in the new crop," he explained. "In order to mention some figure, let us say a hundred thousand dollars, though perhaps he will not need quite that much. If the bank advanced him any such amount, it would have to take a mortgage on the property. There wouldn't be any other way to handle the transaction. So you would have to waive your own rights in the plantation, the rights you have as Captain d'Alvery's wife. You acquired those, automatically, when you married him, you know."

"I suppose I did. I never thought about it, though. You see, Mr. Goldenberg, I married Gervais because I was terribly in love with him—I didn't think about money or anything else. I'm still—I still love him so much I'd do anything I could for him. My rights don't matter. But it matters a lot to have him happy."

Mr. Goldenberg continued to look at her searchingly as she spoke. His admiration increased with his appraisal.

"I can see that you are absolutely sincere, and perhaps, as an old friend, you'll permit me to say, whether Captain d'Alvery is in financial difficulties or not, I consider him a very lucky man," he remarked gently. "But do you think your mother-in-law and your sister-in-law will feel the same way about it that you do? Of course, they have rights in the property, too, since it is inherited."

"I'm sure Cresside would feel the same way that I do, Mr. Goldenberg. She and Gervais quarrel a good deal, but underneath it all they're very fond of each other. And Cresside's a grand person, generous to a fault. I know she'd want to help. . . . Of course, my mother-in-law's a grand person, too," Merry added loyally, but a little hesitatingly. "I wouldn't dare to speak for her until I've talked with her. You see, I'm very ignorant about money, Mr. Goldenberg, and I didn't realize, when I thought of asking you to arrange for a loan, that the bank would have to take a mortgage on Belle Heloise. I do happen to know that Madame Mère has a very strong feeling about mortgages. I've heard her say so a great many times."

Uncomfortably, Merry remembered certain scenes between Gervais and his mother. Madame d'Alvery, from the first, had opposed his plan of restoration. There was plenty of room for them all at the Big House, she insisted. François and Adela Estrade had raised ten children in it without feeling crowded, despite the constant presence of various indigent relatives who made visits of indefinite length, as Philogene d'Alvery had begun by doing. And besides all the elderly aunts and uncles and cousins, Angus Holt had lived there for years. Madame d'Alvery saw no reason for rebuilding the storehouse and the *garçonnière* to create more living space, still less for restoring the cooperage and the blacksmith shop. She was ready to concede that machinery must be safe, if it were in use, but she would rather have seen the mill shut down than equipped with installations which were not paid for. "It is better to have a leaking roof that is your own roof and that no one can take away from you, than one that is watertight and mortgaged to someone else," she said repeatedly. It was her favourite example of a property owner's only sound position. Merry knew that nothing would ever change this viewpoint, for Madame d'Alvery had tried, far more forcefully and persistently than Merry, to stop Gervais' reckless expenditure. But after all, she had not succeeded. Now that money had already been spent on the leaking roof, so to speak, something must be done about repaying it. . . .

"I'll talk to Madame Mère," Merry said, meeting Mr. Goldenberg's bloodshot eyes squarely. "I'll let you know what she says. Of course, it wouldn't be fair to ask you to present this question to the directors and then find that the family wouldn't consent to a mortgage at all. I'll come back to see you again some time before Monday, Mr. Goldenberg. Or else Gervais will come himself. And —and thank you. I can't tell you how grateful I am to you. But I think you know. I hope there'll be something I can do for you some time that will mean as much to you as this means to me."

Merry walked up Third Street to the Boulevard with feelings of mingled relief and dread. She had accomplished the first part of her mission, and this had lifted a load from her heart. Mr. Goldenberg had been generous in every sense of the word—generous and considerate and understanding, as she had thought he would be, for all this was entirely in keeping with his character. Yet before she went to him, she had not been able wholly to suppress a little forking fear that he might betray some natural resentment because she waited until she was in trouble before seeking to renew their acquaintance, that his reception of her might be cool and his manner distant, so that her petition, difficult enough at best to put forward, would be repelled at the outset. Now that fear was lulled, but she still had her husband to face, and she knew that this second ordeal might be harder than the first. However, she realized that she must try to compose herself before seeing her mother, whose antipathy to Gervais had increased, rather than abated, with time. If Merry's agitation was evident, Mrs. Randall would seize upon it and ferret out its source. Resolutely, the girl forced herself to walk slowly, breathing in the sunny air, looking at shop windows as she went along, and trying to divert her thoughts both from the interview which had just ended and the interview which was still ahead of her. As she passed the Confederate Monument, she saw that Pascal Tremblet was sitting alone on the bench in front of it and stopped to speak to him.

"Good-evening, Mr. Tremblet. Where's your partner this fine day?" she asked, as he rose to greet her. But even before he answered her, she knew that her question had been ill-timed. His pinched face had a stricken look, and the gnarled hands clasping the old cane were quivering.

"He's not so well, him, Miss Merry," Pascal said slowly. "He didn't come out to meet me yesterday, so I went to his grandson's house, and I found him in the bed. He said he'd be up again today for sure, if it were pretty weather, and you couldn't ask for prettier weather than this, now could you? But like you see, he isn't here."

"Perhaps he'll come later on. Perhaps something has detained him," Merry said, trying to speak convincingly.

"No, ma'am, I'm not trying to deceive myself. He hasn't come because he isn't able to. Likely he won't ever be, again. I'll be all alone, me, pretty soon."

"Please don't say that, Mr. Tremblet! . . . Have you spoken to Fabian?"

"Not yet, Miss Merry. But Miss Cresside, she stopped by the Monument a while back, and she said she'd do it for me. I'm looking for him to come by almost any time now."

"You're right in counting on Fabian, Mr. Tremblet. He'll do everything he can for you and your friend. I wish I could stay with you until he comes, but I'm on my way to see my mother, and I have to get back to the plantation to feed my baby at six o'clock."

"Yes, Miss Merry, I know how it is. Don't you worry any about me. I'll be all right. I'll just sit here and wait for Fabian."

She went on her way reluctantly, a fresh worry added to those that already burdened her; but she found her mother too preoccupied with her own troubles to notice the unconvincing quality of Merry's determined cheerfulness. Mrs. Randall was rocking back and forth in her little sitting-room, sniffing suspiciously, and she did not even look up when her daughter came in. Merry, who was used to such experiences, stooped to kiss her and spoke to her affectionately.

"Hello, Mother! Aren't you going to tell me you're glad to see me? I was ever so glad that I had a chance to come into town!"

"Well, it's nice you've got something to be glad about. Everything's looking pretty black to me, right now."

"Why, what's the matter?"

"Miss Mittie's lost her job, that's what's the matter. I don't know what's going to become of her or me without her salary."

"Lost her job!" Merry echoed in dismay. "What happened?"

"She got suspicious when the principal didn't say anything to her about next year. All the other teachers had been told they'd be kept, that they'd get formal notices saying so a little later on, same as usual. She didn't hear a word, so she made inquiries. And she found out she was being fired for disloyalty."

"Disloyalty! But Miss Mittie's the soul of loyalty! No one could possibly think she was disloyal."

"I don't know what anybody thinks, but that's what the State superintendent says. Some of the women in that Suffrage crowd she goes with would like to see him lose his own job, because they don't think he's fit for it. He claims Miss Mittie's been one of those working against him. That's disloyalty, as far as he's concerned."

"But *was* she?"

"I don't know, Merry. Miss Mittie won't talk about it herself. All I know is, after this month, she won't have anything to live on, except what she's saved, and that's mighty little. What can a teacher save out of her kind of pay? She can't get a job anywhere else in Louisiana either, when she's been fired in Baton Rouge on account of trouble with the State Superintendent. And she can't go back North. She couldn't qualify to teach there any more. She hasn't tried to keep up with all the newfangled Yankee notions. She's just drifted along, like we do in the South. She never thought she'd have to do anything else."

Merry listened to her mother with a sense of mounting disaster. It was not the first time she had heard of a teacher's displacement on some pretext for which politics were really responsible. Besides, she knew that her mother spoke the truth: Miss Mittie, conscientious and intelligent as she was, had always openly expressed her contempt for modern schoolroom methods, and these expressions would count against her now. Under all these circumstances, it was unlikely that anyone would be able to intercede for her successfully, or that she would be able to re-establish herself, on her own initiative. And without the money from Miss Mittie's board and lodging, Mrs. Randall herself would be almost penniless. The long postponed moment of her mother's dependence on her, which Merry had foreseen when Gervais urged her to marry him, had come at last, and somehow she must cope with this too. But she could not force her tired mind to do so immediately. She continued to sit beside her mother, silent and appalled, while Mrs. Randall went on sniffing and rocking, until she heard Cresside honking outside. Then she rose and went slowly towards the door.

"Just a minute!" she called to her sister-in-law. Cresside called back that there wasn't any hurry, to take her time. Just the same, Merry knew that she must not linger. Philogene would be hungry, Gervais would be annoyed, half a dozen things might have gone wrong during her unannounced absence. She put her arms around Mrs. Randall's bony shoulders and hugged her hard.

"Don't feel so badly, Mummy," she said soothingly, calling her mother by the name she had not used since childhood. "Miss

Mittie'll be paid for one more month, whatever happens. You and she can both manage that long. And before the month's up, I'll think of something I can do to help. I don't know what it'll be, but something. I've got to go now, because my baby needs me even more than you do. But I know you need me too. I'll come back in a few days and we'll talk this over again."

XXIII

AS she went down the steps of her mother's house, Merry decided that she would say nothing about the trouble which had befallen Miss Mittie until she had thought out some way of relieving it. But on the way back to Belle Heloise, she did tell Cresside about her talk with Mr. Goldenberg. She felt that if she were armed with her sister-in-law's support regarding the mortgage, she would be better prepared for the inevitable battle ahead of her, and she was not disappointed about securing this.

"Merry, I do hand it to you for spunk," Cresside said heartily. "I told you that the night you came to Belle Heloise and again the morning Philogene was born, but now I'm ready to tell the world. I know it took guts for you to go to Mr. Goldenberg like that. Of course I'll put the old John Hancock anywhere he wants me to. And I'll do what I can to make *maman* and Gervais see the light of day. I don't suppose I'll get very far with your beloved husband. But we better start right off by reminding him that if he has this money from the First National, he can tell Fletcher to go straight to hell, and that he won't have to dig up any collateral for Bisbee. He can pay for the restoration straight away, and clean up his open note too, writing a sweet little missive to the effect that of course it isn't due for months yet, but that it gives him great pleasure, etc. If he's smart, he'll manage to wedge in a line saying he didn't think of 'formalities' between friends, and that he's sorry Bisbee didn't see it the same way. That ought to give the old skinflint the idea that he won't be coming to Belle Heloise any more, and, believe me, he'll be sorry, and too late. He was lapping up atmosphere along with champagne, and writing bragging letters about both of them back to Peoria, or wherever it is he comes from."

"You always know just what to do, Cresside. I wouldn't have thought of beginning by reminding Gervais he could get rid of Fletcher and Bisbee straight off. I think that's just the way to

300

handle him. Can you think of an equally good way to get around Madame Mère?"

"I haven't yet, but I'm working on it. Just give me time."

The evening did not start off too propitiously. Merry and Cresside had never left the plantation before at the same time, and though Dinah and Lethe had done the best they could with their charges, the twins had sensed the withdrawal of authority and Philogene the absence of his most important source of supply. Vail had fallen down and cut his knee; Sybelle had stuck the corner of her bib into her eye; Philogene had been howling at the top of his lungs for nearly an hour. While Cresside rushed off to get iodine and boric acid water, Merry hastily unbuttoned her dress, and within a few minutes comparative quiet and order were restored; but it was impossible for either girl to answer the questions about the afternoon satisfactorily until the children were in bed and dinner over. When Gervais started back to the *garçonnière*, however, Merry detained him.

"I want to talk to Madame Mère and you together," she said. "I want Cresside to stay in the room while I'm doing it, too. Let's all go into the library, shall we? I've told Lethe she must listen for Philogene, that I wouldn't be back right away."

The session which ensued was stormy from start to finish. Gervais was almost as angry because Merry had been to Mr. Goldenberg without consulting him as he had been over Mr. Bisbee's letter about "formalities." He spoke to her as he had never spoken before, and the flush of embarrassment with which she had begun to tell him of her mission faded to pallor deeper than Cresside's while she listened. Her lovely natural colour did not come back at all that evening, and she had to keep biting her lips to keep from crying. But she could not be cowed, though her husband and her mother-in-law, joining forces for once, declared over and over again that they would never mortgage their ancestral home. Even the taunt that only an outsider would have made such a suggestion, and the reproach that the Estrades would turn over in their graves if they knew of it, failed to move her; and at that point Cresside succeeded in coming to her rescue. She had not thought of going to Mr. Goldenberg herself, she said; but that was only because she did not know him well enough to ask favours of him; she thought it was darn lucky for them all that Merry did. As far as being an outsider went, she was just as much of an Estrade as her mother, and just as much of a d'Alvery as Gervais, too; and she was all for the mortgage. If their ancestors did turn in the graves, perhaps they would wake up and find out that things had changed a good deal since their day, on the whole for the better; but whether they did or not, their descendants might just as well face facts. What did Gervais want to do? Let Fletcher and Bisbee start telling all over town that he was bankrupt?

They parted, completely at odds, and without reaching any definite decision, when Merry had to return to the *garçonnière* to give Philogene his final feeding for the night. Gervais did not speak harshly to Merry again; he ignored her as completely as if she had not been present. He did not lie close beside her with his arms tenderly around her when he went to sleep; instead, for the first time, the width of the bed divided them and it was symbolic of the greater gulf separating them spiritually. Merry lay wide-eyed and wretched, thinking of her mother's troubles as well as her own, and longing to creep over to her husband and beg his forgiveness for having offended him; but she resisted the impulse with the same firmness that she had resisted the attack which had preceded his withdrawal. Morning found them no nearer together, either figuratively or literally, than they had been the night before, and the strained silence between them lasted for several days. Merry knew she had done everything she could and said all there was for her to say. But Cresside kept hammering away at her brother, whenever she saw him, and in the midnight talks with her mother, which had now become habitual, she continued to speak on the subject, less caustically but no less insistently. On Saturday morning she confronted Gervais as he was mounting his horse, and asked him if he were planning to call on Mr. Goldenberg that afternoon.

"I sure am not," he said abruptly. "What gave you the idea that I might?"

"Well, you know the directors' meeting is on Monday, and you also know that Merry promised to give him some kind of an answer before then. She agreed to go herself if you didn't and I think she's done her share in trying to get you out of this mess already. It's taken a lot out of her. I wouldn't put it past you not to mind that, but don't forget it's taking a lot out of Philogene, too. Maybe you haven't noticed that Merry's going around looking more and more like a ghost and that Philogene's howling his head off from hunger."

"So what?"

"So that if you're not going in town today, I think I will. I can go to see Mr. Goldenberg myself. I can tell him that *maman* and Merry and I are all very much in favour of the mortgage and that we hope he'll be able to arrange it. After all, we control the greater part of the property among us."

"You can't lie to him like that. *Maman* isn't in favour of the mortgage."

"Damn right she is. She wasn't to start with, but she is now. Go ask her yourself if you don't believe me, you dumb Dora."

Gervais tied his horse and strode off towards the Big House without answering Cresside. His mother received him reproachfully but calmly.

"Certainly Cresside told you the truth," she said in a cold voice.

"What possible reason could she have for lying to you? I feel exactly as I always have—that it is far better to have a leaking roof that is one's own, than a whole one on which someone else has claim. But since in this case you have already repaired the roof with someone else's money, your creditor must be reimbursed. We cannot repudiate our just debts, Gervais." It was exactly the line of argument on which Merry had counted, but Cresside had facilitated and expedited the process of deduction. "Cresside also consulted me about going to see Mr. Goldenberg herself, in case you declined to do so," Madame d'Alvery continued. "I gave my consent to that, too. Naturally she would ask Fabian to escort her if she made such a visit, so that the family would be represented by one of its male members."

"You don't mean to tell me that Fabian knows all about this mess, too?"

"I have an idea that Cresside may have given him some inkling; they went to see Pola Negri together last night," Madame d'Alvery answered imperturbably. "After all, Fabian was bound to find out about it sooner or later, and Cresside was the best person to tell him. He has always been very fond of her; I do not need to remind you of that. I believe he told her that he would keep the afternoon free until he learned, definitely, whether she would need him or not."

Eventually, Gervais and Cresside went into town together, after a second passage at arms which left them both angrier than the first. She had better learn to hush her mouth and mind her own business, he told her. She would, Cresside retorted, when he stopped spending money like a drunken sailor; maybe he could get away with squandering his wife's and his mother's and his children's, but she wasn't sentimental about her share. . . He thought things had come to a pretty pass when every female d'Alvery was ready to accept money from a German Jew. They weren't accepting money from a German Jew, Cresside replied bluntly; they were going to borrow it from an American bank, if they were lucky. And since a Hoosier Baptist like Melvin Bisbee, who had been lugged out to Belle Heloise by Gervais without consulting anyone, wasn't willing to help them do that, she thought they were darn lucky that a German Jew, who was a friend of Merry's, was willing. . . . Anyway, he would thank her to leave Fabian out of it; if he had wanted Fabian to know, he would have told their cousin himself. Was thazzo? Well, she had wanted Fabian to know about it, so she had told him herself. And that was that. . . .

The recriminations went on and on, but in the end it was Cresside who wore her brother down. Impudently, she suggested that as Fabian would be waiting around for her, she might as well ride into town with Gervais when he went to see Mr. Goldenberg; he could let her off at Somerulos Street before going on to Third; there was no use using up gas for two cars when one would do. He froze into haughty silence after his outburst, as he had before. But this did not affect Cresside in the same way as it had Merry. His sister rejoined him after midday dinner very smartly dressed, and wearing just enough make-up to complete her general air of jauntiness. As they rode along, she made a number of wisecracks, apparently unconcerned, because he gave no sign that he had heard her, and when he left her in front of Fabian's house, she waved to him gaily from the gate.

"Give my best to Mr. Goldenberg," she said pertly. "Tell him I'm sorry I didn't get to see him myself this time. I've been dying to, ever since you told Merry he looked like a Levantine. I haven't the least idea what a Levantine is, but it sounds intriguing. I suppose we'll be having him and Mrs. Goldenberg to our next dinner-party though, and I'll see him then. That is, if he'll come. I wouldn't, if I were in his place, but maybe he'll take a charitable view of our shortcomings, for Merry's sake."

Fabian, who had been watching for her, opened the front door in time to hear her farewell remarks to her brother, and greeted her with a quiet chuckle.

"Hush up and come on in," he said. "What'll you take to celebrate your victory? I see that among you, Tante Isabelle and Merry and you got Gervais completely whipped down. I knew you would. He can win medals and all that in a World War. But there's no hero living who could stand up long against a gynarchy like the one that's getting established at Belle Heloise."

"I haven't the least idea what you're talking about," Cresside said, grinning. "You're as bad with your gynarchy as Gervais is with his Levantine. I wish you'd use words a poor girl can understand. You're right though—Gervais is whipped down at last. It's taken nearly a week and a great deal of moral suasion, but it's done. . . . I'd like a julep, of course."

"I thought you would, and I thought you'd be here about this time, bringing Gervais in chains with you. So it's already made and in the icebox. I'll go and get it for you."

He returned from the kitchen with two beautiful frosted goblets on a silver tray, offered Cresside a cigarette, and sat down on a sofa beside her, with Belizaire at his feet. For a few minutes they sat smoking and sipping their drinks without speaking, enjoying the companionable silence. Then Fabian made a pensive remark.

"I've been wondering, since you spoke to me last night, if there wasn't something I could do to help out. I don't mean by lending Gervais money. Of course I'd be willing to do that, but I know he'd hate it like hell. I really think Merry's plan is a lot better, anyhow. Gervais'll work to pay off that mortgage to the bank as he never'd have worked to pay back a relative who'd loaned him money 'informally.' But I've got another idea."

304

"Feel like telling me what it is?"

"Yes, in a general way. I'd rather not tell you the details until I see how they work out. But, briefly, I think I might go back to Washington. I don't know whether you remember I went there about a year ago when Gervais got all hot and bothered about the Equalization Board. I made some contacts then that I think might be still more useful now. Anyway, it would be worth trying."

"Right away?"

"No, I couldn't go right away. I've got two or three cases coming up that I can't very well leave. And I want to watch the Constitutional Convention fairly closely too—Reid and Pleasant are readying a hell of a fight to boost the Severance Tax and I've got a couple of oil companies among my clients, thank God. But I could go late this summer—that is, I could if I knew what to do with Belizaire. He ran away the last time I left him, and Carmelite was almost beside herself."

"Would you trust him to me?"

"I'd trust anything I had to you, of course. But wouldn't he be an awful nuisance to you? You've never had a dog, and a dog's a lot of fun, but a lot of work too. . . . Snow and Cornet don't count," Fabian added scornfully, reaching out to put his hand on Belizaire's waiting head as he spoke.

"I know they don't. I've always wanted a dog—I mean a real dog—of my own."

"Then why in hell didn't you tell me so?"

"I don't know. Why should I have told you so?"

"Because I'd have seen that you had one."

"Well——" She flushed a little, and spoke with unwonted earnestness. "I don't think I ought to have one of my own," she said. "*Maman* wouldn't like it, and she's put up with a good deal from me already. It isn't fair to worry her with anything else. Besides, the twins take up a good deal of my time. I don't believe I'd have enough to look after a dog too, right now. Perhaps when they're older. . . . I'd like for Vail to have a dog, a real dog. Every boy ought to. And I'd be awfully happy if you'd lend me yours while you're away."

"Well, you may be sure I'll be awfully glad to do it. It's a bargain. How about another julep?"

It was not until the following week, after the Board of Directors had reported favourably on the loan to Belle Heloise, and the necessary documents to provide this had been duly signed, that Merry spoke to Gervais about her mother. She was not waiting for a favourable opportunity, as far as his mood was concerned, since she had ceased to hope for this; but she wanted to be sure one disaster was averted before she tried to deal with another. When all the papers had been passed and the money was actually in the bank, she again invited a general conference as the family left the dinner-table.

"Perhaps Cresside has told you already that I went to see my mother the same day that I went to see Mr. Goldenberg," she said, looking from her husband to her mother-in-law after they were all seated in the library. "Anyway, I'm sorry to say that I found her very unhappy. Our friend and lodger, Miss Mittie Alden, has been unjustly discharged by the State Superintendent of Schools. Of course that means that her salary'll stop when school closes. She won't have much of anything to live on after that, and neither will my mother."

"Gosh, but I'm sorry, Merry!" Cresside exclaimed, while Madame d'Alvery murmured something vaguely though politely sympathetic, and Gervais looked hard at Merry without saying anything.

"When Gervais asked me to marry him, I told him just how poor we were, Madame Mère," Merry went on, turning to her mother-in-law. "I said that the time might come when I'd have to take care of my mother again, just as I did when I worked for Mr. Goldenberg. I'm afraid it's come now. She doesn't own the little house she lives in, and it's in such bad repair that I don't believe she could get another lodger who would help her meet expenses, the way Miss Mittie has. My father didn't provide for her in any way before he died. My brothers left her a little insurance money, but I know that must be almost used up now. Of course I haven't been able to give her much, these last few years." Merry did not speak resentfully; she made a simple statement of an unfortunate fact. "My mother's depended on the money she's been getting from Miss Mittie to keep her going," Merry concluded.

"I think it is greatly to your credit, Merry, that you have such a sense of responsibility to your mother. But it is not clear to me just what you want to do for her."

"Why, *maman*, it must be! It's plain as print! Merry wants to invite her mother to live at Belle Heloise, and Miss Mittie too, just the way your relatives and Angus Holt used to live here! Papa, too, for that matter! A darn good idea, I thould think!"

"Be quiet, Cresside, for a moment, and let Merry speak for herself. . . . Is that what you had in mind, *chère*?"

"Yes, Madame Mère, it is. . . . And I'll never forget that you called me *chère* when you asked me, feeling the way you do about the mortgage too!"

Merry's words ended in a sudden sob. She leapt up and walked quickly across the room; then she knelt down and buried her face in her mother-in-law's lap. Madame d'Alvery looked at her son over the girl's bowed head.

"Since you have insisted on providing so many extra living quarters on this plantation, you are hardly in a position to com-

306

plain if they are used, Gervais," she said. "I certainly shall not do so. . . . Merry, my dear, I beg of you not to weep. You should have been spared this unhappiness, and you would have been, had I known sooner that the need you describe existed. Cresside is right. The situation is similar to many that have prevailed before. . . . I suggest that we offer Mrs. Randall and Miss Alden the rooms above your office and library, Gervais. These would seem to me the most practical for their purposes, and the pleasantest, because of the little kitchen. They will have more privacy in the remodelled storehouse, and more independence, than anywhere else on the place—though of course we will make it clear that we shall expect them to join us for meals at the Big House whenever they feel inclined. We will also make it clear to Miss Alden that in the near future she can be very helpful to us by teaching the children. Personally, I shall be glad to see the old schoolhouse in use again. And, as far as I am concerned, your mother is welcome to whatever we can offer her, Merry. Shall we consider the matter settled? If so, I should like to have a game of bridge before I retire for the night."

XXIV

"I'VE left some old trousers of mine in the dog-house. When Belizaire finds these, he'll know I'm coming back. And I'll put him in the run before I leave. If I don't, he'll break away from you and follow the car. In fact, you'll probably have to keep him in the run or on the leash all the time, for a few days anyhow, to prevent him from making off."

"There isn't any shade in the run. I won't be able to leave him there through the heat of the day. Can't I take him into the house?"

Fabian shook his head. "There are too many doors. You might think you had every screen locked, and the next thing you knew he'd be out of one of them that a servant had inadvertently opened. You can take him into your own room, or on the gallery outside of it, once in a while, if you really want to. But I wouldn't make a practice of it. Pretty soon you'd be a slave to him, and heaven knows that's the last thing I want. Better keep him tied up in the patio. And let Amen lead him back and forth between there and the run and take him for a walk twice a day. Don't you do it. Belizaire's strong enough to pull you right off your feet. You might get a bad fall that way, and hurt your back."

"I don't believe I would. But I'll try to do just as you said about everything, Fabian."

They walked slowly out towards the run, Belizaire following with dragging footsteps. Several times he stopped entirely, looking reproachfully from his master to his newly appointed guardian. Fabian spoke to him, first coaxingly and then sharply, but his habit of obedience was not strong enough to bring about submission to the unwelcome orders. He was finally pulled bodily into the run, and prevented from escaping only by swift manœuvring in closing the gate after him. He immediately sat down on his haunches, and, lifting his head, began to howl, loudly and dismally, as if he were in dire distress and terrible pain.

"That's nothing," Fabian said reassuringly. "He always does that when I leave him in a strange place. He'll stop after a while when he gets accustomed to his new surroundings."

"But this isn't a strange place. You've brought him here dozens of times."

"Yes, but I've always stayed too. And I've never shut him up before. . . . Well, there's no use in having the agony long and drawn out. So long, Cresside."

"So long. And good luck!"

She had been half hoping that he would kiss her good-bye before he went to Washington, though there was no reason why she should expect that he would. He was not demonstrative by nature and they had never been classified by relationship as "kissing cousins." On the rare occasions when he had taken her hand or put his arm around her shoulder, this had never seemed like a caress; it had been merely a gesture made to signify protectiveness and restore confidence. Cresside had no delusions on this score. But she had always welcomed these gestures, and increasingly through the summer she had found herself longing for them; there was something about them which not only imparted a feeling of security, but which filled her with supreme contentment. If an impersonal touch could do this, it seemed reasonable to assume that a kindly kiss could do even more. She stood watching Fabian out of sight, feeling frustrated because she had not found out whether her assumption was correct.

She had no leisure at the moment to brood over this unduly, however, as it was almost time for the twins' supper. They ate this in the patio now, sitting in high chairs on either side of a small table. Though they were enveloped in sizable bibs of Turkish towelling, securely tied round their plump persons, their enthusiastic but bungling attempts to feed themselves required considerable guidance: the silver mugs which they seized needed steadying to avert overflows; the short-handled spoons which they dipped into their porringers had a way of emptying themselves before reaching the hungry pink mouths. Dinah always sat between the

308

wins on one side of the table, turning watchfully from one to the
other; but Cresside, who could forestall accidents more quickly,
usually sat on the other side. Long before their supper was finished
they had begun to be sleepy, and if their naps had been curtailed
for any reason, fussy as well; it took tact and patience to slip the
final mouthfuls down, and afterwards to get the twins settled for
the night. Merry was busy with Philogene at the same hour, so it
was also Cresside who helped Dinah sponge off Vail and Sybelle,
get them into their nightgowns, and tuck them into their cribs
under the enveloping mosquito netting. By the time all this was
done Selah had almost invariably announced dinner, and she had
barely time to freshen up hastily herself. After dinner, Merry and
Gervais sat for a few minutes with Madame d'Alvery; then, if
there were no guests, they went back to the *garçonnière*. It was
now tacitly understood that Mrs. Randall and Miss Mittie would
come to Belle Heloise as soon as their money gave out. But they
were still managing somehow on Napoleon Street, so the family
programme was as yet unaffected by the complications which their
presence would eventually entail. Cresside remained with her
mother until Madame d'Alvery retired; then she generally read for
an hour or two before going to bed. Fabian had never asked her if
she found the evenings at Belle Heloise long and empty; but he
had asked her a number of times whether she had read this or that
which he had recently enjoyed, and upon receiving a negative
answer had given her the book in question, carefully marking the
passages he had especially liked. She had read practically nothing
as a girl, except the "literature" required in the English courses she
took at Convent, all of which she heartily hated, and the more
salacious current novels, which occasionally came up for discussion
in "the gang," and which were theoretically banned in the house.
Now she was becoming tardily aware of a great treasure-house to
which she could retire at will, sure of respite and refreshment.

When she finally put down her book, on the night of Fabian's
departure, she realized that it was already very late and that Belizaire was still howling woefully. She went outdoors and stood close
to the run, speaking to him in comforting tones; but she did not
dare to open the gate and go inside for fear that he would slip
past her and rush off in hopeless pursuit of his master. Momentarily, she succeeded in calming him; but as soon as she stopped
talking to him or moved away ever so slightly from the run, he
began to howl again. While she hesitated, wondering what she had
better do next, Gervais called to her from one of the windows of
his room.

"For heaven's sake, Cresside, stop puttering with that hound and
go to bed! If I'd known you'd make such a fuss over him, I
wouldn't have let Fabian leave him here! Or if I'd known he was
going to raise such a racket either! I haven't had a wink of sleep

L

yet and neither has Merry. Pretty soon he'll wake up the kids too
and then there'll be hell to pay."

"Well, he hasn't waked them up yet, and I don't believe he will
And it isn't late, so you and Merry haven't lost much preciou
sleep. Fabian said he'd probably quiet down before long, and
reckon he will. But he's lonesome."

"*Lonesome!* He's a disturber of the peace. Go back to the house
can't you? If you start disturbing it too, that'll be the last straw."

With a few parting words of encouragement and comfort to
Belizaire, Cresside left the run. She was reluctant to leave he
charge, and she was not greatly concerned about her brother's los
of sleep; however, she was still hopeful that Belizaire woul
eventually quiet down, and it seemed puerile to start an argumen
with Gervais in the middle of the night. She herself tossed and
turned for a long time; but her wakefulness was due less to the
dog's continued outcry, drowning the sorrowful note of a mourning
dove, than to her distress over his misery; she could close her ears t
it, but not her mind. Before dawn she was up and dressed again
feeling she could stand it no more. She longed to let Belizaire out
to take him for a walk herself; but remembering Fabian's fina
words of admonition, she resisted the temptation, and sat waiting
for Amen to come and release the prisoner, forgetting that she wa
down hours earlier than usual and wondering what made the boy
so late. When the unconcerned but good-natured negro finally
appeared on the scene, still yawning, and cautiously inched his way
into the run, slipping on the leash before Belizaire could elude him
Cresside went into the garden-room and sat down at the ol
custom-house desk.

"Dear Fabian (she wrote),
    "Belizaire misses you very much. So do I. This is the firs
time I've ever thought I'd rather be a dog than a girl, but now I do
Because a dog can get up on his hind legs and tell the world jus
how he feels, and a girl has to keep quiet about it. I want to cry
too and I know I mustn't.

                                        "As ever,
                                            "Cresside."

She read the letter over two or three times, sat staring out at the
garden for a few minutes, read the letter again, and tore it up
Then she went out in the patio and waited for Amen to bring
Belizaire back from his walk. Lucie passed her as the maid went up
the outside stairway with Madame d'Alvery's breakfast tray, and
briefly bade the girl good-morning in her usual incurious and re
spectful manner. She did not indicate, by either word or look, that
she was surprised at seeing her young mistress downstairs before
early morning coffee had been served. But a few minutes later she
310

returned with a second tray, and set it down on a small wicker table by Cresside.

"Thazza mighty fine dawg of Mr. Fabian's," she remarked. "Cain't none of us say his name, though, to call him or make much of him. Bellie, that'd be easy. But it don't jes' sound respectful to Mr. Fabian."

"I don't think he'd mind at all. And I think Belizaire would come if you called him that. You can try, anyway."

"Yassum—I'se fixin' to bring you some more coffee right soon."

Lucie was followed after an interval by Dinah, bringing Vail. The twins still spent most of their waking hours in the patio, much of the time in a large play pen, from which they were occasionally released for more freedom of action. Vail could walk very well now, and often succeeded in getting out of bounds unless he was carefully watched. Sybelle tagged after him with more uncertain footsteps, but she already lisped a number of words, while Vail stubbornly declined to say more than two. As these were "Auntie" and "Dinah," however, they sufficed to meet his every requirement; Gervais not infrequently remarked that Vail would grow up a near-mute unless Cresside and Dinah stopped catering to him so slavishly. . . .

Dinah put Vail into Cresside's outstretched arms now before going back upstairs for Sybelle. The girl tossed him up in the air two or three times, while he shouted with glee, and then put him on her knee to "ride a cock horse," a performance in which he heartily co-operated. But when she tried to hold him in her lap he wriggled away from her. Vail demanded boisterous amusement; if he did not get it in one way, he sought it in another. He succeeded in squirming out of Cresside's grasp, but, instead of heading pell-mell towards the lawn, he scrambled over to Belizaire and looked questioningly but joyfully first at the dog and then at Cresside.

"Nice doggy," Cresside said encouragingly. "Pat him, Vail. Look, this way! That's it! Can't you say doggy, Vail?"

"Auntie," Vail responded promptly.

"No, no, not Auntie. Doggy! Sybelle can say doggy, Vail."

"Auntie," reiterated Vail, with characteristic stubbornness.

"My, but you're a mule-headed little boy! I don't know what's going to happen to you when you grow up if someone doesn't teach you to mind."

Cresside looked at him with doting admiration as she spoke. He had always been a beautiful baby, and he was already beginning to show promise of becoming a very handsome child. He was very large for his age, sturdy rather than chubby, and amazingly strong; he handled heavy and unwieldy playthings with complete ease, and when he was angry flung them a considerable distance. His colouring was striking; he had very red cheeks, very blue eyes and very black hair. As his hair was completely straight, it presented a problem: Gervais thought it should be cut like a big boy's, but the other members of the family insisted he was still too young for this, so it was left long and stuck out, rather wildly, in every direction. Cresside and Dinah had both spent endless hours trying to curl it and smooth it, but to absolutely no avail, and its natural disorder was further increased by Vail's habit of running his stubby fingers through it. He did so now as he continued to look from Belizaire to Cresside.

"Doggy," Cresside repeated, patting Belizaire's upraised head and stroking his long ears. Vail eyed her roguishly and began to chuckle.

"Auntie," he said again.

Cresside chuckled herself. She and Vail were laughing together, each enjoying the other's merriment, while Belizaire, momentarily cheered, began to wag his tail when Selah came out on the patio.

"Dat peddler man done come, Miss Cresside," he said. "Him an' his little boy. Dey ain't come in no cart dis time, but in de reddest truck ever been on dis road. De little boy done brung a present for Miss Sybelle he say."

"Ask him if he won't come out here, Selah. Dinah'll be down with Sybelle any minute now."

As it happened, Dinah, with Sybelle in her arms, emerged from the hallway at the same moment that Selah opened the kitchen door for Luigi and Riccardo to pass through. The peddler and his son were both attired in their best, and Riccardo was carrying a long cardboard box with great care under one arm. As they approached the baby girl and her nurse he mutely held this box out. Luigi hastened to explain the nature of the offering.

"Good-a morning, Miss Cresside," he said. "My, my, whata beautiful bambinos! That-a boy, soon he be big like-a my Riccardo. But the leetla girl, how she's look just like-a dolly, with the yellow curls, the pink cheek and oh! such-a beega eyes! Looka now, Sybelle, see what-a my Riccardo bring you! Maybe you think you a-lookin' on yourself in the glass!"

Helpfully, Luigi whisked the lid off the box. Inside lay a huge flaxen-haired baby doll, elaborately dressed in fine muslin and lace ornamented with pink satin ribbons. The doll's waxen eyelids, heavily fringed with dark lashes, were tightly closed; but when Luigi tilted the box, so that her position became upright, her eyes flew open. Watching Sybelle to see if she appreciated this miracle, Luigi next fumbled under the frills for some hidden contraption, and immediately the doll began to bleat, "Mam-ma—Mam-ma!"

"Mam-ma!" echoed Sybelle, thoroughly entranced.

"That's-a-it!" Luigi exclaimed. "This-a dolly bambina say Mamma just-a like you! Go to sleep just-a like you! Wear pretty clothes just-a like you! She all for you, Sybelle. Riccardo bring-a her to

312

you from Nawlins. Take her out the box, Riccardo, so Sybelle can-a see!"

"Suppose we sit down," suggested Cresside, "and put the doll on the table. Then Sybelle can see it better, and touch it too, if she wants to. But we must be careful she doesn't break it. What a magnificent doll that is, Luigi! Much too beautiful for a baby to bang around. We'll have to keep it in a safe place until Sybelle gets older."

"You want-a keep it safe, you keep it safe, but the dolly is-a for Sybelle. We got a fine stock of toys now, but this dolly no come-a out no stock. Riccardo got this dolly just-a for Sybelle. Ain't I got right, Riccardo?"

"Yes," agreed Riccardo, without much enthusiasm. Now that he had delivered the doll a weight was lifted from his mind, and his gaze was no longer focused on the puzzled baby girl in the nurse's arms, or on the pleasant young lady who had invited his father to sit down; he was looking around the patio in search of other attractions. As he caught sight of Belizaire and Vail, his flagging interest revived, and he tugged at his father's arm.

"Look, Papa!" he said. "There's a nice black dog. Can I go over and pat the dog, Papa?"

"Now you listen-a me, Riccardo; you never come here to pat no black dog. You come here to give a dolly to leetle Sybelle."

"But I did give her the doll, Papa. Can't I go over and pat the dog now?"

"Do let him, Luigi," urged Cresside. "That's Fabian d'Alvery's dog, Belizaire. He's very kind to children. You see Vail's made friends with him already."

"That ain't what he come here for."

"I know, Luigi. But let me take him over there for just a minute. I'll bring him right back."

She offered the little boy her hand, which he took willingly, and led him to the farther end of the patio, where Belizaire was chained to the stair landing, with Vail still squatting beside him. "I've been trying to make Vail say doggy, Riccardo," she said. "But I haven't had any luck. Perhaps if you say it he'll try to copy you."

"Doggy," said Riccardo obligingly. "Nice black doggy." He patted Belizaire, staring at him covetously, and reiterated his greeting. Vail looked at the intruder with a belligerent expression, but he neither moved nor spoke until Cresside turned to lead the reluctant Riccardo back towards the table where the others were sitting.

"Auntie," he called after her imperiously. "Auntie!"

Cresside hesitated, biting her lip and looking apologetically at Riccardo. "I'll have to go back and get him if we're to have any peace," she said. "He'll be howling at the top of his lungs in another minute. Run along to your father without me, Riccardo."

Then, as he complied, she retraced her footsteps, picked up the heavy child, and returned to the group gathered around the table with him in her arms. Dinah's expression remained respectfully blank while this went on. But Cresside knew that the nurse, like the peddler, whose astonishment at such indulgence was undisguised, felt she should have left the refractory child where he was or made him walk. With an obstinacy equal to Vail's, she continued to clasp him closely to her, hitching him a little higher on her shoulder. "Selah says you've got a beautiful red truck, Luigi," she said irrelevantly. "I'd like to see it, if you'd show it to me."

"Sure I show you my truck, Miss Cresside," Luigi said proudly. "We carry plenty things now. You remember when I had just Johnny Crooks—stageplanks—sauerkraut candy—alla kind-a stuff like-a that? All on my back, too, in a basket? You remember my cart too, maybe yes? How I got kitchenware—fancy-dress goods— julery in that-a cart also my fruit and-a candy? Now I got-a crockery—ready-made clothes—home furnishings—toys—objects of-a piety—I got a real store now, an' he's all in my truck! Better as what-a you find on Bayou Lafourche, and the onliest-a one on the River Road!"

He led the way around the east wing of the house with exultant footsteps, his son at his side, Cresside with Vail and Dinah with Sybelle following after him. The red truck was parked near the entrance to the butler's pantry, with all the importance of a fire-engine, and a number of little pickaninnies from the quarters, not to mention quite a few of their elders, were gathered around it in awe and excitement. Luigi had not only repainted it since purchasing it from his prosperous cousin, Mike Montagino; he had so materially altered the body that he had succeeded in converting this into a caravan. It was completely enclosed, except for sliding doors on the side and small windows at the rear, which permitted an inviting view of the interior. This was filled to the last inch with an amazing variety of staples and knick-knacks, all arranged with such neatness and precision that, despite the crowding and the small space, there was no confusion. Cresside regarded it all with almost as much enthusiasm as did the pickaninnies.

"Why, Luigi, I never would have dreamed anyone could do such wonders with an ordinary old truck! This is enchanting. People couldn't help wanting to buy everything you've got when you've made it all so attractive!"

"Well, now, you pick-a out one leetla toy for that beega boy you got, also one for new bambino too," Luigi said expansively. "I make-a special price, just-a for you. I wanta you should tell the *Capitano* so soon like he come in. My truck ain't all what I got. I gotta my fancy grocery store too! What-a you think for that, heh?"

"Luigi, you haven't! Where is it?"

314

"Well, it ain't a fancy grocery store yet, Miss Cresside. It's just-a leetla old building on Lafayette Street. But I get me good-a trade bimeby, account she's close-a by the ferry. Not-a no rented place. I buy—for cash-a money too. She's a gonna be fixed up with plate-glass window, showcase, everything."

"Marvellous. I'll bet your wife is crazy about it too."

"You betcha, sure. We got our house in back of the store and now she don't got to take so much-a care for Riccardo no more, account he's a-going to school soon. We do alla work ourself, save-a plenty money thataway. You tella *Capitano* so soon like he come in from the field, no, Miss Cresside?"

She promised faithfully that she would, and as she watched the gaudy truck swing out of sight, with Riccardo sitting up very straight beside his father and Luigi manipulating the wheel with a flourish, she told herself laughingly that she could hardly forget such an amazing piece of news; the rate at which the peddler was forging ahead was nothing short of staggering. She sat thinking about him and the little son of whom he was so proud for some time after she had gone back to the patio. But Gervais, who did not come in until after the twins had been put down for their naps, and who found her busily engaged in brushing Belizaire's tangled coat, greeted her in a way which put her immediately on the defensive and drove the morning's pleasant interlude from her mind.

"I hadn't any idea you'd spend the entire time Fabian was gone dry-nursing his spaniel. You've never shown much interest in our own dogs. In fact, I've heard you say dozens of times you didn't see how anyone could go dog crazy, like Fabian."

"That was a long time ago, before I'd seen much of Belizaire. And I've heard *you* say, dozens of times, that you didn't see why we had specimens like Snow and Cornet in the first place, that we ought to get some *real* dogs at Belle Heloise. I agree with you, for once. I'm going to ask Fabian if he can't get us a puppy the next time Belizaire sires a litter. Vail has noticed him already. He and Sybelle are nearly old enough now to start playing with a puppy."

"They'd have a fat chance of playing with a puppy if you sat and fondled it all the time, the way you're fondling Belizaire."

"Well, naturally I wouldn't. In the first place, the puppy wouldn't need to be tied up. This would be its home and it would be chasing around, having a great old time. It wouldn't be confined and pining for its master, like Belizaire—I've never seen a human being as lonely as that poor dog. In the second place, I wouldn't worry about a puppy the way I'm worrying about Belizaire. It would be ours, and, if anything happened to it, that would be our own hard luck. This is entirely different. Belizaire's all Fabian's got."

"Oh, come on! Fabian's got as good a practice as any lawyer

around here. He's got a very tidy patrimony too, besides what he earns. And he's got the best cook in Baton Rouge and one of the most distinctive houses."

"Oh, for the love of Mike! I mean all that *matters*."

"Well, if you'd ever done half the worrying about cash in your whole life that you've done in the last twenty-four hours about that noisy beast, you'd know it matters a good deal to a man if he doesn't have to worry about it. Fabian's sitting pretty—a darn sight prettier than I am right now, with sugar dropping further and further down every day and money getting tighter and tighter all the time."

"Maybe if you didn't spend so much you wouldn't have to worry so much."

"You talk as if I'd been throwing money to the four winds. I only did what practically every other planter did last year when sugar went up to twenty-six—increased my acreage, improved my machinery, put my whole place in apple-pie order. It didn't seem like extravagance to any of us—it seemed like a sensible investment. How could we tell that sugar would drop to ten before the crop was in and keep right on dropping? We weren't to blame for the drop. If you'd ever bothered to keep informed about current conditions you'd know price-fixing was responsible for that—price-fixing and a market flooded with Cuban sugar."

"I suppose you cleared up all the back debts on the place, didn't you, before you started in on your little improvements? You might as well come clean, Gervais. You can't fool me. You're not satisfied without putting on a big show—Fabian is. His house is cute, but you could get the whole of it into one wing of Belle Heloise. And at that he hasn't got a real home because he hasn't a wife and children. A man can't call a house a home, no matter how cute it is, if there's no one to welcome him when he gets there at night except a cook and a dog."

"Of course he can, if that's his idea of a home. It is Fabian's. He could have had a wife if he'd wanted one easy enough. There are plenty of girls who'd be only too glad to marry him for his money and his position."

"And as if Fabian would want a girl who'd marry him for that! As if he weren't shying off all the time for fear some damn gold-digger would try to do that very thing! Plenty of those babes look as if butter wouldn't melt in their mouths, and they have a line you could hang clothes on! Fabian doesn't intend to get fooled, so he's always on guard. Naturally he's terribly sensitive. You men who are all looks and mighty few brains don't seem to know what it does to a man's pride when he thinks a girl wouldn't want to look at him, much less touch him. He gets the idea *anyone* who married him would be doing it for money because there couldn't be any other reason. And you think Fabian could have got married

316

easy enough if he had wanted to! To a girl worth having! What about Merry? She didn't want him, did she, with all his money and position? Didn't you ever hear of a burnt child fearing the fire? What about a burnt man, then? You darn fool! You make me sick and tired!"

Cresside jumped up and rushed to the garden-room, slamming the door behind her. Gervais stood looking after her, with even more perplexity than annoyance. It was a long time since he had heard her lapse into the sort of expressions she had just used, and it gradually dawned on him that only resentment or rage would have made her revert to them. Obviously she was very angry, though the cause of her anger remained a mystery to him. He was also surprised at her disturbingly shrewd observation about Fabian and his way of life; he had never given her credit for analysing any character or situation with such thoroughness and thoughtfulness. He considered following her, first with the idea of arguing and then with the idea of apologizing. But eventually he decided that nothing would be achieved by argument, and that he did not owe her an apology. He went out to the fields again, dismissing the matter from his mind. But he unwillingly faced it once more when he came back, to find Charles Boylston installed in the patio beside Cresside, who in turn was seated near Belizaire, with her perpetual "baby-sewing" in her hands and an obstinate expression on her face.

"Hello there, Gervais!" Boylston said. "Come here and see if you can't do something with this stubborn sister of yours. I can't. She used to say, every time I asked her to go out with me, that she couldn't leave the twins. Now she says she can't leave Fabian's dog. I never did think she had much of an alibi—after all, Dinah was always here and Merry never left the twins but once—for three days. Now I can't see that Cresside's got any alibi at all. Fabian couldn't have expected her to sit and hold Belizaire's paw all the time he was gone himself."

"Maybe I know as much about what Fabian expected as you do. But we won't go into that. If my alibis don't hold water, I'll give them up and spell things for you in words of one syllable. I'd have done it long ago, but, believe it or not, I was trying to let you off easy. However, the truth is that I don't want to go out with you, that I never did and that I never shall. When you've thought that over you might decide whether it isn't a waste of time for you to come here quite so much."

Again she jumped up and disappeared into the garden-room. Belizaire strained at his leash and whined as she slammed the door behind her. Charles Boylston looked at Gervais in extreme bewilderment.

"I honestly don't know what I've said or done to upset her so much. I'm terribly sorry."

"You needn't be. You didn't upset her—she was upset already. She lit into me this morning, and she has me foxed too—I can't imagine what's got into her. I'll say this for Cresside, she's flip, but she isn't very often downright rude, like she's been today. Everyone except Merry calls me 'edgy,' and I reckon I am sometimes. But I never thought Cresside was."

"She isn't. Of course, she wisecracks about almost everything, but this is different. She can't really mean that she doesn't want me to come here . . . can she?"

"Of course not. She's going through some kind of *crise des nerfs*, Lord knows what for. Come on, let's find Merry and have a drink."

Cresside reappeared at supper-time, undisposed to eat and abnormally silent, but completely controlled and very courteous in a chilly way. After supper Merry proposed bridge and Cresside joined the others agreeably enough. Whatever the cause of her *crise des nerfs*, it had not affected her game; as usual, she played her cards swiftly and skilfully, covering her partner's mistakes without criticizing them, and capitalizing on her opponents'; she won every rubber. But she did not move from the bridge-table when Boylston began his farewells, and, after seeing him off, Merry and Gervais made a dash to the *garçonnière* without going back to the Big House, for it had begun to rain. They discussed Cresside's strange conduct for a few minutes before settling down for the night; but as usual when they were alone they dismissed vexing subjects easily in their preoccupation with each other. When they were almost asleep Gervais muttered drowsily that he was thankful the hound had stopped howling at last, and Merry, with equal drowsiness, murmured she was thankful he was getting used to his quarters. Neither of them suspected that these had been abruptly changed.

For Cresside had lain, a second night, listening to the dog's lament, sounding above the note of the mourning dove, and this time she had decided that she could not stand it. Before, Belizaire had been lonely, but as far as creature comforts were concerned, he was well off; now she knew he must be drenched through and through, that part of his wretchedness should be laid to his dripping condition. She slid out of bed, put on her slippers and bathrobe, and without turning on any lights or making the slightest noise, crept through the twins' room to Dinah's cubby-hole. Then she groped quietly around in the dark until she touched Dinah's substantial shoulder.

"Hush!" she said softly. "The twins are all right—don't wake them up. But it's pouring cats, dogs and billy goats. I can't leave Belizaire out in all this rain. And Mr. Fabian made me promise I wouldn't try to take him out on the leash by myself. Will you come and help me get him in, Dinah?"

318

"I sho' will, Miss Cresside. You step out on the rear gallery, please, ma'am, and I'll come to you right away."

Dinah in deshabille was even more majestic than in the picturesque clothes which she wore in the daytime. She presently appeared, wearing a voluminous crimson robe and a tignon which matched it. She had brought the flashlight that she always kept by her bedside, and she held it steadily before her as she advanced. Then she put her arm around Cresside, supporting her while they went down the stairway to the patio and across the soggy grass to the dog-run. Belizaire was already crouching by the gate, apparently aware that deliverance was at hand. He submitted with docility to the leash and trotted quietly after his rescuers as they retraced their steps across the lawn, up the back stairway and through the rear gallery. When they reached the door leading into the upper hall, Dinah paused.

"What does you want to do with him now, Miss Cresside?"

"I'm going to take him into my room, of course."

"He's mighty wet. He's gwine ter drip all over your pretty rugs. If he lays down on one of 'em, he's gwine ter leave his shape there."

"I don't care about my pretty rugs. I'm going to have him where it's dry. . . . Let's get some bath towels and rub him, and let's try to be quiet so we won't wake *maman*."

"Ah ain't a-gwine make no noise. You climb back on to de bed, Miss Cresside, while I gets you another nightgown. You'se done got soaked to de skin yourself. I'll do de rubbin' after I gets you fixed up. But, Lordy! Dat dog's shaking himself dry dis minute. Look how de raindrops goin' all over the floor, lik' I tol' you. Bellie's gwine be all right, but your carpet, it ain't never gwine be de same again."

"Please stop worrying about the carpet. And please rub Belizaire anyway, even if you do think he's all right. I'll write a letter while you dry him. I won't get out of bed again."

Cresside had raised her arms while she was talking, and Dinah had deftly slipped off the drenched nightgown, swiftly drying the girl's slim body before slipping on another gown that was soft and fresh. Then she took a larger towel, and, getting down on her knees, began to rub Belizaire, singing softly as she did so:

> "Ol' Mr. Owl was settin' on a limb,
> He looked at me, I looked at him.
> Says I, 'Mr. Owl, I's always heard
> Dat you is a mighty wise ol' bird.
> Now dere's sumpin' dat I craves to know,
> Does de one I love, love me or no?
> Won't you tell me dis, Mr. Owl? Please do!'
> But ol' Mr. Owl jes said, 'Whoo-oo-oo!'
> Says I, 'Mr. Owl, I done axed you,

"*Does de one dat I love, love me true?*
You ought to know, you is so wise."'
But ol' Mr. Owl jes blinked his eyes
An' turned his head fus' lef' den right,
Den flew to a limb plumb out of sight.
So I axed again, 'Is my true love true?'
He jes flapped his wings an' said, 'Whoo-oo-oo!'"

While Dinah sang, Cresside sat up and wrote, taking a pad and pencil from her bedside table, and looking over, between every other word, to see if Belizaire were still submissive.

"DEAR FABIAN,

"It is raining very hard tonight, and I could not believe that you would really want me to leave Belizaire out in the run through such terrible weather. He might have drowned. No, I suppose dogs don't drown, do they? But he might have caught pneumonia. So I have brought him into my room. I did not take him on the leash by myself. Dinah helped me. She is rubbing him with a big bath towel now and presently he will be nice and dry, and then he will lie down on the rug by my bed and go to sleep. I shall be awfully glad to have him. It will not be so lonely for him or for me either. Night is the loneliest time, isn't it, when you are missing someone?

"As ever,
"CRESSIDE."

She put down the pad and pencil and looked over at Belizaire again. Dinah had finished drying him, and he was stretched out contentedly in a characteristic position, with his hind legs widely separated and laid flat on the floor, so that he looked almost like a rug himself. He gazed up at her with large grateful eyes and made little grateful sounds in his throat. After Dinah had left and the room was completely dark again, Cresside could still see his eyes, glowing through the darkness; she could still hear the little sounds in the stillness. She was happier than she had been at any moment since Fabian had left. But by and by she reached out for the little pad that lay on the bedside table and tore off the sheet of paper on which she had written. Then she tore this into many small pieces. After that she lay for a long time looking at Belizaire's glowing eyes and listening to the small sounds he made which mingled with the notes of the mourning dove instead of drowning them as his dreadful cries had done. But by and by he went to sleep. He put his head down on his front paws and closed his eyes, and everything was quiet. But Cresside lay and watched and listened just the same.

If they had not brought him in out of the wet, Cresside and

Dinah said to each other, two days later, they would have thought that Belizaire had caught cold in that hard pelting rain. But since he had been brought in and well dried, since he had stopped crying for Fabian and seemed so contented in Cresside's room, they could not understand what ailed him. He grew more and more listless; he could hardly be cajoled into going out with Amen; he could not be tempted into eating anything. When he finally refused to drink water, Cresside told Amen to put on his leash and get him into the car; she was going to take him to the vet, and she thought Amen had better come along. Belizaire lay unprotestingly at her side while she drove up the River Road at top speed; and he was equally apathetic when she got him into town, crawling across the sidewalk and cowering in a corner of the strange-smelling little office where he finally landed. The veterinarian, who was very busy, and who had only one rather bewildered assistant to help him attend to the heterogeneous collection of animals which unhappy owners were crowding upon his attention, said he did not think there was much the matter; however, Miss d'Alvery would have to leave the dog for an examination. How long? Oh, for several hours at least—overnight would be better. . . .

"I don't think Mr. d'Alvery would want him to stay overnight." She remembered what Fabian had said in the first place, when he had gratefully accepted her offer to care for Belizaire: that dogs often picked up diseases when they were put with other animals, that he was thankful to have his in the run at Belle Heloise by himself. On the other hand she did not want to offend this doctor, who represented her only possible source of authentic information and scientific helpfulness. "It's ten o'clock now. Suppose I come back for him at one?"

"Very well, Miss d'Alvery. I can't give you the results of any blood tests by then, I'm afraid. But you can get those tomorrow, if you prefer."

Cresside patted Belizaire's head and told Amen to stay where he was, with the vague idea that he might in some way mitigate the dog's depression. Then, leaving her car parked, she walked around to the telegraph office and hastily wrote out a message, handing it to the clerk and leaving the building before she could change her mind about sending it, as she had in the case of the two little notes.

"Mr. Fabian d'Alvery,
   "Willard Hotel,
      "Washington, D.C.

"Belizaire is sick and I am very much worried. Please come home as soon as you can.

"Cresside."

Having sent the telegram, she did not know exactly what to do next. Finally, she decided to go and sit in Fabian's garden until it was time to call for Belizaire again. As she turned off Third Street, she saw Pascal Tremblet and Preston Vicknair on the bench near the Veterans' Monument, apparently deep in argument. She went over and spoke to them, and they both jumped up, greeting her with delight.

"Why, good-morning, Miss Cresside! It's not often we see you in town. How are the little twins?"

"They're very well, thank you, and so is their baby brother. But Fabian's dog, Belizaire, is sick. Fabian left him with me when he went to Washington himself, and I'm terribly worried. I came in town to bring Belizaire to the vet's."

"Worms, most likely," Pascal said. "They take the life right out of a dog. Has he howled, Miss Cresside, like he was in pain?"

"He's howled, but only at first, from loneliness. Since he's been sick he's been very quiet."

"Then it wouldn't be worms," Preston announced authoritatively. "Mr. Fabian must have looked out for worms anyway. But you take fleas, they suck a dog's blood. I saw that dog scratching, the last time I was at Mr. Fabian's house, and I wanted to ask him then, did he have his dog defleaed regular. But——"

"Fleas!" interrupted Pascal. "Fleas wouldn't hurt him none. Fleas is natural to a dog, Miss Cresside. Don't let Pres pass off any nonsense on you. But mosquitoes, they might get him down, if he was bitten enough. Did you leave him out nights?"

"At first I did. That's what Fabian told me to do. But since we had that hard rain the other night he's been sleeping in my room. . . . I didn't know so many different things could be bad for a dog. But I did know he oughtn't to catch cold and I did know he was lonely. He misses Fabian terribly."

"Well, Miss Cresside, I reckon it ain't only his dog misses him. I was saying to Pres, just before you came along, that this wasn't the same town, with him gone. You see, we sorta got the habit now, going to his house. He's asked us more than ever, since Max died. We were counting up how long it was since he left, and we couldn't hardly believe it was less than a week. Seems more like a month."

"I thought I'd go and sit in his garden while I waited for the report on Belizaire. Wouldn't you like to come with me? I'm sure Carmelite will give us all a cool drink. As far as that goes, I'm sure she'd be glad to give you your dinner, if you'd like to have."

"We wouldn't like to intrude when Mr. Fabian was away, Miss Cresside."

"Nonsense! You wouldn't be intruding. I'm sure he took it for granted you'd keep on going there, just the same, whether he was there or not. But, anyway, I'm asking you now."

Fabian's house and garden seemed very empty without him and his dog, but otherwise the pleasant atmosphere was unchanged:

322

the garden was full of flowers, sunshine and sweet scents; the house was quiet, cool and orderly. Carmelite was moving around the kitchen with calm efficiency. Of course, she could give the gentlemen their dinner, she said, a little haughtily, as if hurt at the implication that there could be the slightest doubt of it; but wouldn't Miss Cresside stay and have it with them? Cresside hesitated for a moment and then called the veterinarian. There was a long wait before he came to the telephone, and she pictured him, still harassed in the turmoil of his office, trying to escape from one anxious patron in order to attend to another; but he finally reminded her, rather curtly, that he had said in the beginning he would like to keep the dog under observation, and that the longer it was left with him the better. He had already taken its temperature and this was 104°; not that this was anything to worry about in itself.

Cresside went back to the kitchen more worried than ever. But she told Carmelite that she would be glad to stay for dinner, and when this was ready she took her place quite naturally at the head of Fabian's table. The two old men were also completely at ease. Cresside had been playing fantan with them after telephoning the veterinarian, getting out the cards from the corner cupboard where Fabian always kept them and setting up the card-table in the same place that he did. In order that Carmelite might not be diverted from her cookery, Cresside had mixed the drinks, too, with her usual skill, serving them on a silver tray lightly overlaid with summer lilac and maidenhair fern, in frosted silver goblets with a ginger lily pierced by a slender tube of green glass on top of each. Then, finding that Carmelite had not picked fresh flowers that day, she had gone out into the garden and done so herself, decorating the dinner-table and the living-room. She had never done this at Belle Heloise; that had long been her mother's province, rightful, however neglected; now it was Merry's, joyfully improved. Cresside could not presume on either. But here there was no one else to do what she had done. She was surprisingly happy in doing it, and touched beyond measure when Pascal, always the more voluble of the two veterans, finally put into words what both felt so strongly.

"It's nice to have you here, Miss Cresside. Not that we don't still miss Mr. Fabian. But you seem to belong here too. Now, if we could just have you both——"

"But you can, of course. I'll come and play hostess any time you like. I'm sure Fabian wouldn't mind at all. Not that he needs me. He's a wonderful host himself."

"Yes, of course. But a house seems that much more homelike when there's a lady in it."

He was saying much the same thing she herself had said to Gervais, Cresside realized, though she had been talking about the effect of a wife, and naturally these two poor old men were not

323

thinking of her in that light—only as Fabian's cousin, who was substituting for him as well as she could at that moment, and who might occasionally supplement his hospitable gestures in the future. But, except for the corroding anxiety about Belizaire, she felt curiously content, as she sat after dinner, pouring the coffee, measuring the brandy and listening to the garrulous veterans as they rambled on. She knew she had made them happy, and she was happy herself in feeling that she "belonged," as they put it, in this pleasant little house, that she fitted so easily into the pattern, that it became her to be there. . . .

The veterinarian was reassuring when she returned to his office; he felt certain there was nothing much the matter with her cousin's dog, he told her; undoubtedly just a touch of distemper. He would give her some medicine to take home with her, which she should administer three times a day; he had already given the first dose. Amen, who had sat patiently in a corner throughout her long absence, now led Belizaire back to the car, and they drove down the River Road again in the peaceful twilight. Cresside was still conscious of the unwonted contentment which had come to her in Fabian's house; but, as the evening wore on, she became disquieted again. Belizaire, instead of lying quietly on a rug, retreated under her bed, and stubbornly stayed there. The bedstead was built so low that, slim as she was, Cresside herself could not creep under it; she could only lie down beside it, begging Belizaire to come out. But her powers of persuasion were inadequate; he rolled over, and then lay, limp, prostrate and unresponsive, his black form swallowed up in the darkness of his hiding-place. She called first Amen and then Dinah, to see if they could accomplish what she failed to do, but, though they tried, perseveringly, their efforts were as futile as her own. Finally, she dismissed them, and lay down on the rug herself. If she got into bed she would not be able to see Belizaire, and though she did not suppose it would make any difference, she felt impelled to keep watch and to listen for his breathing. Over and over again she thought that this had stopped. But very early in the morning he moved slightly, and a little later he crawled towards the foot of the bed and lay down again. The knowledge that he was still alive filled her with thanksgiving, but it did not assuage her fears for the future. She raised herself on her knees and stretched out her arms across the counterpane. Then she buried her face in its overhanging folds.

"Please, God," she prayed. "Please, don't let him die. He's all Fabian's got, and Fabian trusted me with him. I've done the best I could for him, but I reckon I just don't know how to take care of a dog. You'll have to help me——" She stopped, not because the prayer came haltingly, for it was as spontaneous as a child's, but because she was sobbing. She waited until she could form words again, and then she went on: "If You let Belizaire get well, I won't

324

ask for anything else. Not anything. But please help me to do this one thing for Fabian."

She stopped again, no longer inarticulate with tears, but confused when it came to bringing such a prayer to an end. To her present shame, she had not said, in a long time, any of the prayers she had been so carefully taught; she had not gone to church, she had observed no periods of private devotion, and she had always managed to elude the austere priest who had baptized the twins and who had come regularly for years to hear her mother's confessions and say Mass in the invalid's room. So she had almost forgotten the printed patterns. And, in any case, none of the prayers she had learned before would have helped her to word the one she was trying to utter now; no pious mother, no catechism, no missal supplied formulas to use in such a case as this. She was not even sure it was proper to pray for a dog, in the eyes of the Church, or certain Fabian would have approved her petition. For Fabian called himself an unbeliever. He had been reared, like herself, in a Catholic household, baptized and confirmed; during his parents' lifetime he had gone regularly to confession and communion. But that was a long time ago. Since then he had not merely neglected the sacraments, as she had; in his moments of bitterness and gloom, he had denied them. And, after all, this was his dog for which she was praying. Had she any right to invoke Divine aid in the face of his possible resentment? She thought possibly Father Navarre, the saintly man whose aid Gervais had invoked at the time of his hasty marriage, might have been willing and able to give her wise and sympathetic counsel. But Father Navarre had not remained in Baton Rouge; he had gone back to his native swamplands, to the humble trappers and fishermen and moss-gatherers who loved him and whom he loved. Probably he had forgotten all about her by now. Increasingly sorrowful and increasingly perplexed, she went on groping. "I know this is just a dog, I know there aren't any prayers to fit. But somehow he's made me want to pray again, and You know I haven't in a long time. So it ought to count for something. Because if he gets well it will give me faith again. Not just to beg either. To worship too. . . ."

The anxious hours of the next day followed each other laggingly. Amen and Selah came upstairs in the morning and moved Cresside's bed; then they lifted Belizaire up and helped her to give him his medicine, while Dinah stood watchfully by, ready to help too. But Belizaire did not try to resist; he still lay limp and apathetic. After he had been dosed he was put on the upper gallery, so that he would not be able to crawl out of reach again. But this was apparently a needless precaution; he stayed quietly on the clean white bath-mat that Dinah spread for him. Cresside sat beside him, and Lucie, in her usual incurious way, brought trays to her there.

325

Nobody suggested that she should do anything else, and nobody told her she was silly to sit all day beside a sick dog; indeed, one by one, her mother and Merry and Gervais came and sat with her, talking to her in lowered voices, as if they were trying not to disturb Belizaire. Madame d'Alvery told Cresside the story of a pet she had owned when she was a young girl. It was a story Cresside had never heard before and which she would have believed her mother incapable of telling, for it revealed secret stores of tenderness which her daughter had not supposed she possessed. Then, before she left the gallery, she bent down and ran her white, ringed fingers gently over Belizaire's wasted body.

"I do not think he has fever now, Cresside. I think his medicine is helping him."

"I hope so. . . .You don't know, do you, *maman*, whether Amen has come back with a report from the doctor?"

"I believe he has. I believe Gervais will come and tell you about it. Try not to grieve so, *chère*. And tonight, get some sleep."

"I'm going to sleep here. Amen's going to move out my *chaise-longue*. I couldn't stand having Belizaire crawl under the bed again."

"No, it might be better as you have planned it. *Bonsoir, chère*."

"*Bonsoir, maman.*"

The news which Gervais brought in soon afterwards was unalarming. The veterinarian had found a slight infection in Belizaire's blood stream, and he believed that certain injections might be advisable. However, as this treatment was rather drastic, he suggested waiting the return of the dog's master before trying it. Meanwhile, he was sure Miss d'Alvery was doing everything she could.

"And you are, you know," Gervais went on. "You couldn't have done more for Belizaire if he'd been a baby. When it comes to that, no one could do more for a baby than you've done for the twins ever since they were born. You're a steadfast little cuss, Cresside."

"I just happen to care for babies. And—and dogs. In spite of what you said."

"I'm sorry I said what I did. By that I mean I'm sorry for several things I said. I know you don't think I've got much sense. But at that I've got sense enough to realize that I'm just as lucky in my sister as I am in my wife."

"Thanks for those kind words. But you didn't need to tell me that, just because Belizaire is sick."

"I didn't tell you that just because Belizaire is sick. I've been meaning to say so for a long time. But I'm not very good at saying things like that. Fabian's the orator of the family."

Merry came to see Cresside while Gervais was still on the gallery, and for a few minutes their talk centred on the children. Cresside was not to worry because she had not done as much as usual for the twins these last few days, Merry said. They were getting along finely. It was time they learned to manage without "Auntie's" constant attention anyway. They imposed on her, especially Vail. . . . Cresside remonstrated at this statement, but she was too tired for much argument, and after a few moments Merry signalled to Gervais that they had better go. When they left Cresside they both kissed her. She could not remember when Gervais had kissed her before. He was as undemonstrative as most brothers, and therefore it meant all the more to her that he had kissed her now. But not nearly as much, she thought, after Gervais and Merry had gone away arm in arm, as it would have meant if Fabian had kissed her before he started for Washington. She lay for a long time, staring out into the starlight, thinking about the kiss he had not given her and wondering why she could not put it out of her mind. Eventually she went inside and undressed. After she had slipped into her nightgown she happened to think of a thin negligee which she had never worn, and without rhyme or reason she felt she would like to wear it now. She had chosen it because it was so quaintly cut, like an old-fashioned wrapper, and yet so cool and dainty. It was made of pale blue silk, trimmed with tiny tucks and rows of featherstitching, and it had little frills of narrow Valenciennes lace at the neck and wrists. She took it from the shelf of her armoire, where it had lain indefinitely under a pile of filmy modern lingerie, and after she had put it on, she realized she had wanted to wear it because it was the sort of dressing-gown that Fabian would have liked, if he ever noticed such things, or saw them. Still thinking of this, she returned to the gallery and lay down on the *chaise-longue* which Amen had carefully placed beside Belizaire's mat.

Belizaire seemed to be resting quietly. She put out her hand and touched his head. He did not respond by looking up at her, but he made the slight movement which was so reassuring to her, and finding that by lying on her side she could continue to touch him, she nestled down, still caressing him. Except for the gentle wail of the mourning dove the night was very still. Little by little, its quietude seemed to steal into her troubled heart. She was no longer terror-stricken. She knew she had done all she could. She could possess her soul in patience while she continued to await the answer to her prayer. Praying again, she drifted off to sleep. . . .

It was the movement of Belizaire's head beneath her hand which awakened her. She felt that before she heard any sound. Then she was dimly aware that the sick dog was struggling to his feet, that a car was coming into the driveway, and that there was some connection between the two. She sat up, listening and looking around her, still more than half asleep. There was a little light in the sky, enough to show it pale and luminous against the dark trees. She could see Belizaire too, no longer an indefinite black shape, but a clear-cut creature, suddenly alert. Through some strange chance the other dogs were not barking; but the car had stopped, and someone was skirting the lower gallery with cautious footsteps. She swung herself off the *chaise-longue* and ran to the railing, Belizaire staggering along beside her. As she reached it she heard Fabian's reassuring voice.

"Hello, there. I thought you might be outside and I was looking for you. I got your wire and gathered you wanted me to reach here as soon as I could. Can I get in? And may I come up? I'll try not to wake anyone else."

"The front door's unlocked. Of course you may come up. I'm thankful you're here."

"Well, so am I. I'll be with you in just a minute."

He continued to move slowly and quietly, but she could hear him coming closer—into the house, through the lower hall, over the stairs, through the upper hall, to the door of the front gallery. Then he opened this noiselessly and came out. Belizaire gave a weak bark of joy, and crept up to him, fawning at his feet. As Fabian leaned over to stroke the dog, Cresside went toward him too.

"Fabian," she said, and stopped. "Oh, Fabian, I'm so glad you've come home." Her thankfulness welled up in her throat, choking her. For a moment she could not say anything else. But she saw that Fabian was no longer bending over Belizaire, but standing straight and looking at her intently. She made a great effort and managed to go on. "I don't know what happened to him. I must have failed to take good care of him somehow. But I'd have given my right hand if this hadn't happened, when you trusted me with him. I know he's all you've got."

"I haven't got you, by some miracle, have I?" Fabian asked, and took her in his arms.

XXV

SO a kiss was not merely a weird tremulous thrill, that made you throb and tingle as it pierced you through and through. It was not merely a signal of mysterious danger, which beckoned an invitation while flashing a warning. It was not merely the blossom on the tree of knowledge of good and evil, burgeoning into bitter fruit. It was home after exile, safety after danger, joy after sorrow, fulfilment after frustration—all that and so much more besides, for which there were no words. When

328

Fabian lifted his head at last, Cresside looked up at him with such wonderment that her joy was veiled by it.

"I didn't know a kiss could be like that," she whispered. "Of course, I've been wishing, for a long time, that you would kiss me, but I didn't realize why. I only——"

"Well, I didn't know a kiss could be like that either," Fabian replied, interrupting her. "If I had, you'd have been spared all that wishful waiting, because I simply couldn't have held out. It's been hard enough as it was. Why didn't you give me some sort of a hint? You must have known I'm not any good at guessing. And you must have known that was what I desperately wanted to do."

"But I didn't! I'm not good at guessing either! Once I guessed wrong, and since then——"

She stopped short. Fabian put his arms around her again, but this time, instead of raising her face eagerly towards his, she bowed her head.

"What's the matter, darling?" he said. "You don't mean to tell me that one was enough, after all? I thought that was just a sample! Come on, your hair's nice, just as soft as silk." He ran his hand over it again slowly and tenderly. "But I can think of something a lot nicer," he added. "Why, Cresside . . ."

She had begun to cry. She was doing it so quietly that Fabian, observant as he was, had not instantly realized it, and she was trying hard to stop. He spoke to her very gently.

"I thought you were so happy, Cresside. There, I know you were. And that made me happy too. Don't you want me to be happy?"

"Yes. More than anything in the world. But——"

"There aren't any buts. Look, what do you say we go down to the garden-room? I'm afraid we'll wake Tante Isabelle if we stay here, and I don't want to do that just yet. Besides, I think some good strong coffee would go down well, don't you? I've got a thermos in my car—or I can make some fresh, while you dress. I suppose you have to dress? I wish you didn't, though. Whatever it is you're wearing, it's a knockout."

She looked up, her eyes still wet, but her tremulous lips curving into a hesitant smile. "I put it on because I thought you'd like it," she said shyly. "That is, of course, I didn't have any idea you were going to see it, but I thought it was the sort of thing you would like if you did see it."

Fabian laughed. "Well, you certainly guessed right that time. But at that I reckon you'd better put on a dress if you're coming downstairs. We don't want any of the servants drifting into the garden-room and jumping to rash conclusions which unfortunately would be incorrect. After all, I'll have plenty of future chances to see you in an outfit like that, and mighty soon too. I'll give you a little more time than Gervais gave Merry—I mean a little more than he gave her at the last minute, not more than he gave her all the years he was dawdling around. But I shan't give you much. You could get ready to marry me some time the latter part of next week, couldn't you?"

"Fabian, you don't mean that, do you? You don't want to *marry* me?"

"I most assuredly do. I thought you'd gathered that much anyway. And I gathered that you wanted to marry me. This hasn't been a case of 'Love me, love my dog.' It's been just the other way around. I don't see how you could be so upset about Belizaire, if you weren't pretty fond of me. You weren't trifling with my young affections, were you, just now, when you kissed me?"

"I—— Oh, Fabian, you know how much I care! Don't—don't joke about it. You know I'd do anything on earth I could for you. But I can't do that. I can't marry you."

"Darling, I won't joke if you don't want me to. It just seems natural when I'm so happy, that's all. But I won't let you talk nonsense either. Of course you're going to—a week from Saturday or two weeks from Monday, just as you prefer. But not a day later than that. Look, I'm going to take Belizaire down to the kitchen with me. I'll bet I can get him to drink some milk while I make the coffee. I'll meet you in the garden-room in fifteen minutes."

It was considerably longer than that before Cresside joined him. When she did, she found the door into the garden-room wide open and the first rays of morning sunshine gliding into the room. Obviously Fabian had taken time to go out into the garden, for there was a vase of fresh flowers in the centre of the custom house desk, which he had set like a table, with service for two. The inkwell and blotter had been removed to the top of the bookcase and replaced by a white cloth, serviettes, silverware, porcelain, steaming coffee, hot milk, sugar, buttered toast and fig preserves. Chairs were drawn up on either side, facing each other, and Belizaire was stretched out, mat-like, beside one of them. Fabian, with a napkin over his arm and one of Lou Ida's aprons tied around his waist, was standing behind the other. He pulled it out with a flourish.

> "Ma'amselle, s'il vous plait,
> Le déjeuner est pret.
> Le café est bien chaud,
> Le pain grillé est beau,"

he chanted.

Then, after she was seated, he whisked off the apron, threw down the napkin, and took the place opposite her. "I like two lumps in the morning and a real half-and-half mixture," he told her. "Not black, the way I take it the rest of the time. You'll pour it out for me, won't you? You might as well get into practice."

"Fabian, I told you——"

330

"Yes, and I told *you*. We'll discuss that after breakfast. But let's get something inside of us first. Listen, Belizaire is going to be all right. He's drunk nearly a pint of milk already. I think part of the trouble was just that he was pining for me. He always does that when I go away. Flattering, but inconvenient. I don't know what the devil to do with him when I have to leave him. Well, of course, that's probably going to solve itself automatically. He'll get more and more used to you. Except that generally when I go away, you'll go with me."

"Fabian——"

"Eat some of this toast I made, won't you? I think it's good. You haven't asked me yet how I got along in Washington. Don't you want to hear?"

"Yes, of course, but——"

"I think I had pretty good luck. You remember that when I went before, it was primarily to see if there were anything I could do to change the position of the Equalization Board, but of course I was concerned about the general sugar situation, even then. Senator Gay was helpful in all sorts of way. Among others, he got an appointment with Houston, the Secretary of Agriculture, and I went to see him with Gay. The Secretary was co-operative too. He said he'd assign the best man he had for such kinds of work to making experiments in new types of cane. The best man he had was a scientist named Brandes, who'd had a lot of experience in Argentina before coming to the Arlington Bureau."

"Yes? And what then?"

"Well, I don't want to go into too many details. It's all right for you to say you're not bored, but we've got lots of things besides sugar to talk about this morning. The gist of the whole matter is that I went to see Brandes just as soon as I got to Washington last week, and he let me bring some Java cane back with me. It comes in three varieties and it's done well in Argentina. Brandes is confident it could do well in Louisiana too, because Argentina's cane fields are about as far south of the Equator as Louisiana's are north, and the soil's similar, as well as the climatic conditions. I've got a few stalks of these three varieties in my suitcase. And that suitcase is in my car, which as you know is parked outside the butler's pantry right now."

"So that——"

"So that I want that ham-headed brother of yours to plant that Java cane right out here, back of Angus Holt's garden, and see what happens. Of course, I don't know anything about sugar, but it's my guess that if nothing goes wrong, those three or four stalks will produce six or eight stalks each by next fall. Then those could be replanted, and by 1923 there ought to be enough cane to plant three whole rows, one of each variety. After that—well, I reckon we're getting too far ahead of the game. For the moment, I only

331

want to be sure that Gervais plants everything that's in my suit-case—except the shirts and socks—right where he can keep his eye on it."

"Couldn't you and I plant it ourselves?"

"No, I think Gervais had better do it. Not that I don't like the suggestion that we should do things together. And not that you haven't pleased me no end by taking an intelligent interest in this, considering all you've got on your mind anyway. But there are lots of other things for us to do, honey."

While they were talking, Cresside had taken a few swallows of coffee and crumbled a small piece of toast on her plate. Fabian asked her three times to refill his cup and helped himself to four pieces of toast, spreading them lavishly with butter and fig preserves. After he finished, he poured the left-over milk into a saucer and offered it to Belizaire, who began by sniffing at it disdainfully but ended by drinking most of it. Then Fabian stacked the dishes on a tray and carried them back to the kitchen. Through the open door leading into the patio, Cresside could hear him talking to Lou Ida, who evidently had just come in. But when he returned he shut the patio door behind him.

"I don't think anyone's going to disturb us here," he said, and Cresside knew that he must have told Lou Ida, in that quiet way of his which was so much more effective than Gervais' storming, that he did not want anyone to disturb them, and that no one would risk incurring his disfavour by doing so. "So I'll stop joking now. By way of beginning to be serious, I might tell you I'd like it very much if you'd walk into my arms again."

She turned from the window where she was standing and faced him squarely. It was obvious that she was making a great effort to speak calmly, but he could see her clenching and unclenching her small hands while she spoke.

"Fabian, I can't. I didn't think, that first time, how you'd take it. I didn't think of anything, except that I was thankful you were back, for Belizaire's sake, and overjoyed because my wish had come true. But my wish didn't go any farther than a kiss. One kiss."

"Your conscious wish. But there must have been some subconscious wishes in the back of your mind too, Cresside. You couldn't have kissed me like that if there hadn't been."

"Well, I—I reckon there were. I—I care a lot for you, Fabian."

"Couldn't you stop using that word 'care' and say 'love' instead? That's what you mean, isn't it?"

"I suppose it is. I suppose I do love you. Yes, I know I do. But, honestly, I never thought of it like that until this morning. I've only thought that it meant a lot to be with you, because everything that happens while we are together seems natural and pleasant and comforting. We never seem to bore each other or get on each

332

other's nerves. And we seem to understand each other without any explanation. I don't know how to say it, but there's been a sort of effortless harmony."

"You're saying, very beautifully, that we've loved each other for a long time. Because everything's seemed that way to me too, Cresside. Didn't you know that was the way it seemed when a man and a girl fell in love with each other?"

"No, I didn't. I thought when a man and a girl fell in love with each other they were after something else."

She spoke scathingly. Without taking any apparent notice of her tone, Fabian came over to the window and put his arm around her shoulder, easily and impersonally, as he did on the ferry boat.

"Well, of course they are, sooner or later," he said in his quiet way. "But if it's later instead of sooner, they gain a lot in the long run. I'm glad you used the word harmony, Cresside. It almost makes up for having you shy away from the word love. After you'd found out that there was mental and spiritual harmony between us, you guessed that there might be physical harmony too. Well, now you know that there is."

Cresside stood very still, so still that she seemed to become remote and rigid. Fabian's arm slid easily from her shoulder to her waist and held this fast. Involuntarily she relaxed in his embrace, gradually losing her detachment.

"Don't make any mistake about this," he said steadily. "When I asked you to marry me, I wasn't thinking of good companionship. We'd keep on having that, of course—without any barriers, without any separations. But we'd have much more than that. You'll never know what it meant to me, Cresside, when I first began to realize my deformity wasn't repulsive to you, that there was something else about me that made up for it. Because you're so lovely that any man in his senses would want to have you, if he could. You're not going to tell me I can't, are you?"

"I can't say anything else, Fabian."

"Why, darling? Can you tell me?"

"I'll try. But I don't know how to begin."

"I think I can help, if you'll promise not to be hurt by anything I'll say."

"I can't promise you that. But I know you won't mean to hurt me, that you won't any more than you can help."

"All right. Has your refusal to marry me anything to do with Sylvestre Tremaine?"

Again something about her stillness suggested attempted withdrawal. This time Fabian did not try to recapture her. After a long pause she answered, speaking steadily herself.

"Yes. It has a lot to do with Sylvestre. He didn't want to marry me, Fabian."

333

"You're wrong. He'd have given his right hand to marry you."

"When it was too late."

"That's his hard luck—his lasting hard luck. He's going to covet you vainly all his life, Cresside."

"But he didn't always. Not vainly, Fabian. He got what he wanted. All he wanted. Almost without the asking. Because I wanted it too. That's what I thought love meant then."

"Well, you know better now."

His calm rejoinder failed to check her passionate outburst. She went on vehemently, the words coming with a rush at last.

"What good does it do me to know better now? What good does it do either of us? If I'd dreamed you were falling in love with me, I'd have shut you off, the way I shut off Charles Boylston. But I didn't. I thought you were just being kind to me. And sometimes I thought you'd guessed. We've been so close, in so many ways, I didn't see how I could keep a secret from you."

"You couldn't. I did guess."

"You did!"

"Yes, of course. The day you had your bad fall."

"The day I had my bad fall! Why, that was the day Sylvestre and Regine were married! More than two years ago!"

"Yes, it's a long time. I've wanted to marry you for a long time too."

She twisted suddenly around, staring at him unbelievingly. He slackened his hold on her waist so she could turn easily in his arms, but not enough to risk having her break away from him.

"Why, you couldn't! You couldn't have wanted to marry me if you knew!" she gasped.

"But I did. I still do."

"Fabian, you're not going to pretend you don't mind?"

"I'm not going to pretend anything. I do mind. But I don't mind enough to let it make any difference about wanting to marry you. I've told you twice already this morning that I'd like to marry you next week. If you were in love with Sylvestre, that would be different. But you're not. You loathe the very sight of him. When it comes to that, you never really were in love with him, any more than I was ever really in love with Merry. I think we were both awfully lucky that we've got a second chance. So I wish you'd let me go right now to Tante Isabelle and Gervais and tell them to start getting ready for a wedding. They must be awake by this time."

"Fabian, please stop talking about getting married next week. And please let go of me."

"I won't stop talking about getting married. But I'll let go of you if you'll promise not to run away."

"All right. I promise. But I don't feel as if I could stand up any longer. I feel as if I've got to sit down."

334

"I'm sorry, darling. It was terribly selfish of me, not to realize that you'd be getting tired. But it's been so wonderful, holding you this way."

He released her, kissing her half-hidden cheek as he did so, and then pulling the two chairs away from the desk and placing them side by side. When she was seated in one of them, he drew the other still closer and sat down himself, taking her hand in his.

"Is that better?"

"Yes, it is better—not that I didn't think it was wonderful to have you hold me that way too. And I wasn't getting tired exactly. But my knees were beginning to give way and I had a queer feeling in the pit of my stomach."

"Is it gone now?"

"No, not quite. . . . There's something else I've got to tell you, Fabian."

"There's nothing else you have to tell me. You didn't need to tell me about Sylvestre. I knew it already."

"Yes, but I wasn't sure you did. You wouldn't have thought I was playing fair, would you, if I'd married you without telling you?"

"No. But you always do play fair. Of course, you'd have told me sooner or later. You didn't need to agonize over Sylvestre though, this morning, when we were both so happy. You could have told me any time before we got married."

"Fabian, we're not going to get married. It isn't just a question of the past—of Sylvestre. It's a question of the present—of Vail."

"Of Vail?"

"Yes, I can't leave him. He's mine."

She had met his eyes, squarely, all the time she had been speaking. Now she drew a deep breath that ended in a sigh, and, gripping his hand convulsively, hid her face on his shoulder. He reached over and gathered her into his arms again.

"I have a feeling we can talk about this better if we're closer together," he said tenderly. "I'm going to hold you on my lap. There! Are you comfortable, darling?"

"Of course I'm comfortable," she answered, in a strangled voice. "That isn't the point. Didn't you understand what I said to you, Fabian? Merry isn't Vail's mother. I am."

"Yes, I understood. But it wasn't a shock to me."

"You haven't known that all this time too!"

"I've thought so. And it's been a mystery to me how anything like that could be so thoroughly concealed. It's been a mighty well-kept secret. Would you feel like letting me in on it? On the details, I mean. Don't if you'd rather not——"

"But I want to. Of course, some people are in on it already—maman and Gervais and Merry and Doctor Champagne, besides the trained nurses and the upstairs servants."

"What about the priest who baptized the babies? Wasn't it the same sourpuss who comes to hear Tante Isabelle's confessions, about Lord knows what?"

"Yes. But I'm almost sure he didn't catch on. Anyhow, the inscription on the baptismal certificate's mendaciously in order—'Malcolm Vail, legitimate son of Meredith and Gervais d'Alvery'—Merry showed it to me afterwards to reassure me. I wasn't at the ceremony—still couldn't lift my head—and later, when the sourpuss, as you correctly call him, said he'd like to come in and see me before he left, I had Creassy tell him I was asleep. I've always avoided him, so my message was quite in character. I think most of the house servants must have guessed, but you know how jealous they all are about shielding their white folks. They've been wonderful—everyone's been wonderful, when it comes to that. Most of the credit belongs to Merry though."

"To Merry! Why?"

"It was her idea—that the babies could be passed off as twins. When she found out about me and realized that they were due at the same time, she suggested it. She said she was sure we could carry it off. You see, my bad luck had put me out of circulation anyway. Besides, I don't need to tell you how isolated this place is in midwinter—it's a wonder Doctor Champagne managed to get through, considering the state of the River Road! As a matter of fact, Vail and Sybelle *are* twins. That is, they were born the same night. I was taken sick first, but I was sick a lot longer than Merry."

"I'm sorry you had such a terrible time, darling. I was afraid you did. You looked like a ghost for months."

"Oh, but that wasn't just the long labour! I really did hurt my back. I hurt it badly. Everything they said about that was true. I was in a cast, I did have to wear a brace. I was in bed for months on account of my back. But I would have had to stay there anyway. I had pernicious vomiting. I'd begun to have it before I got hurt and I couldn't have hidden it much longer. Of course, Doctor Champagne discovered it right away."

"Cresside, you've been through nearly every sort of hell there is. But I'm going to make up for some of it. I'm going to help you forget about it once we're married."

"But I can't marry you, Fabian. That's what I keep trying to tell you. And I'm trying to tell you too how wonderful Merry was. She kept encouraging me. The others didn't. Not even the doctor. You see, they all thought it would be a blessing in disguise if I lost the baby. They hoped I would. Some of them even . . . I don't need to tell you about that, do I, Fabian?"

"No, you don't need to tell me about that."

"Well, but Merry said I was right to want to go through with it. She said she was sure I could. She told me if I could stand having

336

a hard time physically, she'd keep me from having a hard time otherwise. She convinced the others she and I were right, she made them carry on, she taught them to play their parts without a hitch. I don't see how I could have held out, Fabian, without Merry."

"You would have, some way."

"I don't know. . . . I didn't go downstairs from the day I hurt my back until Vail was three months old. The horrible nausea lasted all the time I was pregnant, and then afterwards, of course, it took me a long time to get my strength back. But nothing that happened to me did Vail any harm. All my vitality went to him. Dr. Champagne said sometimes it happens that way. Vail weighed more than Sybelle when they were born, and I nursed him too, long enough to give him a good start."

Cresside was not speaking in a strangled voice any longer, but in a tone of fierce triumphant pride. Fabian bent his head so that his face touched hers, and clasped her more closely in his arms.

"You couldn't have done all that, darling, no matter how much Merry helped you, if you hadn't had tremendous courage and endurance yourself. If Vail ever finds out that you're his mother, he'll be mighty proud of you."

"But he mustn't ever find out! It would kill me if he did! We've taken every precaution that he shouldn't! Who'd do such a cruel thing as to tell him?"

"I don't know. There are about a dozen people in on this secret already, aren't there? Well, there's an old saying that it's no secret that's known to three. Sooner or later there's almost bound to be a leak. I don't mean an open scandal—I think you're fairly safe from that. But some kind of an allusion to an old mystery—accidental, probably, rather than malicious. For instance, Vail might overhear a private conversation between persons who would have bitten out their tongues rather than betray your secret. But you've got to face the possibility that your son may know the truth, just the way you face everything else, Cresside."

Again he pressed his face to hers and tightened his embrace.

"Except that hereafter I'm going to help you face that—and everything else," he said. "But no matter how much I help, I can see it would be hard for you to leave Vail. I can't imagine why I didn't think of that before, because I've kept threshing over this whole situation for months now. Of course you know I'd be more than glad to have you bring him with you. But that would be a dead give-away that would set tongues wagging. You can't undo everything you've done so far."

"Of course I can't. So of course I can't marry you either."

"That doesn't follow at all. As a matter of fact, it would be a good thing for both of you if you left him."

"A good thing! If I left my own child!"

"You don't want him to know he's your own child. You just said it would kill you if he found it out. Well, then, naturally you want him to believe Merry's his mother. You want him to believe you're his aunt. I should think that would be easier all round if you weren't in the house with him. As it stands you monopolize Vail, Cresside; you can't help it. You always have. And he turns instinctively to you for everything he needs and wants. You feed him, you bathe him, you get him up in the morning and put him to bed at night, you sing to him and play with him. The first word he said wasn't mamma. It was auntie. He doesn't say mamma yet. If you leave him he cries for you, if he's angry you pacify him, if he's ailing you soothe him. I've never seen the slightest sign that he relied on Merry, or that he missed her when she wasn't around; I've never heard him chortle with glee when she appeared. Wouldn't it be a good thing to start changing all that before he gets much older? Answer me honestly, darling."

"I don't know. Yes, I suppose it would. I hadn't thought of it that way before."

"Well, won't you? Of course you'll miss Vail terribly at first, if you leave him, and he'll miss you too—for a few days. But it won't take him any longer than that to get used to a change if you go while he's still a baby. And remember you wouldn't be far from him anyway. You could come and see him whenever you liked. I suppose in the natural course of events you'd be at Belle Heloise every day or two, while I was at the office. And he'd look forward to your visits pretty soon—his aunt's visits. He wouldn't ever think of you as the mother who went off and left him—he'd think of you as the aunt who came to see him. He'd grow up believing Merry was his mother, the way you want him to, unless there were some mischance. And if there were, you'd still be near enough to explain. He'd grow up as Gervais d'Alvery's first-born son, as Sybelle's twin, as little Philogene's elder brother. All that would mean a lot to him, Cresside, now and when he's older too."

"Yes, I know. It's what I've wanted for him, it's what I've tried to get for him. Only I thought I'd be here too."

Her voice was trembling uncontrollably again. So were her hands. Fabian held these fast in his.

"You will, whenever it's best that you should," he said reassuringly. "But it isn't best all the time. Please believe me, Cresside. It isn't best for the boy and it isn't best for you. You oughtn't to live the rest of your life as the outlier of the family circle, in the aftermath of a tragedy. You ought to have a home and a husband of your own and children you could acknowledge as your own. You'd be happy yourself if you did, and you'd give a lot of happiness too." He stopped, halted by his innate reluctance to voice his own desperate loneliness and his own overpowering need. But he

338

knew now that he must do more than admonish her as a mentor; he must appeal to her as a lover. "You don't seem to know what it would mean to me to have you for my wife," he said urgently. "You don't seem to know what it would mean to me to have you for the mother of my son. But the truth is it would mean everything in the world. You've told me that you love me and I believed you. If that's true, don't you love me enough to marry me?"

The story of Fabian and Cresside is taken up again by Mrs. Parkinson Keyes in her sequel to this book, "Vail d'Alvery."